Serge Joncour is a French novelist and screenwriter. He was born in Paris in 1961 and studied philosophy at university before deciding to become a writer. His first novel, *Vu*, was published by Le Dilettante in 1998. He wrote the screenplay for *Sarah's Key* starring Kristin Scott Thomas, released in 2011. His 2016 novel *Repose-toi sur moi* won the Prix Interallié. *Wild Dog* (*Chien loup*), also published by Gallic Books, won the Prix Landerneau des Lecteurs.

Jane Aitken is a publisher and translator from the French.

Louise Rogers Lalaurie is a writer and translator. She is based in France and the UK.

Also by Serge Joncour:

Wild Dog

Lean on Me

Lean on Me

by Serge Joncour

Translated from the French by Jane Aitken and
Louise Rogers Lalaurie

Gallic Books
London

A Gallic Book

First published in France as *Repose-toi sur moi*
Copyright © Flammarion, 2016

English translation copyright © Jane Aitken and Louise Rogers Lalaurie, 2022

First published in Great Britain in 2022 by Gallic Books Ltd
12 Eccleston Street, London, SW1W 9LT

A CIP record for this book is available from the British Library
ISBN 9781910477885

Typeset in Fournier MT by Gallic Books
Printed in the UK by CPI (CR0 4YY)
2 4 6 8 10 9 7 5 3 1

I

Ludovic always took a deep breath before ringing the bell, quickening his pulse in anticipation of a frosty or angry reception. Then he would draw himself up to his full and considerable height, puff out his chest, and wait for the door to open.

But now, at the sight of the elderly woman emerging onto the top step of the small, rather shabby house, he knew he faced a different challenge altogether. He must resist feeling sorry for her.

In the sitting room, Ludovic chose the big armchair on the far side of the coffee table. The old woman took forever to sit down. Ludovic couldn't help thinking she was exaggerating, unless she really did have a bad back, and legs, and more. He waited for her to settle, laid out some documents from the file he had brought, but already she was struggling up out of her chair, and shuffling towards the corridor. She was going to fetch her specs, only she wasn't sure where they were.

Three minutes passed, and still she had not reappeared. An excruciating wait. Pauses such as this always made Ludovic feel awkward and embarrassed. He hated silences, much preferred it when things came together quickly, even if that meant a heated exchange. His visits did sometimes provoke anger, and shouting. More than once, like last week, a guy had even pulled a knife on him. But today was nothing like that. He would never let it show, but he felt ashamed inside. The old lady reminded him of his mother: she was more or less the same age, had the same trouble walking. The likeness had bothered him when she first answered the doorbell. In his work, he relied on his imposing build to make an impression. A stern gaze helped, too. He wasn't trying to scare people, just to show that he would not soften or be swayed by emotion. It worked, as a rule, but sometimes it was hard. It was hardest of all when he felt, as now, that he understood everything about the person whose home he was entering, the little old lady who had invited him down the narrow concrete path and along the hallway of her modest house in Sevran, on the north-eastern edge of Paris. He had figured everything out about this old lady with her shuffling gait, sensed it all straight away. She had spent most of her life here; he spotted the signs of old, die-hard habits, the long-abandoned kennel, the garden no one saw to any more, her husband's shoes tucked under the dresser, though it seemed he was out, or asleep, or in hospital. Ludovic was unsure, for now, where this brave little lady stood in life, though he knew she was in debt, of course – the house was not unpleasant, but there was a whiff of bad luck, and withered hopes.

From the cooking smells that hung in every room, he immediately recognised the old-school cuisine – refried butter, frozen steaks sizzling in a fat-filled pan, Brussels sprouts that had hung around too long outside the fridge. There was the battery-powered radio on the side, and the neatly aligned slippers. And overlaying the rest, the faint, stale odour of last night's supper, the reek of a poor diet – too much fat, possibly too much drink – that he often noticed when he turned up unannounced in people's homes. It was the cumulative impression that struck him every time, the inevitable result of arriving brazen and unexpected at the home of a person you've never met. He had shown her the headed notepaper, with its official-looking red-white-and-blue logo, over the top of the gate and she had signalled for him to step up the path straight away, politely, making no trouble. She was clearly not planning to make a run for it; any attempt on her part would be pathetic indeed, and a very poor reflection on Ludovic. It depressed him to handle situations where people showed bad faith from the start, poisoning the encounter with their lack of scruples, or their downright dishonesty.

The old lady returned with her glasses and asked him if he would like anything to drink, a beer perhaps, or a glass of port, but he refused. To accept a drink would alter the tone. This was not a courtesy call. The real risk in debt collection this way, face to face, was allowing yourself to be deflected, and then there was no way back. Casting his eye over the file, Ludovic realised the woman was not as old as all that. She was seventy-six, according to the date of birth on the forms, but her memory was failing, or she pretended it was, because now she was serving him that glass of port, and one for herself, in two little schooners full to the brim, which she placed carefully on the coffee table. Ludovic made a show of pushing his glass away and taking up most of the table with the papers from his folder. Faced with all these documents, all the letters on red-white-and-blue-headed paper, the woman rose again from her chair. Ludovic sensed her panic. She was plainly affected by his copies of all the reminders she had received. There was no hiding now, the evidence was there in front of her, the debt was real. They had caught up with her.

'You know, Madame Salama, the longer you let this drag on, the worse it gets. I'm here to help you, Madame Salama. That's why I've come, to help you sort this out so that you don't have to worry about it anymore. That's my job, to make sure things don't get out of hand. Do you understand?'

Ludovic attended every meeting equipped with a cardboard folder bearing the debtor's name, written conspicuously on the cover. Just one cardboard folder, not a binder. The technique emphasised his personal approach – he had travelled just for her, he had come to see her alone, whose surname was written in black marker on the red file, rather like a set of doctor's notes. A thick file, stuffed with papers, 90 per cent of which were nothing to do with the case in hand. After two years in this job, Ludovic knew one thing at least: a fat folder was far more intimidating than his own impressive bulk.

'You know, I never really understood all the paperwork, those registered letters and all that…'

'Of course, Madame Salama, but if you'll just sit down again I can explain everything.'

He sensed her anxiety, so he softened his tone, addressed her as one human being to another. 'Don't worry, everyone has unpaid bills. These days it's practically the norm: there's something you need to buy, you get into debt, but then when you've bought it you forget you still have to finish paying for it. It's the system, it steers you into debt…'

'It was for my granddaughter, you see, it wasn't for us.'

'The ring, it was for your granddaughter?'

'Yes, for her wedding.'

'OK, but as far as I can see, she got married two years ago, and the ring is still not paid for. Two years is a long time, don't you think? And apart from the deposit, only one payment's been made, and not a full payment either – is that right?'

'She's got divorced since then. Poor child, she's such a good girl, an absolute love. She hasn't had things easy, believe me, but she really is a good girl.'

'I'm sure she is, Madame Salama, but I haven't come here to talk about your granddaughter. It's the ring I'm concerned about.'

'He left her with two small children; he just took off one day.'

'Right, but from what I can see, your granddaughter's husband isn't mentioned anywhere in the file. You agreed to pay for the ring in instalments, didn't you, Madame Salama? Expecting that he would pay you back?'

'Oh, I don't know any more, it's my husband who deals with all the paperwork; he's always dealt with that side of things.'

'I see. And where is Monsieur Salama?'

'He's in hospital.'

Ludovic's pang of apprehension was justified. He must be careful not to weaken, not to give in to pity.

'I see. But it's your signature on the first cheque. That's definitely yours, isn't it?'

'We use the same chequebook, and I can't remember. You're talking about things that happened three years ago and I've told you, they've got divorced since then.'

'No, this was two years ago. And where is the ring now?'

Ludovic pretended to search through the papers. Already, he could picture the scene, his attempt to retrieve the ring from the granddaughter who has doubtless sold it already. Two screaming kids, a panicked young woman who has lost everything. Maybe she has a new boyfriend, and he's there, standing between them. Ludovic would have to handle him, too, and try to keep a lid on things, stay calm.

He decided to try a little bluff.

'Madame Salama, you wanted to help your granddaughter before, so here's what you're going to do. You're going to help her again, because if you don't, she's the one who will bear the brunt of this. If you do nothing, she'll be the one who has to pay the seven hundred euros.'

'Oh, I don't want her to get into trouble…Oh my goodness, this would have to happen to me. Just my luck. I've never had much luck. Don't tell me you're going to get her into trouble…'

'That's exactly why I'm here, to avoid any trouble for her.

11

Listen to me, I can sort this whole thing out. I represent the jeweller in Livry-Gargan, where you bought the ring. He runs his own business, he's got the shop and the workshop, and lately he's been having a lot of trouble with people who don't pay. He wants people to have their rings on time, so he lets them pay in instalments, but he's the one who suffers if they don't make the payments. I'm sure you understand that. He needs to get paid, or he'll be forced to close. You can see that, I'm sure.'

'Jewellers, they're all thieves…'

'Not this one, Madame Salama, not this one, believe me. So, to resolve this, we're going to do one simple thing. We're going to plan your repayments, over twenty months if you prefer, and so that you don't have to worry, you're going to write out twenty cheques for thirty-five euros that the jeweller will pay in each month, and then we can avoid legal proceedings, or the bailiffs, or anything like that. That won't happen, I promise. There won't be any trouble.'

'That's all I need! For him to drag me through the courts – at my age. Well, let him try. If he wants a fight, he won't be disappointed!'

'Don't upset yourself. I'm just here to make sure no one bothers you any more. We can talk this through. We're going to take this slowly, month by month, you understand, Madame Salama, very slowly. You'll see, if you trust me, Madame Salama, everything will be fine and just like that, thanks to you, everyone will be happy and your granddaughter won't get into any trouble. Agreed? Let's drink to that.'

'Ah no! I don't want that!'

'What?'

'For my granddaughter to get into trouble.'

She took a battered chequebook out of the dresser drawer, and straight away Ludovic was seized with doubt. He prayed she wasn't about to write a series of cheques that would bounce. Already, he pictured himself having to come back in a week's time, but forced to take a quite different tone, to raise his voice to this seventy-six-year-old woman. He crossed his fingers that she would not try to trick him now, that she would act in good faith. She downed her port in one gulp then poured herself a second glass, and he felt more worried still. Even writing the first cheque proved a challenge: she complained that she couldn't do it, the pen wasn't working, there wasn't enough light. She got to her feet one more time and told him to do it. He could write the cheques out for her. She had decided to trust him and cautiously, he decided to trust her too. They would work together. But then, because he had a nose for trouble, because he noticed from the stubs that the last cheque had been written three years ago, because she was wearing two pairs of socks over her tights – not surprising, since the heating was clearly off – he realised this saga was far from over.

Aurore was surrounded by people, almost too many, she felt. The system had gone down and all the check-outs were frozen. Everyone stood in line with full baskets or trolleys; there was no turning back, short of dumping her groceries and walking out, but then what would they have for dinner? She glanced at her phone – it had signal, but there was nothing she could do. The check-out assistants seemed disoriented by the silence, unsure what to do in this unexpected lull. The tills had gone quiet, the chorus of beeps and the hum of the conveyor belts had ceased – there was almost no sound. People exchanged blank looks. Holding a walkie-talkie in one hand and offering chocolates to waiting shoppers with the other, the manager reassured everyone that the system would be back up and running in three or four minutes. Aurore wondered what might happen if she could take these three or four minutes back. Perhaps they would change the course of her life. She broke a sweat, but kept her calm, though she could hardly bear to think of all the time she lost, the time that was stolen from her, and the time it would take to gather her shopping, step back out into the cold and cross her courtyard. To cross that courtyard one more time.

The incident was like a snapshot of her life, lately. Since September, every day had been like this – her time was no longer her own. So many hours demanded of her at the office, so many minutes swallowed up in metro tunnels. Even her children seemed to her like a pair of small, selfish time-thieves, and though he was only there for ten days each month and spent most of those scowling and lurking in his room, Victor, her stepson, made demands on her too, which was perhaps worse still because he took up her time without even wanting to, just by being there, doing nothing, not making his bed or doing his homework, sprawled on the white sofa with his games console when she wished she could sit in that very spot for just one evening, drop her things in the hallway and settle back into the deep, white leather and let everything take care of itself.

The beeps resumed and life carried on. By the time she left Monoprix it was dark outside. At seven thirty on 20 October, the daylight had already fled. The carrier bags cut into the flesh of her fingers. People walked quickly in the cold, as if fearful. As she weaved her way deeper into the side streets the pedestrians, cars and shops shrank back, and soon the only sound was that of her heels tapping on the pavement. Sometimes she felt she would be reduced to this: the beat of passing time, the tick of footsteps fading into the night. And yet she had so much, everything she had ever wanted: responsibilities, a nice apartment, a family. It was just that since September, her whole life had begun to go wrong.

She tapped the code, pushed the carriage door with her foot and faced the dark courtyard. Thinking about it, she realised this was the only time in her day that was truly her own. That was why she needed it so badly. Before the crows had come to roost, this courtyard had been a space apart, a breath of air, a tonic; the moment she stepped out from the lodge, she left the whole city behind. Two towering trees formed a canopy higher than the rooftops, a world of deep silence and peace, a wilderness where tufts of grass grew between uneven paving stones, and bushes formed a dense shrubbery behind a low wall around the base of the trunks. Nature was gaining ground here, all too visibly.

Only the street-facing side of the old town mansion had been renovated, the side in which she lived. The buildings across the courtyard were ancient, with electric wires running along beams three centuries old, untouched since the last refurbishment, decades ago – another world, in which she never set foot. She walked through the woodland scent, skirting the scrap of greenery she could barely see because she had stopped turning on the outside light in September, when the crows arrived. She knew that if she set the light on its timer they would start their hideous cawing, screeching down from the treetops, shriller than an alarm. Just thinking about it sent a shiver down her spine. She had never been comfortable around birds, was even scared of pigeons when they came too close, so a roost of crows was unthinkable.

She had pushed through the carriage door for the first time, with Richard, eight years ago. Walking into the courtyard, she had discovered this patch of green, sheltered from the July heat. It had felt like finding a little piece of countryside in the middle of Paris. It was as cool beneath the tall trees as an air-conditioned room and, before they had even visited the apartment, she had known that this was where they would live. Because of the courtyard: a buffer between her and the outside world.

Aurore switched on the temperamental lamp in the post room cum bin store. The old light bulb glowed amber. She swept the junk mail into the bin and kept hold of the bills. As she left the room, she looked up. The leaves were rustling in the breeze, but the sound did nothing to quell her sense of unease.

She kept the light off in the stairwell too. Sometimes she dreaded she would find them on the landing, imagined seeing them on every floor. She told herself there would come an evening when she could no longer face it, when she would be so paralysed by fear that she would be unable to come home. Richard kept telling her, 'Aurore, they're birds; they're probably more scared of you than you are of them,' but she knew that wasn't true. When they were close by, barely more than arm's-length away, they refused to move, and fixed her with their beady eyes, challenging her. The two crows embodied all the fears that were crowding in on her, everything that was going wrong, the mounting debts, her business partner who no longer spoke to her. Since September everything had been conspiring to frighten her out of her wits.

In the city, people spend their lives making first impressions. Thousands of pairs of eyes, encountered all day long, thousands of fellow creatures who come too close; some you barely notice, others not at all. The impression Ludovic gave was of a big man. Being well-built affected the way he behaved with others. He was careful. This evening, for example, in the overcrowded bus, he was conscious that if he overbalanced even slightly, he might hurt someone, so he held on tight to the rail, because the driver seemed to enjoy making his bus, and the passengers, sway and lurch. Sitting just below him, three elderly ladies appeared tiny, some of the men too. He wasn't sure the women were paying him any attention, but the men were definitely throwing him glances, jealous of his build – a free pass in a crowd.

A young woman climbed aboard with a baby buggy. Everyone tried to make space but still it wouldn't fit. A recorded announcement requested that passengers 'move down inside the bus', and the driver left his seat to enforce the message. It was unbearably squashed now, and people were becoming impatient. Ludovic got off at the next stop. He couldn't bear crowds, the way city people herded together. Back on the street it was the same, people pushing forward, heads down. They adjusted their course, or dodged at the last minute, to avoid bumping into anyone else. They did this automatically, whilst he still had to think about it. You probably had to have lived in Paris for a long time to move instinctively through a dense, fast-moving crowd like this, to go with the flow without having to concentrate.

Before, he had never been conscious of the impact his bulk made on other people. When he was walking in the Célé valley, on the high mountain paths or through the fields, his presence did not have the same weight. His size was insignificant in that landscape, but here, he was forever stepping to one side, making way.

At Pont National, he turned left to walk along the *quais*. The view was wide open, utterly unimpeded. In the city, it takes a river to open up the sky like that. Here, at least, you could see it, even by night. The Seine was the only serene, feminine aspect of Paris. Apart from that, what he saw all around him was a tough, frenetic city, a city conceived by men, the buildings and monuments built by men, the squares, cars and avenues designed by men, the streets cleaned by men, and over there, in the skatepark, hanging out in the cold, like they did under the elevated section of the metro, nothing but men... As he walked along the stone embankment, he knew the guys were looking at him. They were looking at him because he looked at them. He attracted this kind of bravado all the time. He had come from a stressful meeting in Ivry-sur-Seine, just beyond the *périphérique*, south-east of the centre. An hour-long wrangle with an uncooperative, devious couple who had wound him up until he was on the verge of losing his temper. But he had controlled himself. Twice he had given in to anger in similar circumstances. Twice he had blown a fuse. But he wouldn't do it again, he was certain of that. At some point we all acquire a measure of wisdom. Still, appearing by surprise at someone's home to present them with an unpaid bill was always a risky business. And two meltdowns in two years was a good enough record, though 'even once could be once too many'. That was what his boss, Coubressac, had told him when he started. Coubressac had reservations at first, about Ludovic doing home visits – he had known him a long time, seen him play at club level as a rugby forward. He knew he was gentle as a lamb off the field, but he had been a pretty rough number 8, more interested in running down his opponent than in looking for the way through.

If you look strong, you need to be strong, too. At forty-six, Ludovic had lived long enough with his tough, untouchable image. But in reality, he felt crushed by the city. The move to Paris had been a sacrifice, otherwise he would still be in the Célé valley, in spite of the poor yields, and the rumours he could never shake off; in spite of the chemicals that had most likely caused his wife's death, and the case that never came to court. He would still be living as a farmer, because it was in his blood, it was his vocation. But besides the enduring memory of Mathilde, he had to face the fact that, today, five people could not live off forty hectares of land – mostly pasture – hemmed in by the hills. It was remarkable enough that his sister and parents managed to live off it. He took pride in his sacrifice for his sister, and his nephews. He had moved out, stepped aside for his brother-in-law, but that at least meant his parents could live out their lives in peace, with no need to fret over sharing out the inheritance.

It was never easy to leave the land where you were born, especially when you own it outright. But after Mathilde's death, and everything that was said, he could not stay. When the job in Paris had come up, he had said yes, almost as an act of defiance. The older of the Coubressac brothers had been looking for negotiators in the Paris region. He needed people he could trust, not necessarily experienced, but honest and reliable. The Coubressacs' family firm made farm tools, and sponsored a handful of rugby teams around the Célé, including Saint-Sauveur and Gourdon. When Ludovic played in the juniors, and later at club level, the name COUBRESSAC shone out in gold letters on the donor's plaque, at the entrance to the stadium.

Thirty years ago, their oldest son had moved to Paris to start a property business, and quickly discovered the problem of unpaid invoices. He predicted that in times of crisis this could become an easy way to make money. He had been proved right. Now, in France, there were six hundred billion euros of unpaid invoices a year, in a country where most of the State budget was devoted to paying back the national debt, which just showed that debt made the world go round and the main challenge in life was either to get paid or to pay what you owed. And so Coubressac had joined forces with a lawyer to set up a debt collection agency. At first it was just the two of them, but now they employed over forty people. Only three made house visits; the others worked the phones. Debt recovery requires tact and persuasion. After two months' legal training, Ludo started collecting. Paris was a big leap, vast and overwhelming compared to Limoges or Toulouse. It had been a rude awakening. Even though the job seemed made for him, he knew he wouldn't be able to carry on for much longer. Already, after two years, he felt oppressed by the bad luck of others, by the way good people found themselves trapped by the credit card companies, by the muddlers who refused to pay, two utterly contrasting behaviours, both of which had the same outcome. Sooner or later, everyone had to pay their due.

Ludovic preferred to see people face to face. It was more humane, because collection by phone – sitting eight hours a day in an office, chasing up debtors, harassing them for weeks, repeating the same script in the same threatening manner – was not for him. That was why he opted for house calls. And houses were indeed what he visited most. Small, modest villas, rather than apartments, in the inner suburbs, with a name on the bell which he calmly pressed. By phone it felt more like hunting – relentless stalking, designed to panic the debtor by calling them at any time of the day, including late at night and first thing in the morning, by phoning their neighbours, their friends and family, even their workplace, so that everyone knew they owed money, just as if someone had pasted a label marked DEBTOR in the middle of their foreheads. It was harassment and they never let up until the victim cracked. It was cruel.

From reading the files of closed cases, Ludovic knew that house calls produced the best results. He would have hated to spend all day on the phone, anyway. He disliked calling anyone, even family. But more importantly he needed to be on the move, out and about. Sitting down all day would have been unbearable.

When he began debt collecting he had expected some rough cases. He was prepared to deal with near-criminal behaviour but mostly he found himself tackling people who were defeated by life. The low-paid, or the newly unemployed, who had been unable to resist the urge to spend. Sometimes people were just ill-equipped for modern life, and had been scammed or been careless. Of course, sometimes there were people who deliberately avoided paying their rent or a tradesman, if they thought they could get away with it. But they were few, sadly – because it would have so much easier to tackle only the slippery, nasty types. Better for his self-motivation, too; no risk of being overcome with guilt, or pity.

He wasn't proud of his work, but neither did he feel he was in the pay of big business, any more than he was on the side of the debtors he chased. It wasn't quite so clear-cut. As a debt collector he didn't represent the big companies, only ever the sole traders, small-business owners, professionals, the self-employed. They might be jewellers, dentists, plumbers, furniture retailers, builders or architects. Service providers who had let unpaid invoices accumulate and who could not keep on top of the reminders, because getting paid had become a job in itself. They risked bankruptcy. The main reason businesses failed in France was unpaid bills. Tens of thousands of jobs were lost that way each year. And a third of the unpaid bills related to changes of address, sometimes deliberately to avoid paying. In such cases, the creditors were powerless unless they embarked on endless legal, expensive legal proceedings, with no guarantee of success. The big brands had their own debt recovery departments, and used bailiffs, not always legally, but a registered letter from a firm of bailiffs could be very effective. Even then, some debts remained unpaid. That was why Ludovic did not think of himself as a debt collector first and foremost. He told himself he was a righter of wrongs, because he felt the need to justify what he did. It was best if he just never talked about his work. And he wasn't in the habit of opening up to people.

He had lived in Paris for two years now and still he had no friends and scarcely any acquaintances. He saw practically no one. He could manage his time however he liked, provided he attended three debriefings each month at the office. The only people he spoke to otherwise were his 'targets'. Social contact of a sort. His one big fear was coming upon a family scene: parents with small children, a mother with a babe in arms, toddlers running about under her feet, a father out of work. In those cases, the children were always used against him, to make him feel guilty. The parents would say, 'You can't do this to me. Yes, I owe money, but I have four children to feed; you can't do this to us…', and it hurt him to think of the children he would never have with Mathilde. And the pain did not make him kinder, more understanding. On the contrary, it made him seethe with anger and he was afraid that one day he would really go too far – not in response to a raised voice or an bad-tempered gesture, but because of some low blow, a vile attempt to elicit his pity by flaunting a family, exhibiting everything he had been denied. And so, every time he turned up outside a new door, every time he rang a new bell, he feared the worst. Experience had taught him to be very careful. Whatever happened, whatever was said, he'd had his last chance. He must not lose his temper a third time.

Before, there had been a pair of turtle doves nesting in the highest branches. On fine days you could hear them coo above the chirping of other birds, or the blackbird's call. A soothing, refreshing sound, but this September, back from holiday, Aurore had found handfuls of beige feathers scattered beneath the trees. When she looked up, she had seen two quite different birds, intensely black. Two huge crows, their plumage gleaming like gun-metal. Since then there had been no cooing, no turtle doves. The crows had driven them away.

'Or maybe they ate them alive...'

'Honestly, Aurore. Those birds are all you talk about!'

When you confide in a friend, you expect her to agree with you, to understand, without the need for explanation. Not so with Andréa. She had been living in India for the past three years, using her failed fashion label as an excuse to drop everything and start a new life in Madras. A life more authentic, apparently, more like 'really living'. She only came back to Paris twice a year and each time they met, Aurore found her a little crazier, more irrational, no longer on her wavelength at all.

'Life is about staying as true to who you really are as possible, and you, Aurore, are anything but a businesswoman. It's way too cut-throat for you. It's a dog-eat-dog world – I should know...'

Heading back to the office, Aurore told herself she should stop talking about the birds, or everyone would start to think she was crazy. But she knew she must cross the courtyard again tonight. Even at home, she might open her windows and find them right there, in the branches outside. Even when she clapped her hands they did not fly away. She shouldn't have to put up with this. She had read on the internet that new, bigger birds were taking over in Paris because of climate change. There were seagulls everywhere already, and now the crows had come, scaring away the sparrows and swallows. Nature seemed hell-bent on proving the survival of the fittest.

She had read, too, on a science website, that crows were among the most intelligent animals, above even primates in their ability to play tricks and display cunning. Researchers in Japan had observed them placing nuts on the road, to be crushed under the tyres of passing cars. They would wait, then swoop down to retrieve the kernels. This proof of their slyness horrified her – perhaps it was the image of the crushed shells. More than once she had consulted online forums in search of tips for scaring them away, but all she had found were wild, superstitious claims about crows as harbingers of bad luck, and the perils of living alongside them. These were backed up by legends and superstition. Crows had been put on earth to betray mankind. After all, the first creature released from Noah's ark had been a crow that had never returned with news of the end of the Flood because it was too busy pecking flesh from the bodies beached by the retreating waters.

In a strange way, all this struck a chord with her. Since September, everything had been a source of worry. First, the two big orders cancelled by Galeries Lafayette, and then the missing shipment from Asia: 1,200 dresses, suits and bustiers had disappeared without trace. Three serious blows that had brought heavy losses. Next month they would be unable to meet the payroll, and the bank was threatening to cut her off. Any bank would do the same, of course – they weren't interested in lending, in fact they were chasing capital for themselves, to play the markets. When Aurore asked her bank manager for an overdraft extension, she felt she was begging for handouts. Worst of all was Fabian's reaction, so calm and unruffled she almost wondered if the whole disaster was somehow in his interest. Fabian was not only her business partner but a friend from way back when they had studied fashion together and got on so well they had launched their own company. And sure enough, for eight years, with Fabian as commercial director and Aurore as designer, everything had gone well; eight years as co-pilots at the helm, releasing two collections a year, stocked in an ever-growing number of outlets – the perfect double act. But just recently Fabian seemed to have changed. He wanted to take things to the next level, talked about high volumes and cost-cutting, seemed convinced that the only way to keep a foothold in the market was to 'expand, and fast'. Ever since his two trips to Hong Kong and the mysterious meetings he'd held there, he had turned his attention to 'piggyback distribution' – using a bigger fashion group to carry them into new markets, going elsewhere in search of growth and making use of brand capital to diversify the range. He had even talked about going into handbags, or developing a perfume. Like Andréa in India, Fabian had become a completely different person. Over the years, he had become unrecognisable.

Aurore knew a lot about the fashion world. She knew that success meant seizing every opportunity, sometimes sacrificing your initial good intentions in the name of profit. It wasn't enough to produce great designs, you also had to know how to sell them, how to position yourself, how to hang out with the right people to secure store space and press coverage. No designer succeeds by talent alone, but by the size of their contact portfolio and the people skills of their publicist. Aurore had never been naïve about this. 'The more you tell people you love them, the more they'll make out that they love you back...' But Fabian was no longer interested in making clothes, only profit. On top of everything she now found herself having to manage the concerns of their six employees, who could see there was a problem and sensed Aurore's growing anxiety.

That was why it was good to get home, why she had begun almost to long for the weekends. But last Sunday evening, one of the crows had settled on the guard rail just outside the bathroom window, barely a hand's breadth between them when she opened it to shoo the creature away. And it had refused to move. Terrified, panic-stricken, she had lost control, hollering and rapping on the window pane to make as much noise as possible, but the crow had simply moved to a branch just a little further away, and sat peering back at her. Richard had knocked on the bathroom door to check everything was OK. Yes, everything was fine, but since then she had sworn to be rid of the birds, even if she had to get hold of some sort of scare gun – she just wanted them gone. She clung to this idea of getting them out, *out*, as if it would solve all her problems, restore order to every part of her life. But even if she did get rid of them, how could she be sure they would not come back? How could she know they had gone for good and that nothing else in her life would come crashing down? The only way to get rid of them forever was to kill them.

Of course, he had called on Madame Salama a second time. Last week, as she took out the battered old chequebook, he had seen it coming: the first of the series of cheques he had filled out, and which she had signed, had bounced. And worse, the bank account had been closed two years ago. Now, this evening, as Ludovic left her house, he felt stricken. Appalled at the pressure he had brought to bear, even raising his voice to the old lady who pretended not to understand, insisting she let him look inside the dresser, because he was sure there would be cash hidden there. That was where his own grandmother kept her banknotes, under the protective plastic, right at the back of the drawers. And it turned out that Madame Salama did the same. Four fifty-euro notes. But she wanted to keep her cash. She needed money to get to the hospital: it exhausted her to go on the bus and so three times a week she treated herself to a taxi. And suddenly Ludovic did not dare touch the money; the banknotes were her tickets for the journey to visit her husband in hospital. The husband who would never come back here, never again live in the comfort of his home. For as long as she needed a taxi to go and see him, which might be years, Madame Salama would need her orange banknotes.

Faced with this reality, Ludovic had sat down heavily in the armchair beside the little table and sighed as he passed his hand over his face. To ease the atmosphere he had asked for a port, and because he did not know what else to do, he turned the situation on its head.

'Henriette, you're going to have to help me here. I'm pleading with you – you have to help me, otherwise there'll be trouble. Henriette, tell me, you must have another account somewhere. I'm sure you have a savings book or a post office account – everyone has one of those, don't they, Henriette?'

That was why this evening, on leaving her house, he needed more than ever to walk. He had left her neighbourhood and followed a long suburban boulevard, one of the arteries that all end sooner or later at a *porte de Paris*. A bus passed him on the road, heading in the right direction, but he continued on foot through the dismal suburbs, devoid of life – apartment blocks with no shops, disused factories, ill-assorted houses. He felt suddenly very far from the Célé valley, very far from the life he had led before. Were they even part of the same world? He thought of the silence there, of the wide-open space where you could wander without seeing another soul.

Finally, Henriette had taken out her post office book, and he had started again, writing out ten cheques, each for seventy euros – the pill would be harder to swallow this time. He had filled them out one by one and she had signed them, but she had not spoken another word, as if all of a sudden she had understood that it would be better to do things his way. At least now the episode would be closed. She had many other things to worry about but she could sort this out, at least. When he got up to go, this time she did not accompany him to the door, but stayed where she was, silent in her chair, not looking at him as he left. Even more than last time, she reminded him of his mother. He felt dirty for having bled her, drop by drop, of her seven hundred euros. A little old lady! He walked fast, berating himself out loud, talking to himself in a way no one else would dare. The only advantage of being a head higher than the rest, and a good bit heavier too, was that people never remonstrated with him, even when he deserved it. The danger lay in mistaking that for a licence to behave just however he liked.

He headed down the endless boulevard, and tried to rediscover the feeling he got before a match. When you walked down the corridor from the changing room, your metal studs rang out on the concrete and you felt invincible, armoured, focused. But it didn't work. Here, there was always someone to catch his eye: a down-at-heel woman in an exotic, cheap-looking floor-length robe, a market vendor shouting an offer at him. In these soulless suburbs even a smile was enough to catch him off guard. Paris was one of the smallest capitals in the world, contained within the near-perfect circle of the *périphérique*, but when you added the suburbs beyond, it became infinite, a sea of districts as far as the eye could see. And so, after walking for an hour, he climbed aboard one of the buses that had been passing him since he set out. The passengers were noisy and irritable. There was violence in the way the kids messed around, an unpremeditated aggression, the same urgent, combustible energy he had felt at their age. The difference was that he had places that could absorb the impact – tracks for his mountain bike, deserted roads, valleys all around, an environment unfazed by his adolescent outbursts. Here, youngsters were always in trouble, continually running up against something or someone in a series of endlessly reverberating shocks. Standing in the bus, he found it hard to put up with these schoolkids. They were causing havoc, they resented their confinement, and the trouble was, no one said a word. You could take them down with a joke, try to talk to them, but he didn't feel like it today. Nor did he want to tell them off, in case they took it as provocation, in which case tempers would flare. But he knew that all he needed was to grab hold of one of them, isolate him from the rest – the little smart-arse in front of him, for example, the one swinging off the bar and kicking the other kids, while no one did anything about it, they were all getting on his nerves…

'Stop that!'

They stared at him as if he was mad, just some weird old guy. He sensed they were testing the water, staring him down, but they chose not to take it any further.

He needed a goal now, to get back to the river. He was hopelessly adrift in a metropolis he would never understand. The Seine was his only point of reference, his one glimpse of unfettered nature, its flow like a never-ending search for the way out of Paris.

When you go from one suburb to another all day long, taking the metro, then the RER, then a bus, followed by a train, you realise that the city goes on for ever. You go from Paris to Noisy, then from Villemomble or Gagny to Nogent. The easiest way to get about is to return to the central axis each time. After a day criss-crossing Paris, Ludovic had seen enough avenues and apartment buildings, houses and intersections. Now he just wanted to see the Seine, his anchor. The presence of the great river, a stone's throw from his apartment, reassured him that he was not totally cut off from nature. In the city, the river was the one omnipresent, unalterable element of nature. In this city, everything starts from the Seine, and everything returns to it. Like a river in the countryside, it is the origin and lifeblood of human settlement. The Arsenal was like a world apart right in the middle of Paris, a world of old stone and tranquil streets, without cafés or shops. In the evening it was as peaceful as a provincial town, and here he did not feel out of place – as if this quaint corner offered a respite from the arrogant chic that prevailed in central Paris. He had discovered that in Paris you were identified with a place, generally a street or a metro station, in Paris you told people that you lived in such-and-such an area, as if each were a village. The apartment building he lived in was beautifully renovated on the street side. But the buildings at the back of the courtyard were a different matter. There, the façade was grubby, the gutters leaked, and the inhabitants gasped from climbing the steep stairs. This building – his building – was like a tenement block from the post-war years.

An Armenian lady on the second floor had lived there since the Second World War, while on the floor above there was a seventy-eight-year-old woman who seemed almost youthful by comparison, and a little old lady who lived with her two cats. Also on the second floor, there was a woman so quiet you never knew if she was there or not, and two students sharing a one-room apartment – a couple of boys in their twenties who played very loud music. From time to time, Ludovic would yell at them to keep it down for the sake of the elderly neighbours, especially the ninety-year-old couple on the first floor, who were not in the best of health but who clung on, keeping one another alive, so that neither would be forced to leave their home.

The most striking thing in the neighbourhood – and very unusual in overcrowded Paris – was the number of empty flats, their windows never lit. In the renovated front building, there were four large apartments, two of which were rented by the week. But without air-conditioning or a lift, they were often empty. Sometimes tourists would rent them for a few weeks at a time. You could hear their wheeled suitcases when they arrived or left, bogus neighbours who disappeared as quickly as they had come. Then there would be nothing for weeks. In the left-hand wing of the front building, the apartments were not even rented out. All were empty, their owners waiting for the market to push up their value. The advantage of this was that the building was quiet. Beyond that, Ludovic never gave it a thought. Investments in square metres of floorspace, worth ten times the price of a hectare of fertile soil were beyond him, like so much else in Paris.

On his staircase the windows didn't close properly, the stairs creaked. He had done a minimum of work in his apartment, just to make it habitable. He had patched up the central heating pipes and replaced the shower cubicle because the old one leaked. Sometimes one of his neighbours on staircase C called him for help because they saw he was good at DIY, that he had a toolbox and knew how to use it. More than once he had come to the rescue, fixed a sink that had come away from the wall in one apartment, unblocked a U-bend in another, and for the little old lady who lived next door he had even changed all her plugs, though he hated doing electrical work. He helped out his neighbours because he knew that in Paris anything that went wrong was a major catastrophe. A blocked basin, a leak, a door that refused to close immediately became a huge problem, though such things were just part of the normal run of life. Sometimes things break, they get repaired, it goes without saying. On a farm there are always things to be fixed, maintained or fiddled with. In the country, he spent his time doing just that.

His small, one-bed apartment cost him six hundred euros a month, which he found exorbitant though in fact it was a bargain. His boss had found it for him. When you worked in debt recovery there were always agreements to be struck. But when people asked him what he did, he would say he was a legal adviser. He was not naturally talkative, anyway, and certainly not with Parisians, whom he found intimidating in the extreme. They always made him feel like an outsider. It was no better in the outlying districts and towns. He was, of necessity, learning how to find his way around there, but a whole different set of codes applied beyond the *périphérique*, and still he did not understand them. He knew that when people saw him coming they usually took him for a plain-clothes cop, because of his trainers. Several times, gangs of wiry kids with their jeans below their backsides had challenged him, because there was strength in numbers. Groups like these wielded real power in the poorer residential suburbs and the high-rise estates alike. Anyone from beyond their neighbourhood was soon singled out, even more quickly than in the country. He would never have imagined that in a big city an unfamiliar face would be spotted faster than in a tiny hamlet, and treated with the same suspicion. Sometimes when he got out at an RER station, or walked across an anonymous, concrete concourse, he felt watched like a stranger on an evening stroll along the banks of the Célé. He felt it acutely – the instant you moved somewhere else, you were an outsider. Everyone is endlessly 'not from around here'.

It was 9 p.m. when Aurore came through the door. After an interminable discussion with her accountant, she had left the office late and was exhausted. She wanted to step into the all-embracing darkness of her courtyard, but instead found herself bombarded with light from all sides – one lamp above the porch, another by the gate, even the one on the far side of the courtyard. It was almost unheard of for all of them to be triggered at the same time. But worst of all was the cawing, which got louder as she walked through the lodge. There was a hint of frenzy in it this evening, as if something had maddened the birds. Fractious crows were harbingers of doom according to the Romans, or was it the Greeks? She wasn't sure. But this was just too much: some commotion in the courtyard had made the birds more agitated than ever. Sick with fear, Aurore clanged the gate shut behind her and looked towards the shrubbery. She couldn't believe her eyes: the bushes at the foot of the trees were moving. There must be animals rooting around in there – she could hear their growls and sinister cries. Even the ivy-leaves on the tree trunks were trembling now, which made the crows caw louder still... Instinctively, Aurore charged in, swinging her bag and beating it against the bushes. She quite forgot her fear, in her determination to break up the fight and chase the furious creatures away. But it was a man who scrambled to his feet amid the foliage. She stared at him, dumbfounded, as if confronting a burglar. Leaves masked his face but she recognised him as the neighbour she disliked meeting in the courtyard, the one who eyed her with a smile that made her shiver, like the excitable crows overhead.

'What the hell do you think you're doing?'

Ludovic would not reply in similar vein. He kept his calm. A cool head was the strongest weapon against such rude, aggressive behaviour. Up in the trees, the crows' rasping cries were louder still, disturbed by the presence of the humans below. Their cawing took on a shriller, more hysterical pitch now. Ludovic shouldered his way out of the dense tangle of branches, emerging with twigs and ivy stuck to his sweater. As he made to step over the low wall that enclosed the miniature jungle, he raised his arms to show off his catch: two cats held by the scruff of their necks, the poor animals dangling in his grip like freshly caught vermin. He held them high, and stepped towards Aurore.

'You can't hold them like that. You're hurting them!'

'Don't worry about them.'

'You have no business messing around in there. It's full of flowers which I planted.'

With the yowling cats, and the cawing crows, and this guy trampling all over her flowers, it was all Aurore could do to contain her anger.

'I didn't trample your flowers. I was just fetching the cats. They belong to Mademoiselle Mercier, the little old lady on the third floor. She's been frantic with worry, thought she'd lost them, but cats are cowards, really, they never go far.'

Aurore wasn't listening. She was busy inspecting the flowerbeds to check that her flowers and her parsley, sage and basil had survived. She was shaking with rage at this vandal. Ludovic stood watching her, still holding the cats.

'You should give those plants some space. They shouldn't have been put in so close to the hedge, it starves the roots. Box is toxic, you know…'

'What do you know about it?'

'I know that everything needs to be cut back, even the trees – the branches are touching the roofs up there. If there was a strong wind, I hate to think what kind of damage they'd cause…'

'Are you one of the owners here?'

'No, but I know a thing or two about trees.'

Unfazed, he gave her a smug, self-satisfied grin. The most shocking thing for Aurore was the sight of the cats writhing to free themselves from his grasp and scratch him, two unfortunate beasts held captive in the hands of that brute, not to mention the cawing overhead that wouldn't stop and was as wounding to her as the man's smile. This was the first time she had seen the neighbour up close and now she knew exactly why she had never said hello to him.

Ludovic looked up at the birds. Jokingly, he said: 'I think you've annoyed them.'

'There weren't any crows here, before.'

'Before what?'

'Before… You're the one who's annoying them. On purpose, now, it seems.'

'Oh, not at all, I'm a proper nature-lover. See here!' He brandished the cats. 'Anything that makes this much noise is fine by me – they're so full of life!'

Aurore picked up her bags. She'd had enough of the screeching and meowing and this man in her courtyard, which had become a place of terror this evening.

'Hold them properly. I told you, you're hurting them.'

'Don't worry about them. I know what to do with cats…'

'Seems you know a lot about a lot of things.'

'Less than you, by the sound of it.'

As Aurore turned and began heading towards staircase A, he called after her.

'Know what kind of crows they are? Check their beaks – they

39

look like carrion crows to me. They're the worst! Far more likely to attack…'

Aurore plunged into her brightly lit stairwell and raced up the sixty-eight steps that led to her door (if you counted the five steps up from the courtyard). Sixty-eight steps climbed in a state of utter fury, convinced she was now safe from nothing, that there was no peace even in the courtyard where she had once felt protected, and she told herself it was time to buy that pepper spray she had seen online, because she needed something to make her feel secure. She might even go so far as to spray the crows themselves, and anything else that threatened her, because this time she was ready to wipe them out, all of them, everything. No longer on the defensive. Now, she was ready to attack.

Richard had got home before her. Every time this happened, he seemed annoyingly pleased with himself. Aurore dropped her bags at the foot of the breakfast bar as if to shake off the bizarre encounter just now, down in her courtyard. Before taking off her coat, she allowed herself a moment to breathe, to put some measure of distance between herself and the animal frenzy outside. The twins were playing with Vani. Even if Richard got home first, Vani would always stay on to look after the children until Aurore got back. This evening the children were excitable because their half-brother Victor was there – not that he displayed any interest in his younger siblings as he lay on the sofa, playing on the tablet they were always trying to snatch from his grasp. As usual, Richard was deep in conversation on his hands-free phone. Clearly none of them had heard what had gone on outside. The thin little earpiece wire was hidden under Richard's hair, so it looked like he was talking to himself. He was often on the phone, striding up and down as if conversing with someone else in the room that he alone could see. So Richard was home, but at the same time he was in another place else entirely. He always kept his phone with him and often forgot to take off the earpiece, so that while he was there in person, it was hard to tell if his mind was in another realm, somewhere far more important, no doubt.

Without pausing in his conversation, he came over to kiss Aurore on the cheek before squatting on his heels on the living-room rug. It must be a transatlantic call – at this time of the evening he was far more likely to be on the phone to America than to Asia. As so often, he was running through whatever project he and his associates were hatching, juggling deals worth millions of dollars, whereas she had failed even to persuade the bank to extend her overdraft. Being American, Richard usually conducted his calls in English, but had he been speaking French it would have been no easier to work out what he was saying; his conversation was abstruse, peppered with business jargon and cryptic turns of phrase that were incomprehensible to the uninitiated.

Vani had put on a cartoon in an effort to divert the two little ones' attention from their older half-brother. They were laughing and half following the story, but went on bugging Victor, who kept pushing them away. The noise came together in a cacophony of languages, accents, children's and adults' voices, and the loud shrieks and crashes from the cartoon. There were six rooms in this apartment, but for some reason they all had to be here, in the same one. Aurore could still hear the crows' incessant cawing, around and around in her head. They were probably still at it, right outside her windows. As she took off her coat, she glanced into the courtyard to see if the lights were still on. But outside all was dark. The crazy neighbour must have left the scene, taking his cats with him. Just to be sure, she opened a window and leaned out. The branches of the tree were just beyond her reach, swaying in the breeze. The leaves had not yet fallen; Chinese lacquer trees kept their leaves well into the autumn, turning slowly from green to yellow. At least the crows were quiet now, there was no meowing to be heard, the lights had gone out and calm was restored. Peering through the branches, Aurore looked for a lit window across the courtyard. She had never seen where that man lived, but the highest windows of the opposite building were hidden by the trees and those that could be seen further down were covered by blinds or curtains. The sight of the building opposite was somehow depressing; it was like a world where time had stopped. She felt suddenly cold, and closed the window, afraid the man might be watching her, just like this, from his place, in the dark. But she saw nothing when she glanced outside one more time – nothing except the branches moving in the breeze and the dense darkness beyond. He must have a window onto the courtyard, she thought, but which one was it? Richard was behind her.

'Are you sure you're all right?'

'You scared me,' she lied.

They kissed lightly, automatically. And Richard smiled at her – the handsome smile that had won her over from the first – before heading back into the living room to continue his call.

Vani left a little after nine, annoyed to be going home late but not daring to say so. The five of them moved to the dinner table. Richard was an attractive man who frowned a lot. He was one of those people who never really left the office. Often, he would retreat into his own thoughts, concentrating on an idea, a call he needed to make, and it was only natural that he should, in a way: his company was constantly rising to ever greater heights. He had that air of quiet confidence that American business people destined for success often had. Aurore had always admired his casual Anglo-American style. He asked the children questions while they ate, listening to their answers but glancing at his messages. She envied the way he switched seamlessly between topics, and above all how calm he remained in all circumstances. Richard never lost his temper, and she wondered if that was the key to his success: simply never losing his cool. He was thirty-nine, and since making vice-president of Foundproject, he had shone in the role to a remarkable degree; the more responsibilities he took on, the more at ease he seemed. Even his gestures were more expansive. Of course, Aurore was proud of his success, but she knew all too well that a man who never stopped moving up the ladder, who was always aiming higher and higher and dreamed of splitting his time between France and the States, would one day start to look down on her. In fact, for several months already Richard had seemed less eager to answer or return her calls, and some evenings he admitted not even noticing the texts she had sent him at midday. They were lost in the flood of messages, he said. It was only a small thing, but it hurts to realise that the person you live with has stopped noticing your texts.

It was good to be inundated with requests, infinitely preferable to asking for help, as Aurore knew only too well. The business Richard had founded with his partners had just merged with an American group. Now, they were counted among the biggest web-hosting start-ups in Europe. The man she had lived with for eight years was the same man she had fallen in love with, but with a thousand more demands on his time. But still, he fulfilled his role as a father, as evidenced by the fact that this evening his oldest son was here with them. This evening he had three children at the table, a proper family, and he was full of paternal pride, made all the more intense because such moments were rare. In a world where everyone trembled for their future, growing more fearful by the day, Richard was a miracle, so successful it seemed almost contagious. The danger was that success, and the constant demands on his time, would change him. Last week he had been away for two days at a conference, next week he would be in San Francisco for three days. They never talked about it, but Aurore had the firm feeling that Richard was faithful to her, even though he was such an attractive man – handsome, authoritative, but always cheerful with a ready smile.

She wanted to talk to him this evening, ask him what he would do in her place, faced with vanishing orders, late payments that were mounting up, and worst of all, a business partner who had begun avoiding her... But if she opened up to him about her worries here at the table she would panic them all, the whole family, and Richard's perception of her would shift to that of a woman with problems, a mother losing her grip. There was no way she could talk to him, now or later. He was one of those men who needs to be surrounded by successful people, and she knew that if she betrayed the slightest weakness, if she failed, he would never look at her the same way again.

'Would you know a carrion crow if you saw one?'

'Aurore, don't start with your—'

'But would you?'

He had ended up trapped in this role, in a way. By playing the placid, unflappable guy, calm and reliable, he was forced to be that person. But it was exhausting always to play the good guy. He knew perfectly well that the man he tried hard to be did not exist. Especially not right now. Paris disturbed him. Since coming to live here, he found himself constantly knocking into people, barging into them without meaning to, as he passed in the corridors at work, in a metro station, or the hallway of an apartment block. His days in Paris left him wound up almost to breaking point, so that sometimes when he got home in the evening he was ready to lash out and actually hit someone. The fine line he trod constantly at work, the crowds that were everywhere, all the time, vehicles and pedestrians in every direction, the atmosphere of constant friction, the day-to-day stress, left him tense as a coiled spring. That was why he needed to be in the open air.

He returned to the Célé valley every five weeks, driving the six hundred kilometres and staying for two or three days, never more. He went mainly to see his mother. At least he looked out for her as best he could. The others – his sister, his nephews and his brother-in-law – didn't seem to have the time. True, they worked a seventy-two-hour week, always under pressure from the bank, the market price of veal, the weather, the mountain of overdue paperwork. With each year that passed it was more and more difficult to keep a farm running, and everyone was too busy to care for their mother. Though just two years ago, she had been the one who cooked all their meals, and did everything around the house. When they came in from the farm all they had to do was put their feet under the table and their meals, like their beds, were always made. But now that she could no longer do these things, their mother had become a burden, one more thing, like a dead weight. And so Ludovic still went there as often as possible, so as not to lose touch. A family is like a garden; if you can't be bothered to work at it, it will grow wild, and die of neglect.

He was careful to say nothing about the way they were managing the farm. Even when they lumbered themselves with a payment plan for a brand-new tractor and cowshed. It wasn't what he would have done, but they insisted they had no choice. If you run a farm like a business, you're a businessman, not a grower. There was a great deal that bothered him about the way they ran things, but he forced himself to say nothing. He would make no criticism of their handling of the farm that should have been his. A family was a delicate thing, especially when it owned a loss-making farm, five kilometres from the nearest village, an isolated farm shared by multiple generations. It was important that there should be one member of the family who mitigated and shared the burden, who kept themselves above the fray, otherwise everyone went their own way and everything broke apart. He drove the six hundred kilometres to Saint-Sauveur, and he only ever spent two nights there, never more. He would not be a burden to them, and so far it had worked. Nowadays, he stayed up later than they did. Once everyone was in bed, he would go out into the yard to smoke. Outside, there was always the same musical score, the owl and the crickets. Tonight there was no moon. He could see nothing beyond the yard, but he pictured the scene in his mind's eye. He knew every path, every nook and every cranny for twenty kilometres around. A strange feeling: here he knew the landscape practically down to the last

47

millimetre, whilst in Paris he knew nothing about the apartments opposite including the one belonging to that beautiful, highly strung woman, the sour brunette he saw smoking in the courtyard in the evenings, walking in circles around the trees, much as he was doing now. It was after midnight and they had all gone to bed ages ago. When he lived here, he had turned in earlier too, rather than stay up watching television or whatever else; he had gone to bed eager for the next day, wanting the night to pass quickly so that it could be morning again. But nothing he did was like them now.

Each time he came home, he felt his mother's growing absence, as she became more and more cut off in her own world, installed in the sitting room all day, motionless as a stopped clock. He always took her for a walk. He was the only one she would walk with beyond the farmyard. She hadn't really grasped that he no longer lived at Saint-Sauveur. When she saw him reappear in the doorway, she raised her head and looked at him as if he had only left that morning, as if he still worked there. She would ask him what he had done with his morning, though she hadn't seen him for weeks.

She was losing her mind, that was how they put it – she was losing her mind and her present was a day without end, where the clocks didn't work. Yet there was one clock inside her which continued to function; it was the clock that registered the rhythm of the seasons and the work that went with it. It seemed as if that measure of time was a part of her, a sort of inalienable instinct, which meant that she still knew precisely when to sow, when to bring the animals inside, when to make hay and prepare for an incoming storm.

When he took her out, they would cross the bridge, then walk along the riverbank, she holding on to his arm. They would walk like that for more than an hour, not quickly, but getting far enough across their land. The farm occupied the whole of the bottom of the valley, more than forty-five hectares. It was a fertile, sinuous strip that followed the course of the Célé river. On either side, two rocky outcrops rose to more than a hundred metres, twin ramparts that framed the narrow valley like a canyon. In the summer, the western outcrop stole their sun two hours early in the evening. In the morning, on the other hand – because the western hill was lower and broader – the sun rose straight up. Day broke here at the same time as everywhere else, but night fell earlier.

The aim of each walk was to get as far as the old carding shed. The ancient structure was still standing. It was huge, and had been abandoned fifty years ago. His mother had bought it just for the land, and for fifty years they had been saying that they must do something with those buildings. At one time they had used them to store hay and wood. Ludovic and Mathilde had vowed that one day they would open a gîte there. Green tourism was something that worked well in the area – a rural gîte with canoes for hire on the river. Many people were keen to get into green tourism locally, and suddenly there were plenty of buyers for the old carding shed. But his mother would not sell. Ludovic still told himself that he would go ahead with the project he had conceived with Mathilde, though it would be much harder now, and a colossal amount of work. There are projects like that, that live on inside us, and help us to carry on.

On their way back to the farm after a good long walk, Ludovic would be bearing his mother's weight. She flopped against him like a heavy rag doll. With Ludovic's arm wedged firmly under her own, she clung to him, muttering unintelligibly. Perhaps that was why she had produced such a solidly built son, so that she could hang from him like a puppet.

When she got home, still on her son's arm, Gisèle would put

her slippers on awkwardly. That morning they had walked for almost an hour and been all the way round the carding shed, whereas normally, with her daughter or son-in-law, she barely took more than a few steps in the yard. For two years now, she had spent her days in her armchair, gazing out of the window. She watched through the window as if she was watching television. It was extraordinary to spend entire days like that, in complete silence. But sometimes she would talk. She would say that a cow had been saved, or she would reminisce about goodness knows whom, Old Tauriac, their closest neighbour, though he lived three kilometres away, or the postman on his moped, who always had a cigarette in his mouth and who hadn't come for more than thirty-five years. Usually, in the afternoon, they would put the television on for her. They turned it on for the one o'clock news. She liked that, the one o'clock news; it was like going for a walk beyond the immediate vicinity, to an exotic place where the flowers were the same, but the roofs and the landscape were different. But once the news was finished she would turn her gaze straight away to the other windows, the windows onto the real world. There were six of them in the large room and you could see all over the farm from them, apart from to the south because of the kitchen wall and the fireplace. To the west you could see the arable fields, and the vegetables to the east, and you could see a bit of the river as well, and the rocky hills if you looked up. So it was only to the south, where the cowshed was, that you couldn't see, but you could tell what was happening there from the sounds. There were only about fifteen cows, and they returned each evening by themselves, docile, as if trained, as if Ludovic were still there and they were answering his call, although it had been two years since he left – two years since he had left this house, with the bitterness of those who leave their native soil. As for his mother, it was hard to see her sitting in silence. But when she began to talk it was harder still.

'It's a good thing you're here, you know, because your sister and Gilles, try as they might, they would never manage without you.'

'Maman, what are you talking about... There's Papa, he's a big help, isn't he?'

'Good thing you're here.'

That was the point at which Ludo invariably froze, never knowing if he should infantilise his mother, treat her like a little child who didn't understand anything about anything, tell her for the hundredth time that he no longer lived here, that his sister and brother-in-law weren't doing too badly, and tell her, again, that his father, though he was eighty-two, still rose every day at dawn, and saw to the veal calves and the vegetables, and could still handle a tractor better than anyone else. He did not know how to treat his mother as she became more and more confused. Should he be unkind and tell her he was leaving the next day, that he lived in Paris? Should he say, again, that anyway the place wasn't productive enough to support them all, that their income was dwindling as time went by, and the day of the traditional, mixed farm where you did a little bit of everything was over? How could he make her understand that the old ways, which had worked for centuries, did not work anymore? She would never understand.

But it hurt him more than anything when his mother asked for news of Mathilde. 'Why do we never see Mathilde? Is she annoyed with us?' When for the last three years Mathilde had lain in the cemetery.

The dinner seemed to go on for ever. Aurore was surrounded by men all talking loudly, and she felt she would never be able to escape. Already, over the aperitifs, she had decided it would be unbearable. Now she glanced down at her phone. No missed calls, or messages. She felt cut off, a long way from home – a three-hour train ride away, plus an hour in the coach along the motorway that ran past the petrochemical plants of the Rhône valley. An hour watching industrial sites slide past, wreathed in strange smoke. They weren't ghost factories, then, but they were like something from a bygone era. This evening more than ever, she felt out of her depth, abandoned in the cold and wet of downtown Annonay.

Her TGV had left Paris Gare de Lyon at seven o'clock in the morning. She had got up at five. That was the problem with wanting to make 'couture' garments with new fibres, combining sophisticated, stylish designs with technical fabrics. It was testing and took all her skill. To make it easier to keep an eye on all aspects of the business, her rule was that the clothes should be made as close to Paris as possible, and only ever in France. She would never deviate from that. It wasn't just a matter of principle, she also wanted to control the supply chain, be able to trace an item from start to finish, and not have to wait for her stock to arrive from the other side of the world in a container. It mattered hugely to her, too, that her clothes were not made by exploited little girls working seventy hours a week. Fabian could rattle off all the figures he liked, but she would not go back on her initial plan to produce everything in France. Until recently, he had agreed with her on everything and always followed her lead, but for six months now he had been trying to encourage her to sign up with a new partner, a distributor with offices in Europe and Asia, who had convinced him that it was vital to move production out of France. Things had come to a head, and now Fabian left her to manage alone on work trips, no doubt waiting to pounce if she made a mistake. So here she was, at this dinner, surrounded by specialists in high-tech fibres, salesmen used to selling high volumes to sports manufacturers or makers of industrial clothing, experts in paraglider wings, ski outfits or survival blankets. There was no one who knew anything about making luxury lingerie or crossover cardigans. But that was what she wanted, always to innovate, by using new materials or daring to try new fibres. And the others around the table would have the satisfaction of working on individual designs, making fine, elegant pieces using their ultramodern polyester. It would be a challenge, a change from their huge industrial orders, their production lines churning out thousands of items. It would be an achievement for them to make precise, delicate garments, and since midday they had been listening to her. They respected her, and she truly felt they were ready to work with her. She did not for one moment doubt their motivation, but as the day wore on, she realised that it would not be that simple, in spite of their good will, because there was so much they did not understand. They seemed unable to visualise the prints and cuts she had in mind. There were six men and her. Only their accountant was a woman, and she appeared to understand even less than the men. She seemed even more disdainful and uptight than they were fast becoming.

Aurore endured the never-ending dinner. The group was noisy, she thought; they all spoke too loudly. Perhaps as a result of manufacturing kilometres of techno-fibre on vast, deafeningly loud machines, they had become that way themselves. That was all she had seen, all day: gigantic looms that weighed several tons and made a racket like a chorus of power hammers. It was amazing to see a thread a few microns wide begin its journey across forty square metres of hangar, a colossal, blaring production line spooling reels that were more than two metres tall, out of steaming autoclaves. It was the perfect illustration of the paradoxical nature of the operation, using very heavy machinery to produce something so light, a hyper-resistant material created by weaving the finest of threads to the highest possible count. As a fashion designer, the process interested her very much.

And now, after a day of trying to make herself heard above the noise, she was having to do the same this evening. There were three conversations going on at the table, bursts of laughter, and she thought again that she would not be able to bear it much longer. She felt the incomprehension that all designers feel when dealing with manufacturers. She saw the effort it would take to bridge the gap. There were times when the thought that she must be the one to make everything happen left her exhausted. It was easy to draw a design on a piece of paper, a dress was manageable when it was a mere sketch. It was only later that the problems began, especially now that she had to do everything alone. She had to make decisive choices, and no mistakes, negotiate the estimates with each supplier, present her designs to each new customer, and it would be like this until she could take no more and then she would fall apart or say to Fabian, 'OK, you win, we can manufacture in Bulgaria or China or wherever you like, but I can't go on like this…' The price of her independence was this pressure, which weighed on her physically. The brand depended on her and after six months of enduring this on her own – the design, the manufacture, all the problems – there were evenings when she couldn't take it anymore.

'And why don't you want to do business with them?'

'Excuse me?'

'You're brimming with ideas, Madame Dessage, you should make them an offer.'

'I don't understand, make who an offer?'

'Ski suit manufacturers! Or Airtex: Aurore Dessage motifs on the wings of a paraglider – that would add a lot of value, send it sky high!'

That made them all laugh. All afternoon she had been talking to them about little two-piece suits in stretch twill, but they were redirecting her to their target market, customers who ordered by the kilometre and were the mainstay of their business. They knew they were in a strong position because technical fibre on its own accounted for most of the textile industry in France and a large share of exports. As for conventional fabrics, most of the factories had closed.

Cheese was served, then dessert. They passed around the heavy, well-stocked cheese board. She felt as if everything was conspiring to make her aware she didn't belong here. She would much rather have been at home, partly because Richard was in London this evening and Vani had become less and less keen to stay after eight o'clock: she no longer wanted to spend her evenings alone with the children, and claimed she did not feel safe in the old, half-empty apartment block in the middle of Paris. She was worried about break-ins and ghosts. It was even worse now that she had seen the crows. She said it wasn't good to sleep next to a nest of crows. 'In Sri Lanka, we don't like those jungle crows with their feet as long as their beaks, we consider them vermin.' She could frighten everyone in the building with talk like that. Only Richard managed to laugh off their nanny's fears. He enjoyed bringing the subject up, knowing what she would say: 'Do you know they carry disease? You'll see, when the kids get diarrhoea.'

Yesterday, with Vani so anxious, Fabian letting her down, and Richard out of town, Aurore had been sorely tempted to cancel her trip, but she found the strength to persevere. Her work was no less important than Richard's; in fact she was even more indispensable. He was part of a large team, within the kind of structure that spread responsibility between colleagues, whereas she had six members of staff all reporting directly to her, and everything rested on her shoulders. Each time she visited a factory, she was away for twenty-four hours, but it was essential to visit her suppliers, to see the textiles come off the production line, to explain the needs of the business in person, so that she could be sure they understood her.

After dessert, she felt obliged to stay for coffee and liqueurs. She had been seated at the end of the table, next to the engineers and the managing director, and even though they treated her like an important client, they knew perfectly well that the orders she would place would be tiny. To secure a good price, she must convince them, there and then, as she sipped her pear liqueur: haute couture styles in their catalogue would be a source of prestige; it would establish them as makers of high-end textiles, hence it would make good business sense for them, and for her. But they would not budge on price. Even after a two-hour dinner, they held firm. They treated her just like their other customers, the ones who ordered by the kilometre. Her arguments did not sway them. The longer they all lingered around the table, the more they took the upper hand. Their laughter intimidated her. For two months now she had felt out of her depth, and this evening, she was struggling to hide her unease. She felt so small in the face of the fear mounting inside her.

Aurore felt as if everything was spinning out of her control – her company, the twins, her marriage. Richard was away more and more often, clambering so far up the corporate hierarchy, that now he seemed positively out of reach. Meanwhile, she was fighting to turn her company around and find the money to pay her staff and suppliers. She was trying to re-engage with her disinterested business partner, even though she feared he was planning to stab her in the back. She was struggling to reassure her staff, whilst still working on her new designs and trying to keep costs down. Launching her own fashion label had been a big adventure, but now every scrap of fun and excitement had gone.

She went outside to smoke a cigarette, staring blankly across the large square sunk in darkness. Frost twinkled on the ground. Apart from the few vehicles belonging to the restaurant's customers, the parking spaces were all empty. She knew she was catching a cold. She knew, too, that her life had gone wrong. That she was moving from one chapter the next – a bad luck phase that suddenly took on the features of her sinister surroundings. Yes, since the start of the new season, something had changed, as if she was being made to pay for all the years when things had run smoothly. She thought again of the cats dangling from the grasp of that giant, of the man's smug grin, and his confidence in his own strength, like the men here. The memory of her neighbour was mixed up with the vision of the factories that had ground down her morale all day, as if in future her life would be made up of nothing but these depressing journeys, and their attendant humiliations, and empty car parks and deserted towns. And always with people talking about figures and unemployment, and a hopeless future.

'Madame Dessage, shall we go?'

*

Her hotel was some distance from the restaurant. After they had dropped her outside, in the depressing town centre with its empty shops like missing teeth, she first smoked a cigarette, then made her way to the unlit door, but could not find the entry code. Nor was there a night porter, or anyone answering the phone. She was forced to ask drinkers loitering outside the closed bistro to find the number for the hotel manager, or anyone who might know the damned code. So that when she finally reached her room, after fearing that she might have to spend the night outside, she felt an overwhelming need to call someone, anyone, just to hear a voice at the other end of the line that would find the right words to reassure her. Even though it was past midnight, she wanted someone to do her the immense favour of listening and telling her that despite the cold, desolate room she was going to sleep well. She thought about phoning Richard, but she knew that he was at an event sponsored by his company, and she had no desire to intrude into his world and complain and ask for help. In any case what could he do for her while he was away in London?

Sometimes, when faced with an unexpected crossroads in life, we discover that for years we have been walking a tightrope, with no knowledge of whether we are stepping out over a void, or if there is anything – or anyone – strong enough to catch us underneath. And we realise that we do more for others than they do for us. Everything is expected of us. Of course, in this way, children are voracious, greedy, ever-demanding, never grateful. Naturally, we carry our children. But Aurore was thinking of all the other people she must support and to whom she must never reveal her weaknesses, her breaking points, for fear they would test them to the limit. The true givers, the true listeners, were rare indeed.

Again, this evening, Aurore was the last to leave the office. Before going, she just wanted to print out the estimates sent by the Annonay factory, but when she went to the printer, she saw that not a single sheet had come out, and the warning lights were flashing red. She lifted the top and found a sheet jammed inside, covered in ink. She tugged at it, tearing off a strip on which she read the words '...suggest we continue our confidential negotiations on the pre-pack insolvency, so that the period of voluntary liquidation is no longer than two months and the buyers...'

Voluntary liquidation... Straight away, Aurore thought of Fabian. But there had never been any discussion of voluntary liquidation, still less of negotiations to sell the company to new buyers. She stared in puzzlement at the scrap of paper, unsure whether this was a document Fabian had prepared, or whether perhaps it was nothing at all to do with the company. She closed the top of the printer, but as she waited for the machine to reset itself, with the usual series of whirrs and clicks, she searched 'pre-pack insolvency' on her phone. Aurore stared at the top listing. She did not panic, but she feared she understood.

She hadn't exchanged a word with Fabian for days. He had been away last week, and the week before that they had argued. Now, if this scrap of paper really was about their business, it would be worse than a betrayal. The most galling thing was the reference to 'buyers' plural. That meant he had teamed up with goodness knows whom to hatch a plan, and that for weeks or maybe months, he had been fixing a deal behind her back. She did not want to believe it. How could he have pulled this off without her knowledge? Was she really so naïve? It was true that there were aspects of business she didn't fully understand. Perhaps she hadn't read some of the contracts carefully enough, but she had always trusted him, and anyway that had never been her role.

Travelling home on the metro, she felt the same sensation that had overcome her in the hotel room in Annonay: everything was spiralling out of her control. She had felt utterly abandoned then, and three days later she felt the same. Now, as then, she would have liked to be able to call someone for reassurance. But she did not want to alarm anyone, and it would be humiliating to ask for help. She felt she was losing her business; things were slipping from her grasp. She would look pathetic, shameful. She was glad of the packed train carriage; it was comforting to have all these people around her. Living in Paris reassured her – that feeling that she was at the centre of things, surrounded by other lives, other languages, seeing people from all over the world, tourists eager and excited to explore the city, on foot, by bike, aboard a bus, even by rickshaw. The melting pot of delighted foreigners, and all those who had chosen to make their lives here, who had dreamed of moving to Paris, who clung to the idea of Paris and had created this ideal of the city. She needed to feel she was at the centre of all this energy. For fashion, Paris really was the centre of the world, and that was key. In times of economic crisis and uncertainty, Paris would always stand for creativity. It would always be the cradle of haute couture and she was stimulated by that creative exuberance, by the idea that all the top couturiers, jewellers, leather goods manufacturers came here to present their new collections, that Paris was home to the most prestigious runway shows, the best Fashion Week. The vitality buoyed her.

Yet, this evening, fear was uppermost, the fear of no longer being able to design new collections, or take part in shows, and she knew if that happened, she would feel she had been banished. Her brand had encountered problems before, but this time they came from within. She took the torn scrap of paper from her pocket. She could not bear the thought of filing for bankruptcy and losing the brand that bore her name. She would lose her identity, and she could not bear the thought of telling her six employees that she could no longer cope and the business wasn't going to make it, that they were being made redundant despite all the times she had asked them to work late. She could not look them in the eye – Aïcha, Laura, Saïd, Sandrine, Maeva and Ricardo – and tell them that this time it was all over and she was letting them go. She would never be able to do that.

In the crowded metro, she told herself she absolutely had to talk to Fabian, and now. She rang him twice in quick succession. The third time, the call went straight to voicemail. She wouldn't leave a message, that would only forewarn him and she wanted to take him by surprise, to confront him with this scrap of paper so that she could gauge his reaction. Obviously, there would never again be the euphoria of the start-up – the sleepless nights before a runway show, even working through the night sometimes, but always with a terrific team spirit, music pumping in the background. It appalled her to think of the energy she had poured into creating the brand that bore her name. She would not have the strength to start all over again. To start a company in France you either had to be mad, or have a fantastic support network. It had been easy to find supporters as an emerging designer, but she had seen what happened when others stumbled along the way – it was impossible to get back on your feet. In Paris, one failure was a life sentence.

It's never easy to face facts, but she could not ignore the knowledge that the bank would probably withdraw its backing after December. She had two months to get herself back on track, or they would pull the plug.

The train braked sharply, throwing the passengers against each other. She gripped the rail. The carriage was crammed with people, and advancing slowly – there was probably a demonstration above ground, or a visiting head of state. Two men were talking about a suspect package on line 4; others were saying it was on line 2. They spoke as if the incident was part of some video game, merely an inconvenience. Or perhaps there was a bomb. The result was that everyone had transferred onto line 1. There was pushing and shoving, and bodies pressed all around her, too close to make out their faces. She knew that soon she would break a sweat. Luckily, line 1 was automatic, and efficient. Unhuman but efficient. There was no driver, therefore no wasted time. Stop, beep, set off again, seamless as an automated production line. She thought back to the racket of the giant textile looms. At each stop, the stations recycled their cargo of travellers. People poured from the corridors, they came from everywhere, knocking into each other, pressing tighter in the carriage. An unhappy crowd. More than ever, Aurore felt that all was lost. Her back was sweaty, her legs felt as though they would give way. This sudden feeling of abandonment was like a fever. Hadn't Richard left his first wife to move in with her practically overnight? She had felt guilty about it for eight years, as if she had been responsible for the separation, and his wife's unhappiness. One day Richard would do the same thing to her, or perhaps it would be more insidious than that; he would grow more distant little by little, spend more and more time away, increasingly absorbed in his work.

The train pulled into Saint-Paul and she let herself be carried up the escalator, as if being conveyed out of Hell. She arrived in the fresh air, her shirt unbuttoned, assailed by toxic thoughts.

*

When she opened the gate to her courtyard, she looked around at all the windows. Very few were lit and some of those had heavy curtains hiding the light; only hers were blazing, all six of them up there, unimpeded by shutters or blinds. There was no sign of the crows and she relished the silence as she took a few steps over the mossy paving stones. She leaned over to look at the flowers she had planted as bulbs in the spring, and her three-year-old hydrangeas, checking all the plants he had trampled. She peered down at the ground around the bottom of the bushes, trying to see if her basil had survived. The sage had sprung back, but the parsley was ruined. Suddenly they burst out like clay pigeons from a trap. The first screeched past her, inches from her ear, the second erupted from the bushes, beating its broad wings, and smacked into her as it passed. The feeling of those wings was repulsive. She staggered backwards, all the more shocked because tonight she thought they had gone. Perhaps they were doing it on purpose, toying with her, and now here she was on her backside on the freezing cobbles, trembling in shock.

A re you OK now?'
    He had taken her by surprise, and she gave no reply, acting as if he was not there.

She could not bear the manner of this man, asking how she was as if they knew each other. This morning everything was conspiring to make her late; everything was getting on her nerves. She was standing by the letterboxes in the post room, trying to put up a note for everyone, but the tape would not stick to the ageing plaster, so she fixed it to the noticeboard at the back, above the bins, which meant she had had to rewrite it on a bigger piece of paper and reach up awkwardly to position it, which made her later still. Behind her, the man was talking about the cats, assuring her that they would never escape again. Perhaps he was implying that he had had them put down, flaunting his male dominance. When she turned round, she saw him standing in the doorway, dressed in a blazer, not that it made him look smart. He was addressing her with the false bonhomie of a neighbour trying to be friendly. She went over to her letterbox, passing in front of him without really looking his way. But she noticed the combination of the black blazer with trainers and a white T-shirt. A thoroughly yokel get-up.

'Oh, and I wanted to tell you, I've got my eye on your enemies up there.'

She straightened up, said nothing, but shot him a look of inscrutable intensity. She was astonished, and grateful, truth be told. And appalled by his black blazer, those trainers… Yet she had the extraordinary feeling of having been heard. She couldn't think what to say to the man, but it was he who spoke again, doing as she was doing, looking in his letterbox.

'They're pests, those birds, they chase everything else away, and the worst thing is once they've roosted, you can't get rid of them.'

'So it would seem.'

Aurore took out a bundle of papers, flyers and cards.

'It's especially bad for you – it's no good having them right opposite—'

'How would you know—?'

'You don't live on the third floor?'

'No… I meant what do you know about crows?'

'My father used to make us shoot them. They eat everything, and if you kill one, the others come to eat it. They eat each other, they're scavengers.'

He was balling up the flyers from his letterbox as he spoke. Aurore watched his big hands crushing the paper, the same hands from which the cats had dangled, helpless, the other evening. An image of crows pecking at entrails flashed into her mind. Decidedly, everything about this man made her uncomfortable. But here he was, smiling broadly.

'What's that you're pinning up there?'

'My stepson is having a birthday party. There will be lots of people – it's just to warn the neighbours.'

Still smiling his annoying smile, he said, 'Neighbours? The building's full of deaf old people and empty apartments – you won't bother anyone…'

'Well then, let's just say it's to warn you.'

'Oh, you don't need to worry about me. Nothing bothers me!'

He pitched his ball of paper into the half-open bin and departed, with a brief '*au revoir*'. Aurore lingered in the post room so that she wouldn't have to walk with him.

Once in the metro, she kept hearing that 'Nothing bothers me.' Was that really true? she wondered. Though he had said it with such certainty that it really seemed as if nothing did bother him. Perhaps he never let anyone annoy him, never complained. She imagined he might be like that, though she knew it couldn't be entirely true; everyone suffers, everyone has fears and weaknesses, it was just that he was better than most at hiding them – or else he really was very strong, like an armoured vehicle. She pictured his smile, with its hint of provocation – that smile, and that build. That man took up too much space. She pictured him again, planted in front of her, in the doorway to the post room, blocking the light.

'Nothing bothers me.' She had understood what he meant. 'Nothing can get to me, nothing touches me, nothing frightens me.' Suddenly, she found her own fears ridiculous. Like her current fear of being late, of facing her accountant one more time, as she pointed to the red cells on her Excel spreadsheets, more and more red cells. She must confront Fabian, make sure he had nothing to do with that scrap of paper. Or else she could pretend she hadn't seen it, and keep an eye on her inbox, waiting to see exactly how far he would be willing to go to betray her. At lunchtime, she would also have to reassure her team, because they all knew that the next collection was melting away, that there would be no show this spring, and that in two weeks' time there would be nothing left for them to do... She faced an array of challenges this morning, and that was without her everyday worries: the dread that something had happened to her children, her stepson's chaotic eruption into adolescence, hiding weed in his wardrobe, Iris's asthma attacks since the holidays. Her six-year-old daughter's pale face was frail rather than pretty at the moment. She must not let her worries as a mother become apparent to Fabian, still less to the others, but they were there, hidden deep inside her; day after day, they were always there.

'Nothing bothers me.' The expression kept playing in her head and it was annoying her now, just as everything on the way to the metro had annoyed her: the rain, the pedestrians jostling their umbrellas, the stream of backed-up traffic, the scooters weaving in and out. And then, in the metro, everything was worse still. People crammed together, steaming bodies far too close, the damp reek of pallid humanity, like a pack of wet dogs – everything was repulsive this morning, there was no Parisian charm. Today, everything smelled of sour laundry, and she had the overwhelming impression that they were all dirty and sad and damaged more and more by the late October gloom.

'Nothing bothers me' was perhaps a sign of supreme indifference. The man was disturbed by nothing because he was impressed by nothing, cared about nothing, he was totally selfish, alone in the world; since he'd lived in the building, there had been no sign of a wife or friends. Did he really live all alone? She had no idea. Until now she had never given him a second thought; he hadn't existed for her. She suspected that he lived at the top of the building at the back of the courtyard, and the leaves that filled the space between them were protection of a kind; the trees shielded her from the façade opposite.

Several times over the next few days, she found herself looking at the windows across the courtyard. As the leaves began to fall, she could see through the branches, and at night she could see whether the lights were on or not. Outside one window there was a pot of white geraniums, but she could not imagine the man planting delicate flowers in a window box twenty centimetres square. One evening, as they were sipping their tisanes, she suddenly asked Richard if he knew the man who lived in the building opposite, the big burly guy...

'Why are you asking me about him?'

'Oh, you know... have you ever spoken to him?'

'Yes, hello and good evening. He's "one big guy", as we say. But he's kind of weird.'

'Weird?'

'Everything about staircase C is weird. It wouldn't surprise me if it turned out he was squatting some little old lady's apartment, or maybe he's killed her...'

'No, but seriously...'

'I am being serious. Don't you realise that it's because of their filthy cellars and attics that we get all the mice and birds in the neighbourhood. I bet there are rats too. The managing agent told me that on staircase C everyone has cats and it's not because they're animal lovers, it's just so they'll kill the mice. It's like a bygone era over there.'

She knew everything had changed when she caught herself looking out for him. For several days in a row, Aurore collected her mail from the post room, then waited around for a few seconds, thinking she heard footsteps on staircase C. She wanted him to tell her how they had killed the crows when they were kids. Since apparently they could be killed, and since he had mentioned this solution, her original idea had taken shape, though it was almost certainly impracticable, and even the thought of discussing it with him made her feel queasy. This morning as she unlocked her letterbox, she thought she heard his footsteps, so she stood looking through her post, delaying the moment when she would have to leave and face her schedule, overshadowed by two difficult meetings. The meeting with her bank, in the morning, about the unpaid social security contributions from her payroll, and the lunch with her team, would be very wearing. For now, she would just like to see that man whom nothing bothered. She felt it would set her up for the day, and she would get through the two meetings with that same confidence and detachment. The man whom nothing bothered, and his exasperating smile. Just one glimpse, and perhaps some of that supreme confidence would rub off on her. The man who was intimidated by nothing. But he did not appear.

Aurore left the post room and opened her umbrella, slowly and carefully. It was starting to feel more and more autumnal and she disliked the rain that seeped into everything and snarled all of Paris in an interminable traffic jam that made everything more difficult. Footsteps could be heard on staircase C, but as she made her way across the courtyard she saw it was not him but a FedEx delivery man who had got the wrong staircase. An abrupt reminder that she must face her day of files and meetings. She adjusted the large bag on her shoulder and continued across the courtyard, passing through the carriage arch without closing her umbrella. The floor was wet, and her shoes slipped as she tried to pull open the heavy door to the street. Suddenly, for once, it opened on its own, and there he was in front of her, on his way back from a run. Seeing her there, he stood aside to let her pass, offering her the rain-sodden street with that same, almost violent smile. She looked at him, and showed no surprise, but she could not believe that he had been for a run in this deluge, in nothing but shorts and a waterproof K-Way jacket, without even a hood. His face was soaked but it didn't bother him. Yet again, nothing bothered him.

She was almost annoyed that he did not mind the rain. It meant he would never understand her. A man who set off to run bare-headed in a torrential rainstorm was the exact opposite of her, with her umbrella already open and her inappropriate shoes that slid on the wet floor. Yet at exactly that moment she felt the urge to hug him, to absorb some of his strength, just hug him, that was all. She let none of this show in her curt 'Thank you', the cold, aloof way she stepped in front of him. But then she heard him call out behind her. Two words, with perhaps just a hint of irony: 'Good luck!'

She turned to see if he was watching her leave, but he had already gone through to the courtyard. She thought of the matches Richard and the children watched on television, men fighting over a ball in the rain, juvenile hunks with bare legs horsing around in the mud. And that jacket with its rainbow motif – she hadn't looked closely but she had noticed that, a rainbow on a black K-Way, the man standing there dripping water with a rainbow on his chest. Bare-headed and bare-legged. Truly this was a man who seemed untroubled by anything – the rain, the cold, anything in the world. He was either a free spirit or supremely self-absorbed. Around her, everyone walked with their head down in the cold and wet, wrapped up warm under their umbrellas, when all he needed was a pair of shorts and a K-Way. In the midst of the crowd, criss-crossing hurriedly in every direction, she pictured a great mound of superfluous things weighing down upon her, the threats and pettiness all around, and she pictured him, too, the man who fascinated her simply because of his air of natural brute strength. The man who stood firm and unbothered, like a rock.

He could never get over the airs she gave herself, the distance she was always careful to keep. He could only assume she didn't like him, or else she was afraid of him. He knew he could be intimidating; it was something he liked to play on, at times. He hadn't allowed himself to watch her leave because he knew she was wary of him, saw how she held herself aloof whenever their paths crossed. He knew she had nothing against him, but he felt this woman was on the defensive, though he expected nothing from her. He only spoke to her because he enjoyed provoking her, throwing her off her stride by looking her straight in the eye. He hadn't forgotten the evening she shouted at him. His overriding impression was that she lacked confidence in herself, or perhaps it was just her way of reminding him that she lived in the chic part of the building, on staircase A, where apartments sold for two million euros. Not on staircase C.

There was another reason he hadn't turned to watch her go; he was tired of automatically falling into that urban trap. Since coming to Paris he had been surprised at how many times he caught himself following women with his eyes, looking at their legs, staring at a passenger on the bus, not meaning to, but feeling his eye drawn irresistibly to her. He felt sickened by the need to look, exhausted by all this humanity. It wasn't natural to spend your life constantly under the gaze of others. In his valley, he hadn't had to endure other people's curiosity. And it wasn't even curiosity. In Paris people only look at the things they covet; they don't even see the rest, just ignore it, pretending not to see musicians playing in the metro, that battalion of gypsies caterwauling in the corridors beneath Place de la Concorde, hollering louder than their instruments – everyone passes them by as if walking past a poster, and the mute beggars, sometimes just for a glance, no one sees them either. But Ludovic looked, he looked even at the people you shouldn't see, the crazy ones who keep staring at you, waiting for a reaction. These provocative exchanges energised him. In the metro a single out-of-place look could start a fight.

Showered and dressed, it was his turn to become an extra on the Paris streets, walking towards Saint-Paul metro station. The rain had not let up. Behind the bus stop, opposite the church, the young Romanian woman was sitting on a cardboard box, leaning against the glass, barely sheltered. She was hiding her child under her raincoat, which she held stretched out like a makeshift tent. Yanna or Ileana. He had asked her name last summer, making her repeat it several times. She had written the letters on her palm with her index finger, but he still couldn't make it out, maybe she didn't know how to write. That was as far as their conversation went, so every morning he would say, 'Hello, Yanna,' not because he found her attractive, and still less out of charity, but just because she was there. He never gave her money, just a handshake, and not even that every day. Yet she was beautiful, with the gleam of her dark, deep-set eyes. She was beautiful with her slight rain-soaked smile, but no one saw her; he hated them all for pretending not to see her. If she'd been a cat they would have bent down to stroke her and talk to her, but he had never seen anyone talk to the girl, or smile at her, or even look at her. Like his neighbour, who never smiled, but eyed him up and down. The bourgeois neighbour, with her entitled claim to a miserable fifteen square metres of city garden, unaware of his umpteen hectares of land. He told himself he'd give her a proper fright one day, the stuck-up cow, just for the fun of it.

Before going down into the metro, he went for a coffee and bought a packet of cigarettes, as he did every day.

'*Bonjour!*'

No reply, as usual. He went over to the bar, but instead of ordering a strong coffee, he said something else; it just slipped out. 'I said "Morning" and the least you could do is say hello back. OK?'

The astonished waiter turned to the other customers, seeking their support. The manager was standing at the end of the bar and came over. 'What would you like?'

'When I come in I say "Morning", so I expect you to do the same.'

'Morning. Anything else?'

'A strong coffee.'

He felt everyone's discomfort, even at the tables behind him. The Coldplay track sounded especially loud in the embarrassed silence. He would have liked to swallow his coffee in a single gulp, but it was scalding. He felt ridiculous, and couldn't believe that he had lost his temper; he had let that snobby neighbour get to him without realising it. So he gulped the coffee down anyway, and then the glass of water straight after, to calm the burning. Then he slammed a euro on the counter and stormed out.

As he opened the door, the waiter called loudly, 'Have a nice day!' Probably to wind him up, but maybe not. One day he would lose his temper for real, and some poor person would suffer. Just whoever was closest to hand. Payback for all the others.

Whenever he was in Saint-Sauveur, he would take a walk around the vineyard to see how Mathilde's *domaine* was doing. It had been taken over by a guy from Bordeaux who cultivated the vines in a completely different way and who had spent a lot of money doing up the buildings. A sharp reminder of how much time had elapsed since her death, of a chapter that had closed, never to reopen. The second sharp reminder came, like a slap in the face, each time he saw his mother again. Before each trip, he would ask himself how she might seem this time. Would she still be able to go out? Would they still be able to take their walk along the river? He would hire a wheelchair if it came to that. He had seen one in the window of the pharmacy in town, had never noticed they were there until now. Back in her prime, when she was bursting with life and health, his mother had been no saint, and though he had been her favourite, the biggest and strongest in her eyes, he never forgot how harsh she could be at times. She was a tough woman, who had worked sixteen hours a day outdoors and in the house, and that had made her hard and rough like a millstone. Often, it was best to keep out of her way.

He could not forget that she had never liked Mathilde, because Mathilde came from an old wine family, and vineyard owners were a race apart. They had a vast estate which they sprayed with chemicals, and they dressed up like cosmonauts to do it. In the spring, some vineyards even hired planes to do the spraying – an hour of a single-engine plane to douse the plants in who knew what chemicals. It was the chemicals that had killed Mathilde.

But he couldn't say that here – that was one taboo that the large estates shared with the small farms. Yet everyone knew that insecticides killed bees, so why not humans as well?

Another reason his mother disliked Mathilde was that Ludovic had chosen to work on her family's estate, as if he found wine more exciting than their traditional mixed farm. But to keep everyone happy, he would come to the farm every day, too. For four years he had done two days' work in one; he must have been mad, and weak with it, and that was why he knew deep down that he was not as strong as people thought. The truth was, he didn't like to upset anyone. The farm and the estate were only eight kilometres apart, yet they were two completely different worlds, two neighbouring worlds that did not communicate. Luckily the workers on the estate respected him, as did Mathilde's family. He had earned that respect more than once, by pruning the vines for hours on end, row after row, without even a moment's break in the comfortable front seat of the truck. Yet it was hard for him – being tall is no advantage for tending vines; in the winter the vinestocks are barely knee-high, and he had ruined his back by working bent double in the rain and the cold, and steering the little fifty-horsepower tractor for hours, with no cab and no windscreen to protect him from the elements. He could have taken the easy way out, prancing about as a team leader, or working in the cellar, but that stank of nepotism. Perhaps being a wine-grower was more prestigious than being a farmer. He didn't care, it was just that he loved Mathilde and working with her meant being with her, that was all.

Walking around the vines, Ludovic thought back to those tensions, the unspoken grievances, and he almost missed them. Even though they had never married, he considered Mathilde to have been his wife. The months of her illness had been awful – a long, dark tunnel. A battle in which strength counted for nothing. A battle they had lost. He would never talk about his wife's cancer, and in any case, whom would he talk to? He held on to the thought of the little walks they would take together in the hospital corridors, from her room to the coffee machine. Towards the end she found it hard to get out of bed. The two-hundred-metre walk required a superhuman effort, but she did it, until the day when he had gone on his own to fetch the cup of hot espresso she liked, with sugar, and the day when she had stopped talking about drinking coffee, and the day when she had stopped talking about anything. From that day on he would never think of himself as strong, from that day on, he would just pretend. He let his height, his build do the talking, the body he hid inside. He also knew that he would never, could never love again; he would never take the risk. The lack of love in his life was like a chasm inside, a dried-up lake. He knew now that he must live without the vital energy that comes from loving, desiring, kissing another person. He had managed so far, and he certainly wasn't going to meet anyone in Paris.

In the evening, his nephews came home from school. All seven of them ate dinner together, and it was a happy moment. They always let him sit at the head of the table, and when he wasn't there, they left the place empty and waiting for him. His two nephews were fascinated by his life in Paris. At eight and ten, they dreamed of going to see him there, staying for a weekend at least. He told them that his flat was tiny, he only had one bed and they would have to sleep on the floor or camp in the courtyard. They thought he was joking… Their uncle was so big and strong that he had to live in a huge house, even in Paris. Their parents always tried to change the subject, saying they had all the time in the world to go to Paris, and if they wanted to go to one of the big FNAC stores, there was Limoges or Toulouse. 'You know perfectly well your uncle doesn't have room for you in Paris, so stop going on about it…'

'Look, I don't live in a broom cupboard, you know. They can come whenever they like. It'll just be a bit of a squeeze, that's all.'

Each time he came for one of his two-day visits to the farm, he sensed that he made them uncomfortable. His sister was embarrassed to be preparing to take over, to announce to the world that her husband had taken the place of her brother, the rightful heir. As for their father, he just wanted a smooth transition, though he missed Ludo, if only because Gilles was not a hunter. His son-in-law did not approve of hunting and his grandsons took no interest in the farm; they hankered after the big city. But Ludo's father said nothing. He didn't want any trouble.

Ludovic also refrained from saying anything that might upset the family, though he had noticed the barn roof was leaking, the cesspit needed emptying, the ruts in the track were getting deeper, the hedges were too high, and a dozen other signs of neglect, things he would have fixed long ago had he still lived here. After dinner, Ludovic went outside to smoke with Gilles. As always, they walked across to the barn. Ludovic glanced at the equipment as he chatted to his brother-in-law. His questions were direct, and he expected straightforward answers. He was trying to find out if everything was all right, if they were able to pay themselves something at the end of each month. He wanted to help if he could, and he tried to offer advice, without actually appearing to do so. No one tried to push Ludovic aside, they respected his imposing presence, but since the death of his wife they felt sorry for him, too. His father came out to say good night. He was going to bed. It was eight thirty, and that was when he always turned in now. Ludovic punched him playfully on the shoulder, like a boxer taunting his challenger. 'You're still up to it, old man!'

'Eighty-four... Let's see how you are at half my age...'

'I'm already half your age, Papa, more than half, in fact.'

There had always been a kind of nervous tension between them, especially when Ludovic still worked here and had tried to introduce new ideas. His father wanted everything done the way he'd always done it, and they had argued several times, but that was just the way their relationship worked. They spoke freely; each said exactly what he thought, and often they had come to blows – in words only. Now, even at this stage in their lives, they still felt the need to provoke one another, to reach out, too, and touch the other man. Ludovic play-jabbed like a boxer, and his father drew his shoulders in to ward off the punches. Distance had made them awkward. Weeks went by without them seeing each other, and that had strained their bond. It was important to close the divide, restore their relationship, and for them that meant teasing and horsing about.

'Old man, can I borrow the keys to the gun room?'

'What nonsense are you up to now?'

'I just want to borrow a .22.'

'You're going to fire a rifle at this hour?'

'No, I just want to borrow it, that's all! Have you still got that silencer?'

'Eh? What the hell are you planning? Settling a score?'

'You could say that.'

'Right, well, if it's with your brother-in-law here, you've got a clear shot, point-blank. I'll hold him still...'

To prolong the joke, his father clutched Gilles by the shoulders, holding him firmly on the spot.

Gilles shook him off, unamused. Now he was the one to announce he was going to bed. He left them standing out in the yard, but he turned to look back at them from the farmhouse door. They were like a pair of kids. Every time he saw Ludovic and his father enjoying time together, he felt like an interloper, an encumbrance who had stolen someone's place. Yet Ludovic had never shown any resentment. It was hard not to like Ludovic – he had a natural assurance, and he seemed so dependable. But it was hard not to be wary of him, too – there was something slightly disturbing about him, like this ridiculous plan to stash a rifle in the back of his car and take it back to Paris.

It was rare for them all to be together in the large meeting room but this afternoon there was an emergency. Aïcha had just received a call from the factory in Troyes letting her know that an entire batch of stretch jersey dresses was defective. As they came off the production line, the three hundred sheath dresses were oddly misshapen and sagging. Fabian wasted no time in accusing Aurore in front of the others. It was easy for him to cast blame because he had always said it would be better to manufacture them in the Piedmont factory or the one in Bulgaria, both of which were equipped with the latest digital Stoll machines. Aurore had messed up by insisting on her supposedly infallible French supplier. 'I told you that useless bunch would be a disaster; they don't have anyone there under the age of forty!'

There was no time to waste on Fabian's petulant outburst. Aurore needed to act fast. But she thought it strange that the factory had waited until five o'clock on Monday afternoon to warn them. Why had they let the whole weekend go by? They couldn't have manufactured all the dresses in one day. Something wasn't right. Still, she must bounce back and find an immediate solution to rescue the design. Galeries Lafayette wanted the dresses for February, but Fabian had negotiated delivery – and payment – three months sooner, in November. Fabian had signed the deal, and he had been bragging about it for the past six months. Now, in front of their in-house team, it was easy for him to make out that it was Aurore's fault: she wasn't just the designer whose name was on the label, she was also the boss, and for such an important order she should have been there at the factory when it went into production, ready to spend the day checking everything. Of course he could not resist pointing out that Aurore's obstinate refusal to manufacture outside France, precisely so that they could oversee end-to-end production, did not in fact prevent screw-ups. He was playing the part of the prudent, clear-sighted manager, showing off in front of their plainly embarrassed staff, and belittling his partner as a designer out of her depth. Aurore could bear it no longer. She left the meeting and shut herself in her office, to call the factory back.

She had begun working with the factory in earnest two years ago. Prior to that, she had used them just once, to make up some simple polo shirts, but she trusted the team; they boasted a prestigious client list, and they worked with computerised knitting looms. The staff weren't especially young, but she found that oddly reassuring – it comforted her to see the knitters bent over their machines, women in old-fashioned overalls, continually adjusting the needles. But the reality was that they had messed up production of her order of three hundred dresses, which would leave her forty thousand euros out of pocket. The yarn they had used was too fine, and the dresses were loose. She could see it all in the video they had attached, each dress was shapeless, and two sizes too big. This kind of accident never normally happened, and she had sent them the prototype by DHL. They would have had it there in front of them when they started production, with all the measurements and references, and simple human error had screwed it up. She could not believe it. Then she wondered if perhaps she was the one who had made a mistake. Perhaps if ultra-modern or air-jet machines had been used, the 4 per cent of elastane might not have affected the tension so badly. But Sandrine or Aïcha should have anticipated the effect and adjusted the instructions accordingly. Or perhaps not. She no longer knew. What she did know was that she should have been on site when production started. That was the one thing that was certain. Had she been there she would have seen straight away that it wasn't going to work. Or perhaps all those around her were to blame, they no longer understood what she wanted; yes, that was it, clearly no one had understood that these jersey dresses should be close-fitting, stretchy. She had wanted an eye-catching, body-sculpting shape supporting the bust and hips, certainly nothing loose and baggy. Yes, that was it, she was no longer capable of making herself understood. She was no longer a good manager, she had lost that obsessive need to oversee every last detail. A thousand times before, she had felt she was inadequate to the task before her, but she had never let it show. Today was different. Now she felt as if that was all anyone could see, and the truth was, they were right.

The only way to rescue the situation was to go to the factory. She looked up train times, cancelled her three meetings for the next day, including lunch with the bank. She called Volker the head man, told him she would be there tomorrow, and forced herself to be tough – they must take the blame. She told him they should have realised immediately, from the first trial run, that the dresses looked nothing like the prototype. Volker replied coldly that she should have chosen a different thread, or been there at the factory. And he expected payment.

'Madame Dessage, I told you to come here or to send someone in your place.'

'But how come you only told us about this today, on Monday, at five o'clock in the afternoon?'

'We called on Friday. Our shift supervisor even called your partner at home. Your internal communications are not my problem.'

Sometimes, the only person you can turn to is yourself. In her office, with her head in her hands, Aurore tried to convince herself that she was right, to give herself the encouragement she was getting from no one else. She had set her heart on high-end clothes in small, exclusive quantities, made in France. Never anywhere else. The prints and leather-wear were the only exception, produced in Portugal and Italy. She was sure she was right about this, she had an instinct for upcoming trends, and for a long time now she had felt certain the demand for ethical fashion would grow, even if it was more expensive. Clean, humane manufacturing processes were important to her. In her first fashion jobs she had travelled three times to China, and resolved never to set foot in Shenzhen or Guangzhou again, never to pump ammonia into the canals of Shaoxing, never to exploit the child workers of Bangladesh or Bulgaria, who were paid even less than in China, and for three hundred hours a month. She did not want to design dresses knowing that kids of fifteen were risking their lives to make them; she found it morally indefensible.

She did not want to set foot outside her office in case she bumped into Fabian. She could hear him talking – for once, he had come into work – and he seemed almost cheerful. But when she heard him laughing in the design studio on the floor above, as if this disaster was just what he had been waiting for, she knew she had had enough. He was laughing because he had caught her out in front of everyone. She had fallen into his trap, unawares. For months, he must have been hoping this would happen, that she would fail spectacularly. And now she had. Now he was free to finalise his own deal if that was his plan. He would fire her for incompetence or professional misconduct, so that he could get control of the company and take it wherever he wanted.

'So,' she began to Fabian, 'you think my mistake is funny?

And what's more you've known about it since Friday, when they called you. You've known since Friday that something was badly wrong. So what are you playing at? Go on, you can tell us, we're all here. What's your master plan... are you going to fire us all?'

Fabian recoiled, shocked to see her so angry. Then he rallied and calmly addressed the assembled staff: 'As you can see, your boss is a model of self-control!'

He was playing her. And now she was sure. He had engineered this so that they would all be here when the factory called after the weekend. She even wondered if he had altered the yarn specifications himself so that the dresses would be faulty. She couldn't quite bring herself to believe it, but the thought crossed her mind. Since the episode with the guns in Turkey, nothing would surprise her. That day, Fabian had felt so humiliated, so small in front of her, that it was possible he had thought of nothing but revenge ever since. Aurore could stand this no longer. She collected her things and left the office. She jumped into a passing taxi, though it would take her three times as long to get home as it would on the metro. She just needed to sit down and be driven.

She remembered taking a taxi to the airport with Fabian two years ago, for their flight to Istanbul. He had just started to talk about relocating production to cut costs, but relations between them were still amicable. They were old college friends, after all. He had persuaded her to give it a try, start with something small, like hosiery. Aurore had gone along with it and that was why, at the height of summer, they had set off for two days to visit a factory on the outskirts of the Turkish capital. Fabian had organised everything, beginning with a visit to the Dorümek family – a major manufacturer with magnificent premises, state-of-the-art machines and well-trained workers. They had over a thousand employees. Of the management team, three spoke French quite well. Everyone was most welcoming, and everything looked truly excellent when they visited the production lines, which were clean, professional and spacious. Most importantly, there was no sign of exploitation or ill-treatment. Fabian had suggested giving the factory just a few pieces from their next collection, to get an idea of their work. Aurore was happy to comply. She had started to think that perhaps Fabian was right. They needed to focus on the numbers; his obsession with high margins was important in order to attract new investors. In a way, Fabian had won. At the end of the factory visit, Aurore agreed to sign a contract for a line of jersey dresses.

Of course, there had been the obligatory drinks in the managing director's office to celebrate their future working relationship. The windows in the vast air-conditioned room were sealed, but everyone wanted to smoke – a cigarette or a cigar with the excellent champagne – and they had gone out onto the spacious roof terrace overlooking the Bosphorus. In the outdoor heat, one by one, their hosts removed their jackets. Aurore and Fabian saw that the three charming men who had shown them around all day, their welcoming, mild-mannered hosts, who had encouraged them to shake hands with the workforce, were all carrying pistols on their belts. It was common practice here, they explained, when a shocked Aurore asked, 'Why the guns?'

They were baffled by Fabian's and Aurore's horror-struck reaction. It was just to prevent stealing. They'd occasionally had problems in the past, light-fingered employees on the factory floor. 'But not any more,' they said, showing off their weapons.

That had put an end to it. Aurore and Fabian had shared a look of stupefaction and unease. They were surrounded by men with guns and Fabian, despite having organised the trip, was just as shocked as Aurore. Especially when it became clear that the other managers, who had just joined them and with whom they'd had breakfast and lunch, were carrying weapons, too. Without knowing it they had spent the whole day surrounded by armed men. They felt betrayed.

Back in Paris, Fabian had felt guilty, and humiliated. He had been taken for a fool, and Aurore's reaction had not helped: 'So that's what you want us to become, partners with bastards like them. And it's probably even worse in India or China. Cheap production means doing business with people who exploit their workers, you know that as well as I do. When you choose to cut your manufacturing costs by 60 per cent, you make a deal with the devil, you're playing – literally – with fire. Well, you can do it without me!'

After the Turkish episode, Fabian had seemed less obsessed about manufacturing abroad, though it appeared he had spent the last two years secretly planning his revenge. But to ruin an entire order and make it look like her fault, just to get back at her? She could never have imagined he would go that far.

When the flight from Istanbul touched down, they had taken a taxi into town, driving through a sudden downpour. Just like now. She searched in her bag and found the scrap of paper she could not bring herself to throw away: 'pre-pack insolvency'. So this was the trap he had set for her. She would not confront him outright: 'So, Fabian, you've decided to stab me in the back and steal the company from me?' She preferred to let him come to her. She would wait for him to emerge from the undergrowth.

That evening over dinner, unusually, she felt the need to unburden herself. She wanted them to understand that everything wasn't as easy for her as she made it seem. Her children were old enough to hear these things now, and she wanted them to understand why some evenings their mother came home utterly drained and exhausted. The children didn't dare say anything, not even her stepson, and Richard's only response was a shrug, a shrug that was worse than anything he might have said, a shrug that meant, 'Don't let it bother you.' It was coldly condescending and she was profoundly hurt. Richard's shrug implied that he provided for all of them, so she didn't need to fret about her little fashion label and its six employees.

She immediately regretted opening her mouth. But she did have to explain why she needed to go to Troyes the next day, and that she would probably have to stay the night. She also wanted them to feel some sympathy for her, for once. On the other hand, she also knew that if she had been a halfway decent boss, she would already be in Troyes right now. But she hadn't wanted to just leave and abandon the four of them with no warning, because that would have made her a bad wife and mother as well. The fact remained that tomorrow evening they would have to do without her. Richard and the three children were staring at her as if she was making a mountain out of a molehill. The four people she was closest to in the world, however much they loved her, could not even begin to understand, still less put themselves in her shoes, and that was a hard lesson to learn.

Before going to bed, she kissed Richard where he lay, stretched out on the sofa, and asked him to turn down the volume on his basketball game. She didn't want to get into a lengthy discussion, but she asked if he'd heard of pre-pack insolvency. Over the noise of the crowd and the horns, he replied vaguely that yes, he had, it was a new way to take over companies and get rid of the management, with the backing of the commercial courts. It was a bit shady, 'but in France all your laws are a bit weird'.

His answer intrigued her. She wanted to know if a small company like hers should worry about being the target of such a procedure, and who would be able to trigger it?

'You'd have to be very unscrupulous to use it, or crooked, or preferably both.'

She got no sleep that night, but in the morning she resolved not to panic. On the contrary, rather than jumping on the eight o'clock train to Troyes, she booked the eleven o'clock instead. Richard took the children to school. In his way, he was trying to help. Vani would not arrive until early afternoon. Aurore was never usually on her own at home in the morning and savoured the rare treat of a couple of hours to herself. She wouldn't go back to bed or sit on the large white sofa, she was simply going to take her time. She would enjoy not having to hurry. Instead of a hasty shower, she took a long bath. Twenty minutes without the radio, or any other noise, and with no one banging on the bathroom door, was the height of luxury. There was so much steam that when she got out of the bath the mirror was misted over. She opened the window to clear it.

With a towel round her waist, she unhurriedly applied sweet almond oil to her shoulders and breasts, checked her nails and spent a long time brushing her hair, bringing back memories of a childhood ritual. All the while, the bathroom window remained half open, and the condensation evaporated in the cold air. Her train was in an hour. She would call a taxi. She needed to make sure she had all the documents she needed, including the original order form with the specifications. It would be a tense meeting and she must be firm. She wasn't going all that way to hear their excuses, she was going to put things right. She didn't mind how they did it, but they were going to make the dresses properly, even if it meant adjusting them by hand, one by one, and bringing in extra seamstresses. She was determined to save those dresses.

Deep in thought about the day ahead, she had completely forgotten the open bathroom window. Now, feeling cold, she closed it quickly, but then something struck her, and she opened it again. She couldn't believe what she was hearing. She stuck her head out. There was a long silence, then the sound of birds. Not the crows, but the gentle cooing of turtle doves.

She could scarcely believe her ears. First, it was mid-November, but second and more importantly, the doves had disappeared three months ago. But there it was again – the peaceful, gentle sound of turtle doves was echoing around the courtyard. They had come back! In spite of the cold, Aurore opened the window wide and leaned out to look into the trees. The highest branches towered above her, spreading over the enclosed space. She searched for the doves in the tangle of near-leafless branches. She feared she would see the two spectral crows, but no, the turtle doves were really there, perched together, making little movements of their heads as if timidly reclaiming their territory.

She watched them for a moment, with the wet towel still around her waist. She was shivering but she was so relieved they had come back that she almost felt cheerful despite the stressful day ahead. The doves were a good omen.

She was still not in a hurry. As she went down the stairs she looked carefully at the trees through the landing window on every floor, just to make sure the crows were not lying in wait for her. In the courtyard she walked all around the shrubbery, looking up in the air like a child searching for a kite, and when she spotted the two cream-coloured birds, she felt real joy. She almost forgot that she was supposed to be catching a train.

In the post room, she hastily opened her letterbox and slipped her hand inside without looking. Instantly, she pulled it back, as if she had found a nest of snakes coiled against the cold metal. She bent down to look inside at the horror she had felt with her fingertips. Her hand was still trembling from the shock. What she saw was a compact posy of thick, hard black feathers tied up with a red ribbon. There was no note or message, and with a shudder of alarm she realised that that man was trying to provoke her, or threaten her.

Gingerly, she lifted the bundle out. The crows' feathers had been tied like a trophy. She feared this might be worse than a threat; perhaps this was his way of apologising, or worse, a token of interest, which would be hideously embarrassing, coming as it did from a resident of the building directly opposite her own.

On the train, with no phone signal, and no newspaper, she took the curious feathers out of her bag. She had decided to bring them with her, and she examined them sceptically. She should have been thinking about the crucial meeting ahead, steeling herself for an angry confrontation with the manufacturer who had caused her such trouble, stoking her sense of righteous indignation. It was so easy to doubt yourself, especially when you needed to be firm and assert your standpoint. She stared at the passing countryside, wondered how she would find the strength to be hard-headed and force them to re-work the dresses there and then. Could she make them see they should have called her sooner? Would she have the guts to ask them outright why they hadn't noticed a problem with the thickness of the yarn? Since yesterday, she had been wondering if they would try to put all the blame on her. They would probably just say she should have been there on the day they went into production. In the middle of nowhere, aboard the deserted inter-city train, she felt more alone than ever. Without thinking, she stroked her cheek with the feathers. She was playing absent-mindedly with a trophy made from the feathers of her enemies. The crows had intimidated her, but now they were vanquished, liquidated. She was sure that man had killed them, and the thought was both terrible and endearing. She did not know him, but on some irrational level, he had invaded her thoughts just as fully as the crows. She determined not to think about him, she would deny him the right to exist in her thoughts, yet he intrigued her. There are people like that, who make a big impression, and even if you don't know them, even if instinctively you don't trust them, you feel drawn to them. Perhaps there was such a thing as a man who could make you feel strong, a stranger who could lift you up when your family no longer even thought of doing so and you didn't feel you could ask them. It would be unthinkable to make an ally of him, still less a friend, or anything else, and yet knowing he was there reassured her. It seemed almost as if he was there with her now. She remembered him pushing open the carriage door the other morning, appearing in front of her. He had seemed to fill the considerable space under the entrance archway, to inhabit it with confidence. He made you feel, inexplicably, as if, with him there, nothing bad could happen to you, and everything would work out. As a landscape punctuated by telegraph poles flashed by, she became convinced that she would feel stronger if he were close by. Even the crows had seemed to fear him that evening when he had searched about under the trees for the cats. Perhaps he was the kind of man who was always ready to help out. In that case, there was no harm in getting to know him. Except that a relationship of any kind with a man who lived in her building, right there on the other side of the courtyard, would be impossible. For so many reasons, it would be impossible.

She rolled her trophy of feathers between her fingers. She would have liked to think it was a sign. For months those harbingers of doom, those hideous crows, had terrorised her. But now she held them in her hand. Now she could do whatever she wanted with the objects of her terror. They would never frighten her again; on the contrary, she was making use of that fear now, just as she should have done with so many things in her life.

The atmosphere was tense. They were surprised by the feathers she was handling as if they were a fan or a pen, but no one dared say anything.

Volker led her through the factory floor to inspect the stock. It was just the two of them now; the shift supervisor did not want to be involved. Aurore knew the message Volker was sending as he walked her through the vast workshops. This was a show of might. The array of machines, working at full tilt, was intended to impress her and emphasise that they, the manufacturers, were the stronger party. She was just a small-time client with a petty complaint.

They passed through double metal doors and into a warren of corridors and stairs. The air was cold. Volker walked in front of Aurore, saying nothing. As they made their way down the long corridor, she tried to reconcile her different roles. She was the intransigent boss, the designer out of her depth, and the mother who worried whether she would get home that night. She was the wife who did not know whether Richard would be in Paris that evening or not, the client who had been let down, and the concerned manufacturer. She was all those things at once, but when she had in front of her the three hundred dresses sealed in the transparent packaging that she herself had designed, with her initials in script, she became Aurore Dessage once again. She was a brand, a brand close to collapse.

Faced with the enormity of the disaster she suppressed a surge of panic. She picked up one of the packets at random, removed the dress from its packaging and let it hang from her fingertips. It was terrible, the weave slack and lifeless. The dress was nothing like the vision she had committed to paper. She felt she was confronting an intimate truth about herself, and the shock was a devastating blow. Every one of the three hundred dresses was in the same state. She controlled her anger, but her exasperation grew unchecked, and she steeled herself to stare Volker coldly in the eye and tell him he must repair the damage. He must stop work immediately on all other projects and set his teams to remake her dresses. She did not care if he had to pay them overtime, or recruit legions of extra hands, but she would not leave until they had started work on the dresses, all of them, by casting off the edges or re-doing the rib trims. Technically, it would be possible to save them all. Facing him, she found the strength to insist that he take charge of the recovery operation and that he ask his staff, or staff borrowed from another workshop, to unpack and unfold the dresses, to unravel the rib trims and re-do them by hand. That was what she was asking of him. She reminded him that she had emailed him instructions and sketches and had had the prototype delivered so that he would know exactly what she wanted. It was up to them to make sure that their production followed the specifications and, if they had worked properly with the programmer, they would have seen straight away that something was wrong. Instead of pressing ahead they should have halted production to find out where the problem lay. They should have asked themselves whether they might use a different yarn. And they should have called her. They should have called and spoken to her in person before they made all the dresses.

Volker was very taken aback. He hadn't expected her to insist they fix the dresses one by one. Sensing that he was on the back foot, Aurore pressed her point. Clutching her crow-feather trophy, she gave vent to the anger that had been building up inside her for three months. It had pained her to see the loss of respect she had suffered in so many eyes, to see people distance themselves from her. It was painful that her children needed her less, that Richard was talking seriously about dividing his time between Paris and the United States, about renting an apartment over there, as if Paris was too small for his grandiose ambitions. He resented France's social system, too, though he had liked it well enough the day he was winched up into a helicopter and taken for emergency surgery after a rock-climbing accident. He had been astonished that he could be looked after and patched up, and have his leg plastered that same day, with no one asking for money upfront. He had liked France very much indeed that day, but now he kept changing his mind with the supreme confidence of someone for whom anything is possible. He could afford to invest tens of thousands of euros in an unknown enterprise, just as he could move out of one home and into another in the space of twenty-four hours. Richard wasn't really much help to her, she realised; he didn't make her feel great about herself and nor did Fabian, with his treachery, or Aïcha, on her design team, and all the others who never bothered to apologise when they arrived late for work. Then there was Gaëlle, their publicity director, who always claimed she worked best from home. Aurore knew that, little by little, she was losing control of everyone around her. Maybe that was the way of the world, people became more distant, they left you and then one fine day you found yourself all alone with no power over anything, and no influence over the course of events.

At the far end of the factory floor, Volker was making calls. He had understood that she was not going to leave without a solution. She would probably stay the night, spend hours deliberating with them, ask the managing director to have dinner with her, because suddenly he was available whereas before he had supposedly been abroad. She had brought her overnight things and would not be leaving Troyes until tomorrow. She would keep up the pressure. With luck, they would start unpacking the desperate dresses that very afternoon, and then they would reshape each one and bring it back to life.

II

It was the first time she had set foot on this staircase and she was surprised at how dark and narrow it was. Very different from her own building. The steps were so narrow it was actually quite hard to get a foothold. It was starting to get dark, but she did not turn on the light. On the first landing she looked out of the window. The courtyard appeared quite different from this angle, not at all the same as the view from her apartment. She could see the broad, pale façade of her building opposite, with its renovated stonework in perfect condition. In this building, the windows were tiny, the stairs ancient and the parquet cracked. She was astonished to discover such a different world just a few steps from her own front door. Parisians were more likely to travel to the other side of the world than they were to visit the staircase opposite. She could see her own windows from here; they were all dark.

Her train had pulled into the Gare de l'Est at five o'clock that afternoon. After twenty-four stress-filled hours in Troyes, a weight had been lifted from her shoulders. She felt light, but exhausted. When she entered the courtyard, she had seen the turtle doves with their delicate beige-pink plumage, sitting on a branch close to the tree trunk. She had wondered, on her journey back, if they would still be here, if she had dreamed the whole thing, if the man really had killed the crows, and why. She had decided to call at his apartment when she got home, though the thought scared her a little. To kill birds like that in the middle of Paris, he must be crazy. But she could not help admiring his crime.

Halfway up the stairs, she peered through the landing window to look into the tree, and felt a little dizzy; she had barely slept the night before, but her insistence had paid off. At five o'clock in the morning the seamstresses had begun to resize the dresses. They would be done one by one, and it would take three days, but the consignment, every pallet, would be saved.

The panes on the third floor were dirty, and it was hard to open the window – the wood was damp and swollen. She pulled hard, and eventually it opened with a loud, unsettling groan. She leaned out. The top floor on this side was slightly lower than the building opposite. She could see into her apartment and make out the tops of the sitting-room and kitchen walls, but the trees screened the bathroom from view. It was the first time she had seen her home, her own small world, from the outside. Clearly Vani had not yet brought the children back from school, and Victor was not home either. The apartment was deserted, silent, and she wanted to be there, to savour the peace and quiet, rest on the sofa or take a bath. She would come and thank the man another time. She would wait until their paths crossed in the courtyard; there was no urgency, and truth be told, she felt a little uneasy. Now that she was almost outside his door, she no longer felt like paying him a visit. She was afraid. The two doves were right there. She saw how close the branches of the tree came to this building; some actually touched the wall. When she tried to close the window, the old wood grunted and squeaked like a wounded animal. Even slamming her hand hard against them, the two frames refused to fit together. So she pushed harder, but there was nothing to be done. Now she felt trapped on this blasted staircase…

'What are you doing?' To her right, an old lady was staring at her through her partly opened door.

'I'm so sorry, I live opposite, on the other side of the courtyard, Madame Dessage – you know me, we sometimes bump into each other downstairs.'

'Possibly. I heard a noise, so… Are you looking for someone?'

The little old lady had put her security chain on. Aurore went over to her and apologised, repeating that she lived opposite. She had come up to get a better look at the turtle doves. The woman brightened, and opened her door fully. 'Oh yes, you've seen? He made them leave!'

'Made who leave?'

'The crows! My goodness, they were awful, they drove my cats wild.'

Aurore was relieved to have hit on the perfect pretext for her visit to staircase C, and to discover that she was not the only one to have been bothered by the evil birds. But her relief was tinged with disappointment. If the guy really had killed the crows, he had done it for this old lady and her cats.

'So it was the big, tall man who…?'

'Ludovic, yes! I call him Ludo. We're lucky to have him.'

Aurore thought of the feather trophy in her bag. She had thought he was sending her a message, but maybe he had just been showing off, bragging after the kill.

'Listen, when you see him, could you thank him from me?'

'Yes, of course, but thank him for what?'

'He'll understand.'

'Well, he brings me my baguette every evening, so I'll definitely be seeing him. But tell me, are you the young woman who lives opposite, with the children? I wanted to tell you that sometimes they lean out of your Velux up there, in the roof, and one evening they even tried to climb out, into the tree.'

Aurore was a mother again, a mother reacting with panic as she pictured the scene, Iris and Noé sneaking up to the roof, following their half-brother.

'Are you sure? Which window can you see them from?'

'Come in, I'll show you.'

The old lady had plenty to say. Aurore spotted her name by the doorbell: Mademoiselle Mercier, a name she had seen forever on one of the letterboxes in the post room, without knowing who she was. As she listened, she reflected that lately she had seen this little old lady, moving slowly about the courtyard or out in the street, less and less often. Probably because of the winter weather or because of the too-steep stairs. She must find it hard to get up the three flights. The two cats from the other evening were lying curled up together in a sort of cushion basket. They didn't move except to raise their heads and stare lazily at Aurore, then they settled back to sleep. She wondered if the woman had any children or friends, but quickly understood that she was very much alone in the world, alone with her TV tuned permanently to a news channel, the sound turned down. Her only visitors were the care staff twice a day and, of course, Ludovic. Aurore felt guilty for never having spoken to the woman, apart from a brief *bonjour-bonsoir*. She felt guilty that she had never bothered to ask which floor she lived on, or to find out who she was. Though she quickly realised the old lady was almost too chatty when encouraged, as now. She complained about all the apartments that were either empty or let to tourists; she complained about the owners who were never there, and said that the building had become a joyless place. 'It used to be lively here, with children playing in the courtyard and lots of people. But now it's just sad.' But the worst thing, for her, was the Airbnb lets because, 'those apartments are either occupied, and there's too much noise, or they're empty for weeks, and it's silent.'

'You shouldn't be allowed to rent an apartment as if it was a hotel room. And the people who rent them are not proper neighbours, they don't really live here. Anyway, at the moment, they're all empty!'

'But, Mademoiselle Mercier, it's only sometimes, and don't you think it's a good thing that people come from all over the world to visit Paris?'

'You're not going to rent out your apartment to tourists, are you?'

'No, I live there with my husband and children; we're there all the time!'

Aurore sensed the old lady's confusion; the world that played out on the TV behind her was becoming incomprehensible. It was a world that was moving on without her.

'Have you lived here a long time?'

The woman could not help laughing. 'I was born here. In 1934!'

Aurore did a quick calculation and was amazed that anyone could live in the same apartment all that time. It was actually unimaginable to be so sedentary, and sad, but just at that moment, there was a lively series of little knocks on the door and the woman's face lit up.

'I told you…!'

Mademoiselle Mercier went to open the door, without putting the chain on this time. Ludovic stood outside on the landing and although he spotted Aurore immediately, he bent down to give the old lady a kiss on both cheeks, and handed her a half-baguette. The two cats were already at his feet, rubbing their heads against his shoes and twisting round his calves. He paid them no attention, not even bending down to stroke them.

'I see you have a visitor, Odette, so I won't stay.'

Aurore came over, not knowing quite what to say. But it was he who spoke, smiling as always. 'So, you found my little present?'

'Yes, I wanted to thank you…' She was playing it down, making light of the gesture, almost forgetting her disappointment at his reason for killing the crows, and for whom. Then, with a slight shudder of disgust, she said, 'Can I ask how you did it?'

From out on the landing, Ludovic gave a joking reply: 'Ah, well! I wouldn't want to upset anyone's tender sensibilities here…'

And now he looked down at the cats, still rubbing themselves against his legs.

Aurore recognised the irritating self-assurance of a person who considers themselves superior. She didn't like the tone he slipped into all too easily, the tone of perpetual irony, of a man who treated everything as a joke.

'But did you kill them or not?'

'Yes, and I did it for you, when I saw how they were ruining your life. I told myself I couldn't let you suffer like that.'

Now Aurore was unsure whether she should believe him. Was he being sincere? Concerned for her well-being?

'I see,' the old lady intervened, 'and there was I thinking you'd frightened the vile creatures away for the sake of my cats.'

'*Chère Odette*, your cats can look after themselves, believe me.'

Aurore could see how well the two of them got along. The old lady insisted Ludovic should come inside. She took him by the arm, like a dear friend, and seemed thoroughly cheered by his presence, full of admiration for her splendid neighbour, whom she clearly regarded as a surrogate son. Ludovic led her over to the window. Aurore followed. He explained how he had shot the crows, where they had fallen, how he had managed to shoot one without the other flying off. It was basic stuff, he told them. He used to go out shooting in the country, where he lived before. He acknowledged they might find that shocking. He was disconcertingly frank, concealed nothing, didn't try to spare their feelings. Quite the opposite, perhaps.

'You mean you used a shotgun?'

'No, a rifle.'

Again, Aurore felt how terribly far his world was from hers. A man who thought it was perfectly normal to shoot birds. It didn't bother him in the least. He talked about the courtyard as if it was a country estate, or a forest with him as gamekeeper. When he gestured to show how it had all happened, he might have been indicating a vast sweep of land.

'Well, look, I don't know how to thank you.'

'Just try saying the words.'

Ludovic felt a certain satisfaction in forcing the woman from staircase A to say it to his face.

Aurore stepped forward and shook Ludovic's hand. He shook hers firmly in response. Through the window she could see there were lights on now in her apartment. The children must have come back from sport. She was mesmerised by this unaccustomed glimpse of her daily life, which she had never before viewed as a spectator. Her apartment had come to life without her. Seen from here, everything astonished her – her home, full of activity, across the courtyard, this hand that was still holding hers, though she had quite forgotten it. Ludovic turned and followed her gaze.

'I understand how strange that must be for you...'

'Yes.'

Ludovic was standing in front of her, blocking her view a little. Stepping aside, he told her to come closer to the window. She discovered her home, there in plain sight, especially with all the lights on. For now, there were still a few leaves on the trees. Soon there would be none, and then you really would be able to see everything. She had six windows overlooking the courtyard,

106

plus the three Velux windows above. She wondered if this man ever watched them. Had he been spying on them? She glanced at him. He was staring at the apartment opposite, too.

'It's true, in winter, you can see everything opposite really well from here… You seem surprised!'

Aurore repeated simply that it was a strange experience for her, but she was unable to take her eyes off her apartment; it was fascinating. She would have liked to wait until Richard returned, or to see herself walk along the corridor. Suddenly she couldn't help but ask Ludovic, 'And can you see all this from your place too?'

'I have both tree trunks directly in front of my windows, so I'd have to lean out to the side, but, yes, I can see your apartment, just a bit lower down. I don't look, though, obviously.'

Aurore was annoyed with herself for asking. She moved away from the window, but Ludovic stayed where he was, tilting his head to follow the two children moving back and forth inside the big apartment. She wondered what kind of hold he wanted over her, and what he might expect of her. Nothing, perhaps.

'It looks big, your place.'

'Well, time I was getting back.'

She made it sound as if she lived a long way away, as if she was not from round here, and certainly not from this side of the building. She just wanted to get away and be on her own territory, over there, on the other side, where everything was clean and alive. She said goodbye to them both, and Mademoiselle Mercier made her promise to come back soon. Aurore nodded, but without much enthusiasm, unconvinced she would do anything of the kind. She shook Ludovic's hand as she left, but he said he had something to show her in the courtyard, and went down ahead of her without saying goodbye to Odette. Aurore gripped the banister rail to avoid slipping on the treacherous stairs.

Ludovic had advised her to hold tight, perhaps that was why he had gone in front.

When she found herself in the courtyard with him she felt guilty, as if being there with this man was somehow wrong, as if she was worried about being seen. Ludovic went over to the bushes, but before stepping in amongst them he turned back to her with a deadly serious expression. 'What I'm going to show you here is strictly between ourselves. No one else must know because it's against the law. I could get into serious trouble if it got out.'

He asked her to follow him into the tiny courtyard forest. Aurore felt a small thrill, like a child playing a game, as she entered the dense shrubbery behind him. She almost wanted to thank him for reminding her so forcibly of her childhood. She found his air of mystery rather absurd, but touching, and she was a little afraid to discover what he was about to show her. They hadn't gone more than three metres into the tangle of viburnum, rhododendrons and elder, but it felt as dense as a jungle. There, in the middle of the shrubbery, they were both hidden by foliage, cut off from the world. It was almost dark now, and the courtyard light on its time-switch would turn off soon. Ludovic showed Aurore two little clumps of feathers clinging to the tree branches, then he pointed at the loose, damp earth, and with the same serious manner told her that that was where the crows were, because he hadn't wanted to put them in with the rubbish, and because it would help keep other crows away. The visible feathers would make them think there had been an attack by predators. Aurore said nothing. She was disgusted by the thought of the two birds under her feet, but then she raised her head and saw the turtle doves, light and miraculous, the very opposite of the buried black crows. And hovering between the two potent symbols was the face of this man. A man as strong as the tree he was resting his hand against. He genuinely seemed to have no idea how deeply he had touched her. She was amazed at his intuition, how he had guessed what she wanted, understood her, without her saying anything. This perfect stranger had become instantaneously close to her, the only person, among so many, who had listened. She would have liked to express her gratitude for his understanding, but in these cold, damp natural surroundings, in this unusual and very uncomfortable situation, the words would not come. She was worried that someone would find them here. Then the light went off, and everything went dark, and she still didn't know what to say. But she did want to thank him because there was no lovelier gift she could have received in this age of arrogant self-satisfaction, no greater sign of thoughtful consideration than to anticipate another person's needs, and so rather than find the words, she took this man in her arms, as if wrapping them round the tree trunk, and all that she could say was 'thank you', several times, into his ear, with an intensity that he probably found hard to understand. The strength of the body she was holding fortified her. He was warm and powerful and she had not felt anything so human for years. Ludovic did not ask himself what he should do, he was so bowled over by the smell of her perfume, the jojoba scent of her soft hair, and by feeling this woman's body against his. He was astounded to find himself in her arms. It was like the sudden intoxication of a too-potent liqueur and he let himself be submerged by a force that robbed him of words, as if his years devoid of tenderness had come to a miraculous end. He held her as tightly as she held him, telling himself he would not let go until she did. But she moved even closer, letting her bag fall to the damp earth with its covering of dead leaves. She felt the solid strength of this man. Just now, when everything in her life was a trial, she had found an anchor, a fixed point while everything else spun out of her control. Ludovic wondered if he should kiss her;

he was desperate to, but he did not want to panic her and ruin any part of this dazzling moment. It was rare for him to be taken by surprise, and he was as incredulous as he was overcome.

When you suddenly find yourself kissing someone, it's because you can no longer bear to have any distance between you. Even pressed close together, you feel you are still too far apart, and you want to melt into one another. It was she who took the initiative; the flesh of his lips was so soft that she did not even have time to wonder what she was doing, had not the slightest moment of hesitation, so badly did she want his lips again. She threw herself back against the tree, and felt a wish had been granted. For years the courtyard had given her energy; it had been an enclave of serene happiness, and now it was living up to its promise. For once, she was at the very heart of her refuge from the world. It was dark now, and inside the dense shrubbery everything was darker still. They were perfectly hidden. She felt the man's hands on her neck, then on her breasts, as if he might lift her from the ground. She opened her eyes just to see if this was really happening. She was panic-stricken for a moment; there was still time to think clearly and to stop it all, but then she thought of the spirit of this man, of the black feathers she had stroked against her cheek, like a premonition of this total embrace. He was so big he might have hurt her, but he was gentle, in control. She felt light in his arms, which surprised and delighted her. It felt thrillingly sinful to be kissing this man under her own windows, thumbing her nose at her life and everyone who had sneered at or underestimated her. In spite of herself, she found herself murmuring, 'This can't be happening... it can't be happening...'

Ludovic drew back, though she wanted him to go on, to insist. But if he had insisted, she would have hated him. He had shown consideration, respected her slight hesitation, and now she wanted him even more. They gazed at each other though they could barely make each other's faces. Then the entrance light came on, and the light over the gate to the courtyard, and finally the courtyard light itself. Aurore buried her face in Ludovic's neck, shrinking back, though they were already hidden. They mustn't move in the tangle of foliage, and now it had become a game, she felt all the excitement and danger of playing hide-and-seek. Footsteps rang out, crossing the cobbles to the post room, there was the familiar sound of its metal door opening, the time-switch being pressed again, and at last the footsteps retreating towards staircase C or B. Aurore knew it was not Richard, and he never went to the letterboxes. She could not tear herself away from Ludovic, her partner in this game, and he was not moving either, not making a sound. She put her hands on his buttocks and found them firm and muscular, tight against his jeans. She pulled this big kid, more imposing than a man, closer still; he felt as strong as the tree and she could not let him go. Suddenly from above, she heard Iris yelling at her brother. Her children. Her astonishing, amazing children still, for a few moments more, such a long way off.

She did not often get the chance to take a bath before dinner, but as she slipped her key into the lock she felt that she could not do anything else – she would have a long soak in the bath and wash away any lingering scent from her encounter. When Iris and Noé looked along the corridor and saw her appear, they ran towards her. They seemed literally to float from the sofa into her arms. She bent down and hugged them both, and after the arms of the man the hug felt light, gentle and unreal. She rediscovered the smell of her children and she held them as if she had not seen them for a year. She felt herself pass, with no shame or unease, from the ardent desire she had felt for the man to exquisite tenderness. It was a surprising extension of the same feeling. She closed her eyes to rid herself of any guilt, suddenly overcome by the enormity of what she had just done, out there in the courtyard. As she held her children she wanted to ask them to forgive her for the soaring happiness from which she was gently descending, for the desire she still felt – a desire that still buoyed her – and for the exhilaration that had absolutely nothing to do with either Iris or Noé.

Locked in the bathroom, this time she made as much steam as possible. With the windows closed, she let the cloud of vapour build until she was completely enveloped. Already, she was wondering how to react if she encountered Ludovic again. It would be hard to avoid seeing him, given that he lived right there, through the branches outside the window. He had liberated her courtyard, rid it of menace, and, anyway, was it even possible for her not to see him again? But really she should not, for so many reasons, not least the simple fact that he lived here, behind one of the windows opposite, and that made it mad, dangerous and impossible. Thinking back on what had happened, the two of them hiding like children among the bushes, it seemed both appalling and wonderful. She had forgotten that carefree feeling of falling into someone's arms – it was a reminder of childhood, the guilty, irresistible attraction of the boy in your class, the heady intoxication of teenage bad behaviour. She would have liked to go to sleep right there in the bathroom so that she did not have to think about it. Then everything would right itself. She would have liked to be far away, very far, and the feeling was so strong that she felt she already was. At the other end of the apartment, in the sitting room, she heard her stepson, Victor, who had just come home and was already demanding that Iris and Noé leave him alone. And she knew that, little by little, all these things were going to suck her back in; little by little, things would return to normal and the evening would take its course: Vani would leave, she would have to prepare dinner, Richard would come home, he would get off his motorbike taxi as fresh, energetic and full of life as if it was the beginning of the day. She knew that a word, a look, a peck on the lips from Richard would remind her of what their life together was, the life of a fulfilled couple, successful right across the board, with plenty still to do, and new territory to conquer.

She would have liked to be out of the bath before he was home – perhaps he had sent her a text or a voicemail to let her know what time he would be back, to ask if she had bought bread, if she had got home all right. Or perhaps he hadn't. For once it would be she who had not seen his text, and that was a very good thing. She lay in the hot bath, her eyes closed, picturing what she would do when she got out. She would wipe the steam from the mirror, fearful of seeing herself; she would turn, open the window a little, and look cautiously out, trying to see what he might be doing at that moment, just over there, opposite, wondering what he was thinking. It would be simple enough to find out – just chop one or two of the branches that obscured her view and call out in the direction of one of the windows across the courtyard, just below.

She opened her eyes and sat up so quickly in the slippery bath that the water slapped over the side. For goodness' sake! What on earth had she been thinking of, kissing that man when she had idea who he was? Deep in her cloud of steam, she began to panic, thinking of the life she had patiently built with Richard and the children, and she told herself she had made a terrible mistake in offering herself to this stranger. It was worse than opening their door to a predator – the image flashed before her eyes – it was as if that man's presence had taken the place of the crows, and she knew that the space he now occupied was far greater. He would be much more of a threat, much more intrusive and now he would never leave her alone.

Other people exist even in their absence. She had no idea what to think about that man. In just a few hours, he had come to have an enormous effect on her life. She would have liked to stop thinking about him, to erase his insistent presence from her mind. She was obsessed with him, to an alarming degree.

That morning, as she emerged into the courtyard, she was worried she would bump into him. She did not visit the post room and hurried in the direction of the street, determined to limit the possibility of seeing him. A chance encounter would mean confronting the unavoidable reality of the situation. She didn't know what had come over her the evening before. Perhaps fatigue after her trip to Troyes, the sense of adventure, something new, when she had set foot in the other staircase, that feeling of being a long way from home, even though it was on her doorstep. She had been so damned stupid. She promised herself that if their paths crossed, she would act as if he wasn't there. In any case, in this building, all the neighbours were like ghosts, distant possibilities. The thought reassured her.

She took a back route to the metro, down the little street behind the church of Saint-Paul, where she was far less likely to bump into anyone. There were no cars or people, and it came out a bit further along on another street that was scarcely any busier, before rejoining the crowded boulevard. She walked the length of a cold, damp square from where there suddenly rose the strident cawing of crows, echoing loudly amid the drab vegetation that subsisted there. She looked across and saw half a dozen of the birds perched on the back of a bench. She took fright at the thought that they, too, might take it into their heads to torment her, that they would get into the courtyard while she was away or follow her, unless they had resorted to this miserable little square because they were fearful of coming to her building; the man had told her that when they smelled the remains of their buried brothers they would not come back, they would be scared away forever.

Still, the fear overwhelmed her again, real and intact. She was haunted by the thought that these frightening creatures might be stalking her. Beady in the black mass of their glossy plumage, their little eyes watched her go by, as if they had a score to settle. Perhaps, with their sharp intelligence, they had understood, and knew that in this city she was their worst enemy. She was glad to come out on the avenue; it was like a return to civilisation, with the noise of the traffic drowning everything. She joined the orderly crowds of commuters on autopilot, walking towards the metro, pouring down the stairs, sucked in by the great draught at every station entrance, a gigantic rush of oxygen that was the network's only guarantee of a continuous flow of breathable air.

What she had always underestimated about herself, and tried to silence, was her deep-seated need for reassurance. It was the thing she craved most of all. Probably they all did, these people boarding the carriages with her, all of whom seemed to be clutching their bags – rucksacks or satchels for the men, handbags for the women – plainly everyone was holding on to something precious, something intensely personal, a little bit of home that they carried with them, something to help them through the day, holding it tight like a parent's hand. Once in the carriage, standing or sitting, most looked down at their phones, but still kept a tight grip on their bags. That morning, Aurore decided they were all like her; a crowd of children seeking reassurance.

And throughout the day she saw the same need in each member of her team. Her first task was to reassure them all, one by one, about the three hundred dresses. The mistake was being corrected. But then there were all the other things, the state of the finances, the fact that Fabian was once again absent, and all the other questions they were asking. But to calm their anxiety, she first had to feel calm herself… The day was difficult and joyless.

In the evening, after dinner, Richard asked her what was wrong. She was acting strangely, she hadn't said a word for two days. After her trip to Troyes and her sleepless night away, she had spent the afternoon negotiating with the bank. It was humiliating to keep asking for extensions on her loans, knowing they would probably not be granted, because the bank manager needed reassurances of her own. Everything was a worry. Aurore answered truthfully that she was exhausted. At the very end of the evening, before bed, as they were making themselves hot drinks in mugs brought back from the States, Richard hovered close as if he genuinely wanted to talk, but he just said again that he had found her distant lately. He asked her two or three questions about her work, and whether anyone had brought up the subject of the pre-pack insolvency. She dreaded the moment he would adopt the exasperating, superior tone he always used when offering advice, as if looking down from the great height of his own success. And there it was: Richard told her that he had given it some thought. She should look to new investors, but it wouldn't be easy. He said this condescendingly. As a tech expert, he had looked at the numbers. Textiles were a dying industry in France. A sector that had once employed a million people had, over the last two decades, shrunk to fewer than five thousand. It was finished, viable only as a niche market. He delivered his statistical arguments with the self-assurance of the movers and shakers of the business world. She ought to have felt encouraged that Richard was talking to her again, but instead it worried her even more. She realised he felt sorry for her, and she did not need that. They spoke in French, but his American accent was particularly pronounced this evening.

'You know, Aurore, it's not really for me to say this, but I think you should network more. Networking is so important – you've got to make connections, and you don't have enough of them. Friends are the building blocks of business. It's what friendship is for!'

It was already midnight, but Richard's ringtone sounded. He ignored it, a sign that the conversation they were having mattered to him, but when it rang again, he finally picked up and, with a smile, switched his attention to some far-distant place. He switched languages, too, talking in English now, but whether to Singapore or to London, it was impossible to tell. Aurore went over to the window. In spite of herself, several times during the evening she had felt impelled to look out. At night, the panes reflected across the courtyard like mirrors. Several times, she had opened the window to hear the silence and look across at the building opposite, but she could see nothing through the trees. The windows of the other building were partly obscured by the branches, or unlit and their curtains drawn. And yet she felt she was being watched, though she herself could see nothing. It panicked her to think that the man on the other side had a rifle. She reassured herself that he was clearly neither crazy nor bad. His was not a malevolent spirit, but still, he haunted her thoughts, and it bothered her now more than ever.

She had never wanted curtains – she wanted the apartment to be filled with light. Even at night the bare windows had never bothered her. Everything could be seen openly. Apart from the bathroom which had a little curtain, the whole apartment was on show. Now, however, she thought she might go to the Saint-Pierre market this weekend and buy some fabric. Not that they had anything to hide. But perhaps she felt the urge to keep people from seeing too far inside herself.

He stood on the landing and listened. There was shouting coming from inside, even before he rang the bell. He waited for a couple of minutes to judge the situation. What he heard was the sound of a young couple unable to cope with their kids. There were obviously two or three children, and their parents had lost control of the mess and unruly behaviour in an apartment that was probably quite small, in the middle of a series of blocks built in the 1970s – a dated but well-kept building, in a town on the north-eastern edge of Paris, a place with the oddly bright-sounding name of Bondy.

Before going up to their floor, Ludovic had cast an eye over the tall stockades at the far end of the car park, a soundproof wall that ran all the way along the back of the buildings but failed to wholly shut out the muffled roar of the motorway behind. Probably, the higher up in the building you were, the more intrusive the noise became. Coupled with the view of the river of cars far below, and the exhaust fumes. The kind of hell that could drive you crazy over time. Sure enough, the people he had come to see lived on the top floor.

The people inside were all hollering at one another. He could hear adults shouting and children crying, and from experience he knew that it was never a good idea to show up in the middle of a heated argument, especially one involving a couple. A couple arguing is like a grenade primed to go off in the face of the first person who interrupts. It was dangerous to come between a couple in conflict, especially if they had been drinking. He had done it one evening on Place Wilson, Toulouse, and never again.

At the sound of the bell, the flat's occupants fell silent. It was the young woman who came to the door. It was often the women who answered – they were more likely to face things head on. Ludovic stood on the mat outside, well clear of the door, and asked if he could speak to Monsieur Jaddar. Behind the woman, at the end of the hallway, he saw three small, blank faces staring at him. He could have lightened the mood with a little wave of his hand, but he wanted to preserve the tension, keep things ice-cold, with no hint of friendliness. The young woman did not invite him in, but when Ludovic saw the guy's face above those of the children, he stepped forward and walked down the corridor, holding out his hand and immediately introducing himself. He mentioned the Musculator gym and the two clients who had hired him, Sonia and Mathéo.

'You've got a nerve, bothering us in our own home with that shit!'

The young woman behind him was setting the tone. Ludovic noted that the man had shown no reaction. He had obviously been taken by surprise. He had not expected the business of the missing equipment to catch up with him here at home, without any warning.

'Madame, do you work with Monsieur Jaddar? No? Well, if you don't mind, I need to speak to the person in charge of Fitness Furniture. He's the person I've come to see, and he may be your husband or your boyfriend, but the only reason I'm here is because you don't have an office, and since there's no home address given in the register of companies either, I had to do a spot of research. And now I've found you.'

Sensing trouble, the guy scratched his head, but it was the girl who flared up again. 'You've got no right to come into people's houses like this!'

'Let me be clear, I am here on business, sent by two clients, so when I step inside your home, it's no different from entering an office, or a shop, if you prefer.'

Ludovic sensed this would escalate if he did not calm the young woman down. The guy was still deciding how he should handle the situation. Should he play the innocent or come clean? As for the kids, they stood stock-still, terrified and silent. Worst of all, Ludovic felt trapped in the corridor. He could not see this ending well. There were six of them in the narrow, dark hallway, and he had to move things along fast or the pressure would build, like the trigger on an air-gun.

'Look, why don't we sit down? I can explain everything.'

Ludovic seated himself at the head of the dining table, forcing the other two to sit either side of him, if only so that they could see all the papers he was spreading out. The arrangement gave Ludovic the upper hand, and he spoke forcefully so that he would not be interrupted.

'Since I'm here, let me give you some advice. The best thing for you would be to avoid this getting as far as the courts, because you wouldn't have a leg to stand on, Monsieur Jaddar. You are listed as a dealer in gym equipment on the website of Fitness Furniture, which you run. Three months ago, you received a down payment of eleven thousand euros to supply Sonia Delio and Mathéo Casas with two treadmills and three weight machines. Sonia Delio and Mathéo Casas had planned to open their gym before the end of the year. Perhaps you are unaware, but they borrowed the money here and there, and especially from their parents, plus a bank loan, so that they could buy the equipment and fit out their premises. They've completed all the work, but they haven't heard anything from you, Monsieur Jaddar, for the past three months, despite sending you dozens of emails and five recorded-delivery letters. As for your website, Fitness Furniture,

I see there are no legal notices, which is itself an irregularity, as far as I'm concerned, and no CONTACT US section, either. Which is strange, wouldn't you say? Mademoiselle Delio and Monsieur Casas have no operating cash flow, and now all they're hoping is that you will return their advance payment. You might object that they could have taken you to court themselves, but Mathéo Casas has something of a history in that regard, and they prefer to use our agency. For our part, we have undertaken to find a speedy resolution to the problem. Do you understand?'

Jaddar and the woman did not react. The children began to finger the paperwork Ludovic had spread out. Ludovic waited for the parents to tell them to stop, but they did nothing, so he calmly gathered everything up.

'Monsieur Jaddar, have you been to China?'

'No.'

'So you import equipment from a manufacturer in China without having met them?'

'We're in touch by email.'

'Ah, in what language?'

'English.'

'You speak English?'

'I get by, and there's always Google Translate.'

'I see. And your training and background are in what exactly, sales or sport?'

'I was a trainer at a gym in Saint-Denis, right? I know all the gear, all the machines!'

'Fine. So are you a wholesaler or do you sell second-hand equipment through your website? Because I've studied the market prices, and the equipment you're offering is three times cheaper – that's quite a big discount, wouldn't you say?'

Ludovic always tried to speak clearly, but he often found that the people he dealt with showed tremendous difficulty understanding him, compounded no doubt by their extreme bad faith. Since he was a kid, he had always liked to play the responsible older brother and found genuine satisfaction in solving other people's problems; it was a role he enjoyed, managing difficult situations. But with these two, he felt that by acting as the reasonable adviser and trying to be calm and clear, he was uniting them against him. Not that they were bad people; rather he sensed that they were utterly inexperienced, frightened and lost.

'Listen, I'm sure you wanted to run a decent business. You set up on your own, and for that alone I congratulate you. But you have to know the people you're dealing with, and as I understand it, you've never even met your suppliers – you've never actually seen the equipment, have you?'

'We have.'

'So what's going on here? Your Chinese suppliers have cheated you? Is that it?'

At that point the guy, who had been made to feel small in front of his woman and the children, lost it completely and thumped the table so hard it tipped over, sending the pile of papers flying, whilst yelling that no one would ever cheat him, and certainly not the Chinese and certainly not in sport. 'No one hustles me, you hear?'

Ludovic thought the woman would join in, but it was the kids who began to cry, pressing their faces against their mother's legs while the man continued his rant. Ludovic rose to try to restore calm, keeping in mind the whole time that this guy had screwed over two young people who had taken a genuine business risk and borrowed from their family. For their sakes, he asked Jaddar to sit down and get a grip, but this made things worse.

'No one tells me to sit down in my own home, so take all this paperwork and get out!'

Weighing more than a hundred kilos counted for nothing against a man so riled up that he had lost all self-control. Jaddar was ready to come to blows, capable of grabbing a knife or anything else – a man in that state might do something he would later regret. Ludo kept his distance, asking the guy to be reasonable and listen to the proposition he had come to make, but then the woman raised her voice, too, screaming at him to get out. The kids, paralysed at first by their mother's anger, began to holler as well, and the parents shouted even louder as a result. The tension was unbearable. Ludovic said nothing. If he backed down, gathered up his papers and left, he would demonstrate that he was powerless; it would solve nothing and, worse, it would mean he could never come back, because next time they wouldn't even open the door. If, on the other hand, he acted like them and started shouting, it would get them even more worked up. Reacting physically would be worse still, demeaning the guy's authority in front of his kids and enraging him further. He might call in the neighbours, or a few friends nearby. Ludovic had experienced that before. He could see no way out, and now both the man and the woman were trying to grab his arms and pull him out into the corridor. He pushed them off brusquely and began to gather up his folder and papers that were strewn across the room. As he bent to pick a sheet of paper up off the floor, the guy put his foot on it. Rather than catch him by the ankle, Ludovic attempted a bluff. He said he was going to leave, and that outside in the car park he would be taking photographs of the guy's car to add to the file because now it would have to be seized as compensation.

This was a risky strategy for two reasons. First, because he had no idea whether they owned a car or not, and second, because he had no authority to seize assets of any kind. But guys like this invariably had a flash car – the basic accessory, especially for a small-time swindler who reckons he's mastered the art of the deal. They always drove an in-your-face 4×4 to bolster the illusion of their social standing.

He saw at once that he had hit the bullseye. As soon as he left the apartment the guy threw on a jacket and followed him out and down the stairs, which was exactly what Ludovic had wanted – to get him away from his partner and kids, and avoid a confrontation that would be hard to control in front of his family. But down on the ground floor, there was no chance of speaking to the guy one-on-one: a group of kids was playing a frenzied ball game in the hallway. The noise was unbelievable. They would have to talk outside, but as he stood poised to open the door, Ludovic knew perfectly well that he had no idea where the guy's car was parked. Left or right? Or straight ahead? And which car was he looking for? The kids ignored them and carried on playing. If anything, they were kicking their blasted ball harder and harder.

Ludovic was stuck. The guy was silent now. He wanted to get him up against the wall, make him spit out an apology for the things he had called him. But if he laid a hand on him, the kids would get involved, and maybe bring in reinforcements… He knew, too, that once he was out of the door he would be stuck on the other side, with no way back in. Furious that he had backed himself into this corner, Ludovic turned to Jaddar and looked him in the eye, making no attempt to conceal the anger that had been building inside him for the past twenty minutes. With his jaw clenched and eyes wide open, he felt sure he could stare the guy down.

'Spit it out. What's going on here? You've screwed them over, or the Chinese have screwed you?'

The guy was clearly used to confrontations like this. He was spectacularly unimpressed. Behind them, the kids carried on shooting against the walls. The din reverberated around the hallway, it hurt Ludovic's eardrums and he felt his blood pressure rise as he continued staring at the guy, who gave no response. When an especially loud shriek coincided with the ball smashing into the end of the row of metal letterboxes, Ludovic lost control. In a flash of rage, he grabbed Jaddar by the jacket and marched him backwards along the hallway, pinning him against the wall at the end under the staircase.

'Don't be a jerk, you've been done over by the Chinese, haven't you?'

The sight of two grown men seizing one another by the collar did not faze the footballing kids one bit. They didn't even stop to stare. Ludovic sensed that he had taken the guy by surprise, and he pressed home his advantage, slipping a hand into the back pocket of the man's jeans, loose over narrow hips. The big electronic key was there; all he had to do was grab it and carry through the bluff by going out into the car park. He would see which car responded when he clicked to unlock.

A big 4×4 lit up to his left – a black BMW X6. Ludovic felt sickened at the sight of it, the kind of vehicle that was worth thirty thousand euros and cost a fortune to run. It looked brand new.

'Wait, what? You'd steal from two young people trying to get their business off the ground at the same time as treating yourself to a car like that? Bought with their money! What kind of scumbag are you?'

Ludovic got into the driver's seat, leaving the door open. The guy made a sudden grab for the key, but Ludovic caught him by the wrist and bent it back in an armlock. Jaddar was forced to his knees, writhing in pain.

'Where's their equipment?'

'I don't know.'

'How does it work, eh? You buy second-hand equipment and resell it as new?'

'There's no scam. I haven't done anything wrong.'

'So where is it?'

'I don't know... It's stuck in a container, or it never left, I have no idea. Sometimes they take six months to deliver.'

'You know, I really like it when people try to take me for a ride. Play me for a fool. You know why? Because when people do that, it means they're underestimating me, and that's a mistake no one should ever make.'

'It's coming, all the gear. I just don't know when, that's all...'

'Forget the gear. I'm not interested in the gear. What I want is the money. You took the money, now you give it back. Let me tell you – your money, your business, your hustles, that's up to you. I don't even care if you could afford to buy this car, I'm not the police, but if you have any self-respect you will pay them back right now because if I submit this case to the courts, it's going to cost you, big time. You know you'll have to pay 50 per cent straight away in fines, that's sixteen thousand euros for your little game, and that's not even taking into account the time you'll spend behind bars, so as we're here, why don't you write me a cheque and then you'll be able to look at yourself in the mirror, OK? And if your equipment shows up one day, well, so much the better; you can try eating it, or sell it to some other sucker, I don't care, but I swear, if you don't pay this debt now, I won't give up. I promise you, I will not give up.'

Ludovic released the armlock. He knew from Jaddar's lack of reaction that he had won. The fake tough guy was rubbing his forearm; the fight had gone out of him and he slumped, not even trying to recover his car key. Ludovic sensed he was ready to let it go and take out his chequebook. Sometimes, talking like a tough-love father figure made the other decide to listen. He was no psychologist, but he knew how to get them eating out of his hand. Living on the farm, he'd faced opposition a thousand times, every possible way, from a horse, a mule, a runaway dog, a headstrong bull. You had to take control, bring them round. It was the same with rugby, work on the other guy to take him down.

He made the most of his natural advantage. He knew the source of his strength – not his arms, nor the torso that caused his shirts to strain at the seams, but his cool head. Yet he never made the mistake of seeing himself as some kind of superman. You came out on top by playing on the fears and shortcomings that made other people weak. There was a flaw in everyone; you just had to find it. Even at school, he had often had the upper hand, but being top dog was not without its dangers. There was always a temptation to manipulate people, to misuse your power, going back on your promises to be good. Here – both out in the *banlieue* and in the centre of Paris, even in his own building – everyone's faultlines were clear to see. And if he wanted to make use of them, he had only to find a way in.

A trap. For three days now, Aurore knew she had fallen into a trap. All that man had wanted was to fuck her, to feel her all over, and now he would be preening himself, triumphant. Three days after the event, she felt nothing but the bitter taste of wrongdoing. With hindsight, she could scarcely believe she had done it. Best to forget, to erase the moment as if it had never happened, except the man lived opposite. Just thinking about it made her wary of her own windows, the trees, even her turtle doves, all of them witnesses capable of betraying her secret.

Every evening, when she pushed open the heavy carriage door and stepped into the courtyard, she saw the tiny jungle and stifled her dread that the trees might talk. Every morning, she walked down her staircase filled with apprehension. What if he was there? She had no idea what she would say to him, and dreaded his reaction even more. No doubt their embrace, the passionate kisses, the intimate caresses had turned him on and he would want more; he would never understand. She trembled each time she thought of him, but from fear far more than desire. She could not explain what she had done – to have given herself, without thinking, to an unknown man, a man who killed birds, a man with a gun. It was sheer madness. She told herself the terror would subside, but three days later came the master stroke, the incident that poured oil on the flames. That morning, she had been shut up in a room on the first floor at work with her accountant, poring over spreadsheets since nine o'clock sharp.

And as she faced the other woman – her demeanour increasingly tense and severe – Aurore had felt she was truly on trial. Here, too, everything pointed to her guilt.

The sound of sewing machines rose from the floor below. The women were putting together two new prototypes, a crucial moment when the sketches became a reality. Aurore loved the sound of the garments being assembled – it gave an impression, at least, that the business was doing well. Despite the fact there was no money for the coming year, she had started work on a new, if small, collection. It would keep everyone busy, so they wouldn't have time to think too hard about what was going on.

In meetings, Aurore always kept her phone to hand, with the sound off, but set to vibrate. For the third time that month, her accountant Fabienne Nguyen was summing up the case for the prosecution. Fabienne had dominated her life recently, calling her every day – yet another thing preying on her mind. A faint Vietnamese accent hardened her diction; she was punctilious, focused, methodical, and attractive in spite of her tight-lipped smile. Aurore registered every point raised, every warning delivered. The end of the tax year was approaching, but the outstanding unpaid orders – ninety-two thousand euros' worth of merchandise that had vanished en route to Asia – meant she was unable to finalise the accounts.

'Aurore, I know it's always difficult to secure payment from overseas clients, but it's been over a hundred and twenty days now, do you realise that? Now that your bank has called time, I honestly don't see how we're going to get through this – they've got to pay, do you see? There's no hiding from the numbers.'

Aurore listened as she examined the spreadsheets. Dozens of cells scrolled past with every click, all of them red, and superimposed on these were visions of Ludovic emerging from the trees or pressing the bell to their apartment, kissing her in front of Richard, while the woman sitting opposite her held a knife to her throat.

'... and if we add in your unpaid tax, frankly, Aurore, I don't see how...'

Aurore felt herself suffocating, and when her phone buzzed on the table she welcomed it like a breath of fresh air, relieved to have the chance to escape for a smoke in the corridor. But the number displayed was her own, the landline at home, and straight away she knew something was wrong. Vani never called; she took care of everything and never waited to be told what to do. Aurore apologised to Fabienne, who shot her a furious look as if to say, 'Tell me you're not going to answer that.' But Aurore was already speaking to her nanny, who was panicking so much she was incapable of explaining what had happened. What little French she had mastered deserted her now, and all she could say was, 'Bang, a big bang!' Words that turned Aurore's blood to ice, because she could hear Iris and Noé wailing in the background, begging to talk to their mother – all the more distressing since Aurore had no idea what was going on.

Water was still trickling down to the courtyard and the staircase was slippery as she bounded up the steps through the last of the torrent that had poured over the polished wood. When she reached their landing, the door to her home stood wide open in spite of the cold. From here she could see down her hallway to her kitchen and part of the sitting room, as far as the ivory-coloured carpet that was soaking wet, thick and spongy now. All around her, the floor was a broad, shining pool and when she stepped inside the apartment, the chaos was clear to see – the kitchen cupboards shattered, the worktop in pieces, the wreckage of the oven and hotplates strewn over the tiled floor. But what shocked her most of all when she turned to look into the sitting room, what struck her like a thunderbolt was the sight of him settled on the big white sofa, that man, with Iris and Noé sitting either side of him.

The children rushed to greet her, brave little survivors of their ordeal. But the man did not move. Aurore was stunned. She bent down to hug the twins tightly, overwhelmed as never before by their sweet smell. She should have been reassured to find them safe and well, but at that moment a multitude of hideous thoughts were racing through her mind. That man, making himself comfortable in her sitting room, looked to her like a predator, a harmful presence she would never be rid of, the very reincarnation of the crows, except that he was not content to remain out there among the branches; no, far worse than that, he had entered her home and sat enthroned amid the wreckage. She sensed that she would never free herself from him now.

Holding her children close, she felt deeply sickened – sickened by her own self, by the sheer folly of having kissed that man; sickened by the thought that this perfect stranger had possessed her mouth, her body, that she had held his buttocks in her hands. Even to think of it revolted her, and though she understood nothing of the present situation, she sensed an impending crisis, as if the three-hundred-litre boiler that had come crashing down, this meteorite that had landed right there in her kitchen, had just shattered her life into a thousand pieces, and the harmony she had known before would never return.

Vani emerged from the bathroom with the mop and a big bucket. The nylon overall she always wore was soaked and dirty. The two women stared at one another, their faces flooded with guilt. And Vani stated outright, 'This is not my fault,' at the very moment that Aurore wanted to say precisely the same thing: 'This isn't my fault, all this mayhem, the shame of not being home when it happened, and above all the presence of this man here, all this mess, it's not my fault…' With his usual infuriating coolness, Ludovic got up from the white sofa and crossed the room to Vani. Aurore stared in disbelief as her nanny, usually so shy, allowed Ludovic to put his arm around her shoulders and pat her on the back.

'We have this lady to thank, because without her, believe me, we wouldn't be standing here now. Or we'd be up to our thighs in water!'

He continued speaking with the same extravagant calm, explaining how, just minutes before, over in his apartment, he had heard what sounded like an explosion, a huge bang. He had glanced out into the courtyard, but with all the windows shut and nothing unusual to be seen outside, he told himself it must have come from further away, perhaps a different building, or the next street. But immediately afterwards he had heard cries, the terrified screams of Vani and the children at the sight of the huge boiler that had broken free, three hundred kilos that had shattered the kitchen units and torn out the water pipes as it fell, so that they were all left gushing like geysers – a great tide of cold water, about to engulf the apartment and the rest of the building.

'If she hadn't screamed so loudly, I would have closed my window, and what would have happened then does not bear thinking about.'

Aurore found it hard to commute her judgement of this man, who had terrified her moments before. She could not imagine being suddenly grateful, thanking him for the second time in eight days, yet he had raced over to her apartment and had had the good sense – amid the panic and chaos – to turn the water off at the stopcock, without which the pipes would still be gushing and the water level rising, so that the parquet floor, the wiring and appliances, everything would have been ruined. The apartment below would have been flooded, not to mention the staircase – a disaster a hundred times worse than the damage she saw before her now.

Ludovic went into the kitchen behind the breakfast bar and began pointing out the damage like a works foreman.

'I've called a plumber I did some work for once; he'll be here within an hour. He'll solder the pipes up there, so you'll have water for tonight, but I should warn you, there won't be any hot water. For the rest, you'll have to speak to the cowboy who installed the boiler; I'd call him straight away if I were you – have you got his number?'

'No. Not here, I don't know, I don't know where it is…'

'You've got his invoice somewhere?'

Aurore stood close to the breakfast bar but did not venture into the kitchen, as if to keep her distance from the nightmare.

'Yes, probably. I must have the architect's number some-where... Just look at it, I can't believe it.'

'Well, call the architect now.'

'I just need to take a minute. I was so scared, I need to sit down.'

'Your guy had some funny ideas, anyway – fixing a boiler with concrete plugs, in plaster...'

Aurore stared at this discomfitingly kind man. She wondered how far she was beholden to him now, and above all what he might expect in return. At the same time, she noticed how carefully he tiptoed over the wet tiles, so as not to leave dirty footprints. His unruffled air had calmed them all down. Vani stood behind him, saying nothing but hanging on his every word, as if expecting him to give instructions. The children were in a state of shock, but no longer terrified, it seemed. They stared at the man, who was standing on a stool now and reaching up easily to the ceiling.

'See here, this section, all this is plaster, and the worst of it is they didn't even fix it to the beam, because there are beams boxed in above your ceiling, did you know that? Oak. Much stronger than concrete, they should have fixed it to those!'

Faced with the spectacle of her ruined kitchen, Aurore wanted only to stop thinking and wait for everything to sort itself out, because she couldn't deal with any more emergencies. Her life was too busy, too full of drama; she just wanted to step down and be on a level with her children, not the grown-up on whom everyone relied, and so she went and sat down on the big white sofa.

Ludovic was still talking, perched now atop the breakfast bar, but she wasn't listening.

'Up here! Hello?'

'Yes, I see where you are.'

'So, just come over here for a second.'

'No, I can't move.'

In every life, however grand or perfect, logistical issues invariably catch up with you. At times it seems they will never leave you alone, accumulating all around until you can see nothing else. Ludovic sensed this woman's disarray. She sat with her children around her, looking lost. He climbed down and tiptoed around the bar, through the debris, then walked over to her, wiping dust off his hands.

'You know what, there's something we can do — we'll take a photograph of the kitchen as it is, and you're going to text it to your architect, and two minutes later you're going to call him and ask why they didn't attach the thing to a proper support.'

'I don't understand.'

'Just send him the picture, then call him, and when it's ringing, pass the phone to me, OK?'

She stared at Ludovic with a mixture of disbelief and irritation. He bent down and knelt in front of her so that their faces were level. He explained his thinking.

'You've got to spur the guy into action, do you see? Tomorrow morning, he's got to send a couple of men round to sort out the work because he's messed up in a very big way. You've got to make him move.'

'Is this how you really are?'

'I'm sorry?'

'No… nothing. It's just that I was so afraid when I got here just now, really I was terrified, and now, I'm still scared.'

'Scared of what?'

Aurore was surprised by her sudden feeling of indignation. How could this man who had kissed her, who had grasped her body with his great long-fingered hands, how could he let nothing, absolutely nothing, show? Not the slightest hint of their furtive liaison.

'I'll tell you what, Aurore, come with me.'

He shouldn't have called her by her first name. Vani looked surprised. Ludovic got to his feet and returned to the kitchen, Aurore following close behind. Doggedly, he pushed the boiler aside and made sure everything was clearly visible in the photograph. She watched as he worked, gazing at the broad, muscular shoulders that strained against his T-shirt. He was bending over, exposing a strip of bare skin on his lower back, like a gap in the clouds. He had two small dimples, fixed points in the ripple of muscles. She noticed the cheap, coarse denim of his jeans, and the label – a brand for tall, broad men. It was so cold outside, how could this guy walk about in just a T-shirt?

'So, are you going to take the picture?'

She took several photographs, then Ludovic began shifting the shattered units, to clear the room. He even heaved the huge boiler out onto the landing. Watching him, Aurore sensed a pure force of nature at work. Not the power that comes with professional standing or social status – no, this man's power was simple, human, clean.

Methodically, he cleared the kitchen then asked Aurore to dial the architect's number. He launched into a strongly worded voicemail, detailing the extent of the damage, Aurore tried to get him to soften his tone, whispering that the guy was a friend of her husband's, that he would call back without fail as soon as he was able, that if he was in Paris he would almost certainly come round that evening. Vani took a beer from the fridge and offered it to Ludovic.

'No thanks, Vani. I'll be going now. . ..'

Aurore accompanied him to the door. They shook hands, nothing more, but Ludo made her an offer.

'If you want some hot water, you can come over—'

'No, thank you, we'll be fine.'

She stepped out onto the landing, pulled the door shut behind her and crossed to the stairwell, where Ludovic had begun walking down.

'Our paths are certain to cross again, here, but I wanted to tell you that we mustn't see one another any more, if you see what I mean, we mustn't—'

Ludovic turned to face her, his expression blank.

She went on: 'Well, I mean, we should talk one day. I just want to understand.'

'Understand what?'

'Why you're doing all this, the crows, the boiler, I don't know…'

Ludovic climbed back up to the landing. Watching him, she knew she should never have spoken, he was incapable of understanding, or worse, he would try to kiss her.

Facing her, he answered calmly: 'Aurore, you have nothing to fear from me. I'm here, that's all. I don't expect anything from you – on the contrary. But something's bothering you, clearly.'

'What would you know? What gives you the right to say that?'

She spoke sharply, infuriated at his ability to guess her thoughts. She turned and went back inside, closing the door behind her. He stood for a moment in the stairwell, then left. At least he'd seen inside that apartment, the one he had pictured in his mind's eye for two years now, not that it had ever preoccupied him especially; he was just curious. That woman represented everything he loathed about Paris, everything he rejected, everything he should avoid, and yet he found himself attracted to her. To everything about her.

It was sheer madness, but she did it anyway. She climbed the staircase; not her own, which was across the courtyard, beyond the dirty window panes that she tried not to look at. She took each step on tiptoe, fearing more than anything else that she might meet someone on her way up. Fortunately, the place seemed dead. She reached the third floor far more breathless than when she climbed her own three storeys. She walked the length of the dark hallway, concentrating on the creaking parquet floor, dismissing any other thoughts. She had been working up to coming here for six days now, because she had seen no sign of him; he hadn't even come to find out how the repairs were progressing, or to bask in the glory of having saved the situation, and yet six days was ample time for him to have rung their doorbell, to have turned up one evening to remind everyone what a perfect neighbour he was. But no, he had done nothing of the kind. Or perhaps he had left. And so this evening, climbing the unfamiliar staircase, she felt a little afraid: afraid of seeing him, but afraid, too, that he had gone, that he didn't live here any more, that the man had disappeared. She feared and hoped all of this in equal measure.

When she knocked on his door and was met with silence, she prayed that he would not answer, and that everything would be resolved when she turned on her heel and was released from the trap she had set herself. But the door opened. He showed no sign of surprise when he saw her there on the landing; he just smiled at her, and she stared at him, refusing to let the smile draw her in. Then he asked her inside. She said nothing, but walked through into his hallway, where he stood aside to let her pass. She was so consumed by guilt, by an overwhelming sense of shame, that she was unable to speak. Casting not a single glance around the spartan one-bed apartment, saying not a word, she went straight to the window and stared across at her own home, noting what could be seen of her world from his.

'I just wanted to say thank you, and to apologise, too,' she said, without turning round.

He said nothing. He was probably pulling a face behind her back. Or perhaps not. She didn't turn to look. On the other side of the trees, she saw glimpses of the large white apartment, her home, behind the screen of branches laid bare by the onset of autumn. A few leaves remained, and they hid her to an extent, as if granting her permission to be here. She leaned forward and fitted the puzzle together – her six windows, the window boxes, the three Velux windows in the top rooms, her spacious home, the place where she should be right now. Still saying nothing, he drew closer and placed his hand on the nape of her neck. She gave no reaction, but concentrated on the scene outside, the criss-crossing branches – a comforting screen. Gazing at her apartment from over here, she felt liberated from the demands of the life that awaited her there. For reassurance, just so she could hear his voice, so that he could speak one word at least, she asked why their paths hadn't crossed since last week. He said, 'People run into one another far less often in winter, and I was away for three days.' There were a thousand questions she could ask – Where had he gone? Who was he really? – as if it were possible to know everything about a person, to truly know them, in a matter of minutes.

'Can you see them?'

'Who?'

'Your two birds.'

She had forgotten them, but there they were, huddled together in a ball, ready to face the night – the sweet and touching sight of two kindred spirits lost in the utter cold, as the daylight faded. She wanted to say something about them, but he moved his hand further up the nape of her neck and she felt his fingers in her hair, like a slow, gentle comb that sent waves through the rest of her body. He had addressed her intimately, called her *tu*, and she had accepted it, but felt incapable of addressing him the same way; it felt wrong, almost impolite, and so she was left speechless, giving in to the unexpected wave of excitement that made her close her eyes and shut out the light that had just come on in the opposite building, and for a second she saw herself at home, in her bathroom, slipping into her bath, in sight of the draughty window. Standing here in this cold, soulless apartment she felt the same enveloping warmth as when she lowered herself into the bath, when the water rose up around her, covering her body. When she opened her eyes once more the light had gone out on the other side and she wondered if, in spite of the trees, anyone could see her. Someone probably could; the top floor of this building was slightly lower than the building opposite. But while it might be possible to see her, who would think to look outside, contorting themselves to peer through the trees; who would think to look for her here? Richard was in Kiev and wouldn't be back till tomorrow night. Vani would be clearing away the children's tea things or doing the ironing; no doubt the children were playing in their bedroom... For a moment, she sensed precisely what was going on, and she reproached herself for not being there. But already she felt his other hand moving down the jacket of her work suit to her waist, and a little lower. She closed her eyes and he pressed his body close to hers, not too hard, and yet she felt utterly overwhelmed by his bulk, his presence, was aware of his warmth. He seemed even taller and broader up close. She felt him behind her, bending over her; he rested his chin on her head, held her more firmly, and she was overcome by a force of nature, at once powerful and gentle. She felt the dizzying temptation of things that both transport and terrify us, and, fearing she might lose her footing altogether, she opened her eyes and saw that the lights had come on in her kitchen and sitting room; the sun was just beginning to go down, and she pictured Vani washing the children's bowls. Victor must be home, because the two Velux windows in his mezzanine room were lit now, and the round window at the end, all those lights on when it was barely getting dark, but they reassured her, like beacons, the watchful guardians of her well-planned everyday life, telling her that everything was still there, on the other side of the courtyard, waiting for her. And so she could stray without scruples, she was not lost in some faraway place, she could not be out of her depth so close to the shore. Knowing that her home was just there, within sight, like a lighthouse for a yacht sailing out into the storm, she could explore her fear and still see the way back. She remembered childhood games of hide-and-seek, when you try to disappear without even leaving the room.

He tugged the curtain across sharply, shutting out the view, and she felt he was tossing her into deep water; there was nothing left to hold on to. She turned. She should have felt outrage at his gesture. She did feel outraged, in fact, and in anger she seized his mouth and bit his soft, full lips, the lips that formed a smile that told her to be wary, a smile full of serene arrogance, a smile so troubling that she seized it like a fruit straight from the tree and bit into it harder still. He shuddered in slight pain, a sign of fragility despite his bulk, and she felt the same way she had that evening under the trees, the troubling, all-enveloping embrace of a body she knew she could gradually tame, and the sheer adventure of allowing herself to be led. If his grip tightened too much, she recoiled very slightly, just enough for him to relax his hold straight away. She felt astonishing power: here was a colossus whose reactions she could anticipate and rein in. With his mouth on hers, she lost all control and let his hands move wherever they wanted. She felt like a little girl running wild and free, in the full knowledge that what she was doing was wrong, an irreparable mistake, an irremediable transgression, and she kissed this man wildly, and immediately felt transported far, far away, and her dull anguish did little to dampen her ardour. She gripped his backside, wished her hands could hold the whole thing at once. Feeling her grasp, he tensed and she remembered the irresistible attraction of statues, the need she always felt to touch them, to know their curves physically. Stroking this man's body took her desire to new levels – the overwhelming sensation of holding him, a need to master his forms, his contours, the more so because his silence enhanced his sensual strength further still. How could someone so robust be so gentle and docile? He let out a small sigh, almost a gasp, then took her hand and placed it on his crotch as if challenging her, offering himself to her completely, and the feel of it, rigid and hard, tipped her overboard.

'Take it!'

She heard her own words in reply: 'Take me, go on! Take me,' then other words, vulgar, filthy, disturbing – all the words she no longer felt able to say to the father of her children – came pouring out now, sweeping her back to her days as a flirtatious teenager, feigning confidence, going out with men much older than her. She was the seventeen-year-old *provocatrice* who hung out in nightclubs; she relived the years when she always fell for older men, putting on a show for her girlfriends: nothing was more erotic than offering herself to a man of thirty. Though he didn't know it, this man was taking her back to all those parts of herself she had buried for too long, her boldness, crudeness, and this violent, urgent desire, so far from the pale imitation in her life now.

They heard the familiar, irritating sound of a wheeled suitcase being dragged across the cobbled courtyard. Aurore thought of Richard, then told herself it must be tourists arriving at their holiday apartment. She couldn't bear the noise, and she pushed the man over to the small bed, barely a double, and they crashed down onto it. She found herself on top of him, gazing down at the assured athlete, who had lost all control now. She enjoyed second-guessing his needs, lifted her skirt and sat astride him, relishing her power, subjecting him to the torment of her movements, back and forth, watching his frantic arousal. She touched her panties, knowing she would find them wet; she wanted him inside her, all of him, but first she wanted to rub herself against him; the thin cotton aroused her still more, pressing against her, keeping him from her. She was waiting for him to tense the muscles in his back and sit up, twist and rise like a horse that has fallen, and she would be carried along. She did not want him to be gentle now, but she could not tell him that, and he must have read it in her face because he sat up just at that moment, lifting her as if she were light as a feather. She clung to him and he turned her over, laid her on the soulless bedspread and pushed against her taut panties, then pulled them down and sank inside her, a leap into the void for them both. She forgot herself completely, forgot about the smell of cold tobacco that doubtless lingered in her hair – she had smoked so many cigarettes today – and the sticky feeling under her armpits, now that her whole body was freshly covered in sweat. She heard herself say, 'Harder. . .', caught between his wild movements and the mattress bouncing beneath. 'Harder,' she said again, finding no words to match her passion. His broad chest was like that of a beast devouring her, his arms two barriers against the world, and her hands were once more on his buttocks, now bared, as she dug her nails in to urge him on. In a gasp, she heard him utter words she did not understand. Her head was in his hands, two great paws that shielded her like a helmet, muffling her hearing, and that was when the fear struck her, as if suddenly she had become aware of him pumping deep inside her, stirring a thousand fantasies. His grasp brought her to her senses, she tensed, and panicked, as if at the scene of an accident. He was heavy and deeply aroused, but he stopped the instant he saw that something was wrong. He looked into her eyes and asked, 'What is it?' She didn't dare say that she had taken fright because he hadn't used a condom, that she – that they hadn't given it a moment's thought. She had stopped taking the pill two years ago; she felt ashamed, but she would never tell this man that she and Richard no longer made love. To fall pregnant would be her worst nightmare, and there, in a fraction of a second, she felt as if all the people she had cast from her mind – her husband, her children, Victor, even Vani – were there somewhere, in the room, all crying out, 'And they didn't even use a condom…!' The image was appalling and she began to cry, her face still clasped between the hands of this thunderstruck titan. He stared at her, uncomprehending, but wrapped her in his arms, and she clung to this man who had gone too far, too fast, who had disarmed her; she clung to him to make him understand that everything was all right, she just wanted him to talk to her.

'Talk to me, talk to me.'

She hadn't smoked in bed in ages, probably not for ten years. He smoked Marlboro Reds, the ones she had smoked before she switched to her thin, delicate Lights. Smoking in a closed room took her back to the forbidden thrills of childhood.

'Who are you?'

'How am I supposed to answer that?'

'Help me!'

'It's OK. I'm here.'

'No, help me to know who you are.'

'I'm a man who smokes indoors at home.'

'Who doesn't even open the windows for air.'

'Exactly. Well, I open them a crack sometimes, if I'm too hot at night. And there it is. I live in a one-bedroom apartment opposite yours, and when you knock on my door, I'm here.'

'Do you live alone here?'

'What do you think?'

She glanced around the bedroom, and the sitting room beyond. There wasn't even a door between the two.

'But you see people? You have friends, a job?'

'Hell, we go from sex straight to an interrogation...'

'I'm sorry. I felt afraid, all of a sudden. And we didn't use a condom, and I just got frightened, that's all.'

'I'll be honest with you: I don't have any.'

'Any condoms?'

'I lost my wife three years ago, and since then I haven't... Well, I've never met anyone else. That's it.'

Aurore did not know what to do with the words she had just heard. They echoed her own fear, after all. She was the one who had wanted them to talk, but in view of what he had just said she had no idea what to say next and certainly didn't want to ask him for more details, nor to find out how he had lost his wife, a wife whose presence had just been summoned into this bland bedroom, and suddenly she was no longer afraid, but felt on a rather more equal footing with this man she barely knew. She placed her cigarette in the ashtray on the bedside table; the last time she had seen an ashtray beside a bed was in her father's bedroom, twenty years before he gave up smoking. No one smoked in bed now, except this man from another place, a guy with legs longer than his bed. She took him in her arms, adopted a brighter tone, to encourage him to talk some more, to lighten the atmosphere.

'But don't tell me there aren't women at work desperate for that arse. You must know how grabbable it is.'

'Well, no one does grab it… Or – which is worse? – they do, and I don't even notice!'

'Are there women at your work?'

'Mine isn't really the sort of job where you get to meet people.'

'What do you do?'

'Debt recovery.'

She shot him a look of surprise he was unable to fathom.

'What? Does that shock you?'

'No. Not at all. So how does that work?'

'Simple, really. I recover money on behalf of people who really need it from people who need it even more… If you see what I mean.'

'Yes. I see exactly what you mean.'

She never usually saw Paris from the front seat. In a taxi, she always sat in the back, never beside the driver. She and Richard no longer had a car and no one she knew in Paris used their car. She was rediscovering what it was like to see the city from this perspective, along with the unsettling feeling of sitting next to this man, all the time privately fearing she was lying to herself, concealing her own ulterior motives. All she had done was mention the meeting, but it was he who had suggested coming along. She had agreed straight away – out of bravado or weakness, she did not know.

Sometimes you think you're interested in other people when really you're just using them. Doubtless she was lying to herself. Of course she was, but the benefit to her was immense. And the thought of Ludovic's presence at this meeting was reassuring to her. Perhaps he could help – he was used to awkward situations in his job, could sniff out underhand tricks. But above all, though she would never admit it, asking him to come along was a way to legitimise his presence in her life. If they were caught one day, talking in the courtyard or somewhere else, he wouldn't be a complete stranger, nor a possible lover, but a man who was helping her out at work.

'Are you afraid, Aurore?'

'Afraid of what?'

Since leaving the car park at Place de la Bastille, Aurore had gripped the handle above the passenger window, as if she was in some sort of danger.

'The suspension isn't great. It bounces about on the cobbles, is that it?'

'No, no, your car's great, it's just a bit, well…Why did you get one so small?'

Ludovic did not want to tell her they were in his wife's Twingo, that the car had a history all of its own, one he could not let go. He kept the Twingo because it was practical; he never used it in Paris, or only on the rare occasions when he went for a drink with colleagues in the city's livelier neighbourhoods. Mostly, he used it to drive to his parents' place, six hundred kilometres down the motorway, window open, one elbow resting on the nearside doorframe, because with the rush of air and the deafening din, he was certain never to go over the speed limit. Driving with the window open was his way of staying on the right side of the law. He knew his own nature: with a more powerful car it would be too tempting to hit the open, empty road in the dead of night and put his foot down. Truly instinctive people are the ones who know how to control themselves – that was what they were told in rugby, each time one of them blew a fuse. He fought constantly against the urge to go too far, with alcohol, at the wheel, on a motorbike: anything that gave him an adrenaline rush had to be kept in check. When you've spent fifteen years playing a contact sport, a sport that since childhood has taught you to grab people, to crash into them, it's hard to suddenly stop touching, colliding, to channel all the energy you poured into the game. Even at forty-six years of age, it was hard for him to manage his impulses, to divert his aggression, and above all to avoid turning to anything – whether alcohol or food – that might compensate for the temptation of breaking the rules.

Aurore sat back, enjoying the ride. She never felt at ease like this on the back of Richard's scooter, especially when he slalomed endlessly through the traffic and her helmet cut her off from everything around her, dulling every sound and smell. Ludovic was in no hurry, driving smoothly and carefully.

'Best to say you're a friend who's chosen to come with me?'

'I don't imagine the guy was born yesterday. Don't worry about it. Introduce me as an adviser, an external consultant, and it'll be fine. He's not going to ask for my CV!'

It had rained all night. Inevitably, the traffic was appalling. Rue de Rivoli moved slowly, inexorably, like a heavy flow of lava, a procession of the resigned, the unavoidably late. But at Place de la Concorde, along the axis of the Champs-Élysées, there was a dazzling break in the overcast sky, far off on the horizon, towards La Défense. Skyscrapers emerged from the clouds and the sun's rays lit their myriad windows. The towers of La Défense stood sparkling like gleaming sword hilts. La Défense was another city, angular and unreal. Aurore hated the place; even the thought of having to go there left her demoralised. Alone, she would never have made it. All the more so because Kobzham was a tough character, confident of his power, and not given to making gestures. With over two hundred shops, and concessions in top stores all over the world, he knew he was indispensable. He was Aurore's only real way in to the Asian market; the problem was that for the last three months and more, he had owed her ninety-two thousand euros.

She knew Kobzham would be unperturbed by Ludovic's presence, but she wanted him to know she would be taken for a fool no longer – a fool who supplies twelve hundred garments, payable within ninety days, a naïve dupe who offers herself up with hands and feet tied – that was what sapped her morale more than anything, to have been such easy prey, and to be unable to say as much to his face. At least with Ludovic there, she would feel able to speak up. Because she couldn't rely on Fabian for this: he wanted to hear nothing more about this Kobzham character.

Deep underground in the car park, everything changed. Walking among the slumbering cars, Aurore wondered if she was making a huge mistake. But it was too late now. Ludovic said nothing. He was still very much there, but cold, or concentrated on the task ahead, she couldn't tell. She didn't know him, after all. She knew him even less than she knew Kobzham. But while Kobzham was plainly a cunning, opportunistic businessman, the kind of crucial distributor who would exact his price one way or another, she had no idea who Ludovic truly was, nor what kind of risk she might be taking by getting him involved in her business deals. They summoned the lift; it took ages to arrive. Ludovic smiled at her but said nothing. They stepped into the cabin, and he took her hand. She pictured Iris and Noé, who had been talking about their neighbour ever since the accident with the boiler. He was their saviour, a gentle giant; they asked when he would come to see them again. A sign that they, at least, instinctively liked him, trusted him, and wanted him in their lives.

Above all, Ludovic had come along to this meeting to be with her, for a stolen, unexpected moment together. At the same time, he was genuinely curious to meet this character. Was he truly the piece of filth she had described, or a wholesaler with whom she should have exercised greater caution, insured her merchandise, taken nothing on trust?

The lift rose slowly and smoothly. Bizarrely, it stopped at every other floor. Each time, no one stood waiting to step aboard, and it continued on its way to the forty-second floor. The hallway outside the office suite led to a vast reception area staffed by three assistants, seated behind a desk. One of the young women led them to a waiting room, equally vast, and lavishly decorated in the worst possible neo-Roman taste, but with an extraordinary view over the west of Paris and the departing storm clouds.

Ludovic was struck by the luxury – a little over the top, perhaps, but impressive nonetheless. An odd map of the world was displayed on the wall, supposedly antique and drawn in black ink. Odd because Asia lay at the centre, and France was right at the edge, top left and very far away. It seemed the company had the entire floor to itself. Ludovic had no idea what he was getting into here. He had spotted the two cameras above the reception desk; obviously this guy was a major player and, if he was a bastard, he was a bastard big-time. He felt a moment of uncertainty, mostly because he wasn't a part of this deal and had no business here, other than to help out the very beautiful woman who had just taken his hand once more, this woman whose gaze fascinated him and blew him away, the dark, wondering eyes that blinked while looking deep into his, eyes that trained themselves on him, then shifted to another place and escaped him, as if they were already far in the distance, two quick and gentle butterflies he longed to catch.

They sat down on the huge sofa. Aurore was close beside him on the deep leather. He stared at her legs, gleaming in their nylon stockings. Flesh-coloured stockings that rose to a mirage of shadow, a skirt that had ridden up as she sat, just as it had earlier in the car. He had to stop himself laying his hand there, touching, however lightly, the firm, slender thighs he had kissed. He had the taste of her on the tip of his tongue, the delicate hint of mango, her lips like the pulp of persimmons, and feeling her so close to him, he wanted to bury his face in her neck, bite into her scent, savour her skin. She straightened up and looked him in the face, reading his mind, but now was not the time.

After ten minutes, no one had come to fetch them. Ludovic got to his feet. He needed to smoke, to move, to do something. Sitting beside this woman, whom he saw so little, and being unable to embrace or touch her was torture. Catching one another's eye was difficult enough. Aurore gestured for him to sit down again. She held out her hand and their fingers entwined, painfully tight and hard, to stop them from taking each other there and then on the deep, opulent sofa. Ludovic avoided looking at her, but he slipped the hand she held between her legs, her demurely crossed thighs, slid his palm into the soft, total darkness, felt its fascinating warmth and texture, and then, boldly, he touched his index finger to the seam of her stockings, in the fold between her legs. The outline of her panties, the feel of her yearning, was impossible to resist. She stared him straight in the eye, then threw her head back and uncrossed her legs, permitting him to plunge his forearm beneath her skirt. Wordlessly, savagely, he twisted his fist into her. She shuddered with the sweet pain, then caught his forearm with both hands; she was holding him back this time, controlling his firm, supple body, gripping his arm to keep him where she wanted him. She wanted to feel this man deep inside, wanted him to break his way in, any part of him, all of him, there in her belly; she wanted to draw him in once more, and most exciting of all was the knowledge that this man was capable of just that, of taking her right there, of making everything around them disappear and making love to her as if the world had ceased to exist. He was physically modest, she knew that, but capable of anything, and so she permitted his great hand to warm itself on the nylon of her stockings, opened her legs a little further to ease the twisting of his wrist, so that his hand was free to stroke her contours, the tips of his fingers searching for a way through the nylon, his index finger pressing unsuccessfully against the mesh. She smiled. A few nylon threads stood in the way of this colossus, and then – sheer madness – he leaned towards her, shifted his body till he was facing her, and then swooped down on her like

154

a wild beast, kneeling before her to bury his head between her thighs. He was mad, and the thought drove her wild; she glanced at the door that remained firmly closed, prayed it would stay that way. She could have pushed him away but his mouth had found the right place and he kissed it through the fabric, like biting into an orange, and the sound of sucking made the fruit juicier still. He was wild, and she was enthralled, staring fixedly at the door, her body utterly, sensually captive in his hands as they clasped her thighs and held them easily, submissively open; she could no longer move, and his mouth felt so intensely good against the nylon of her stockings, the softest part of his solid, unpredictable body against her own tender flesh, amid the folds of fabric and shadow, and she wanted more, she wanted his lips there, against her own. She took his mouth first, then knelt down with him, both of them at the foot of the long, black sofa, on their knees in the deep-pile carpet with Paris spread out behind them, and, closing her eyes, Aurore thought again, very hard, of the door, that it must not open, though he seemed perfectly unconcerned, as if the thought of them both being discovered there, in that impossible, unthinkable position, didn't bother him at all – these were the acts of madness this man brought her to; this was the folly he transported her to, a recklessness she longed to indulge.

Suddenly, they heard sounds through the wall, a door slamming shut in the offices, voices, people talking. Instantly, Ludovic threw himself back onto the sofa. Aurore got to her feet. Her legs were weak and her head was spinning. She smoothed her skirt, and Ludovic reached out from where he sat, guiding her back to her place beside him. She stared at him in astonishment, as if to say: 'What did you just do to me?' He kept control, gave a few short puffs, like a long-jumper preparing to leap. He wouldn't show it, but he was shaken, and sprang smartly to his feet when the door opened. Aurore read the surprise on Kobzham's face — he had expected to find her, but certainly not this other guy, and he was thrown. For once, he suppressed the fake smile he always wore. But his opening question, addressed to Aurore, was quick and sardonic.

'Are you together?'

I just want you to tell me quite simply what's going on: have the twelve hundred pieces been sold or not?'

'My dear Aurore, as you well know, with our Chinese friends, things are not always that simple. That's not how they think…'

'Madame Dessage's question is perfectly clear: as the distributor, you agreed to take six hundred dresses, two hundred and fifty suits and three hundred and fifty bustiers. The question is: have these pieces been sold or not?'

'Now listen here, I have no idea who you are, but let me tell you you're making a big mistake: you're thinking like a Westerner. The Chinese don't think in terms of "sold" or "unsold"; it's never black or white. Pardon me for saying so, but *you* have no idea what you're talking about… And where's your card?'

'What card?'

'Your business card. I'm afraid you can't just turn up like this, with no introduction.'

Without getting up from his seat, Ludovic reached for a sheet of paper and a pen on Kobzham's desk, then wrote in large letters LUDOVIC BARRÈRE.

'There, if that puts your mind at ease.'

Kobzham gave no reaction. He folded the sheet that Ludovic had held out to him, first into four, and then smaller and smaller again, as if trying to make it disappear. Aurore repeated her questions about her consignment of merchandise, but Kobzham gave no further explanation, stating simply that he had cleared it all with Fabian, that Fabian was his point of contact and that he never went behind people's backs, on principle. Then he sidestepped the issue with talk of restructuring his Asian network. Since June, his brother had been running the distribution hub from Hong Kong, and soon they would be manufacturing on the spot, through joint ventures with Chinese enterprises. The Chinese were in difficulty, and now was the time to press home their advantage. He was straying off topic, making no mention of the twelve hundred garments, perhaps trying to tell them their order was derisory, that his future lay above and beyond such small fry.

When Aurore had told him about the problem, Ludovic had immediately assumed this was basic, if clumsy, wheeler-dealing – the distributor was maximising his cut by paying his clients six months late. But here, he saw the scale of this man's business; his offices shared an address with the headquarters of a freight and shipping-container company, in which he probably held shares. A connection that opened every door, exempted him from customs duties and probably gave him a prime seat on the VAT merry-go-round, too. Ludovic knew the guy would never give in: he held all the cards, and the merchandise. He was in a position of absolute strength. He caught the whiff of a much more sophisticated racket and wondered if Fabian had given too much ground in the negotiations, been eaten alive, and no longer wanted to confront the man who was sitting opposite them now. At the same time, he thought it strange that Kobzham was keeping his cool in front of Aurore – he was her debtor, after all, and legally at fault. He wasn't even trying to come up with an excuse, to plead internal problems or other difficulties. On the contrary, he showed the assurance of a man in complete control. For an instant, Ludovic wondered if Fabian and Kobzham were in this together, if one racket concealed another.

In his sixties, dapper in a three-piece suit, Kobzham presided over the room from behind his large, transparent glass desk, which was perfectly empty, unencumbered by work in progress. Everything was carefully calculated to impress. He was silhouetted against a vast wall of plate glass, strutting about with nothing behind him as if floating in the sky like a god. Beyond, there lay an extraordinary view of Paris, an unbroken panorama that completed the perfect illusion: he was master of all he surveyed.

'And yet, when I see your offices, your obvious professionalism, I find it hard to believe you don't know precisely which pieces have sold and which have not. Or perhaps there was a problem with one of your containers. Or a troublesome retailer that you prefer not to admit. We may imagine any number of things, and since Madame Dessage is here now, perhaps the simplest thing would be to tell her the truth.'

'Truth is never the priority in China... Never!'

'Well, here we're in France, not China, and you placed the order six months ago. Our question is simple: when are you going to pay?'

'I never talk business with a man in trainers.'

Ludovic took the comment like a punch in the face; it went straight to the complex he had about Parisians in general. He was caught off guard. Certainly, he had no business here at all, far outside his usual frame of reference. And now, pointedly, Kobzham was addressing only Aurore. Even when Ludovic asked him a question, he stared straight at Aurore and gave his answer to her.

'Listen, my dear, let me remind you, I'm your distributor, not your agent. This is a proper partnership, with clearly defined terms drawn up in consultation with your associate. Now, if you're not up to speed with what's going on in your own business, there is nothing, dear Aurore, absolutely nothing, I can do for you.'

'And what exactly is that supposed to mean?'

'I'm not talking to *you*.'

'Shame, because there are a couple of things I'd like to ask…'

'I have nothing whatever to say to you, Monsieur.'

'Then let me tell you, instead: what I see is that for the past six months Madame Dessage has been waiting for payment for merchandise under a contract that stipulates ninety-day terms. Merchandise that isn't even insured, and which you distribute through shops in China and Taiwan. But I've done some research, and it seems the group that operates the shops has filed for bankruptcy… So, where's the merchandise now? Who's to say it hasn't been re-labelled and sold through another group – and if we did a little digging, I wouldn't be surprised to find the man behind that group was… you.'

'What the hell do you think you're accusing me of? Black marketeering, is that it?'

'You refuse to answer, so I'm forced to come up with a hypothesis.'

'Aurore, I'd be wary of your new friends, they look like trouble to me.'

Aurore was seething with rage at Kobzham, but she let nothing show. She had a horror of raised voices, and knew she was caught in the crossfire. Kobzham coolly prepared a cigar, took his time lighting it, then contemplated it, saying nothing. Aurore wished she had never got Ludovic mixed up in this. Kobzham had always been courteous in the extreme, but his insincere warmth made every business transaction feel like a friendly exchange, the better to soften his adversary. That had to stop now. Here, today, she wanted to make him pay. First, he would pay the ninety-two thousand euros, because the money was vital for her business. And second, she would make him pay for stringing her along like a kid for months on end. He would pay for his insufferable arrogance. She felt cheated, defiled, humiliated, dirty.

'Monsieur Kobzham, we'll keep it simple: as things stand, Aurore Dessage, the brand and the businesswoman, is not asking when you will pay her, but demanding that you pay her here and now.'

'Now listen, big guy, it's clear you don't have much experience in this business, but if one day you manage to place your merchandise with Colette, or Harrods, even Joyce in HK – which, by the way, I hope you do – you'd better know there's no way they'll pay within ninety days. They insist on three times that – they won't pay you for a year. One year!'

'First, no one calls me "big guy", and second, even if they won't pay for a year, at least they still pay in the end… They're not in the business of siphoning off merchandise then selling it on the sly. You don't have to be a big shot to do that. Just a particular kind of bastard…'

Kobzham jumped to his feet, dropping his cigar beside the ashtray.

'Who the hell do you think you are, to talk to me like that?'

Ludovic rose too, and the two men stood, each one out of his chair, unsure what would happen next.

Aurore stood up too and tugged Ludovic's sleeve, urging him to sit down.

'No, Jean-Louis… Ludovic, wait, we should all calm down…'

'Aurore, I really don't know who you're working with these days, but I'd have expected better from you, truly. Watch out, Aurore, Paris is a small world. I find your new methods very disappointing.'

'Don't try to shift the blame. You're the one stringing her along!'

'No, Ludovic, wait…'

'Think you can frighten me by coming here with some hired

161

muscle? What the hell does this guy think he's doing? Do you really think he can scare me?'

'No, Jean-Louis, I brought Ludovic along today because he helps us out with our more delicate contracts.'

'Delicate? Well, he doesn't seem to be treading very carefully here. What is it you're after? You want to burn your bridges in Asia, is that it?'

'I'm not here to talk about Aurore's future in Asia, but about the ninety-two thousand euros...'

Ludovic spoke the words with ice-cold rage, slamming his fist on the desk top despite himself.

Back in his chair, Kobzham swivelled round, deliberately turning his back on them. All that could be heard now was the gentle hum of the air conditioning, like some opportune but short-lived attempt to calm things down. A new confrontation was inevitable. Ludovic broke the silence, speaking in measured tones.

'So, tell us about the deal you've struck with Fabian.'

'Aurore, would you care to let your friend and me talk in private for a couple of minutes?'

'No. Aurore's the boss and if you have something to say, you can say it to her.'

Kobzham spun round suddenly, glared at Ludovic and hissed: 'I have something to say to you in private. Scared, are you?'

'I'm only here to accompany Aurore; we're both staying.'

'Please, spare us the love-struck adolescent act, at your age!'

He walked around the desk and stood close beside Aurore as if to escort her to the door.

'Aurore, I have just one thing to say to your friend, and one thing only, and I would rather say it to him in private, if you'll allow me...'

Shocked at the sudden turn of the conversation, Aurore left

the office without hesitation. Kobzham returned to his seat, and gazed at Ludovic over his joined hands. Ludovic stared back, demonstrating that he was not in the least scared. A long silence followed, then Kobzham asked: 'What the hell are you playing at, with a girl like her?'

Ludovic hadn't expected this opening shot, and gave no reply.

'You should see yourself, in your cheap shirt and your cruise captain's blazer, your trainers and jeans – do you honestly think for one minute that you're up to this? If you want me to believe you work in fashion, well, think again; an eight-year-old kid could see you've never set foot in a couture workshop...'

'So?'

'So, can't you see she's using you? I have no idea who you are, my friend, but I saw through you straight away. You're clever, a bit of a trickster, like me, but small-time. No vision...'

Ludovic made a show of listening to the guy calmly. He wanted to see how far he could take this.

'You're not up to it. Just look at yourself. You really think she's going to fall for a guy like you, fresh from the sticks? She's so far out of your league, she's leading you by the nose like a prize bull, and believe me, son, you'll pay for it.'

'Don't try to change the subject. I'm just here to help with a little housework...'

'And what's more, you take me for a fool. Am I right? You really take me for a fool. You'd have me believe you work for her, when I know you're fucking her. I can even prove it. So *you're* playing *me* for a fool. I'd say we're even.'

Ludovic remained impassive, but the words had hit home. Perhaps this man had seen them in the waiting room. Now he was the one who was unsure where to turn next.

'I'll tell you this, Ludovic Barrère, there's one thing I wish for you: never to hear my name again, agreed? Never to see me again, because I'm warning you, your pathetic little show here is borderline intimidation, threatening behaviour, even false impersonation.'

'Sure. You've forgotten blackmail and extortion.'

'You don't know how right you are. You thought you'd come here, right into my office, and shake me up, but you've made a big mistake, big man. You saw the three girls outside in reception, saw them take down every visitor's name. Did you see the cameras behind them? Well, let me tell you this: if I so much as break a fingernail tonight, or if tomorrow I slip on the stairs, you'll be the one that gets the blame, OK? Attempted threats and coercion – check the penal code, I can bring a whole army of lawyers down on your head for trying to intimidate me, and you'll be coughing up your pitiful wages till the day you retire – do you hear me? And believe me, if I bruise, or get bitten by my own dog, two weeks from now, I'll swear it was you… I can break you whenever I want. Break you into tiny pieces.'

When they resurfaced at the exit from the car park, Aurore could not face the journey back across Paris. Not straight away. She had attended fraught meetings before, with suppliers and banks. Highly charged meetings where it seemed the future of the business was hanging by a thread. She had experienced moments of high tension, but nothing like this. This had been the worst meeting of her life, a brutal, bare-knuckled fight that had left her thoroughly shaken. She felt wounded, humiliated, and doubly so because it had taken place in the presence of this man, the man she had only just met, and who was seeing her now in her very worst light. To have both found themselves unable to escape such a barrage of ferocity was not a good sign, she thought; it did not augur well for them.

They reached the Bois de Boulogne, and she directed Ludovic along broad, wooded avenues that were unknown to him. He had never come to this part of Paris, where the buildings were replaced by trees. They went over a crossroads and she told him to park in front of La Grande Cascade. It was five o'clock. Tea time. In the restaurant's vast dining area, tables laid with white cloths stretched out in all directions, and there was almost no one about. At the back of the room, workers were busy putting up Christmas decorations. Ludovic found the place rather dated – retro luxury, all gold paint and red velvet. Huge windows and stunning outdoor terraces overlooked the surrounding greenery. The place felt like a gilded lodge, buried deep in the woods. He saw it as a world apart, a fantasy that the staff were decking out with garlands of pine branches and baubles. Suddenly, they were very far from La Défense.

The waiter guided them to a table on the far side of the room, near the windows. Ludovic glanced down at his faded canvas trainers, and thought of Kobzham's remark. The bastard had opened an old wound – his class consciousness. He knew he should brush off the insinuation, but it haunted him. He walked behind Aurore, and speculated on the correct form – should he be in front of her or behind her? As he followed her, he gazed at the fine leather coat that subtly defined her waist. Her silhouette glided between the tables, and her fur stole matched the sway of her hair. He followed her scent, warm and alive. They sat down, and he glanced at their reflection in a huge mirror. It was true, everything set them apart from one another.

'Is this table OK?'

'Yes.'

He confessed to Aurore that he had never heard of this restaurant, had no idea a place like this, straddling city and woods, even existed in Paris. To admit this small fact relieved him of a mild sense of shame. In truth, he felt he would never fully know this city. Each neighbourhood was a different Paris; there were as many Parises as there were metro stations. Viewed from afar, Paris was a monolithic entity, the capital where everything was decided, where journalists would report on a protest setting off from Place de la République, as if there was only one such square in the whole of France. Paris had always made him feel inferior, though he was reluctant to admit it, and living here only made things worse.

Aurore began to share stories of past visits to this part of the city. Listening to her, Ludovic discovered a childhood a world away from his own. She had often come here as a girl, with her parents and her sisters. Her father played polo in the Bois, and she told Ludovic about the swimming pool nearby, the stables, parties right here at La Grande Cascade. In his mind's eye he caught glimpses of a luxurious lifestyle, and that bastard's comment rang in his ears one more time. He had no place here with this woman. He glanced again at the mirror. They made an odd couple, for sure. Kobzham had poisoned him with the truth. It was crushing to realise that someone was not for you, that they were out of your league. He swore Kobzham would pay; the duplicitous bastard had touched a raw nerve when he insinuated that he had no place anywhere within reach of Aurore, who just at that moment placed her slender, white hand gently over the rock of his clenched fist.

'Are you sure you're all right?'

'Yes, everything's fine.'

For a while, they were both lost in silent thought. Outside, a truck was manoeuvring into the restaurant's parking area, transporting a huge Christmas tree. Aurore kept her hand on his closed fist. She was stroking it now, and then she opened it, coaxing him like a feral cat that she wanted to tame. Ludovic stared at her long, soft hand in his, her slender fingers. He opened his broad palm and she caressed it with porcelain fingers that danced playfully like a child turning somersaults, gracefully twisting the air. She sent tremors through his body, and hers too. They said nothing; there was an awkwardness between them, having just encountered their first shared experience of failure. Aurore swore to herself that she would cut her losses, avoid confrontation. She would never risk an open attack on Kobzham; she hated to fall out with anybody. At worst she would agree a reduced price; she was prepared to let it go, to accept that she had been taken for a ride, and move on. But it was a profoundly humiliating, even suicidal solution for the company. She had two weeks to balance the accounts, to find the hundred and fifty thousand euros that would get them out of the red, but she had no desire to think about that now. She carried on stroking the tough skin of his palm. She admired him, in a way. Recovering money was a trade. A tawdry, even dishonourable trade, and yet this money was vital to her. As was her own trade, her business: the truth of the matter struck her head on.

'Are you angry with me?'

'For what?'

'For my problems. I never talk about them as a rule, not to anyone, so it felt good to have you there.'

'At least he's shown his true colours.'

'I already had my doubts.'

She held back from saying more, from telling him about the sheet of paper stuck in the printer, of her suspicions about Kobzham and Fabian, the low trick they were about to play on her – though she could not be sure. She did not want Ludovic to fly off the handle again, and with Fabian this time...

'But tell me: can you really afford to say goodbye to ninety-two thousand euros?'

'No. Especially not right now. But I want nothing more to do with that guy, I don't want to do business with him ever again, I just want to drop it. I think I feel frightened.'

'Of what?'

'I don't know. Everything. Everything frightens me. Everything worries me.'

Ludovic wanted to reply, but she carried on talking.

'I'm not cut out for this. I don't think I'm cut out to succeed. The more I have, the more I'm frightened of losing it all. You see? I'm frightened that something will happen to my children, my husband, to me, even to you, now... I shouldn't be saying this to you, but I'm not very strong. At least I don't think I am.'

'But Aurore, your brand is terrific. Everyone respects you,

apart from that idiot. You should take pride in—'

'Fashion… It's a small world. When things are going fine, everyone wants a piece of you: the press, buyers, clients. Everyone thinks you're great; people fight for a front seat at your shows. But at the first sign of weakness, they drop you.'

'Wait, he's just trying to trip you up. You're not going to let him get away with it, not him. You should go after him, no hesitation, Aurore. He's a big fish!'

'Exactly. Which is why I can't touch him. Everyone leaves the biggest fish in the pond alone. That's why they're the biggest.'

Ludovic sensed the comment was aimed at him, as if she sought to imply that extracting money from small-time debtors, spending your life sorting out household debts, was pitiful, even contemptible.

'I just want to design clothes, do you understand? I don't want to fight. But being a designer means being in business. It's all about the numbers. I hated that at first. I just wanted to make clothes – clothes that mean something to people, do you see what I mean? Clothes you feel have been made for you alone, a scarf that's been knitted for no one but you. You don't wear it like a scarf you bought in Zara – it makes you feel differently. I can't explain it…'

Aurore's hand lay forgotten in his. She felt defeated, discouraged, beside herself. She wanted to drop everything, stop pretending she was the boss. It hurt her deeply to see her business falter. It was like watching a sick child that fails to get better; there was the same feeling of powerlessness, of being overwhelmed. There's nothing you can do, and everyone is turning their back. You feel total panic. That was why she refused even to consider that Fabian might be double-crossing her. It hurt her too deeply that someone she had counted a friend was doing everything he could, behind her back, to bring her down.

She looked out of the window at the bare chestnut trees outside. She told herself she was facing two more crows, two more harmful creatures: Fabian and Kobzham. She felt Ludovic's solid grip around her hand.

Two waiters hurried over apologising for the wait, which was due to the delivery of the Christmas tree. Ludovic had seen them helping to lift the tall pine off the truck. In a perfectly choreographed pas de deux, they laid out an arsenal of tea-cups, silver cutlery, spoons and dainty cake plates. Aurore retrieved her hand. When the waiters had gone, Ludovic rearranged everything – the cups, the teabags, the spoons, the milk jugs and plates – which they had set out so meticulously, but the wrong way around. Aurore stared as slowly, carefully, he took each item, cleared space on the table, poured hot water into Aurore's cup, closed his fist around the milk jug's belly, lifted the scalding teapot not by its handle but with his fingers around the rim, apparently feeling no pain. You can tell a great deal about a person by the way they handle things. Ludovic had a reassuringly solid grip. They did not speak. Aurore realised that her phone had been turned off for two hours. She fished it out from the bottom of her bag, but did not turn it on. The Christmas tree was brought in through a door at the rear, carried by six members of staff to the centre of the room, where they stood it upright. Even undecorated, the tree changed the atmosphere altogether. Now it felt like Christmas, the festive season, with all its attendant fun and anguish, a fantasy that would soon take over everything – delightful, stressful, and centred on family life. Suddenly, Aurore shuddered and pressed her hand to her mouth. She had just realised she still hadn't bought her own Christmas tree. She hadn't given a moment's thought to the decorations, or the tree, that year. She was a terrible mother.

'We've got my car, I can help. We'll buy one and put it in the back.'

'No, I'd rather see to it on my own. It's not up to you to do that.'

'As you wish.'

She hadn't meant to be short with him, but the last thing she wanted was to muddy things.

'You know, Iris and Noé talk about you all the time, ever since the boiler fell down. They think you saved our home. Which is fair enough. I think you made a big impression on them. Sometimes they ask me when we're going to see you again.'

Ludovic smiled awkwardly. He had no idea what to say, the more so because her comment was in no way an invitation; absolutely nothing of the kind.

He had been sitting in the young couple's overheated studio apartment for more than an hour. The boy had been out of a job for three months, the girl worked from home, freelance, writing articles for a website. They spoke in low voices – the couple had just had a baby that lay sleeping in its cot. Their place was small, with just one window, which they kept closed. The negotiations were progressing calmly, but Ludovic felt the sweat trickling down his back, covering his body. By the end, he was soaked. It was suffocating in there, but he didn't like to tell them, especially because the boy was having a hard time, terrified that the business of the repairs to their car had caught up with him. The girl was anxious, too. They both agreed to all of Ludovic's suggestions, and made no attempt to make light of it all. When he sensed he was being mistaken for a bailiff or a cop, it made Ludovic feel uncomfortable, but he took advantage of the situation to keep the upper hand. Now that he thought about it, he regretted that he had failed to put on such an intimidating show with Kobzham. He was sharp and effective here, but he had noticed over the past two years that the more a debtor owed, the less daunted they seemed. It was painful to note each time how the weakest players were the most honest, the most ashamed. The less they owed, the more they suffered, while those with huge debts rose above the whole business, and seemed not to care.

They both accompanied him to the door, as they might a visiting doctor. It had been so hot in there, he walked the entire length of the Cours de Vincennes in a stiff, cold breeze, just to breathe some fresh air. His T-shirt was damp beneath his jacket. Unusually, he found himself shivering, and thought he would catch cold. For once, this job sickened him. Jesus, it was so easy to get the little people to pay that he felt furious at his inability to persuade the other guy to cough up yesterday; infuriated that he had left the office suite in La Défense without securing even the smallest of promises. On the contrary, Kobzham had wiped the floor with him, changed the subject, turned the spotlight on his clothes, on Aurore. Eaten him for breakfast. He wished he had shaken the bastard up, punched his ugly face. His arrogance, his condescending tone made Ludovic feel sick to the stomach, and he told himself he would not let it go. If Aurore asked him, formally, to take care of the guy, he swore he would make him pay.

He entered a café on the corner of Rue des Pyrénées, a depressing *bar-tabac* with a handful of clients seated along the counter. No one answered his general greeting, as so often, and he said it again, much louder, so that they all looked in his direction. One or two muttered *Bonjour* under their breath, and the barman turned to face him, surprised by the manner of his entrance. Ludovic ordered a hot toddy, something he never drank, had never ordered in a café before. He wouldn't admit it, but he needed a shot of alcohol.

Still unable to get warm, he took the no. 86 bus rather than walk the rest of the way home. At four o'clock it was already full with the early rush-hour crowd. As always, he gripped the overhead bar with both hands. In the open space of Place de la Nation, a shaft of dazzling sunlight shone into the bus, illuminating a cloud of dust, and he suddenly pictured billions of bacteria floating inside the vehicle, specks of saliva or viral particles, and the thought of his hands on the metal bar, made filthy by thousands of other hands, disgusted him. He could see the air he was breathing in, imagined the traces on the palms of his hands – because he always gripped the metal tightly, just to feel the muscles in his back working. He told himself he would buy a pair of gloves before heading back to his apartment.

He got off the bus and headed for the menswear department in the local Monoprix store. He shopped at the first-floor supermarket, but never visited the clothes section as a rule – too many pastels, too many close-fitting shirts, trendy caps, colourful scarves. There was nothing for him there. They were sold out of gloves. He made a circuit of the menswear section, looking for something plain, or smart, even chic. The shirts went up to a size L, as if everyone around here was a male model. The trousers would just about fit. He took down a few pairs of jeans, unfolded them, then folded them away again awkwardly. He looked at the suit trousers but was unable to get them back onto their hangers. He was annoyed now. Even before trying anything on, this was turning into an ordeal. He was embarrassed to enter the changing cubicle, with its thin, ill-fitting curtain, to struggle to get undressed in a confined space, just a few paces from where two female shop assistants were tidying the shelves. But he took five items of clothing – three pairs of jeans and two pairs of pleat-fronted trousers – chosen more or less at random in the biggest sizes he could find, and stepped inside.

He took off his trousers and tried to sling them over the top of the cubicle wall, but a section of the curtain got caught up and revealed him, standing in his underpants, to the two assistants. Hurriedly, he snatched the curtain back down, then stepped into the most generously cut smart trousers, pulling them up as far as his knees, where they were already beginning to strain. He forced them up to his thighs, like a diver squeezing into a wetsuit. With even greater difficulty, he managed to get the trousers down again and extricated himself, hopping on one foot, bumping his shoulder repeatedly against the cubicle wall to maintain his balance. Seen from outside, the whole structure was probably shaking. Indeed the two sales assistants stood staring at the cabin as it shuddered like a rocket on a launch pad. One of them moved closer, concerned that this rather odd customer might bring the flimsy structure crashing down in his desperate bid to find something in his size.

'Is everything all right, Monsieur?'

'No, not at all, nothing fits!'

Ludovic threw propriety to the winds and pulled back the cubicle curtain. There, in his underpants, he showed her the two pairs of jeans he had just tried. The other trousers lay on the floor at his feet. Calmly, the sales assistant asked him to pick them up.

'You've taken a size 48, Monsieur. Obviously it's not going to fit you.'

'That was the biggest size I could find.'

'Try a 52, that's the biggest size we have in stock. Or look at the American models, W39, L34, for example.'

The other sales assistant, a young black woman, joined them. She was as eager to help as her colleague, but could not disguise her amusement at the sight of this man in his underpants and socks, standing in a puddle of discarded trousers.

'I'm sorry, Monsieur, but I don't think you'd fit a 52, either.'

'Well, have you got anything above a size 52, or not?'

After another ten minutes trying things on, Ludovic was once again pouring with sweat, exhausted by the effort of dressing and undressing in a mere two cubic metres of airspace. He just wanted a new pair of trousers. Any style, just so long as they were new. Surrounded by the pile of disjointed trousers, he thought again of Kobzham. The guy would have laughed long and hard to see him here, stranded in a changing cubicle, with two shop assistants coming to his rescue.

The store's security guard, a tall black man who generally stood beside the main entrance, came over to ask if there was a problem. Ludovic often saw the guy, but had never spoken to him. The security staff avoided any sign of familiarity with the regular shoppers, lest they be suspected of connivance. But this time, the usually silent guard offered an opinion.

'Thing is, you won't find anything in your size, Monsieur. There's nothing to fit you here – this is Monoprix.'

Ludovic knew what he meant: Monoprix was not for the likes of him. Everything here was designed for a thinner, more sophisticated class of man. These were clothes for young, snake-hipped city types, an élite to which he would never belong, and now Kobzham was not alone in rubbing his face in the fact – the entire store had joined in, all the thousands of styles and sizes, elegantly arranged on the shelves, even the two sales assistants and the security guard, everything conspired to make him understand that this was not for him, that he had no place here.

He could stand it no longer, and to make matters worse he realised that even his underpants were no good, unfashionable, out of date. The stand opposite, and the mannequins along the top, displayed sleek, well-fitting boxers of all kinds – but only boxers, as if every urban male knew he must dress for the prize fight of daily existence. One of the sales assistants disappeared and returned with a pair of jogging pants; vast, hideous, cream-coloured tracksuit bottoms. She assured him that these were the only thing in the store that would fit.

Even the security guard objected.

'Seriously, Lucie, you're not going to try and sell those to the gentleman?'

Lucie stated again that these were the only thing in Ludovic's size. Ludovic's patience was at an end. Never before had he mobilised three people to help him try on a pair of trousers. At the sight of him dangling the tracksuit bottoms distastefully at arm's length, the other three burst out laughing.

'They'd make a great pair of PJs…' the security guard observed, drily.

Ludovic made ready to put his own jeans back on. The sales assistant asked to see the label first, but it was so faded it was illegible.

'You should try online, Monsieur, or a specialist shop for larger men.'

Plainly, they were all telling him to leave, but in a good-natured way. The security guard was taller even than Ludovic, but very slim, while the two sales assistants were generously built. One of the women was so broad he doubted anyone could put two arms around her, while the other had a very curvaceous but well-proportioned figure, happily plus-sized, a powerful woman with delicate features – the face of a princess and an XXL body. In spite of himself, Ludovic had made them all warm to him. There was a complicity between them now, they had shared a moment of light relief, and they had no desire to return to their everyday tasks. He offered to help them fold up the trousers.

'Oh no, Monsieur, we'll see to that. It's best left to a professional.'

He stared at his reflection in the mirror. He paid little attention to his body now, but back when he was training professionally, he would work out in front of the mirrors at the gym – he and his teammates watching themselves do warm-ups and squat thrusts to fill out the thighs. He thought the cubicle mirror made him look bigger, broader than he was in reality – or perhaps he really did look that way. You can never know how others see you. Before putting his jacket back on, he flexed his biceps and pecs, straining the fabric of his T-shirt – an adolescent reflex that spoke of his suppressed urge to fight. The fact was, Kobzham had got inside his head. It was rare for Ludovic to let anyone get to him to that extent, but the bastard had goaded him and thrown him with a few well-placed words, dismissing him as a provincial nobody, though he knew nothing about where Ludovic came from. Perhaps he had guessed; perhaps it was just that obvious. He had rarely had such bile spat in his face. It was sheer, cold defiance. There was no question of violence, however: no, this guy had far more pernicious tools up his sleeve. It maddened him to think that Aurore was prepared to let it go, not even to get paid. The very idea enraged him. As he walked home, he thought how good it would feel to really get under the guy's skin, to scare the crap out of him and make him cough up — if not the money, then at least an apology.

Aurore remembered how blissfully happy she and Richard had been to wake up together every day when they first moved in. Then the children had come along, their careers had taken off, and the mornings had sped up, then changed completely.

At Ludovic's side, lying on his bed late in the afternoon, she was finding a completely different, no less blissful but far more fleeting kind of happiness. The excitement of seeing each other without knowing when the next time would come. The unexpected feeling of emptiness that began when they parted, disappearing from each other's lives despite only a courtyard standing between them. This afternoon they had met at his apartment. The morning after La Grande Cascade, she had slipped a note into his letterbox, telling him that she would come to his place the following Monday at about 5 o'clock in the afternoon. This was the first time she had arranged a meeting by dropping him a note, but there was no other safe way of getting in touch, not by telephone nor by email. Aurore found herself enjoying the uncertainty, the lightness and excitement of a liaison governed by chance and desire, more precious by far than habitual, everyday encounters, or trysts arranged far in advance. She felt good in the company of this man, who listened. The times they met, she told herself, would be like parentheses, interludes, a chain of scattered, exotic islands in her life, and she would move from island to island, anticipating the next while savouring the memory of the last.

'But that guy can't be the only distributor with access to Asia. You can find someone else.'

'Perhaps. He's the best placed, for sure, and anyway, I don't have a forthcoming collection. I don't know when we'll do another. We haven't got the money.'

'You could hire my company to take it on. That would keep it out of the courts. We have bailiffs who help us out on the side. But I don't think Kobzham is the type to be impressed by official-looking letters on headed paper. I think he just has to be shifted.'

Aurore had no idea what he meant by 'shifted'. She didn't want to think about that, not now. Calmly, she rested her chin in her hand and gazed at this person who could say ferocious things but always kept his composure; who was capable of killing crows in cold blood and making a bouquet out of their feathers, of making love like a savage while speaking softly into the hollow of her ear, talking filth in a gentle voice, as if whispering a poem. This unfathomable man. Sometimes his body frightened her. She felt Ludovic's arm where it lay across her belly. It was heavy, and she told herself that if he put all his weight on top of her, she would suffocate. This man could inflict pain, without even realising it.

But what she saw above all was that she could tell him everything. She never talked to anyone about her troubles at work, nor how hard she found it, at times, to put up with her children, how she longed to be alone and do nothing, to stretch out selfishly on the white sofa. All the things she was unable to say for fear of being taken for a bad mother or a bad boss. Again she felt she lacked the strength to be the boss, the mother, the wife, the creative designer, the nursemaid to so many people, not forgetting the dutiful daughter to her anxious, newly retired and penniless parents, and daughter-in-law to Richard's parents, who lived on the other side of the Atlantic, a daughter-in-law who was always bright and cheerful. She had had enough of all that right now; sometimes just being herself felt like too much. If worst came to worst, she could let it all go, let her business go to ruin and say yes to Richard, who was dying to go back to the States, to start her life over. But that really was the worst of all solutions. First, she did not want to live over there, and still less as Richard's dependent wife. She could not bear the idea of relying on a man to support her. That was why she must save her label, if for that reason alone.

'Ludovic, hold me in your arms.'

At least with this man, she felt as if she stood apart from these things, outside her life. She could tell him everything and, miraculously, he would listen. She found it hard to talk to other people; she didn't wish to burden them with her problems. But he seemed unshakeable, standing firm as a rampart, a supporting wall. He could endure anything, hear anything. That was what this man gave her above all else: his ability to listen, without judging. He understood her, and yet he appeared to expect nothing in return. It seemed he was there to help her more than to love her, and she wondered if you could devote your love to helping someone; whether helping them was already a kind of love, especially when the help was one-way. Why was he doing this?

'Ludovic, can I ask you a question?'

'Yes.'

'What am I to you?'

'I wish I knew.'

'No, you can do better than that. Tell me what I represent to you.'

'Something I... Something I didn't expect.'

'Something?'

'I don't know how to answer your question, Aurore. To me you're—'

181

He stopped short, concerned he would say too much. What he felt for her, he kept to himself – he would never tell her how he wanted to surround her, embrace her, nor the way the scent of her was always on his mind, even when she wasn't there. How could he explain the need simply to smell her perfume, to have her close, to breathe her in? He saw she was waiting for an answer, that she seemed almost worried, and so he took her hand. He was about to speak…Yet to admit these feelings at forty-six years of age felt puerile. Telling her she mattered so much to him already, that he thought of her constantly, that he loved her, in a way – for he surely did – would only scare her away. Besides, his feelings were absurd: this woman had a life in which he could play no part, other than to turn it upside down, though perhaps she was looking for precisely that. He would make things even more complicated if he told her that since Mathilde, no one had mattered so much, that for three years he hadn't kissed or touched another woman. It upset him to think of Mathilde here and now. For the first time since her death, since knowing Aurore, he felt he was being unfaithful.

Aurore looked at him, with no idea of the thoughts behind that closed expression. She didn't understand why his answer was so long coming, so she interpreted his silence, told herself she had made him feel awkward, uncomfortable with her questions, that her girlish demands bored him, she was just an easy conquest, a woman who was close at hand, in the building opposite. But no, that wasn't possible, he wouldn't have gone with her to the meeting with Kobzham, and then there were the crows… She didn't know any more. She pressed his hand firmly. At times, she was terrified they would be found out, that someone would see her with this man's hand in hers. It was impossible, they kept themselves hidden, but the terror haunted her, and then she knew she didn't care, and he began to speak.

'You know…'

But that was all he said. He bit his lip. He wouldn't answer her question. She stared out through the window, then back at his face, atop the great bulk of his body, and she was surprised to see that his eyes were shining. He was still there, lying next to her, as solid and straightforward as ever, but his eyes were moist, as if holding back tears, and suddenly his hand in hers felt fragile, and she had the dizzying realisation, as if for the first time, that she was capable of hurting him.

For once, she was home early enough to bath the children. She made time for a moment alone with them. The twins played together in the tub, thrilled that their mother was there. They were happy and excited – perhaps too excited – and they laughed loudly and splashed the water everywhere. Aurore ought to have been filled with joy at the spectacle of such fun and games, the great ritual of bathtime, but deep down, it irritated her a little. She was thinking about him, on the other side of the courtyard. It was unforgiveable, but she found herself gazing at the window, dreaming of opening it and flying away, fleeing the noise and obligations of her life to join him in the small, dated apartment just over there, to nestle in his arms and let the chaos subside. Her children were shouting right in her ear, but gradually the noise seemed to fade into the distance, as if she was listening to them from outside, through the window, as if she was perched on a branch of the tree, free as the two turtle doves.

When the children had been put to bed, she waited to eat dinner with Richard. He came home after 10 p.m. The meal was basic: cold salmon with blinis and a green salad. He loved to keep things simple, just a simple supper, a simple chat, everything plain and simple. For dessert, they finished the children's tea-time cakes – plain and simple cakes from Lenôtre. She wanted to talk to him about Kobzham, find out what he thought, what he would do in her position, but she felt pathetic discussing a sordid matter of ninety-two thousand euros, the more so because since they had sat down to eat, Richard had spoken of nothing but a string of sensational projects: a new ethical start-up he truly believed in; vaccines that would prove an absolute goldmine over the long term; a worldwide contract for a Concierge app, for which they had secured the seed money; a joint venture between a smartphone brand and a manufacturer of wind turbines in San Francisco; and finally a design for an app that would display your energy reserves on wearables, like the petrol gauge in a car.

'Sometimes you think you're tired when you aren't really, or the other way around – you feel great, when in reality you're running on empty, and that's when you get sick... The app would tell you when you need to drink or eat something, or how long you should run, or sleep.'

He continued talking as he helped clear the table. Richard was always thinking about work, 24/7. Life was his working day. He made everything sound easy and achievable, everything was simple, you just needed to spot the people with the ideas and connect them to the people with the money, and let the adventure begin – a few thousand or a few million euros, and they were on their way. And the more she learned about this brave new world, the pettier she felt it would be to bring up her own stories, to tell him about the ninety-two thousand euros she was owed and unable to recover, and which could jeopardise her entire business. With the dishwasher switched on, she sat, exhausted, at the breakfast bar.

'Aurore, is something the matter?'

'No, nothing.'

Richard came and sat beside her, put his arm around her shoulders, and the feel of it was acutely awkward, especially this evening, just a few hours after two other arms had held her with all their might. She even flushed at the thought. But Richard remained oblivious.

'Aurore, you can tell me.'

To make the feeling go away, to erase Ludovic's face which had superimposed itself on Richard's, Aurore told him that, basically, she was caught between a debtor she didn't trust, and her associate, whom she suspected of trying to drop her.

'Fabian? But he's your friend, isn't he?'

'Perhaps, but I can't help thinking he's in league with Kobzham, to— I don't know, perhaps to force us to file for bankruptcy so they can both make a grab for the business.'

'How could they do that?'

'By pushing us to the brink of receivership, then taking over at the last minute.'

'Is that why you were telling me about the pre-pack insolvency?'

'I don't know, I don't know any more.'

'Because a stunt like that would be self-dealing. It's a crime.'

'Not in France. Perhaps in the US. But not in France.'

'Don't tell me corporate law is less strict in France than in the US! In any case, fraudulently overstating liabilities is constructive bankruptcy and that, even in France, is an imprisonable offence. I can get our lawyers onto it, if you like, and I swear those two bastards will find themselves banned from running a company. They might even wind up in jail.'

'No, Richard, what I just said— I'm not even sure that's what they're doing. It just crossed my mind, that's all. I don't think Fabian would be capable of anything so low.'

She knew Richard had never liked Fabian. An undefined jealousy kept him at arm's length. She didn't want to talk about it any more; most of all, she didn't want to show herself in that light, as a woman forced to fight, in an increasingly messy situation. The power balance in a couple shifts depending on one or other partner's career, and while Richard succeeded at everything he did, she felt almost guilty about her own failures.

'You know, Aurore, going into business is like stepping into a boxing ring. You've got to start jabbing at the opposition, throwing punches straight away, or they'll strike the first blow. But in the ring, everyone can see what's happening, at least everything's clear. In business, it's all below the belt, and that wouldn't surprise me from Fabian. I always said, to me, Fabian's small fry, and the little fish in the pond always dream of being the biggest – and you know why? So they can eat the guys who were trying to eat them before. That's business. Hit him hard, Aurore!'

'Stop talking to me as if I was a child. Or one of those pimply engineers you're always interviewing.'

'Hey, calm down. I'm only trying to help.'

'Don't tell me what to do, what to think...'

'Look, you do whatever you think is best, but I'm going to speak to Lathman & Cleary about this. I'll call them tomorrow, just for an opinion.'

And he closed the discussion with a gesture that left her speechless. He stroked her face with his hand, then gave her a peck on the side of her head. A simple, ever so slightly paternalistic kiss.

'No, Richard, you aren't going to speak to anyone about this. I may be completely wrong, perhaps everything will work out. I've taken advice. Everything will work itself out.'

'Advice?'

'Yes, I asked a debt recovery firm for advice, and it's fine. Everything will work out.'

'But Aurore, legal counsel is what you need, not *advice*. You can't do anything nowadays without lawyering up, I'll call them tomorrow and—'

'No. No. I don't want to get things mixed up. We always swore we wouldn't mix work and family.'

'Listen, if I get Lathman & Cleary on the case, you'd better believe—'

'Richard, tonight I just wanted to talk to you about it, so that you'd understand why I've been… a bit odd lately, that's all. Don't worry, I'm going to sort it out. I don't need your lawyers.'

'Crazy. In France, you only have to say the word "lawyer" and everyone runs scared. But Aurore, hiring a lawyer, it's like going to the dentist: don't wait till it hurts. No one knows how to think ahead in this country.'

'That's enough. Your same old line about us Frenchies…'

'But it's true. Being a genius isn't enough. The ones who make it aren't the most talented, they're the ones who stay ahead of the game.'

'I'm not a genius, I just– well, you know nothing about the fashion industry.'

It was past midnight when they climbed separately into the queen-size bed they had bought when they moved to the apartment. Richard had changed the subject. He chuckled at something in his Twitter feed. Sometimes he talked to himself, in English. Talked to his tablet like a person whose hands he was holding in real life. Though he was sitting beside Aurore, his mind was in another place entirely. Then from time to time, he would come back down to earth and show her something she absolutely must see, bewitching images of abandoned cities, or pink glaciers melting into ice-blue water, volcanoes in the snow, things of no relevance to him whatever; and then he would reply to incoming emails, and move on to Russian car crash videos and all kinds of other, sometimes violent stuff. How could he sleep after all that? Aurore asked him to turn down the volume on his headphones. She turned away, lying on her side, and picked up the book she had been trying and failing to read for the past two weeks. Each time she picked it up she struggled to remember who was who, reading back over the last five pages to pick up the thread and reacquaint herself with the characters she had forgotten.

She thought again of Ludovic's apartment and wondered what he did at night before falling asleep. Did he lie in bed letting his mind wander as she was, or sit fully clothed on top of the covers, smoking for hours? Perhaps he went straight to sleep. She fell asleep thinking of him. The big bedroom was bathed in the blue, wavering light that Richard's tablet projected onto the walls. It was like being underwater.

Sitting on his bed, Ludovic stared at the light coming from Aurore's window. Knowing her to be so close and yet so unreachable was becoming harder and harder to bear. Now, through the naked branches, he had a clear view of the apartment opposite. He envied the man who lived there with Aurore, envied and hated him without even knowing him, without any valid reason, but there was nothing he could do. The man was an irritation, pure and simple. An obstacle.

On the weekends he spent with his parents, no one asked questions, no one dared say anything, though they all thought it, had all noticed he never went to visit his wife's grave. For three years, his father and his sister had been the ones to place flowers, pull out weeds, glance at the face in the framed porcelain medallion, the smile that was forever that of a radiant woman in her forties.

But now, today, without a word to anyone, Ludovic had gone there, as if to seek forgiveness. Since Mathilde's death, he had never left her, never even thought about another woman, not for a one-night stand or even a kiss. He would never have thought he could go three years without making love, without touching a woman, caught in a kind of drought that spread from deep inside, a total absence of desire. He thought that living in Paris would make it easier to move on from Mathilde, to forget her, but in fact it made everything worse. He longed not only for her but for the countryside, compounding his pain. There was no real reason for his abstinence, no moral obligation or sense of loyalty, and he was the only one who knew: his love life or lack of it was no concern of anyone else, and three years without making love was not something you boasted about in general. When he thought about it, it had saddened him, but today he realised that ultimately, his abstinence had saved him from regrets, and from guilt. But now something was different. What he was experiencing with Aurore might be no more than a fling, a moment out of time, but the fact remained that she was there, very much there, and never out of his thoughts.

He stood before the grave as if waiting for forgiveness, but it was too late – for forgiveness and all the rest. He saw the fresh flowers, the plastic pots of chrysanthemums for All Saints' Day, and he pictured his father placing the large tub of flowers here on the slab itself, near the photograph, at a slightly crooked angle. His sister would never have left it there: she would have positioned the flowers at the foot of the tomb, in the little rectangle of gravel, and she would have chosen a smaller, more delicate pot. His father's gesture was clumsy, but moving, and it moved him now, so that he didn't dare touch the misplaced pot and was incapable of laying a hand on the stone. The thought that a body so warm, so alive, could turn ice-cold and hard to that extent, was beyond him. And he had no religious belief, no faith in God or prayer; he did not look to some form of afterlife for an explanation: he just knew that it was possible to love a woman completely until suddenly she was no longer there, and it fell to you to keep her memory, like all the others in this place. He did not know what remained of his wife, here in this cemetery. To him, she wasn't here at all, but running through rows of vines, busy at work around the vats, overseeing the bottling, rallying everyone for the grape harvest. Mathilde was always out on the slopes, she never stopped. Her vines, her wine, the mission to continue her father's work, to improve and modernise – it had been an obsession for her. Mathilde was always working – there's no other way for a wine-maker. She was insatiable, full of life, except for the last three months. But that image of her, he would not keep.

He gazed around the small, deserted, ice-cold cemetery. True, there were not many here, and still, it was strange to think of her there in the tomb. To tell the truth, Ludovic did not feel sad, especially, but disorientated and numb. Beyond the cemetery wall, the woods descended into the valley, threaded with paths along which they had ridden their trailbikes as kids, unaware they were spoiling the peace, not even giving a thought to the poor little cemetery. But this morning, listen as he might, there was nothing, not a sound, only the distant call of the crows as they rose into the air above the fields. And he thought of Aurore, and felt guilty straight away. Sometimes in the summer holidays they would come to the cemetery to drink beer and smoke goodness knows what, never once thinking that they were being disrespectful. When you're fifteen years old, there's no such thing as death. They had made a racket then, too, and he regretted it, thirty years later. But in summer, the cemetery was alive with birdsong and the hum of bumblebees and wasps, and cicadas on the warm stones, from June to August. In summer, the cemetery was almost cheerful, but now, in late November, death had taken the upper hand.

He found it impossible to focus, to clear his mind, to think of nothing, as they did in the yoga classes Aurore had described. He stood with his hands clasped before him, as if in prayer, but it seemed he was pretending, posing in front of the tomb but unable to connect with God or anyone else, and certainly not Mathilde. He knew this pose was nothing like his true self. In fact, since walking into the cemetery, his vision of Mathilde had dwindled more than ever, no image of her came to mind, there was nothing here to conjure her, not even the black-and-white photograph in the recently polished medallion. Mathilde had always been so full of colour, so open and bright, so full of health it could wear a person out.

He stared down at the ground, as if to apologise, and saw the new shoes he had bought in Paris that Friday, leather shoes with pointy toes that made his feet – already a size 47 – seem interminably long. And the stiff, new leather cut into his heel, so that he could no longer flex his ankles. He felt immobilised, like a statue, stiff as everyone around him here, and worst of all he hadn't bought the shoes to please Mathilde... And with that thought he turned and walked quickly away; his feet hurt him too much to run, but he got out of that place as fast as he could. The old iron gate creaked when it was opened, but the loud grinding sound, and the final clang when it shut was far worse. As a kid, when they were told to come to ceremonies for a grandparent, or a neighbour, he tended to stay over by the gate, and he came to know the sound of it by heart. It was a sound for other people; he never once thought it would concern him. The noisy gate was the one truly eternal thing in this place, the only true sign from the Almighty, above.

Always, in the evening, his father was the one to bring in the cows. Before supper, Ludovic would go with him, but he was a tourist here now, no help, because giving his father a hand would signal to the old man that he was no longer able to carry out the task alone. The gesture would have been misplaced, in any case, because most of the cows knew exactly where to go. Even when they had spent the day out in a distant field, they came of their own accord, as if they had been trained.

At these times, Ludovic stood back and watched the old man at work. He still knew how to manoeuvre the heavy gates on their rusted hinges, museum pieces that were becoming harder and harder to close. It took some muscle to heave all that ironwork, and a knack to bolt them shut. His father talked to his herd, patted the cows' sides, inspected them in the dim, yellow light of the old cowshed. He kept a good eye on them, slipping between the huge creatures, perfectly in his element among the steaming, six-hundred-kilo beasts, monsters of a kind, but unwittingly so; monsters so fragile, so vulnerable that it was said if you left one alone, completely alone, in a field, she would stop eating after two days, and then let herself die.

'Hey! Oh! Are you daydreaming or something?'

His father must have bent down; Ludovic couldn't see him amid the dark mass of cattle, but he could hear him calling for Ludovic to come and see. He already knew why: he wanted to show him a new calf, born just two days ago, like a sleepy soft toy with angelic eyes and a coat so silky it's impossible to resist stroking it – but you mustn't touch them, his father said, the fragile little monsters. His father got to his feet and signalled to Ludovic to join him. After a whole life spent among cattle, Lucien still smiled the same smile when he saw a newborn calf; he couldn't help it, he had to show the creature off. Ludovic leaned on the edge of the stall and called across to him:

'Don't worry, I can see him very well from here.'

'Come and look, I tell you, come and see his eyes, like a couple of marbles, you've never seen the like, and she bore him out there in the field, in a pool of water. He must have lain there for two hours, in the water, he was half drowned when I lifted him up, and look, he's come back to life. Look at that, lovely little thing...'

'Yes! I'll have a good look at him tomorrow.'

His father was crouching down again somewhere in the damp half-light, which was alive with the rustle of hay and the soft lowing of the cows. Truth be told, from where he stood, Ludovic could no more see the calf than he could see Lucien. His father stood up, and Ludovic caught sight of his wicked grin in the gloom as he called out:

'Frightened of getting your new shoes dirty, is that it?'

194

At supper, everyone was talking about this and that, but loudly – even the voices of Ludovic's young nephews were raised. It had never bothered Ludovic before, but now that his mother no longer spoke, now that she sat walled in silence, now that every conversation was carried on without her, he found them increasingly difficult to bear. No one spoke to his mother any more, except to ask if she wanted more soup or vegetables. People asked her if she was thirsty, too, but then they filled her glass anyway, without waiting for her to reply.

Most shamefully of all, everyone spoke to her as if she were a child, and when she failed to answer, even with a look or a frown, they would answer in her place. Ludovic was sensitive to these details, but he blamed no one. After all, they were the ones who lived here with her, all year round. In a way, this was no longer his home. He knew that family conflicts could sometimes arise out of next to nothing, a misplaced or misinterpreted remark that sparked a shouting match. As for the work on the farm, Ludovic tried not to ask them too many questions, and the others all talked so much that in any case they often told him everything of their own accord. A host of things that were no longer any concern of his – and he had never much cared for the scraps of gossip, what X had said to Y in the nearby market town, or one of the villages round about. But this evening, nonetheless, purely to goad his brother-in-law – and knowing he would fall into the trap – Ludovic asked him why he had planted a small patch of onions right there in front of the house, in the old garden, when they grew onions by the ton out in the fields. Their barn was always full of onions, carefully stored ready for sale to the hypermarkets and greengrocers.

His sister answered, as if to get between the two men.

'Why have we planted onions in the garden? Why do you think? To eat!'

'Sure, but does that mean you're not eating the ones that grow out in the fields? Won't you eat the ones you sell any more?'

No one said a word. No one dared talk about pesticides in front of Ludovic. He remained utterly convinced that his wife had died because of the chemicals they used on the vineyard, and no one broached the subject with him. But what he saw – while they all refused to admit that Mathilde really had died because of the filth they sprayed – was that they were all eating untreated onions behind his back: they were all suspicious of pesticides now.

Back when Ludovic lived here, he had always enjoyed the respect of his family and the wider community. People knew he was headstrong, so no one dared say anything about his wife's death. But he could tell they all thought that the chemicals had nothing to do with her cancer, that Mathilde had fallen ill out of sheer bad luck. The years went by, and now they had come around to his point of view, though not one of them would admit it to his face. A simple patch of onions had spoken in their place.

After coffee, Ludovic went out to the yard to smoke. A fine drizzle was falling. His new shoes made him unsteady on the beaten earth, the soles slipped, but he wanted to walk across to the barn nonetheless. A door slammed shut behind him. In the halo of light he saw Gilles coming out after him into the cold. His brother-in-law caught up with him in the middle of the yard. He didn't smoke, and so Ludovic knew that he had something to say.

'It's a funny thing, Ludo, we've been getting freak hailstorms here. We had two in June, and after that it was dry as a bone for weeks, and hot – thirty-five degrees – and the onions get leaf scorch, like the strawberries, and all the rest. The weather's changing, believe me, nothing's the same, and we have to adapt.'

'You're telling me this like I've been gone twenty years.'

'No, but really, the weather's changing fast. Nature's getting crazier by the year.'

'Perhaps, but if you spaced out the rows, rather than spraying it all with that filth… How do you manage to keep the containers out of sight, by the way? I never see them in the barn. Do you hide them so I can't see them?'

Ludovic hurried over towards the barn to get out of the drizzle. His T-shirt was already damp, and to his intense irritation he kept slipping on the surface of the yard, on his native soil, the farm where he was born. It annoyed him to be losing his balance, especially with Gilles walking close behind him.

'Why would I keep the stuff out of sight? I've got nothing to hide. And I'll do what I want in my own place, OK?'

Ludovic stopped outside the barn and stared hard at his brother-in-law.

'No, this is *our* place. There's a difference, see?'

Gilles was walking slower now, though the rain was coming down harder.

'What's the matter with you, Ludo?'

Gilles stopped walking altogether. He stood stock-still in the rain before turning and walking back to the house, calling out in disgust:

'You've changed, Ludo, you've changed… Is this what Paris has done to you? You're not the same.'

Ludovic stood in the entrance to the barn.

'And why do you think I'm in Paris, you fucking idiot?'

Gilles carried on walking, shouting over his shoulder:

'I never asked you to sacrifice yourself for my sake. I married your sister, not you.'

When you've spoken harshly, you may regret it, but you know, too, that things have gone too far, what's done is done. The dog came and stood at his feet, gazing up at Ludovic, understanding nothing. It was dark, but he knew the dog was hoping to go out in the fields, to chase cats or foxes, or hares, anything that darted out in front, so that he could tear after it and catch it. For all his sweet spaniel face, his gentle gaze, this cute dog had one burning desire in life – to chase after an animal that ran slower than him, to hunt down anything that moved. Ludovic stroked his neck, and the dog sniffed the air, savouring the scent of a host of possible trophies, not even to eat, but for the sheer pleasure of the chase. His cheerful, good-natured face belied the one thing he longed for: his master's permission to kill.

After six hours on the road, Ludovic stood outside the carriage entrance to his building. It was past midnight, but he could hear sounds coming from inside. His back ached, and his eyes were tired after six hundred kilometres of white lines on the road. The racket distracted him, and he had to check his phone for the entry code. He had left his car, as usual, beside the canal below Place de la Bastille, from where he had carried the two heavy crates of preserves and soups prepared for him by his sister to feed him, of course, but also to assuage her guilt at having taken over the farm. Arms laden with food, he composed the six-digit number with tremendous difficulty, then shouldered the door, holding his phone between his teeth. He was exhausted, and all he wanted was to stretch out on his bed and think of nothing at all. But the moment he stepped into the lodge, he saw something was amiss. The unusual level of noise told him that the big holiday-let apartment on the second floor was occupied – six rooms, a hundred-and-twenty square metres, in the refurbished building, and so expensive that it was often empty, or taken only by rich American families, three generations all together, living the Parisian dream. But they were quiet, as a rule. Young people rented it too, sometimes – ten students pooling their resources to share the eight-hundred-euros-a-night, and when that happened, it was less quiet.

From the middle of the courtyard, Ludovic glanced up at the second-floor windows. They were all brightly lit, and wide open despite the cold. Voices and music poured out from a small crowd of people dancing and talking loudly, determined to have a good time, probably drunk, and completely forgetting that other people lived there too. The apartment was directly below Aurore's, and Ludovic thought of her straight away, unable to sleep. He smiled fondly at the thought of her lying there, close by, at this very moment. He did not know when they would see one another again, unless she had left a note in his letterbox – their private text-messaging system. Or perhaps they might run into one another tomorrow. There was nothing in his letterbox, no post, and above all, no note, not the least sign of life. This woman's ability to disappear without trace was truly astonishing, and the more so because she lived right here. He could see her bedroom window, just by looking up. There was a light on there, too. They weren't asleep. The music was horribly loud in the courtyard, but worst of all was the muffled thump of the bass that seemed to beat directly against the eardrums, right inside your head. Ludovic caught something in the torrent of noise, and he stopped to listen. Everyone was talking English, but one voice stood out, louder than the rest, a man who was shouting to make himself heard – in English, too. It had to be Richard. Richard, who had clearly gone downstairs to his new, temporary neighbours to ask them to turn it down, and had apparently got drawn into an argument. Ludovic set the crates down on the ground and walked out into the middle of the courtyard, the better to hear what was going on. He couldn't understand their words, but clearly voices were being raised in an angry exchange. Ludovic hesitated. He wondered if he should go up to the apartment, not so much to try and calm things down as to get a closer look at Richard, whom he had seen only in passing up to now. Here was a chance to meet him properly, to come face to face with the man about whom he felt more than a passing curiosity, the guy who had succeeded at everything; in a way, the total opposite of himself. The globetrotting, smartly dressed, young hotshot American was his antithesis.

Intrigued, Ludovic entered staircase A, a broad flight of freestone steps with curved edges and tiled half-landings between the floors. The higher he climbed, the worse it got: the music was some kind of insidious, thudding rap, and the bass notes reverberated through the entire building, underscoring the laughter and sharp voices that filled the stairwell. It was past midnight and the noise was intolerable. When Ludovic came within sight of the second floor landing, Richard noticed him straight away, greeting the providential neighbour and corroborating witness with evident relief.

'Aha! You can hear it over there, too?'

Ludovic climbed the last few steps before answering. He gripped Richard's proffered hand, a sign that the American recognised him, that he knew exactly who he was, though Aurore couldn't possibly have talked about him to her husband. Ludovic stared straight at him, as if the revellers had ceased to exist. At last, here he was, Richard himself. He hadn't imagined he would be quite so good-looking, nor so young. Everything about him oozed dynamism, even his habit of sweeping back his hair. To be fair, he was plainly furious, too. Ludovic noted every detail, despite the circumstances. Richard was wearing grey trousers, very elegant shoes – long, slender loafers, smartly polished, with no heel – and a roll-neck cashmere sweater, also grey, all of which suited him perfectly. He was slim, and he radiated a kind of natural-born sense of style. Ludovic could scarcely believe he was standing there in front of him, Aurore's husband, right there.

'Did you come about the noise?'

'Yes, of course, it's all any of us can hear.'

Facing Richard, a gaggle of partygoers took it in turns to stand in the doorway, all of them young and clearly determined not to go to bed. A series of girls poked their heads around the door then disappeared inside the apartment, unbothered by the presence of the party poopers out on the landing. A handful of boys gathered around the ringleaders, as back-up in their negotiations with Richard. Ludovic felt old, and utterly out of place. These guys were all dressed stylishly, too, in white shirts, some were even wearing suits, as if they were on a special night out. They were svelte and young, of that peculiar category of human being that succeeds in looking relaxed and elegant all at once.

Richard resumed discussions with a trio of guys who had stood their ground outside the apartment's double front door. He seemed to be trying to get their agreement on something, perhaps a time by which the party would end. Ludovic let him take charge – his own English was inadequate to the task, and even Richard could barely make himself heard. He glanced back to where Ludovic was standing, a few steps down the stairs.

'Are they American?' Ludovic asked.

'Ah no,' said Richard, walking over to him. 'All Australians.'

Suddenly, he seemed to relax, laughing as he added, loudly above the din:

'My fellow Americans would never be so bad-mannered as to disturb one of their own, right under his windows… But the Aussies are a strange bunch, even their accent is terrible. I can't make out a word they say. It's like they're all, what's your word, *péquenots* – a bunch of hicks from the sticks!'

'Uh, yeah…'

Ludovic balked at the word, but good-looking Richard thought it highly amusing. All he saw here was a clutch of sub-humans on some juvenile bender, hiring themselves a holiday let because a hotel would never tolerate such behaviour. Ludovic studied the excitable partygoers, quite fascinated to know they were Australians. They seemed to be having fun. He almost envied their boldness, to have come here from the other side of the world for a week-long blast beneath the plaster mouldings of a bourgeois Parisian apartment, getting their fill of the sights of the French capital and partying by night. Not bad for a bunch of hicks.

He leaned on the banisters, enjoying the show. Richard was looking for back-up.

'They'd never get away with this in a hotel!'

'Absolutely not. How long have they been here?'

'Since Friday. This is the third night we've had of this, but tomorrow is Monday, and I can't take it any more.'

'If they're bothering you to that extent, you should call the police.'

'They're not bothering you?'

'My place is across the courtyard, I'm a heavy sleeper. Nothing bothers me – I don't notice the noise.'

He knew this would annoy Richard; knew that his show of detached calm would ruffle the American's feathers. He pictured himself telling Aurore the same thing, the first time they had spoken. Unsure how to respond, Richard began addressing another guy this time, taller and visibly less drunk, more clear-headed than the others. They talked like revellers in a nightclub, their faces close together, gesturing comically with their hands, Mediterranean-style. Two others appeared in the doorway, and Richard continued to play the smooth diplomat, keeping his cool. The guy had class, and Ludovic couldn't help admiring him just a little. He harboured a serious inferiority complex with regard to Parisians in general, but an American Parisian was even more daunting. Above all, and quite objectively, he could see that this guy had it all. He was almost ten years younger than Ludovic, with a great job, a superb apartment, kids. And he was

Aurore's husband. Ludovic could scarcely believe that the guy had achieved all this before the age of forty. It gave him pause for thought, and it hurt, like the deafening racket, the voices all around him, the youngsters who laughed and hollered, ecstatic with joy at this thumping, fast-paced, atrocious music. And all after six hours of motorway driving. He hated the whole lot of them.

But at that moment, without really understanding why, he saw the three guys staring straight at him, with a questioning look in their eye. Richard was still speaking, but what he was telling them, Ludovic had no idea. Ludovic stared back, sensing that Richard was talking about him, at which moment all three turned around and went back inside, closing the apartment door behind them. The talking continued, but the music was turned down.

Richard descended the few steps to where Ludovic was standing. He was smiling broadly.

'*Yes!*'

He held out his clenched fist for a basketball-style bump, a gesture Ludovic loathed. He held out his open hand in return, and Richard shook it in the traditional way.

'Did you get what just happened?'

'No.'

'I told them you were a plain-clothes cop, and that you were about to call for back-up, if they didn't turn the sound down straight away. You showed up just at the right moment, you might say!'

'Bravo. Quick thinking.'

Richard was still gripping his hand. Now, he thumped Ludovic's back, too.

'You know what the kids call you, Monsieur Ludo, since that business with the boiler? You're *Superplumber!*'

'What does that mean?'

'*Superplombier!*' Richard translated the title into French. 'You really are a kind of superhero up at our place!'

Ludovic had no idea how to respond to this. Aurore must have talked about him since 'the business with the boiler', and the news baffled him. People often slapped him on the shoulder like this, a broad set of shoulders seems to invite the gesture, like the hind quarters of a prize bull, a horse's rump. A series of friendly pats, to feel the quality of the beast.

'Come on up, we'll have a whisky.'

'No. Thank you.'

Ludovic turned away and wished Richard goodnight. The guy was annoying him now, with his dynamism and good cheer, his intelligence, too. He found it impossible to understand why Aurore was distancing herself from Richard, for him. Last time, she had even told him she felt closer to him than to her husband. How could that be? He felt a shudder of jealousy, even a kind of humiliation, as he lifted the crates, back down in the courtyard, and began the climb up his steep, old staircase. The other guy had passed him off as a cop, after all, just like that. He had used him, played with him, without asking his permission. Richard was disarmingly quick and clever, with a kind of unthinking arrogance.

Once inside his own apartment, Ludovic hurried to take a long shower. He tried hard to wash it all away, the carefree Australians, the arrogant, far too good-looking husband, the six-hour road trip in the Twingo that killed his back every time, but the image that haunted him more than anything this evening was that of his mother, walled in silence; his mother, gone forever, and the others all around her, who no longer ate the vegetables they sold, and Mathilde, at whose tomb he had kept vigil, and Aurore in her bed, just across the courtyard.

This evening, at the end of a long weekend, he reflected that there was a lot on his mind, troubles that refused to go away. He pulled on a pair of underpants and a T-shirt, drank one of the lukewarm beers his sister had slipped into the crates of produce. In her excessive kindness, she had even given him some saucisson and fresh bread. His sister annoyed him, if he thought about it. She overdid her generosity, as if she wanted to be sure he would leave for Paris, that he wouldn't be back any time soon to get under their feet, that was doubtless what she was thinking: the provisions were one way to keep him at a distance…

Ultimately, when he really thought about his life, he saw that he was surrounded by a fair few bastards, and people who were either indifferent to him, or selfish, or spiteful.

For the past half-hour, the Australians had decided to play nicely. With their windows closed, all that could be heard was a loud but bearable background noise. The apartment would be choked with smoke, but at least the racket had stopped. Ludovic leaned on his windowsill to light a cigarette, not so much for the smoke as out of curiosity. As they entered the month of December, the building opposite was clearly visible through the now-naked branches, close but at the same time so very far away. The tall ceilings of the first- and second-floor apartments lifted the whole block with them. At times, he felt he was looking at a brand-new luxury yacht, from the deck of a rickety old sailing-boat. This evening, after seeing Richard, but with no news of Aurore for the past five days, no sign of life at all, Ludovic told himself it would be best to keep away from that woman, this building, everything. To her, he was just a passing lover, a welcome adventure in her troubled existence. Perhaps she was counting on him to help her recover her money, but he should expect nothing more from a princess who was selfishly leading him on.

What bothered him most of all was that for the past fortnight, he had been thinking about her a great deal; indeed, he thought of nothing else. It was an effort for him not to leave a note in her letterbox, not to try an approach of some kind, when he wanted desperately to see her again; he missed her body, her company, for so many reasons. It had been years since he had truly opened up and talked to another human being. But now she knew everything about him, and he dared not admit it, but he felt attached to her, dangerously attached. Barely a month ago, she had avoided him, refused even to look at him when they passed one another. Perhaps she had even been wary of him, whereas she had stood out to him from the first – she was completely beyond his reach because she was beautiful, because every time he saw her, she was wearing a new, flattering outfit; she smelled good – he knew when she had crossed the courtyard just before him, because her perfume lingered in the post room; she was the emblem of a certain ideal, *la Parisienne*, *la femme bourgeoise*, distant, indifferent, the symbol of the women he saw on the city's streets but never met.

Her bedroom light was out. Was she asleep? Were they asleep in one another's arms, or perhaps very much awake… He peered through the branches, looking for the two birds. They were no longer there. The only light shining down into the courtyard now came from the Australians' windows. He could see well enough in the half-light, but there was no sign of the turtle doves. He scanned the courtyard and spotted them at the very top of the building, on the chimney stack to the left, each bird perched atop its own pot, keeping warm, not huddled together. The image of Aurore rose before his eyes, asleep, her face half-submerged in a pool of hair, and he thought of the immense effort he would have to make not to see her again. He had never asked 'When can we meet again?' He never gave the slightest hint of his impatience.

It was the only way not to alarm her, to please her by affecting indifference. But the role was becoming harder than ever to play.

Suddenly, the speakers blasted out in the building opposite, and the Australians all began to sing. Then they turned up the volume even more, and the noise was unbearable all over again, invasive even with the windows shut. Ludovic stayed where he was and watched. He knew already that the windows on the third floor would light up, that Richard would play the bad cop this time and call the police, for real. He was certain to do something. At precisely that moment, the lights came on in Aurore's bedroom, and then the rest of the apartment, followed by the whole of staircase A. Ludovic heard a doorbell ringing frantically in the midst of the din. Richard must be ringing the bell of the apartment on the floor below his and, getting no answer, growing wild with rage. Ludovic couldn't see what was going on, but he followed the scene with amusement, anticipating what would happen next. He thought he could make out Richard's voice amongst all the others, Richard's voice raised to a new, furiously angry pitch. He was losing his cool now, for sure. 'On your own now, friend...' he muttered to himself, and he felt a certain satisfaction at the thought of the slightly built husband unable to keep a lid on his temper, pushed beyond his limits, properly shaken and enraged. Ludovic lit another cigarette and leaned his elbows on his windowsill, in spite of the cold, just for the pleasure of hearing the guy opposite blow a fuse. At this angle, he couldn't see entirely what was happening on the landing, nor on the staircase, but he pictured the scene clearly in his mind's eye, savoured the spectacle. And then he heard angry shouts, accusations piling one on top of the other in an escalating climate of fury, and he recognised the soundtrack of a situation getting out of hand. When gestures, words, even shouts spiralled beyond control, it was a sign that words were no longer enough, and they were doubtless coming to blows. It annoyed him to hear the evident sounds of a fight, but not to see it. And so he pulled on his jeans, laced his trainers tight so that he would not lose his footing if it came to it and, leaving his door ajar, he tumbled down the stairs just as fast as he raced up the two floors opposite, ready to join in.

Out on the landing there was the same appalling racket, but not a soul in sight, so he entered the apartment and came upon the always shocking sight of two men throwing punches hard at one another in the hallway, careless of their own injuries, while the others tried to pull them apart. Richard looked quite different now – nasty, aggressive, dishevelled, overwhelmed by his own anger and spurred on by that of his opponent. How could someone so polished lose his cool to that extent? Ludovic threw himself into the chaos, like a moviegoer crossing the screen. Apart from the small group in the hallway, the rest of the party were still dancing in the large sitting room at the far end as if nothing was the matter. They were drunk or disinhibited, and their high spirits hit him like a slap, these unbearable, good-for-nothing, stupid kids, who hadn't even noticed he was there, weren't even remotely bothered by his presence, and that appalling music, the rap, that was heavy, relentless, but above all loud, much, much too loud. 'Fuck, that music…' Ludovic stopped thinking after that, clenching his jaw, stony-faced. When you grab someone by the collar you take a step into the unknown, and it's all in the eyes: you might weigh a hundred kilos, but the look in your eyes is how you show them you're ready to eat them alive. He pulled the blond guy who had pinned Richard to the floor back up onto his feet, stood him up straight to stare him in the eye, and hit him without a word, just threw his fist into the face of this person who had the arrogance not to be afraid of him. Caught on the chin, he crumpled back down to the floor; the impact didn't only knock him out, but stunned everyone else too. But if you're going to fight, you need to get straight in, no warning shots, no empty taunts. You have to throw in all the rage you feel, all at once, the fear of being unable to go on, the boiler simmering with a thousand grudges, deep inside… The others formed a circle around him, just like in a match, when he still played, and they would launch into another tackle when they came out of a scrum, and that's what he did now: he walked right up the rest of them and caught hold of another one, before they even had time to think of fighting back, and he punched the guy right in the stomach, and everyone yelled out and the circle broke apart. They thought he'd gone crazy, perhaps he was armed; they had no idea that he was releasing the frustration he could bear no longer, the endless waiting for a sign from Aurore, while Richard was sleeping with her night after night. He couldn't care less about these Australians and their noisy party, they could carry on dancing in the sitting room, it was Richard he wanted to destroy, to eradicate. Without knowing what he was doing, he stormed over to the sound system and tore out the amplifier, pulling two cables that toppled a pair of tall, slim speakers, and everything stopped dead. He hurled the amp to the floor as if smashing a coconut. He hated that they were all there, beneath Aurore's bed, with their easy lives, and he saw that he was going too far, but he was drunk on the heady excitement of the fight, especially now they were all pulling back, tails between their legs.

The second boy was clutching his stomach but the tall blond still hadn't got to his feet. Ludovic had caught him right under the chin, cricked his neck, perhaps concussed him, but this was going on too long. The others were crouching around him and Richard looked as stupefied as if he'd been the one on the receiving end of Ludovic's fist. Ludovic was beyond all that. The frightened girls would be saying terrible things about him, they stared at him as if

210

he was a crazed killer bursting into a prayer meeting, but reading the fear in the others' eyes made him want to fight some more, and he hollered, 'Don't piss me off…' No one dared approach him when he got into this state, even if there were ten of them against him, they just stood there, open-mouthed, nothing but a bunch of stupid, drunk kids. There was nothing bad about them, he'd just brought them all back down to earth. He had no desire to speak to Richard, no need of support from anyone. He glanced down at the other guy on the floor. They would call an ambulance or he'd get over it by himself, he didn't care. He walked away, no more noise, no more music, and as they all bent over their casualty, he hurried away down the stairs, stamping his feet hard on each step to release the sudden, bizarre feeling of hatred that had risen inside him.

When he re-entered his apartment, his window was still open. It was cold, but he left it that way, and without turning on the light he sat on his bed to take off his trainers and lie down. There was no more noise coming from outside, only voices, an earnest, shaky conversation. He had to calm down. Through the trees, up there, lights were still blazing, and he dreaded the sound of an ambulance. He exhaled slowly, he had to calm down. It was always horrible to realise he had gone too far. He had always been afraid of giving one punch too many, of losing control of his impulses. Even as a kid, when he was playing, his mother would say 'Stop it! You don't know your own strength…' He needed to close the window and calm down but he dared not look outside and see what he could hear. He pictured the scene, they'd been asking for it, after all, he reassured himself by repeating the words, but still, no good ever came of it when he got carried away. It was Aurore's fault, and Richard's, he knew that all right; the two of them were making him act like an idiot, and it was then that he heard, far off in the silent streets behind their building, the sound of an ambulance siren, the two-tone shriek, loud then quiet, coming closer and closer, and he felt sick to the stomach when the ambulance stopped, right outside the carriage entrance to their courtyard, with its engine running.

III

Nothing worries him. Nothing will ever worry him. After what he'd been through, nothing would frighten him ever again. When you've watched the illness take its toll, day after day, on the face of the woman you love, when you have measured, day after day, the extent of your powerlessness against the other's affliction, when you have been cast adrift for months on a sea of anguish, so that you talk about nothing but death, when you hang by the thread of the latest test result, a fresh diagnosis, day after day, endlessly confronted with your own, utter inability to do anything at all, and when you are forced to admit that despite all the love in the world there is nothing you can do for her, nothing, after all that, there is nothing at all that can frighten you. That was the source of his strength: he had lost too much already, and now, nothing worried him, nothing could scare him or daunt him, nothing.

On Tuesday evening, Ludovic turned on the TV when he got home, and lay fully clothed on his bed. He always watched the regional news bulletins on channel 303 and France 3, so that he felt, just a little, as if he were back there, on the farm. For two days, he had waited to be contacted with news about the Australians. He knew the incident would come back to hit him in the face, one way or another. Either the owner of the apartment would show up, or the police – there were plenty of people waiting to talk to him about the fist fight, the wrecked amp, the guy he had knocked out flat, the extent of whose injuries he still did not know. Nor did he want to know. Richard should have been the first to come and talk to him, or perhaps Aurore, but so far, nothing.

The ambulance had stayed for over an hour in the end. In the darkness, with his window ajar, Ludovic had heard everything, all the comings and goings, the second ambulance that had pulled up in the street outside, the sound of its engine overlaying the first, and then other vehicles, doors slamming, the metal courtyard gate that had opened and shut several times in quick succession, voices under the trees. After the second ambulance, four police officers had arrived. From behind his window, Ludovic had tried to follow what was going on. He could see one end of the sitting room in the second-floor apartment the Australians had rented. In the courtyard, a police officer and two paramedics were talking, but from up high, he could hear nothing but the loud, ceaseless crackle of their radios.

He heard Aurore's doorbell being rung, and that worried him. The police must have asked Richard for an explanation of events, as the upstairs neighbour, or the neighbour who had called to complain about the noise. They would want to know if he had thrown the punch, or someone else... Ludovic listened but could make out only jumbled fragments of conversation, in French and English. The exchanges were mostly quiet; no one seemed particularly effusive or nervous, rather there was a sense of icy calm, underscored by the sound of all the vehicles with their engines still running, and the hissing radios.

After a long while, two of the Australians had come down to the courtyard, followed by the police and the paramedics, and lastly the injured man, who was carried off on a stretcher, clearly fitted with a neck brace and hooked up to a drip. Ludovic watched them go back and forth, dreading just one thing – that he would see all the faces turn to look up at his building, his window, where he stood just a few steps back in the semi-darkness. He feared they had already given his name, that someone would file a complaint, but not one of the people coming and going below looked his way – a sign that Richard had said nothing. No one else knew who he was, whether he was really a cop or not, nor where he lived. Silence fell at last, no more voices, engines, music, nothing. But still he was unable to sleep.

The trouble with looking so strong was that nobody ever worried about him. Everyone always assumed he could rise above anything, that the natural authority he had exerted over the other kids in his class extended to everything else, that it was somehow his duty to grow up faster than the rest and be bothered by nothing at all. It was other people who had corralled him into the role of the big, strong guy, beginning with his parents, who took a certain animal pride in it. And anxious not to disappoint them, he had played the game, never let anything show. When he had a ferocious cold he would dismiss the fever, the burning throat, while others piled on the agony, eager for attention and pity, their faces so white you'd think they were afflicted with tonsillitis, or a bad case of the flu. But even when he was ill, Ludovic denied it and kept a healthy, rosy hue. He wanted to deflect attention, to be free, left in peace. But then he did the same with his feelings: he would let nothing show, keep it all locked up inside. So that sometimes he had seemed insensitive, or indifferent. At school, in the valley and round about, everyone had thought him invincible, when deep down he was unsure he exerted even the slightest control over anything.

And now for two days, fear had welled up inside him, the specific fear that his hot-blooded upper cut would come back to haunt him. We choose, every moment, to resist or relent, to dismiss or be overwhelmed by something that has bothered us. Being strong means disregarding the threat, underestimating it quite deliberately. To overestimate danger is a sign of weakness. But the other evening, he had frightened himself very badly.

The Australians left on the Monday. Or at least, they were no longer there on Monday night. The large apartment was plunged into darkness again, and would doubtless stay that way for a few weeks before new holiday guests arrived from goodness knows where. Ludovic obsessed over the business of the fight. He didn't know whether the guy had just been taken for a check-up, or whether he was still in hospital – a punch in the face can turn very nasty. And he was renting this apartment undeclared, from his boss, so there was every reason to deflect attention now. So far, the other people in the building had seen him as a quiet type, discreet, helpful, unexceptional. He didn't want to lose their trust.

With his feet up on the bedspread he watched the second, regional half of the hour-long seven o'clock news. He knew for certain that at that moment, his mother would be in front of the TV. She watched that part of the programme every evening. His sister or his nephews would put her in front of the television and watch with her. Sometimes, in winter, even his father would join them for the Midi-Pyrénées edition, on channel 303, covering south-west France. From Paris, it seemed like another country, but the programme comforted him, took him back to familiar but distant concerns. The sight of those far-off landscapes wrapped him in a blanket of nostalgia. He was transported, far away. But when three sharp knocks sounded on the door his thoughts turned instantly to the Australians, the police, the guys from the letting agency – anyone liable to cause trouble. He had barely opened the door before she fell into his arms, nestled close and hugged him with all her might. Ludovic was unable to shut the door. He glanced anxiously out into the corridor, to make sure no one had seen them. Aurore clung to him eagerly, hungrily, breathing deeply as if to fill herself with a too-long-awaited scent. In an instant, he felt his fear and anger subside. It seemed to him that each time he saw her, she was more ardent, more passionate. He sensed how much she longed to see him, and he knew the risk she was taking by coming over to his staircase, showing up at his door. It was obvious she had feelings for him. Perhaps recklessly she had allowed him to become too important in her life and would come to regret it. He could not know.

'Ludovic, I can't, I just can't.'

'Can't what?'

'Can I see you?'

'I'm right here, Aurore, you're seeing me now!'

'No, I'm late, Richard's gone to the States for two days, I have to get home. Can you do the day after tomorrow?'

'Yes, of course. Here?'

'No, La Grande Cascade, where we went before.'

He held back from pointing out that it was on the other side of Paris, that on Thursday afternoon he had two appointments north-east of the city, in the exact opposite direction from the Bois de Boulogne, that the place and time were inconvenient. He just told her it was stupid to fix a rendezvous so far away when here, they had one another 'within arm's reach', you might say...

'No. We need to talk. When we meet here we talk, but mostly we do a lot else besides, as you well know, and there are things I need to say. Serious things. Do you see?'

'Is this to do with the Australian? Is there any news?'

'No one gives a damn about the Australian. You did the right thing. Don't worry about that. You did the right thing.'

'So what do you want to talk about?'

She held his face in her hands and again, her clasp was astonishingly tight. She kissed him hard, and he allowed himself to sink into her embrace. This woman dizzied him, overwhelmed him. She had come from outside. Her coat, her skin, her face, were all cold, her breath too. She was adamant that she could not risk getting home late. He cupped her face in his hands to return her kiss, he wanted to stop her from leaving, to overpower her with desire, to break her resistance by taking her in his arms, but she pulled away, took a step back and stared him in the eye.

'I love you. You know that.'

He had no idea what to say, nor whether he should say anything at all. She wasn't expecting an answer, she had spoken on impulse. He felt incapable of telling her 'Me too. I love you, too.' It seemed impossible, though he wanted to, very badly. Stupidly, he was afraid Mathilde might hear, and so he said simply:

'Aurore, stay for a moment…'

'No. The day after tomorrow, five o'clock!'

He stood at his wide-open door, but she had already disappeared from the corridor and for a moment it seemed he had imagined her, but her perfume lingered, it was on his face, in his mouth, he was bewitched like never before. Behind him, on the TV, he heard the end of a news report about a wolf. It had been attacking flocks of sheep and leaving them for dead, for the sheer thrill of the kill. But where? Not anywhere near his farm, surely. He thought Aurore would reproach him for attacking the Australian, that she would take it badly, but in fact she had thanked him, as she had for the crows. Whenever he went on the attack, whenever he resolved a situation through violence, she thanked him. He thought that what she loved in him was the wolf, not the sheep.

M ademoiselle, lie down.'
      'You leave me alone, you—!'
'Listen to me, lie down. You'll see what I mean. When you lie down you feel calm straight away, it's physiological, you can't lie down and feel angry, believe me, it's the one thing I remember from my years of first aid!'

'Get off me! You've got no fucking business here!'

'Please, let's all keep calm. Go on, lie down, Madame Belsanne—'

'Don't you call me Madame... Fuck's sake!'

Ludovic tried to ignore the insults and stay calm in front of this young woman, but the sly landlord had shown up at the apartment too, unannounced, and the sight of him had driven his tenant wild. She was furious, spitting a torrent of abuse and trying to hit them both with her balled-up fists. The situation – and possibly her inebriated state – had aggravated her fury. Glancing quickly around the apartment, Ludovic spotted the wine box beside the kitchen sink. The fact that she'd been drinking certainly didn't help matters. Ludovic could feel the landlord standing quietly at his back. There was nothing the old guy could do here, but his young tenant had blown a fuse when she saw him. In a cruel fit of rage she had even kicked the artificial Christmas tree near the window and sent it flying into the middle of the room, lights and all. The tiny bulbs had stopped flashing, and the sight of the symbol of childhood joy lying broken on the floor tore at Ludovic's heartstrings. He knew above all that he should not try to pick up the pieces, that he would lose whatever authority he had by bending down to clear the mess, but he did it anyway, because it hurt him to see the tree like that. They had to quieten things down, restore calm, because the truth was he wanted to send the owner away, too. The guy had no business showing up like this. The young woman was touched to see him crouch down to pick up the tree and reassemble it hastily. She muttered a barely audible 'Thank you'. Ludovic tried to ease the situation by guiding her to the sofa and asking her to sit down, even encouraging her to lie back and stretch out her legs. But she resisted, jumped to her feet and lunged at the landlord, grabbing his collar and hurling a stream of insults. The poor man was completely overwhelmed. In his panicked state, he began hollering back. Ludovic was caught between them. And yet things had gone well with Madame Belsanne at first. Clearly, she hoped he would take pity on her, but at least they had managed to talk things through. Ludovic dreaded the situation would go on and on, Aurore would be waiting for him in front of La Grande Cascade at five o'clock, on the other side of Paris, so to save time and avoid the endless changes on the metro and RER, he had driven to his appointment with Madame Belsanne. But she lived on the opposite side of Paris from the Bois de Boulogne, and the traffic was bad today.

The young woman owed five months' rent. Her landlord was retired, aged seventy-five, and rented two apartments: this one, and a small studio on the edge of Villeparisis, on the city's far north-eastern rim. The problem was that both tenants had been defaulting on their rent, and there was no termination clause in either of their contracts. Worst of all, Madame Belsanne was the tenant of the ground-floor apartment in the landlord's own small house. His debtor was right there, permanently under his nose. He lived above her and saw her every day. And it was winter now, so the annual rent amnesty applied, and he didn't dare take her to court, not to mention what that would cost, and even if a judge did rule that she should be evicted in the spring, he knew from experience that the procedure was never-ending, it would take at least a year, or more, and she had two children, so the judge was certain to refuse to have her evicted, and all he could do then was make a claim against the State for the money he'd lost, and that was never-ending, too. Which was why the landlord had called Coubressac's agency, persuaded that he stood a better chance of recovering the debt that way. At least they would give his tenant a fright, perhaps she would even leave of her own accord, and failing that, as a last resort, there was Process 24, a wholly illicit practice that was widely used, in secret. It was against every law, people knew about it by word-of-mouth only, and some landlords had no hesitation whatever in applying it.

As far as Ludovic could gather, the situation had become hopeless since the woman's partner had disappeared, leaving her with the two children. Ludovic took a good look at the landlord. He wasn't that old, but he looked done in. He had retreated from inside his tenant's apartment, trying hard not to stumble, and stood now in the front doorway, trembling with rage, incapable of speaking, even to swear, breathless with the stress of having to deal with a woman far younger and quicker than he was.

'Monsieur Costa, I've already told you, I don't need you here. Madame Belsanne is perfectly able to deal with this. Let me settle things with her, just the two of us.'

'But this stupid cow lives downstairs, in my house, the house I built, all the houses around here, and the apartment blocks in Gagny, we built the whole damn lot.'

'What's that supposed to mean, you stupid old fool?'

'This is my place!'

'No, Monsieur Costa, this is your tenant's private home.'

'No, this is my place, and that scum is on my property!'

'You're the scum, the pair of you. Your wife puts all the machines on at night, on purpose, to keep the children awake – the spin cycle going full tilt, every night. You're the scum!'

At that, Costa stepped forward into the middle of the room once more. Ludovic stood in his way.

'And what about you, and those men who come round here every night. Don't tell me we're keeping you awake, the place is a fucking whorehouse!'

'What did you just say, you old bastard? What did you just say—?'

Ludovic stood firm between the two of them and asked the man to step back. He struggled not to raise his own voice, not to signal that anything had thrown him off his guard. Clearly, landlord and tenant alike had a short fuse, the slightest thing would set them off. Daily life around here must be unbearable. But all he wanted was to get away, and not be late for his date with Aurore, on the other side of Paris. It would take him over an hour to reach the Bois de Boulogne at this time of day, but the situation here was turning nasty, with both parties spitting their simmering hatred, their profound disgust at one another. The atmosphere was thick. To cool things down, Ludovic decided to put the old man firmly in his place. He knew only too well that the young woman would never calm down while the landlord still had a foot in the door of her apartment.

'Monsieur Costa, I'm going to ask you to leave. I have come to see Madame Belsanne, and she's the person I need to speak to. You have no business here.'

Shaken by the hollered insults, the landlord stepped back once again, as far as the door, but did not leave, and the more his tenant shrieked at him to get out, the more stubbornly he stood his ground.

Ludovic had taken care to come in the afternoon, knowing the children would still be at school, so that they would be spared just this sort of scene. Any other negotiator would not have been so sensitive. On the contrary, they took advantage of such things, turned up at the end of the day so that everything was tense and sordid. When he had checked out the property a couple of weeks ago, he had seen straight away that this was a risky case. The set-up was fraught with difficulty: a landlord and his debtor living one on top of the other, under the same roof, was far from ideal.

At last, he persuaded Costa to leave and climb the steps to his own place. The guy's legs were trembling with rage. The door closed behind him, and the apartment was quiet once more. Ludovic tested the young woman by pointing to the wine box beside the sink. 'Shall we have a glass?' he asked. 'I think I need one!'

The speed with which she filled two large glasses to the brim, and her eagerness to gulp hers down, told him what he needed to know. He noted the photographs of the kids posted all over the kitchen walls, and decided that intimidation would be the line of least resistance. He would take out the papers bearing the bailiff's letterhead, suggest they draw up an inventory of her possessions to see what she might sell in order to cover her rental arrears, and float vague threats regarding care of the children.

'He says I don't pay, but it's not true. The social security people pay part of it, they give it to him direct, so why's the old bastard complaining? He's got his own house, his own garden, I'm not even allowed to go in it, and when my kids play ball out the front, he yells at them.'

'Were you and the children's father married?'

'Nope.'

'And do you know where he lives now?'

'I don't *wanna* know.'

'You're aware that the rental is in his name, too? Even if he lives somewhere else, even if he's vanished, he has to help you to pay the rent here.'

'We weren't married, that bastard doesn't owe me shit. I *never* wanna see him again.'

'But did he recognise the children as his own?'

'None of your business…'

At this, her anger subsided and she fell silent. Now that the landlord had left and she was sitting down, she seemed drained, as if all the rage had been wrung out of her.

Time was getting on. Ludovic dug deep to preserve his calm. He began his recital of the horrific litany of forms to be filled. That always seemed to strike home. But this girl looked so lost that he found it near-impossible to harden his tone and play the hard-bitten negotiator. He focused on what he stood to get out of this sorry business. Four thousand euros. Two thousand for him, and two thousand for the agency. The landlord was at the end of his tether, and Ludovic knew he would be easily persuaded to turn to 'Process 24'; no doubt at all that the old guy would be ready to pay four thousand euros to turn the big guns on his tenant. Ludovic had only handled one such case before now. First, you familiarised yourself with your tenant's habits, then you fixed a date and then, very quickly, you changed all the locks while they were out. Their furniture and possessions were carried out onto the street, and the site was secured with a dog handler for at least twenty-four hours. Process 24 evictions were so traumatic that the tenants never thought to file a complaint for unlawful entry. Their mind was focused on one thing only – finding somewhere to sleep that night, getting their things back indoors somewhere, and dealing with the crisis at hand.

Ludovic made a show of reading through all the papers,

wondering what tone to adopt. They sat together in the silence that followed the storm. Unsure where to start, he looked up from his folder and across at the young woman. He saw Aurore leaving Kobzham's office, every bit as helpless and wounded, and in this young woman's eyes he saw the same look of desperate disdain, though he knew the two cases were utterly dissimilar, that Aurore's situation was altogether more clear-cut and solid, her life far more comfortable than this semi-squalor, and yet there was the same sense of powerlessness, the rock-bottom distress of a woman who knows reality has caught up with her, that everything is about to crumble around her, that nothing is certain, that nothing stands up; a woman about to lose her footing altogether, though she dares not admit it. There, in front of him, she fingered her empty glass, not daring to fill it all over again.

What he saw now, what he found admirable and deserving of respect, was that Madame Belsanne had given up all pretence of appealing to his sense of pity. She was making no secret of her disarray, seeking no excuses. She made no attempt to put it all down to bad luck, nor to lay the blame on anyone else.

'And your husband, I mean, the father of the children, what does he do?'

'I told you, I don't wanna talk about him, I don't wanna hear anythin' about him, ever again.'

'Listen, Mélina, you're going to have to help me here... Mélina...'

Surprised to be called by her first name, she looked up. Clearly, she was unused to be being addressed as a fellow human being.

'In a nutshell, what kind of guy is your ex? He's on the edge, has a short fuse, is that it?'

'That's it.'

He tried to get around the *périphérique* as fast as possible, determined to get there before Aurore. But on this wet afternoon, the traffic was heavy and progress was maddeningly slow. The stress of finding yourself trapped in the throng of other people, forced to deal with your frustration, to stay calm while cursing everyone around you, was an intrinsic part of city life. Stuck in this traffic jam, he was being impeded by thousands of people clustered together to form a compact, enervating blockade, an obstruction. Everyone in the city got in his way, it seemed.

She had asked to see him. It seemed urgent. But seeing Aurore again was all that mattered. It was as if his sole aim was to hold her, to cut himself off from the world and swim in her fragrance. Even the thought of her forced him to take a deep breath, as the longing – the need – to make love to her rose in him like an obsession. Before Aurore, there had been years without the touch of another body, the scent of another person's skin, the soft feel of their hair. What made her more desirable still was the desire he seemed to arouse in her, the way she was when they held one another tight, when she pressed her head into his chest with all her might, as if to hide herself in him, curl up deep inside. It drove him wild to feel the need she had of him, this woman who had everything. He surged forward at every break in the traffic, determined to get there first, determined not to find Aurore waiting for him alone in the huge dining room at La Grande Cascade, or outside on the steps to the terrace. He pressed down on the accelerator, threading through the tightly packed cars. He wanted to see Aurore again, and he wanted to get as far away as possible from the meeting with the young Belsanne woman, conscious that he had been very stupid indeed. Finally, just as he was about to leave, he had taken an insane risk, turning the situation on its head. No threats or scaremongering. He had whispered to her what she must do. He had given in at the sight of this young mother. He was incapable of treating her badly. 'Mélina, the truth is, Costa has no power to throw you out. In fact, you're the one who could file a complaint against him, yes... For unauthorised intrusion into your home. He had no right to come inside like that just now, you can report him for insulting and threatening behaviour, just make a simple statement at the police station, tell them everything he said to you just now, and he's the one who'll be called in for questioning. If it goes to court, it won't end well for him. You could ask him about the rent again tomorrow, and when he comes into your place and shouts at you, you can film it secretly on your phone... I'm telling you this for free, Mélina, you can do whatever you want, but I swear you can bring the old guy down. You didn't hear this from me, you understand? I haven't said a word...'

Access to La Grande Cascade was sealed off. A line of black saloons filled the parking area, letting out groups of men in suits and long coats who hurried into the restaurant, eager not to stand about in the cold. Ludovic parked a short distance from the chauffeured limos, the taxis and company cars. He got out of the Twingo, lit a cigarette and surveyed the scene. The restaurant had been booked out for a conference or seminar. A red-and-white plastic gazebo had been erected over the steps bearing the logo of a company, or some new-technology jamboree: 'World Big Data'.

He was more than ten minutes early. He preferred that. He liked the idea of waiting for Aurore, taking the time to focus on her and nothing else. Since they had begun seeing one another, he had rediscovered the excitement of looking forward to a date, the uncertainty that gripped him until the very last moment – there was always the possibility that she would not show up. If she was late, or prevented from coming, there was no way she could contact him. He savoured the suspense. It had been years since he felt the delicious anguish of waiting for a woman, when seeing her again is all that matters, when you strain for the moment of reunion, when there is nothing else on your mind, nothing else at stake, simply to see one another again, with the perpetual risk that one of you will ditch the other, or bail out, that it will all fall through, one way or another. To wait for another person is already a shared experience, of a kind. Ludovic wondered why she wanted to see him here, now. Most likely, she wanted him to do something, to give her a hand in some way. He saw the towers of La Défense in the distance, and it seemed as if Kobzham was looking down on him once again. Would Aurore go so far as to formally request him to recover her money from that son of a bitch, make him pay one way or another? He relished the prospect. He would do whatever she asked. Standing there in the icy breeze, Ludovic shivered. He felt the cold more keenly since moving to Paris. In the country, being outside was never unpleasant; he was always moving, working, never standing around, not even when he was out shooting. He liked to feel a blast of cold, a sudden shower of rain, liked to walk in the snow or the hot sun, but here, at the intersection of two broad, tree-lined roads, busy thoroughfares stretching endlessly into the distance, he began to shake, as if his body registered the exact moment, the very second at which he had caught a chill. Strange to think of it like that, but he stood stock-still all the same, toughing it out as he always did. He would beat the cold. He lit another cigarette to warm up, and the smell of it calmed him. Resting his elbows on the roof of the car, he felt an adolescent flutter of excitement. Aurore would not leave him. At the very beginning of an affair, the other person is an obsession: you think about them all the time. Whatever went before is non-existent. The past is reduced to an insignificant but prodigal thing that served solely to bring you to this moment, as if the only purpose of life itself had been to fulfil your need to find the other person.

It was dark now, and he began to worry. What if something had happened? She had no way of letting him know, and if she called the restaurant, he wasn't there. Loving this woman meant taking endless risks. Not only was she married, but married to an unquestionably capable, brilliant man. She was far beyond his reach, in every sense, and yet she was faltering, out of her depth. A terrifying thought crossed his mind: to date, the only person in the world who knew about their affair was Kobzham. Thoughts jostled in his mind, like the cars that continued to pour into the parking area. From a distance, Ludovic watched the smart crowd milling about in the vast salons, groups of men chatting amongst themselves, white-jacketed waiters plying the room with trays of champagne. Until now, he had never felt ashamed of his jeans and trainers, but if Aurore insisted on entering the restaurant this evening, she would blend in with everyone else, while he most certainly would not. Not dressed like this.

It was twenty past five, and pitch dark. After the fourth cigarette, he told himself that his infatuation with this woman would lead nowhere; best to retreat now and keep a cool head. More than anything, he feared he might do something stupid, become mixed up in a world in which he had no place. He should keep his distance, cut loose. The incident with the Australian had been a warning, a sign that nothing good would come of their affair. Essentially, he knew nothing about her and, more importantly, there were things she did not know about him. He should have told her what his life had been for the past three years, but was it really fair to burden her with his pain? Aurore wanted reassurance from him. She wanted him to be strong, afraid of nothing. That much he understood.

He was coughing hard now. He was wearing just a T-shirt under the thin blazer. There were clothes in the back of the car, but he did not want her to see him in his huntsman's sweater and a zip-up fleece. He stood out in the cold, surprised that there was still no sign of Aurore. The icy wind brought a damp drizzle now, and he rummaged in the back of the car for a handkerchief, anything. The jumble of belongings included a pair of camouflage trousers, boots, even the rifle in its holder – he'd forgotten to put it back in the gun cupboard at the farm on his last visit, hadn't given it a thought, perhaps subconsciously he wanted it there, and that was sheer stupidity, too, especially since his gun licence was out of date, he should have renewed it online, he'd get around to it one day at the office, though in fact he didn't care, he never went shooting now. He retrieved a couple of old pieces of kitchen paper from the pockets of the trousers, and blew his nose, but he needed more, much more, and his cough had hollowed now, rising from somewhere deep down inside his back. A taxi pulled up on the other side of the four-lane road. The windows were tinted but he knew that the person getting out of the black saloon would be her. It took her forever to pay the driver. The traffic was fast-flowing at this point. Ludovic signalled to Aurore to take care crossing the road, and stepped out into the middle. There was no central reservation, but a broad strip of white paint. She hurried towards him, not waiting to look around before crossing, and he was touched to see her determination, the way she rushed to greet him. They met in the middle of the road. Wordlessly, she buried her head in his jacket; she wanted him to wrap himself around her, she was cold. Ludovic said, 'Come on, we can't stay here...' but she clung to him tighter still, pressed her head to his chest. 'No, wait. Wait just a minute...' Ludovic disliked feeling quite so exposed. The car headlamps swept over them like spotlights. Aurore pressed tight against him, clinging to him as if he were immune to harm. To her, he was a man to whom nothing bad could happen, who knew no fear, and true enough, that was exactly the image he tried hard to project, but just right now he was dreadfully cold, and sensed danger all around them. It was all he could think of: what if a big, two-seater scooter came too close, or a truck, or a car pulled out of its lane? People were sounding their horns at them now. 'Come on, Aurore, we can't stay here...' But Aurore would not move. Worse still, she was holding him tighter than ever, and speaking in a low voice. 'Ludovic, it's all over... I need you...' She repeated the words like a tender plea, not releasing her grip even slightly, 'I need you.'

He had no idea what she meant, but he felt a sudden, overwhelming anxiety. He wanted to look into her eyes, ask her what had happened now, but the scent of her hair overwhelmed him, and the feel of her body, warm inside her clothes. He felt intoxicated, paralysed, profoundly moved: she was giving herself to him, body and soul. Even now, just by enfolding her in his open jacket, just by being here, he was protecting her, as if he could dismiss all her past disappointments, her present difficulties. He thought again of Mélina Belsanne, the way her eyes had lit up when she understood that he was prepared to sacrifice his client's tranquillity to keep a roof over her head. She had taken it as a sign of blessing from the world at large. Here, now, he sensed that Aurore was hoping for something every bit as miraculous.

Glancing towards the restaurant, she understood why Ludovic had stayed out on the road. More than anything, she regretted that they could not go inside, to the huge dining room, to drink tea somewhere warm and safe, sheltered by the greenery under the great glass roof. She had been looking forward to that moment all day, and now she felt tears in her eyes.

'You, see, nothing goes to plan…'

'Well, thank goodness,' Ludovic replied, 'or we would never have met.'

She looked up into his face, she wanted him to look her in the eye. Her expression was disarming. She was utterly at a loss, confirmed by the whisper he could barely hear through the din of the cars and motorbikes. Hauntingly, she said over and over:

'It's worse than the crows…'

'What do you mean?'

'The accountant has told me everything. This time Fabian wants to shoot me down, do you understand? Literally shoot me down in flames…'

The children were playing upstairs. Aurore called for them, louder each time, but they gave no reply. They must have heard her and chosen not to answer. Another sign of her diminishing control over everything. She called louder still, hollering their names, and still they pretended they hadn't heard.

She couldn't believe it. The sheer ingratitude of her children, the calculated indifference of these two small creatures who could not live without her. Two tiny mammals who, without her, would be unable to find food, would have no chance of survival whatever and despite that, despite all the time she spent with them, they acted as if she wasn't there, as if she didn't exist. This wasn't the first time they had pretended not to hear her. But tonight, after the apocalyptic week she had just lived through, it seemed harder to bear than ever.

She crouched down beside the bath she had just filled with warm water – the perfect temperature, hot but not too hot. Since the new boiler had been installed, the water came out scalding, dangerously hot, and she was forced to adjust the flow of the two old-fashioned porcelain and brass taps, alternating the hot and cold, just like in the old days. The water plummeted, boiling and bubbling, into the bath, and she heard the twins thudding on the wooden floor overhead. They were play-fighting with their half-brother, and all three were especially wild this evening because it was the start of the holidays. Two weeks off school, and more dependent on her than ever.

She dreaded the onset of the winter holidays. This time of year always spelled trouble for her. Past mid-December, the relentless countdown began, and she found herself living in a kind of sealed airlock from day to day, with more and more people in the apartment and everywhere else, and the pressure mounting up to Christmas Eve, then New Year's Eve... Even the thought of it horrified her. But this year was worse than ever. She would have to decide over the holiday period whether to give up or fight her associate. She would have a hard time planning her counterattack and managing her family over the next two weeks, during which time she had to plan their festivities, buy gifts for everybody, organise meals and travel plans, starting with a visit to her parents in Brittany. And before that, Richard's parents would visit Paris for a week, as they did every year. Every year they travelled from Philadelphia to spend Christmas with their grandchildren, and so it would be until Richard's sister decided to embrace motherhood herself. For as long as Kathleen remained childless, her parents would travel six thousand kilometres to celebrate a perfect Happy Christmas in France, surrounded by gifts and decorations, everyone around the tree, and a splendid meal on the table. Aurore experienced the holiday season more and more as a kind of personal sacrifice, and this year would be worse than ever. If she decided to attack Fabian and Kobzham, she would still have to put on a good show meanwhile and take charge of the celebrations while marshalling her defence team, briefing lawyers and reporting the secret agreement between her associate and the man who owed her ninety-two thousand euros. They had deliberately chosen to step out into the light in late December, knowing full well that she would find it near-impossible to round on them in the two-week period during which everything came to a halt. Above all, she did not want Richard mixed up in this, especially with his parents there from Saturday onwards. To mix work and family was a huge risk. If she asked his advice, Richard would take it as a cry for help, and respond with a fine show of condescension – the successful, well-connected husband riding to the rescue of his wife's business. But if he were to unleash his pack of lawyers, set Lathman & Cleary on the case, there could be no doubt: they would bring Fabian and Kobzham down for fraudulent overstatement of liabilities, forgery, embezzlement and bankruptcy fraud. Without Richard, she could do nothing, she lacked the clout even to organise a meeting with a lawyer on the eve of the Christmas holidays. They would tell her to book a date in January and by then it would be too late. And what would be left of her company after that, she had no idea.

She dipped her hand into the frothy water. Bubbles were filling the tub. The children could see to their own bathtime, but she wanted them down here now. The water was lovely, inviting and aromatic, with her vetiver-scented bubble bath. It felt strangely as if she was discovering her own smell, the scent of her body. She thought of how Ludovic would bury his face in her neck, inhale the vetiver on her skin, and now each time she smelled her own perfume, she felt his presence, the animal way he sniffed her and held her close. She turned off the taps, got to her feet and glanced out over the little curtain that hung across the bathroom window. She pressed her nose to the glass and cupped her hands around her eyes, peering out into the darkness of the courtyard. Ludovic was there somewhere, through the branches. Knowing he was there was sweet and maddening at the same time. The leaves were all gone now, and the branches and twigs stood bare. His windows were just opposite, but dark. He was not back yet, or his curtains were already drawn. When he wasn't with her, he disappeared completely, no messages, texts or calls, no emails, no way to connect. She knew almost nothing about him. From what he told her, he spent his evenings watching television, zapping from one channel to the next. Sometimes he went for a drink with the guys from work. He liked to go to bed early. No one in

Paris went to bed early. He got up at six each morning to go for a run, or to start work first thing, catching people by surprise while they were still at home. She regretted not asking him more about himself. Their conversation revolved around her, in fact. Her problems. And as a result, she knew hardly anything about him. Perhaps he preferred it that way; perhaps he didn't want to talk about his past, or he was just naturally outward-looking, an altruist who existed for other people. But can anyone truly exist for other people and expect nothing in return?

She kept her face pressed to the glass, focused on the lifeless window opposite. She regretted confiding in him quite so openly the other evening, in the little café where they had finally taken shelter. She should never have gone into detail, and yet Ludovic had seen the underhand coup coming. One meeting with Kobzham, and he had caught the scent. He saw straight away that the guy was manipulating Fabian, that both of them were capable of setting a trap for her. What he did not know was that she had already fallen into it. The day before yesterday the accountant, Fabienne Nguyen, had called at eight o'clock in the morning, on the day before the beginning of the holidays – something she never did as a rule. She wanted to see Aurore immediately and, rather than come to the office, she asked her to come to her apartment. Over coffee in the small kitchen, she told Aurore everything. Fabian had made her swear not to say a thing, but she could not keep something like this to herself, least of all keep it a secret from Aurore, whom she liked and respected. Towards the end of October, Fabian had asked her to collect all the accounting and finance documents, the end-of-year accounts from the preceding year and even their company registration details and the names and addresses of all salaried staff. She had understood immediately what that meant. He was starting insolvency proceedings, but he assured her that this would be a

236

special case: the company already had a purchaser. Fabian was taking advantage of a new article of company law, introduced in 2014, that allowed businesses to restructure and file their own recovery plan with the commercial courts, thereby avoiding official receivership, and effectively taking matters into their own hands. He had told the accountant that no one else should know – and especially not Aurore. They needed to be sure that nothing stood in the way of the plan's successful completion. There could be no risk of a counter-offer.

And so now everything made sense. For the past six months, Fabian and Kobzham had been deliberately sabotaging the accounts, doing everything in their power to undermine the company – hence the unpaid orders, the deliveries that had gone astray. The plan was to bleed the company to the point of insolvency, so that Kobzham, with his brother as intermediary, would be seen as a saviour, stepping in to take over, with six hundred thousand euros upfront to relaunch the brand and a million euros to invest in the company after that, to reassure the courts, the accountants and the lawyers, and guarantee his takeover. Her brand was being stolen from her, and there was nothing she could do.

Fabienne explained that the manoeuvre, treacherous as it was, would ensure a second life for the company. The problem was, they planned to keep the Aurore Dessage brand, but not Aurore herself. She would be thrown off the board and hired as a contractor. She would supply design sketches as requested, and all subsequent decisions would be theirs alone. They could manufacture the clothes wherever they wanted, shut down the Paris workshop and relocate the production of the prototypes. Plainly, the aim was to capitalise on her name, her image, to use Aurore Dessage to market a whole range of products, from fragrances to bags, jewellery, anything at all.

Aurore had taken the news on the chin, unable to confide in anyone. Nor would she dare. The only person she could tell was Ludovic. Deep down, she was ashamed. She felt humiliated, ridiculed. She had been manipulated and made to look a fool, for months. She did not want to tell anyone else about it, least of all Richard, least of all now, during the compulsory end-of-year festivities, two weeks of forced fun and seasonal joy. And so there, in the café, she had confided everything to the man about whom she knew so little, told him how the two bastards were licking their lips, how she felt hunted, because at court on the fifth of January they would eat her alive.

She regretted her confession now, because Ludovic had frightened her. Never had she seen such an expression on a man's face – a look of pure, hard hatred. His entire body had tensed as she spoke, transformed, disfigured by an anger that seemed to distance him from her. He sniffed constantly and blew his nose hard, too, so that his face turned red, amplifying his bad boy appearance. He said nothing but gripped his coffee cup tight in his fist until it seemed it might shatter in the palm of his hand, breathing hard like a bull preparing to charge.

Aurore rested her head against the glass, gazing out at the windows opposite, and thought about what Richard had told her, the way Ludovic had punched the Australian. Richard assured her their neighbour was crazy, wrong in the head, they should be wary of him, and with hindsight Aurore was alarmed at the thought. Shouts from behind her back startled her out of her reverie. Iris and Noé had wanted to frighten her, and they had succeeded in making her jump out of her skin. They came over to the window, lifted the little curtain and pressed their faces to the cold glass, like Aurore. They wanted to see what she was looking at, out in the courtyard. It was pitch dark. Only the light from their bathroom shone palely among the branches. The two trees would sleep now, for months ahead. Beyond them only small patches of light showed in the façade opposite. Just as in a forest, life in the courtyard was suspended in winter, a slumbering scene where no one walked any more, the trees inert and waiting for spring.

The twins were so excited tonight that in the end she decided to stay and keep an eye on them in the bath. Usually, they washed themselves, but the tub was huge and more than once they had given her a fright, especially since Iris had almost drowned that summer in a swimming pool in the Lubéron. Aurore could still hear the smack of her legs as they splashed the surface of the water, the cries they had taken for shouts of amusement. There had been plenty of people playing in the pool that day, but no one had noticed that Iris was drowning. Lost amid the chatter and the diving bodies, Iris had gesticulated in despair with her leg caught in her rubber ring and her head under the water, unable to right herself. The incident was seared on Aurore's memory for life. And here, the bath was deep and wide, reached by a flight of three steps – the previous owner's Pharaonic fantasy, that Aurore had decided to keep. The bathtub was impressive. And scary, and the children had been afraid of it at first.

She returned to the window, wanted to see if Ludovic was back yet, couldn't understand why he still wasn't home; though he owed her no account of where he went or what he did, she just needed to know what he was doing right at that moment. In the gloom, she saw the two turtle doves alight on the farthest branches. Where had they come from? What did their lives consist of? The children splashed about behind her back, drenching the bathroom floor. Aurore thought of the crows, of the terror that had haunted her, and from there her thoughts circled back to her confession to Ludovic in the small café. The more she divulged, the more distant he had seemed. He was once more the unsettling giant she had avoided for two years. Noé and Iris were still yelling, and she tried not to shout as she told Noé to let Iris go. He was pretending to strangle his sister. She hated games like these, hated seeing the children so overexcited. Her eyes had become accustomed to the dark and now she was certain, there were no lights on in his apartment. What the hell was he up to? And then she heard a dull sound, the sort of sound that stops everything dead. Noé had pushed Iris, she had slipped and hit her head on the side of the bath. The room froze in the still, glassy silence of the aftermath of an accident. Iris was expressionless, apparently unable to move. Noé was in shock, uncomprehending. Aurore pressed her hands to her face in horror and told herself this was all her fault, it would never had happened if she had kept an eye on them, everything was her fault. She watched for a glimmer of expression on her daughter's face, bent over her and, at the sight of her mother, the child's face passed from stunned shock to pain, her cheeks turned pink, tears sprang from her eyes and she burst out wailing. She had had a terrible fright, but she was unharmed.

Aurore knelt and clutched Iris tight against her. She clung to her wet child, and Iris clung back, attached every part of her body to her mother's, all three of them held one another fast, and Aurore felt her clothes soaking on contact. They lost themselves in a deep, deep hug, and all was calm. Aurore didn't dare move. Danger stalks, your whole life long, ready to destroy everything at any moment. Aurore turned her head to the window, she saw again the two crows buried in the ground, she thought of Fabian and Kobzham, and she passed from one moment of dread to the next.

He'd taken three sachets at once, and now he was trembling all over. He glanced at the leaflet and saw the stuff was packed with taurine, vitamin C and caffeine. He was an idiot to have taken three, the pharmacist had said no more than one a day, but he'd had enough of this flu, and the coughing was driving him crazy. The taurine would be coursing through his system, mixing with the coffee he'd already drunk, and now this evening he could not stop shaking.

It was ten past seven. Ludovic had been parked at the foot of the apartment block on Boulevard Suchet, beside the Bois de Boulogne, for over an hour. He'd had time to think. He had come here the day before to check the place out from the same spot, set back from the splendid, but somehow annoying Art Deco façades that lined the edges of the Bois, their entranceways gleaming like a series of palace hotels. This was a Paris unknown to him, though the existence of such luxury came as no surprise. It was just that he never came here. The Paris he drove and trudged around for work was the exact opposite – the north and east, the estates beyond the *périphérique*. Never the 16th arrondissement. From down below, you could picture the huge apartments that ran the length of the brightly lit balconies. At ground level, iron railings surrounded well-tended flowerbeds. Opposite, the Bois de Boulogne extended into the distance. The only cars to be seen along this avenue were top-of-the-range saloons. Everything here talked money. In one sense, Aurore was part of this world, of the bourgeoisie at whose feet he now sat, in the Twingo. His perennial complex about this city and its people gnawed even harder now. More than ever it seemed he had nothing to offer her but his brute strength, his only bargaining chip, but right now he felt weak and feverish as a sick child.

He pictured himself on another evening three years before, in the height of summer, when he had come out of the hospital and sat in this same car, this same seat. Before turning the key in the ignition he had sat for a long while, motionless, incapable of moving, his hands on the steering wheel, just like now. Except that three years ago, his strength had served no purpose. He had been unable to do anything for Mathilde. The vilest thing about that disease is its obstinacy, its determination, the feeling of utter helplessness that it provokes, time and again. Even now, he still could not accept that Mathilde had lost the battle, that there was nothing he could do. During her illness, the only way he could help was to visit her every evening in Toulouse, drive the hundred-plus kilometres after work to bring her a different pot of soup each time. They had believed in the soup. Towards the end, it was all she could take. She ate nothing but soups made with vegetables from their place in the Célé valley, and even the smell of it when she opened the clip-jar, the living aroma of real food, was enough to take her on a journey, transport her far from her hospital room. Ludovic would help her to eat, and with each spoonful he thought she would find new strength, that she would revive as she lapped the juice of the vegetables grown in the soil that had given birth to them both, and because the doctors could see no way to rid her of the cancer, they believed in the soup, too, they were happy for him to bring it in every evening, if it meant she would eat and regain even a little of the flesh that was deserting her. Every night for three months, Ludovic had driven from the farm to Toulouse and back, and every evening at about ten o'clock he would sit, disillusioned and defeated, at this same steering wheel, and drive in the light of the setting sun, with the image of Mathilde lying in her bed. To live through such a thing was inhuman, but live through it he must, driving for over an hour with the empty jar placed beside him on the passenger seat, the soup she could never finish, and every evening he drank what was left in a single gulp, knowing that the next day he would drive back in the opposite direction with the jar filled up once again, and the hope that these journeys would continue for as long as they possibly could, or that they would cease. He no longer knew which.

Twenty past seven.

Aurore was not Mathilde, Paris was not the Célé valley, but this was still the same car, the same empty seat beside him, only the glass clip-jar was gone. From this same seat, night after night, he had watched the sun give up and go, in spectacular style, and when he reached the farm he would extinguish the headlights and sit in total darkness. It was dark here, too, but cold and wet, and the image in his head was Aurore, a woman in peril, but who wanted no one to know, a woman who expected nothing from him, perhaps. Yet she had explained everything in the little café, every last detail, out of a need to confide, or perhaps in hope of something more.

Perhaps it had been a sign, or perhaps nothing, but when they had tried to enter La Grande Cascade, the doorman had stood in their way. They could not come in, the restaurant was booked for a private dinner. Aurore had insisted, imploring the man to let them in, just for a pot of tea in a corner, just a tea, but the guy had refused. She had been desperately disappointed, wounded that La Grande Cascade, her childhood haunt, had turned them both away. They had drunk their tea in a bar-café in Boulogne-Billancourt, a mediocre place on a long avenue, with a counter selling cigarettes and lottery tickets, the first place they had come to. The shabby décor had made her even more miserable, and perhaps that was why she had begun to talk. Sitting opposite her, he had struggled to conceal his astonishment, tried to react coolly to the news, as if no scheme hatched by Kobzham would surprise him. But it was a low blow all the same, and not how he had imagined the world of fashion. Those sons of bitches would show their hand right before Christmas and New Year, giving her no time to respond. Business was amoral, he knew that, but what was truly sickening here was that their scheme had been made possible because there were people on Kobzham's side in the commercial courts themselves. To pull off a deal like that you'd need the presiding judge right there in your pocket. You'd need to know him personally. Perhaps even socialise with him. The brazen privilege of Parisian networks, in business as in everything else. Your network was your passport, it opened doors, bent the rules, and while there was no law against cultivating allies in this life, to do so through the commercial courts, and bring this woman down, was filthy work indeed.

Ludovic did not know Fabian, but he pictured the bastard he undoubtedly was, an opportunist who invariably sides with the strongest. As for Kobzham, he'd seen through him straight away. Now he had the guy's address, knew a little about his habits, the daily thirty-minute jog he bragged about, every evening after work, the run he had taken yesterday and would do again today. It was seven thirty-five when Ludovic saw him emerge from the building, dressed in black jogging bottoms like the day before, headphones over his ears, a black beanie pulled down low over his forehead, and his dog running off the leash behind him. Just like the day before, he crossed the avenue and headed towards the wood, taking quick, short steps as he ran.

Taurine can really get you pumping. Ludovic's hands tensed on the steering wheel as he anticipated the selfish pleasure he would take in scaring the shit out of that bastard, forcing him to his knees. He wanted to shake him up, that was all, but good and hard, to read the terror on his face until he blubbed like a child, that piece of filth. For once in his life the guy would be down on all fours, feeling like he was nothing at all. That fake tycoon, the bastard who had treated him like a provincial nobody, would beg him for mercy. Ludovic would give Kobzham the fright of his life. He saw it as a kind of release. He spent his days playing the hard man to extract money from the little people, down on their luck, living hand-to-mouth. But now he had hooked a big fish, a big-time fraudster, and rich with it, not some no-hoper.

He planned to take him on the home run when he'd be tired and breathless. The coach had taught them that in training: it was best to tackle when a guy was out of breath, the shock to the system was all the greater. There was a reason Aurore had told him about Kobzham's ritual when he got home from work, always to go out again straight away for his run. There was a reason she had given him all the details. The only thing she hadn't mentioned was that dog, a boxer who ran a short distance behind his master. Kobzham always ran with his dog. As yesterday, he had crossed the avenue almost without looking, though admittedly the risk was small, there was hardly any traffic along here. Then, as before, he had set off along Allée des Fortifications, before disappearing into the woods along a narrow footpath. The dog was clearly trained. It maintained a constant distance. It seemed Kobzham ran for forty minutes each time. The day before, he had come home visibly exhausted, dragging his feet, pouring sweat despite the cold. The guy was running on empty.

The dashboard read seven forty. He would have preferred to wait a week, properly get his bearings, but Aurore had pointed something else out, too: the bastard took a holiday over the festive season, every year. One week skiing and another in Florida. Ludovic had no desire to ruminate over his rage over the next fourteen nights, keeping a tight lid on his seething hatred until he could pounce in January. Seven forty-five. Ludovic got out of the Twingo. Glancing at the windows in the apartment buildings, he could see no one. No spectators for what he was about to do. He headed towards the footpath that led into the wood. He had hoped there would be enough time to find a tree he could hide behind, so that he could jump out at the last minute. Fortunately, it was cold, with a fine drizzle, and there was no one out in the wood. Nothing but that dog, who barked twice some way off. The sound told him the dog knew the outing was over but wanted to run some more. It was trying to make itself heard over the music turned up loud in his master's headphones. Thirty metres away, further into the wood, Ludovic spotted the flash of reflective armbands. The bastard had changed direction, he was running off the path, through the trees, kicking through the dead leaves – to excite the dog, no doubt. The boxer barked again. Kobzham ran heavily, but still he covered plenty of ground. He headed around to the right behind the chestnut trees. He was taking a different route tonight. There was no time to think. Pumped on adrenaline and energy pills, his pulse at a hundred and thirty, Ludovic plunged off to his right, through the trees. He would have preferred to catch Kobzham face to face, leap out in front of him, give him a proper fright, stare him in the eye, but now he would come at him from behind, and the shock would be all the greater. In the inky darkness, he quickened his pace, drawing level with his prey. He could tell the dog had spotted him. He held his car keys in his left fist, sticking out between his fingers like claws in case the animal went on the attack. He approached his target without difficulty, ready to catch him by the collar. The idiot couldn't hear a thing – the hiss of his headphones had been audible some distance away. Ludovic caught him by the shoulder, pulled at his hoodie with one hand, as if grabbing a chicken or cat, and Kobzham stopped dead in his tracks, froze as if he had just hit a wall. Clearly panicked, on a reflex, he turned to see who had caught hold of him, what creature had gripped him in its claws. Ludovic was wild with rage. He wanted to confront the guy face to face, but suddenly Kobzham collapsed and sank to the ground, as if broken. Before Ludovic could comprehend what had happened, the dog was upon him. Trained or not, it was angry, and quick, sinking its teeth into his ankles. Ludovic struck at its muzzle with his fist and scored a direct hit, just as he would out hunting with a crazed beagle, separated from the pack. With its snout sliced open by the car key, the boxer shrieked high and loud like a hound that's been gored by a boar, or lost control of its prey. It scarpered, bewildered and terrified. Ludovic's hand was smeared in blood – the boxer's blood. The dog was badly hurt. Kobzham lay face down on the ground, motionless. What was going on? He hadn't even hit the bastard. He felt confused and overwhelmed. He had blood all over him, but it was the dog's. He knew not to bend over Kobzham. He stood waiting for a sign of movement, for the guy to get to his feet, look him in the eye. But with his prey out cold, his plan was meaningless. Ludovic was there in the wood, at a loss, half-crouching with his hands on his knees, feeling oddly out of breath. He stared all around. There was no one. It was cold, and the rain was coming down hard now. There was no sound but the clatter of drops on the dead leaves and the background hiss of Kobzham's headphones, hysterically pumping out some unrecognisable music, enervating as the whine of a swarm of bees. Perhaps now he should bend over his victim? He wasn't sure. He didn't want to touch Kobzham. Calling for an ambulance would land him in endless trouble. But he knew his first aid. Rugby isn't war but it gives a young man sight of another man down, the horrifying spectacle of a man collapsed and unresponsive on the ground. He wanted to check Kobzham was breathing, find his pulse, just to be sure, but he felt unable to touch him, and all this blood made everything strange. The little blue diodes on the guy's pulse monitor spelled ERROR, flashing like the hazard lights on a broken-down vehicle. Jesus, it was hard, even when they simulated the gesture in training, pumping two clenched fists into the mannequin's sternum, it was impossible, shocking and counterintuitive, even on a latex dummy, but when it came to it all you could do was concentrate on saving a life, think of nothing but that: Save. This. Life. Except that here on the ground was a life he cared nothing whatsoever about, that represented everything he most despised, that disgusted him. There was still no one else in sight, nothing but oaks and chestnut trees. He took it as a sign. The forest concurred. The trees closed in around him, as if to say 'Do nothing, do not touch, everything here will keep quiet.' The dog had fled, and there was no life here now but his own.

Now the running man is a man who has taken fright, a man racing to escape the twists and turns of a drama that has become a murder mystery, the running man is saving his skin, because he knows he has landed himself in a bad business that could lose him everything, in a world that is not his own, a world where he has no place. And so he runs, takes flight in the anonymity of the damp earth that swallows his steps. His tracks are washed instantly away by the rain.

Emerging from the wood, Ludovic slowed down, walked at a normal pace. He crossed the deserted avenue as if he were the only human left on Earth, looked up at the apartment buildings, saw their windows lit, their warm glow, the Christmas lights, and still no one was looking out, no one would see him. In this rain, the outside world ceased to exist.

The trouble was, Mathilde's old red Twingo stood out on an avenue like this. People would notice it. Luckily, he passed few cars and sailed through a series of green lights. The traffic was heavy around Porte Maillot, but he blended with the other vehicles now. He drove up Avenue de la Grande Armée, and the traffic was worse still. He circled the Arc de Triomphe at Place de l'Étoile and headed down the Champs-Élysées. He wanted to disappear in the mass of cars and, as luck would have it, the avenue was crammed with people who had driven in from all over to admire the Christmas lights and show them to their children. The traffic was at a standstill, all the way to Concorde. He could not believe what he had done. The idea that he had left a man for dead terrified him. His blood froze at every police or ambulance siren. Every car horn sent his fear burrowing deeper inside. 'It's impossible, I didn't do that, I couldn't...' He repeated the words like a mantra. He was stuck in the middle of the Champs-Élysées, with no way out. The gridlock extended left and right of the main thoroughfare. Cars began sounding their horns for the fun of it, like drivers in a wedding motorcade, others because they were desperate to move ahead. The result was a heady mix of stress and euphoria, with a sprinkling of festive fun. The millions of lights strung in the trees twinkled like a long river of diamonds. Unusually, the cars around him were all occupied by groups of people. He was the only person driving alone. He felt people were staring at him because he was the only one alone in his car and because he had just left a man for dead, and of course it would show, it would show that he had just killed someone. 'But I didn't kill him,' he would have to explain, if the dog reappeared or was found wounded and covered in blood, and if someone had seen him get out of his car and disappear into the woods, someone smoking at their open window, then all hell would be let loose. Yet he had done nothing. He kept his hands on the wheel, as if driving normally, at speed, though the traffic was stationary. He was still running away but running on the spot. He felt trapped, trapped by everyone around him, trapped by Aurore first and foremost, she had used him, she had been using him from the very beginning, though she had never asked outright. He never once realised what she was up to, but still he had ended up doing exactly what she wanted. If he had confided in someone close, a friend, they would have told him not to get mixed up in this. He had everything to lose by getting entangled in this woman's troubles. He had already lost the farm, and Mathilde, and the vineyard, and now he would lose what little he had left. For once, he saw it plain as day – he lost everything by thinking himself more capable than everyone else. Because he always refused any offers of help. He almost felt he should ask the people in the cars all around him, 'What should I do?' But he knew that to look at him, this big man in his little car, hunched so his head wouldn't touch the roof, shoulders broader than the driver's seat, no one would think he was desperate, and he would never admit it. Especially not to them, in the car right next to his, five kids playing their music at full blast, dancing in the seats of their BMW, ostentatiously passing a joint from hand to hand. Ludovic stared at them, and they didn't like it. The guys in front stared back defiantly and said something he couldn't hear through the music and closed windows. They were probably hurling insults. In Paris, there were people who would challenge you to a fight for a misplaced look. He would not turn away, but he lowered his eyes. Games like these were never-ending.

Dear God, all he had wanted was to scare Kobzham a little, and he had died of fright. There were guys he would have liked to call then – Jean, or Mathis, or Éric, the ex-fly-half, he always kept a clear head, or Thierry, his cousin, who sold agricultural equipment, or the English guy, Joss, or Bardas, the ex-teacher.

But what would he say? 'I left a man lying on the ground, I just wanted to frighten him, I didn't try to help him back up…' And then he would have to explain everything from the very beginning, over the phone, when as a rule, he never called anyone. None of them would drop him, he knew that, none of them would think badly of him, but they would all say the same thing: 'You've been an idiot.' When you keep your own stupidity bottled up inside, with everything else, it's never a good sign.

She ached all over this morning; her body was ordering her not to get out of bed. Since Richard's parents had arrived, Aurore had been hit with a ferocious case of flu, two days of all-consuming fever, and she had stayed in bed, lacking even the strength to sit up and read or watch TV. Everything exhausted her. It had been years since she spent two days in bed, not eating, never once getting up.

At the first symptoms, she had searched the internet, looking for miracle cures, and found dozens of remedies, too many. People always said the holiday season was the prime time for epidemics, not because viruses suddenly got worse, it was just sociology in action, all those families getting together in enclosed spaces, passing their bugs around.

She found the holiday season harder than ever. The week after Christmas, they would go to her parents for New Year, and by then Richard's parents would be gone. Before returning to the States they wanted to fit in a trip to Italy, to see one of his father's sisters. In Paris, they had to be taken everywhere, especially since they spoke no French.

She hated doing nothing, but she had no choice. She felt dizzy the moment she got out of bed. She reached out a hand to her bedside table to check a weather app and find out if this cold snap would last, but her head span even when she tried to sit up, and she fell back onto her pillows. The advantage was that she was home alone, they had all gone out. Richard escorted his parents like an ambassador receiving distinguished guests. Each time, he wanted to show them how magical Paris could be, how splendid and successful his life was here. He felt guilty for living so far away, no doubt, and oversaw every visit with a carefully planned programme of activities. This year, he had promised to take them all to the Disneyland Hotel on his VIP pass, and they had set off for two days in the Cinderella Suite – a two-day interlude in the land of fake enchanted castles. Thanks to Richard, they would watch the switch-on ceremony for the Christmas tree, and the festival of lights. The children were overjoyed to be visiting this supposed fairyland, but at least Aurore was spared.

Her festive dread was compounded by anxiety at the annual two-week closure of the business. As a rule, they closed only for the few days between Christmas and New Year. She missed thinking about the next collection – this was the first time she had no sight of what lay ahead. Everything was out of her control, and it pained her to know it. When she had announced to the team that the workshop would be closed for two weeks – at least – it was plain that everyone was more concerned than pleased at the chance of some time off.

Aurore lay half awake, floating between her dark thoughts and sleep. Time and again she reflected on being forced to relinquish her brand. Ten years of work erased at a stroke. She could not carry on under Fabian's and Kobzham's orders, she would not forsake her power of decision to do those men's bidding, but if she dropped everything and left, abandoned the staff and the workshop to their fate, she would feel desperately guilty. There was no solution. All she could see was that, inevitably, she would be beholden to Richard. She would be forced to let him take the initiative and call in his lawyers from Lathman & Cleary. The thought sickened her, but here too, she had no choice.

*

Around midday, she took a sachet of Fervex. The powdered drink smelled pleasantly of rum, and helped unblock a stuffy nose. Each time she took a dose she felt strangely light-headed, her senses muffled as if drugged. The Fervex took away the urge to blow her nose, or to think. After the second dose she was drenched in sweat. She felt as if she was floating out to sea on an inflatable mattress. Little by little she felt drowsy, and her anxiety ebbed. Flu was the perfect escape, in fact. She sank into a deep sleep.

Aurore awoke at two forty-two in the afternoon, though she swore she had been asleep for hours. The day was so overcast it seemed almost dark outside. Her phone showed a whole series of missed calls. She had not felt it buzz. Sandrine and Aïcha were top of the list, they would be full of questions, worried about the rumoured takeover, and the mere sight of their names awoke the guilt that had haunted her for months: she was a bad, unworthy boss. Richard's name appeared just once. But, strangely, Fabian had called five times. Five times in the space of an hour, though it had been three months since he had returned any of her calls. For three months, the bastard had been doing everything to avoid her. And now, just when she fell ill, he was bombarding her with calls on a Saturday, the first day of the holidays. She kept the phone close to hand, unsure what to do. She had no desire to talk to him, and certainly not the strength. Worst of all, he was calling from the mainline phone at the office. Fabian was alone at the office right now. He was Evil itself. She was in bed with a high fever and now suddenly he wanted to talk.

She thought he probably wanted to confess everything. Perhaps he thought he would take her by surprise. But why call five times in one hour? All she wanted was to go back to sleep, to forget everything until tomorrow. She laid her phone on the bed but felt the characteristic buzz of an incoming text. She opened the new message. Fabian again, from his mobile this time. KOBZHAM HAS HAD AN ACCIDENT. NEED TO SPEAK URGENTLY, WE NEED A PLAN B!

Suddenly the world was swirling around her. The fever, the Fervex, and a crashing wave of paranoia made her headache worse than ever. She rested her elbows at her side, closed her eyes and struggled not be drawn into the great black hole that yawned right before her eyes. She felt worse than delirious, a thousand images flashing through her mind. First, the text meant he knew that she knew. He knew that Fabienne Nguyen had told her everything, and that meant the accountant had been on his and Kobzham's side from the start. But the keyword in all this, the word that rang out in the silence with hideous foreboding, was ACCIDENT. Kobzham had had an accident. But what sort of accident? Was it serious? Had he killed himself or broken an ankle? There would be no talk of Plan B for a broken ankle. Was he dead? More than anything else, Fabian's blatant arrogance, his abject cynicism, took her breath away. He didn't doubt for one second that she would want to speak to him. For months he had been plotting behind her back and now he was calling her to discuss 'Plan B' as if nothing had happened, as if he hadn't been trying to shoot her down for months. What kind of filth had he become? Aurore found it hard to catch her breath. She sat up in bed, cupping her phone in her hand, staring as if hypnotised at the message that disappeared when the screen went black and reappeared each time she tapped it with her finger. Again, the word loomed large, the only word she could see now: ACCIDENT. She texted back. WHAT SORT OF ACCIDENT? and sent the message almost in spite of herself. She was trembling now, feeling unsteady as she waited for his answer, praying that he would text straight back to tell her it was nothing serious, a prang on his scooter, or while skiing, and straight away her dread would melt away, the obsessive premonitions, visions of criminal acts, and Ludovic's black look when he had clenched his jaw in the café, the barbaric rage he exuded, that expression devoid of humanity. But there was no answer from Fabian. Idiot. Each second lasted minutes, the wait was interminable, but she needed to know, she was burning to know…

Aurore jumped when the phone buzzed in her hand. NO IDEA! JOGGING. This, too, was repugnant. Three words, not even a sentence. It was flippant, vague – it betrayed the detachment she had appreciated when they first teamed up, and thinking of that, she knew that it tore her apart to lose him, to sever their connection. He had counted for so much, for years now. Going into business together had been fun, exciting, she had liked his evasive style at the time, he stood out from the crowd, but now she felt she could kill him.

How to answer that text? She was afraid to find out more. Most of all, she did not want to hear his voice. And it was up to him to call her, anyway, to explain himself. But they had too much to say to one another and the conversation was bound to turn sour. She got out of bed, steadying herself on the bedroom furniture. She pulled on her jogging bottoms and walked to the bathroom. The sky was desperately low and overcast. It was early afternoon, but already lights were on in the building, though not Ludovic's. The two windows of his small apartment were visible through the trees. He wasn't there. Or he was sitting in the shadows, mulling over his crime. No, that was impossible, that was the fever playing tricks. She wished she had his number. Her coquettish insistence that they should not take each other's contact details seemed pathetic now; she ought to have been above such things, because she absolutely must speak to him. He would reassure her, tell her he had nothing to do with it. The idea that this man might have played a part in someone else's death was atrocious, this man so close by, who lived there, right opposite her, and within her, most of all. Her complexion was white and livid in the mirror, as if she had dabbed herself all over with talc. She didn't feel able to go out; she could barely stand; even there in the warm bathroom she was shivering. She no longer knew what she should do, and anyway there was nothing to be done, so she went back to bed, and sank beneath the quilt like a person sinking into oblivion. It would all come to an end, everyone would leave her in peace, beyond the reach of this world, no more messages, no more Wi-Fi, nothing to stop her sleeping, no more problems, she just wanted to sleep and ride the carousel of her dreams. In truth everything would have been simpler if she had just gone with them to Disneyland.

When Ludovic opened his door and saw her outside on the landing, he had no idea of the effort she had made to get there, no inkling of how hard it had been for her to cross the frozen courtyard and climb the stairs. Unlike the others, staircase C was draughty; there was no door at the bottom, and the windows on each floor were unsealed. It was literally freezing there in winter. Aurore wore jogging bottoms under a tightly belted coat, and her old Converses for slippers. It was unusual to see her dressed like that, and he feared he understood why she was there. What he sensed when she melted against him was how scared she was, scared to talk to him, scared to ask what had happened, scared of what he might say in reply. Without a word, Ludovic rested his head on Aurore's and caressed the slender nape of her neck, holding her close. He could tell she was feverish, and sick. So was he, but it didn't show. Aurore stepped back. She detached herself from him to look into his face, saying nothing. Ludovic could see what was troubling her, the words she could not speak, the question she felt unable to ask. He saw that she knew, and that yes, Kobzham was dead. All that night he had told himself that perhaps the guy had got to his feet after he'd gone, that he had just passed out momentarily.

'Listen, I don't know what happened. It was so quick. I didn't even get the chance to frighten him properly. Well, no, I did frighten him, obviously…What did they tell you?'

Aurore wanted Ludovic to hold her again, close against him,

and not talk about it, but now he was the one who pushed her gently away, held her at arm's length. He stared into her face and asked if they had found the dog.

'What dog? Why are you talking about a dog?'

Ludovic took her firmly by the shoulders, still holding her at a distance. There was no tenderness, no show of affection now.

'Aurore, it's vital I know: did he die instantly, and have they found the dog? I slashed it, really badly.'

'Slashed?'

'Yes, I hit it hard, with a key in my fist. I swiped at it, there was a huge gash, and blood, and if they find his dog – I don't know, they'll wonder why the dog got hit and, most of all, by whom.'

Aurore pushed against Ludovic's arms to get close to him again, nestle against his body.

'But wait! So... you didn't kill him!'

She pronounced the words slowly, as if to convince some divine tribunal.

'No, I didn't kill him. But he is dead.'

She held him tight, clinging to this man with what strength she could muster, the devil she knew and loved, and there was fear and desire, death and delight in their embrace. She felt she could lose herself entirely, swirling round and round in these arms, transported in a spiral that would take them both down forever. They had become more than two chance lovers from different and opposite worlds. From this day forward, she knew she was irrevocably tied to this man, they were bound together, chained, by the insane, foolish act he had committed for her. She knew she had led him into Kobzham's path, and that had sealed their pact. She hadn't asked him to do anything, but it was her fault that the man she loved had brought about the death of the man she hated. Suddenly, everything became clear, and the clarity was terrifying. She was the guilty one. She wanted to turn out the light and sit on the bed, so that they could both stay there on the old divan and hold one another without speaking. All she wanted was for him to hold her tight, and to nestle deep in his arms. She was leading him now, to the bed. She led him and he followed, meekly. They lay down in the semi-darkness. Aurore lay on top of him, feeling strangely light, like a feather, and there they stayed, one on the other, speaking not a word. Aurore closed her eyes. She was finding it hard to breathe, her throat hurt and her nose was blocked, but still she detected that fragrance, her fragrance, the shower gel she had given him, the gel he washed himself with every day. She detected her own smell on him, and she felt at home in this man's arms. Opening her eyes, she turned her head to one side and saw the top of her own windows across the courtyard. The Christmas tree lights were flashing in the sitting room. She had left the bathroom light on when she went out, the bedroom light too. Her life was waiting for her there, on the other side, with the flashing Christmas tree and the festivities to come. Her family would be back tomorrow and yet here she was, in this small, shabby one-bed apartment, in this ancient, run-down building, a whole other universe at the same address, and again she was lost in the vast sidestep she had taken.

'What are you going to do?'

'Nothing, Aurore, there's nothing to be done.'

'No, for the holidays. What will you do?'

'I'll go down to my parents' place. Next week.'

She pondered the image for a moment. She knew nothing about his parents, the farm, his home region, the southernmost part of the Corrèze, the northernmost part of the Lot. They were meaningless to her, beyond the usual clichés about 'deepest France'.

'What difference does the dog make?'

'If it ran off, there'll be no trouble, but if it found its way home with its face covered in blood, people will ask questions, for sure.'

Ludovic sat up, taking Aurore with him.

'Aurore, I have to know whether the dog got away or not, I have to know whether Kobzham died on the spot, or not.'

'But what does it change?'

'Was it Fabian who called you?'

'He tried to call but I didn't answer. We texted.'

'So call him, now.'

'No. I don't want to talk to him. And I don't want to be asking him questions about the dog, all of a sudden!'

'Aurore, I have to know, because he could put two and two together. You have to tell me what he knows.'

With difficulty, Aurore shifted to sit on the bed. Her aches and pains were reviving, and she was overcome with cold. She took her phone from her coat pocket. There was a new message. Richard had called, five minutes ago, while she lay clinging to this man's body. She would listen to the message later. She felt good here, despite the fever, despite the fear, despite the shadows that loomed. Here at least she felt ferociously alive, her heart pounding blood into every last fibre of her muscles, her entire body pulsing with desire and fever. In the half-light she saw Ludovic sitting on the edge of the bed, a wounded statue, and the sight of this creature, powerful but vulnerable, indestructible but reeling, touched her even more than ever. She found him even more handsome. More than the fever and the fear, she felt an irrational, intoxicating desire to possess him, for them to possess one another, to make a new place, a new entity together, in an intense, heady, loving embrace. She sat with the phone in her hand. It frightened her to think such things; it frightened her to choose chaos over a simple, ready-made life, but she had been brought down, toppled, by this damaged man, this man who had dared to take real risks for her. For once, she was the one who would come to his aid.

'OK, I'll call him. But all I want to do is insult him, the idiot, he's the reason we're in this mess...'

'Aurore, we just need to know what he knows, so he's not one step ahead. Do you understand? Because if he suspects anything, well that'll be it. He could bring you down, and me with you.'

Aurore stared at Ludovic and said nothing. It astonished her to see how anxious, even panic-stricken he was. He seemed calm, but he was panicking inside. She found Fabian's last text and clicked on it to call him back, then she turned away from Ludovic and moved to the window. She wanted space, but not to leave here. She was utterly unprepared for a conversation with Fabian; had no idea how to begin. When he answered the call, she said simply, 'It's me.' A long silence followed and then, closing her eyes, Aurore summoned the courage to continue.

'What happened?'

'He collapsed while out jogging, a hundred metres from his place, in the Bois.'

'Who told you?'

'His wife called this morning, and his brother, too, from Hong Kong.'

'But why did you say he'd had an accident?'

'Because he had a heart attack.'

'And he died straight away?'

'How should I know? I'm not a doctor.'

They fell silent. Neither knew what to say next, how to say the things they needed to say. It was a shock to talk again after ignoring one another for months.

'OK. Listen, Aurore, I know the accountant has spoken to

you. I told her to tell you, but it's for the good of the company, do you understand?'

'And the dog?'

'What about the dog? No one gives a fuck about his dog!'

Aurore turned to Ludovic. He almost felt like smiling. Their eyes had become accustomed to the dark, and they could see one another quite clearly now. She was shining with relief. She wanted to show him, to tell him that no one was bothered about the dog. That the shadows were retreating. Ludovic lifted his eyes and saw Aurore smiling at him. He could see clearly that she was smiling. But Fabian carried on talking.

'Aurore, we need to raise some cash urgently. His brother wants to carry on…'

'But did he die instantly?'

'Aurore, I'm talking about what's going to happen next.'

'Because you've decided to talk to me again, now? You've been planning a coup with that guy for the past six months, plotting and scheming for six months to get me out of the picture and now you want to talk?'

'But we were going to speak to you. We were going to speak to you, we just couldn't risk anything getting out, that was all.'

Aurore was not ready to discuss this, partly for fear of saying too much, and partly because she needed time to talk to her lawyers. She couldn't think right now.

'We need to move fast, I've got two weeks to come up with a solution.'

'What do you mean, *you've* got two weeks?'

'Yes, *I've* got everything clear in my head. I'm waiting to find out when his brother plans to come to Paris. For the funeral, no doubt, and anyway, it's all finalised with the group. They were all in agreement as far as I'm aware.'

'Just stop! We're not going to work with these guys! You're

talking about taking up with his brother! Before Jean-Louis's even cold? You're worse than they are!'

Fabian let that go. Aurore regretted flying off the handle. For her, the first and most urgent thing was to sort out the lawyers, ask Richard for help and go on the attack, as quickly as they could, leaving Fabian no time to plot with Kobzham's brother, because if he went ahead she would lose any say in the company's future, and whatever power she still had. Fabian was silent, certain he held all the cards. He waited a moment, then made matters worse by asking coldly:

'Have you calmed down now?'

Aurore said nothing. She was livid. All she wanted was to cut the call, cut him dead there and then. After all, she'd gleaned the information she required and, as for the rest, the battle was only just beginning. She could clinch the case with Lathman & Cleary and they would bring the bastard down.

'Aurore, who's the guy you took along to try and frighten Kobzham?'

The question took her breath away. Aurore knew Ludovic was watching her, catching every crumb of her end of the conversation, but in a fraction of a second, in spite of herself, her expression changed utterly. She turned away, stared towards to the window, towards her apartment, as if she preferred Ludovic not to hear now, not to try and piece together what was being said.

'So who is he?'

'Why do you ask?'

'So I know whether I need to mention him, or not.'

'Mention him to whom?'

'Well, that's just it, I don't know yet.'

'Did Kobzham tell you about that?'

'Yes, and I can tell you he was beside himself – your trip to his offices, with some hired muscle to back you up.'

Aurore had no idea what to say or what attitude to take. She turned to look at Ludovic. He was staring her straight in the eye, and she was unable to suppress a shudder. Dear God, what kind of mess have I dragged him into…

And with that, she moved into the other room.

'Listen, he was an advisor. I needed to take advice. You were busy folding up the business behind my back so that you could bring our debtors in by the back door – I had every reason to be alarmed, you can see that.'

'I'm acting for the good of the brand!'

'Don't give me that. My co-director sinks the business so he can hand it over to a consortium of buyers and kick me out? You think that's acceptable behaviour?'

'Aurore, we need to grow, ten times over, we need to get into fragrance and cosmetics, or we're dead.'

'You weren't like this before, Fabian. All you're interested in now is the figures. Do you see what you're doing? Stealing my name, making me work for hire. You think I'm going to let you get away with it?'

'You're the one who turned up with a hit-man.'

'He's not a—'

'Well that's how it looks from here!'

Aurore returned to the bedroom. Ludovic had pieced together their conversation. He signalled to Aurore from the bed, though she had no idea what he was trying to say. Between the vile sound of Fabian's voice and Ludovic's strange, unfathomable gesture, she felt utterly lost. She walked as far as she could, to the bathroom, and tried to get some measure of control over the situation. She told Fabian she had been in touch with her lawyers, that they were examining the case, that she would make him pay for this. Fabian replied with superhuman calm.

'Aurore, don't even think about dragging this through the courts. You're no longer in a position to attack me, anyway.'

'What do you mean?'

'We need to talk face to face, Aurore. I need to see you, because this changes everything.'

'What changes everything?'

'Kobzham told me the guy you're hanging around with threatened him. And there's proof.'

'That's wrong, he was bluffing.'

'Come over, I'm at the office.'

'No. Not now. I can't. I can't go out. I'm sick, in bed. I've got the flu.'

'Tomorrow?'

'On a Sunday? You'll be at the office on a Sunday?'

'See you tomorrow, Aurore.'

She held the phone in her hand like a smoking gun. She walked back to the bedroom. Ludovic fixed her with a hard stare he could find no way to soften. Aurore was at a loss. How could she fight down her powerlessness, her fever, her aches and pains? She felt overwhelmed.

'What do you think? What can he do to us?'

Ludovic said nothing. He rubbed his cheeks and forehead to rid himself of the jinx, the persistent dread that worked like a poison, tensing, freezing the muscles in his face. He made as if to push himself up off the bed, but Aurore came over and told him not to move. He sat on the edge of the mattress. Aurore lay beside him and rested her head on his knee. The fear was all pervasive, but she nestled against him as if she never wanted to move again. Minutes passed, and Ludovic sat quietly stroking her hair. Then, staring out at the windows opposite, he told her she had better go home, they would be wondering where she had gone. Aurore didn't answer. She didn't tell him she was alone tonight, that there was no one home, that they had the whole night to themselves, just the two of them. She didn't dare confess the fact, couldn't find the words. Perhaps he didn't want her there, perhaps he just wanted to be alone.

'What if I slept here?' she asked, at length.

Ludovic had no idea what to say. Was she teasing him, or testing him, and why now? His confusion compounded his sense of unease. Nothing made sense. Given the circumstances, he could not believe she would provoke him like this, that she was prepared to risk sleeping here with him when her family were waiting for her across the courtyard.

'Well?'

'I don't know, Aurore, I don't know what you mean by "sleep"… And they're waiting for you over there.'

'I'm on my own, they've all gone away. I can sleep with you tonight, eat with you, be here with you.'

She stretched and pressed closer against his thighs as she spoke.

'My place is your place,' Ludovic reassured her.

Aurore reached her arms around his waist and nestled tight against him. She held him like her pillow when she was preparing to sleep. And she really was falling asleep. She was already fast asleep. He felt her slow, regular breathing. Gently, he stroked her face with the tips of his fingers. She gave no reaction. She was breathing like a child with a cold. Ludovic was stuck. He dared not move. From where he sat, he saw the trees outside in the darkness, and the top of the windows opposite, the regular, rhythmic flash of the Christmas tree lights. His chest hurt, and his throat, but he wanted a cigarette, wanted to reach out and grab the packet, but he did not want to wake her, nor to smoke beside her. But still, he needed a cigarette, because this business had left him panic-stricken. Not only the dog, but the knowledge that Kobzham had spoken to Fabian about him. Now Fabian could play them for a pair of fools. Now, Fabian held all the cards. The only way to find out what the bastard had on him was to corner him and ask him outright. But there was nothing either he or Aurore could do right now. She was sleeping. So he sat and brooded in the silent darkness. He thought it all through. He could picture the scene, Fabian telling Kobzham's entourage all about him, then talking to the police, reporting his so-called threats. The family would make the connection with the wounded dog, and he risked what he considered to be a fully justified charge – not assault but 'failure to assist a person in danger', maybe even involuntary manslaughter. His non-crime would come back to bite him, and Aurore too. She had no idea of the trouble they were in. To worry her further would achieve nothing. At worst it might drive her away, and he was afraid of losing this woman. He did not possess her in any way at all, but already he was terrified that she might leave. It maddened him that he was unable to move, unable to smoke, but he sat tight, still stroking her face.

Thirty minutes later, Aurore was still asleep, motionless with her head against his knee, quiet and peaceful. He had been running his hand through her dark brown hair all this time. It calmed him to stroke her. Like a drug. He thought of Mathilde asleep towards the end, how he had soothed her to sleep like a child. He looked at Aurore, at her fine features, her neck, her eyelids, her angelic face deep and far away in sleep. But she was not an angel, nor heaven-sent. Perhaps even the exact opposite. Sitting motionless for so long, holding his position, was making his back hurt. His legs, too. He ached all over. He was trapped. Aurore was actually hurting him. Perhaps, since the very beginning, this woman had instilled him with a kind of sweet poison. He himself felt toxic, sick. She was influencing him, manipulating him without a second thought – he could see that now and together, unawares, they had drifted very far off course, to the limits of acceptable behaviour. Ever since they began seeing one another they had plotted and schemed, sinking ever deeper, simply by following the natural bent of their shared soul. This affair was hurting them both.

The room was plunged in darkness. His perspective shifted. She had led him from the outset, he had done whatever she wanted, and more, but now they had gone too far. Ludovic understood why Coubressac had sent him a text that afternoon, why he wanted to see him on Monday morning. Perhaps Kobzham had been making enquiries, had found out where he worked. Perhaps he, or Fabian, had called Coubressac and demanded an explanation, to find out whether they really had sent someone out to La Défense, and to tell them the visit had not ended well. Anything was possible. He stared at the lit windows opposite, still stroking Aurore's face, running his fingertips over her features. It didn't matter whether she was using him, or not, that wasn't the problem. What he knew for sure was that she was here beside him and his role was not to alarm her, but to protect her, to keep her close. What she had given him was immense, immeasurable. If only this, to have her here, asleep with her head on his knee, and to stroke her with the tips of his fingers. It felt complete. It brought a deep sense of calm. Above all, he would not worry her, and the way to do that was always to anticipate her fear. Now he was sure: Fabian had put two and two together, the guy would be on their tail, and soon he would be blocking the road they were travelling together.

Five years, Ludo! If the guy was alive when you ran off, and on top of that there's a witness, well, you're fucked.'

'But I didn't hit him!'

'Sure, but you didn't save him either. The exact opposite. Cut your losses, mate, get yourself out of the shit. Hold on, someone else is calling me. Stay there, I'll be right back!'

Ludovic was sitting on a café terrace, his empty coffee cup in front of him on the table – a double espresso. On such a cold day, he was the only customer sitting outdoors. The waiter had switched on the heater, but he loathed the sensation of roasting under a grill. He preferred the cold and shifted two places along the terrace. Across the street, the grocery store was preparing for the evening rush. But when it was this cold, people preferred to shop in the warm aisles at Monoprix. Hardly anyone was out. He watched the Tunisian grocer going about his business. Ludovic had just bought two bags of vegetables. The team of four assistants spent their lives in the big shop, whose front was open to the elements. They froze in winter, despite the little radiator plugged in next to the till. From time to time, three of them would huddle in the cramped space behind the counter, less than a square metre, to feel the benefit of the faint heat. The huddle brought them together in more ways than one: they were always laughing together.

He had gone out without waking Aurore. He had slipped a pillow under her head in place of his knee and now, albeit in unusual circumstances, he rediscovered the satisfaction of knowing that someone was waiting for him at home, that he was not alone in this world. Solitude echoes loudest of all in the city. He would have thought the opposite was true, that living alone in the city would be a good thing, a blessing, compensation for all the hours spent going about as part of the throng. But no. The three Tunisians saw him cough and signalled from across the street. He should join them around the radiator, they joked, there was a space free. Never had he had such a bad cough. He signalled back that everything was all right. From where he sat, the bank of fruit outside their shop looked fake, especially the oranges and apples, which had a varnished, artificial appearance, as if they had been waxed or glazed. But the vegetables looked natural enough.

He had bought potatoes, leeks, turnips and celery. Not cabbage because it always makes such a stink. He would surprise her with a freshly made soup; she would wake up to the aroma of vegetables cooking. His ringtone sounded. Mathis was calling back. Mathis worked for his father's insurance firm in Brive, though he had studied law. He lived in Figeac. They'd been friends since they were eleven or twelve years old, played for the same club: Villeneuve. Mathis was bright and energetic, a scrum-half, captain of the team, the sort of guy who always spoke his mind.

'But you were working for Coubressac when you screwed up?'

'Mathis, I didn't screw up, I just wanted to turn him around to face me. I didn't lay a finger on him, he collapsed all by himself.'

'But you knocked him, slightly?'

'No, I barely even touched his shoulder.'

'Sure, but you were lying in wait for him, planning to attack him. That's a criminal offence, and I repeat, if you're guilty of failure to assist, and threatening behaviour on top of that, well, there's no need to spell it out. You take my meaning.'

'I know how it looks on paper, yes.'

'So it was for Coubressac?'

'No.'

'You're moonlighting? Working on the side?'

'No.'

'Listen, Ludo, I don't know what to say, but you'd better pray the police – or the gendarmerie, I'm not sure how these things work in Paris – don't open an investigation. Get down on your knees and pray they don't press charges.'

'Who could do that?'

'If there's any doubt, the police can do it themselves. Otherwise, someone files a complaint. But if he didn't die immediately, and you left him lying there, you're in deep shit. You do realise that? Are you sure you didn't hit him, even a single punch?'

'I just caught hold of him by the shoulder, that's all!'

'Yeah. But Ludo, I of all people should know, I've played with you: you'd never hit another player, but you can hurt them all the same.'

'I told you I barely touched him.'

'And who knew you were mixed up with this guy?'

'No one. Just someone who works with him. An associate.'

'That's bad. You're big enough to know what to do, but in a job like yours, avoid taking extra work on the side, you know that. You're treading a fine line at the best of times.'

'This has nothing to do with my work. Debt recovery is child's play, believe me.'

'Yes. So I see.'

'Fuck it – I've told you, it had nothing to do with work!'

'So who was it for?'

'A girlfriend.'

'Don't tell me you've fallen for some woman!'

'Mathis, I don't need you to preach, I just need advice.'

'Well, you'd better cross your fingers the associate doesn't start digging. Who else could connect you to this?'

'There's no one. No one apart from him.'

'But there is, Ludo…'

'Damn it, there isn't!'

'The woman, Ludo. She knows about it, does she not?'

Waking in the darkness with nothing familiar around her, she felt afraid. She lay huddled on a strange bed, emerging from a deep sleep, and when she opened her eyes she had no idea where she was. She panicked. She was still wearing her coat but shivering with cold. She sat up to shake off the bad dream, and everything came back to her in an instant: the lights in her apartment opposite, the unlit Velux windows in the mezzanine that told her the children were not there, that there was no one at home.

She glanced at her phone. No messages. Nothing. She had slept for over an hour, and the world had carried on without her. This small moment of time out had done her good. She did not know whether she should wait for Ludovic to come back, or go home. For now, all she wanted was to slip between the covers of this bed – she was so cold, and yet somehow she could not. She felt around the bedside table to switch on the old-fashioned lamp. There was nothing here to make her feel at ease, nothing that made her want to stay and settle in. She felt as if she was very far away, sleeping overnight in some makeshift hotel, as she had done the other night in Annonay, on that ghastly evening for which she felt, nonetheless, a kind of nostalgia. He might have left her a note, a sign, but no, this man was a creature of intuition, he could always figure things out, and he thought that others functioned the same way. She looked across the courtyard and felt an overpowering desire to be back in her own home, among her own comforts, her familiar surroundings, her bed. At the same time, she wanted to see him again. Looking around the apartment, she found nothing remarkable, nothing on the shelves, no papers, just a row of old books that he probably never read, a whole collection of Reader's Digest editions with their pseudo gilded spines, Maupassant, Dostoyevsky, but there were none of his things lying around, no ornaments, no photographs, no magazines. How could he live here for two years, leaving not the slightest trace? Just two pairs of trainers and some new leather loafers lined up beside the kitchen bar. There was nothing in the kitchen, either. But the kitchen cupboards were carefully arranged, with a complete set of cooking pans, and neatly stacked plates. In the fridge, there was only butter, some cheese, a tin of tuna and a carton of orange juice. It was strange to see the inside of a fridge so empty. She understood now what it was that fascinated her about him. This man kept to the bare essentials.

She was still running a fever, but her throat felt much less sore. She felt a little fuzzy – the Fervex still doing its work – and lethargic, weak. She looked across the courtyard again, told herself that it would be best to go home, she could make herself a cup of tea, go back to sleep, wait for Richard to call, and tomorrow evening they would all be home. She could wait for them there, comfortable and warm. At that moment, her phone rang. It was Fabian again. With scathing irony, he told her he had just spoken by phone to Tania, Kobzham's wife, and to his brother, who was following events from Hong Kong and would arrive tomorrow. He understood better now why she had been so eager for news of the dog. Aurore heard him speak, but the words escaped her, like a voice-over in a film, a voice from very far away. The dog had been picked up that morning near the Porte d'Auteuil, its mouth covered in blood. Some people had seen it from a distance but didn't dare approach it, and finally someone had called the police. It wore no collar, but was tattooed with a registration number, and Kobzham's wife had collected it from a veterinary surgery in Neuilly.

'Your guy packs quite a punch, to break the jaw of a great big boxer like that.'

'You're imagining things, Fabian.'

'I'm compiling my case, Aurore, piecing together my information, keeping it all to hand in case you set your lawyers on me.'

'Don't tell me it's come to this, Fabian. You know perfectly well what shit you've got us into.'

'Forgive me, Aurore, but you waded into this particular pile of shit all by yourself. My only concern is the brand, its future, nothing else. The rest is your business entirely. You've mixed everything up, Aurore... business, sex, and it's done you no good at all, as you can see.'

Exhausted, disorientated, Aurore decided he was probably right. She was almost ready to switch sides, take his point of view, admit that she was at fault. He was the one who had been plotting his takeover for months and yet, listening to him now, she felt she was in the wrong, she had sided with the bad guys, while he had been doing the right thing. He was the innocent one. He actually believed they had conspired to murder, and he could prove it. As she cut the call, she realised there was nothing to stop him contacting Richard, the police, but Richard above all. Fabian could tell him about Ludovic, the hit-man. She thought of the children. He could destroy her in their eyes, too. Kicking her out and taking control of the company was a side issue compared to this.

At the foot of the bed she found a box of aspirin and some multivitamins. Their love affair was hurting them both, she told herself, like the cold Ludovic had caught while waiting for her in the rain. He had passed it on to her when they kissed, and they would pass it back and forth forever, and never stop doing one another harm.

She lay back on the bed, and peered in the half-light at the old quilted bedspread with its outdated print. It occurred to her that she had been a little girl when this fabric was woven. Her grandmother in Brittany had this exact same bedspread. She curled up again, snuggling her head beneath the two pillows to keep warm. It felt good to fall asleep once more in the lair of this generous man, this hapless wild beast.

He looked through into the bedroom. Aurore was still sleeping, but the little bedside light was on now. She must have woken, then gone back to sleep. She had chosen to stay. Climbing the stairs, he had been certain he would find her gone, that she would have preferred to go back home.

He closed the bedroom door, then peeled and prepared the vegetables before stewing them in the pressure cooker. The small apartment filled with the timeless aroma of soup. A turnip, leeks and a bunch of celery. He had been right to leave out the cabbage. He opened the window and leaned out to smoke a cigarette. The smell of the soup wafted outside. After the soups his mother had prepared for months for Mathilde, it was his turn to make some for a very different woman, in very different circumstances. Once again, soup was playing a role in his relationship with a woman. As if that was all he could offer, a measure of rustic comfort. Perhaps this was just his way – he felt he existed only when helping others in need. Or perhaps it was the other way around, that invariably he made the people around him fragile, and vulnerable, like him.

The big apartment opposite looked more impressive still through the bare branches of the trees. He would never be able to offer such luxury to anyone. He had never lived in such a huge space, with so many creature comforts. He found it hard to believe Aurore would prefer to go back to sleep in his old bed, and not return to the apartment that seemed somehow to be waiting for her. He thought again about what Mathis had implied. True,

278

Aurore was the only person who knew everything and, if she turned against him, if she dropped him, he would have to watch them both – Fabian and her. He was their plaything.

She was there at his back before he realised she had got out of bed, though he prided himself on never being taken by surprise. She had walked over to where he stood and nestled close into his back to protect herself from the cold air outside. Ludovic stubbed out his cigarette and closed the window.

'It was the smell of the soup that woke me up. I felt like I was a little girl again. Ludovic, can I take a cigarette?'

'Not recommended for a sore throat.'

'Just one. I need it.'

Ludovic gave her one and moved away. She opened the window and stepped forward to let the smoke rise on the cold air. Then without turning around, as calmly as she could, she said:

'You know, they've found the dog.'

Ludovic turned down the gas under the pressure-cooker and switched on the big kitchen light.

'Did Fabian tell you?'

'Yes. He'd already made the connection, anyway. I mean, Kobzham had spoken to him about you, about the shouting, the threats.'

Ludovic joined her at the window and took her cigarette, sucking at it needily.

'And so you reckon that's his bargaining chip: if you stick your nose into his affairs, he'll hand me over to the police?'

'He didn't put it like that, but yes, I reckon that's what he's planning.'

'Bastard. And now, he's a free agent.'

'Kobzham's brother arrives tomorrow and he'll be taking over, I think. They worked together, anyhow. But I'm sure Fabian has already told him about you.'

'Yep. At the same time, he has no real proof. We had one shouting match, that doesn't mean a thing.'

Ludovic tried to put on a show of confidence. He could try and forget his conversation with Mathis, but he knew this business would catch up with him – and him alone – sooner or later. He dragged on the cigarette, burning it down to the filter in one breath, then stubbed it into the window box that hung, forgotten, from the guard rail.

'Well, listen. First of all, tonight, we're going to eat a good supper. We'll forget all about this for now, OK? And tomorrow is another day, as my grandmother used to say.'

He laid the table, sliced a plate of bread, folded triangles of kitchen paper. A humble table, but nothing was missing. Aurore shut the window and stood gazing out. She hardly dared think any more. She was hypnotised by the scene outside, the courtyard where nothing was happening. Two youths entered from the street. They lit the yard and climbed noisily up staircase C. Then nothing. Perhaps the others were watching her, ghosts behind the drawn curtains. She closed the curtains.

They ate the soup like a couple of runaways in a mountain chalet, far away from it all, gathering their strength for the many dangers that lay ahead. True enough, the broth did them good; the change in Aurore was palpable. The colour returned to her face, her cheeks were red. Ludovic cleared the dishes. He told her he had bought a cake for Christmas – a chocolate *bûche*. She watched him, admired the resolute strength he demonstrated each time he picked up an item in the kitchen. This man was reliable, trustworthy, she knew it in her heart of hearts. At least he would never change, while everyone around her transformed like shape-shifters, beginning with her own children. No one else seemed to notice, but they changed from month to month, revealing themselves as they metamorphosed. They grew taller and their faces changed, and one day even their voices would be different. Richard changed constantly, too, in his way. He accrued power and confidence, more and more convinced that everything revolved around him. Above all, Fabian had changed, from an ally to a traitor; and the others at work had changed, too. When things began to go wrong, they had become suspicious. They no longer listened to her, no longer respected her. Through all this, Ludovic was the only certainty, and since they had not one single acquaintance in common, she could tell him everything; there was no risk of him repeating it to anyone. Their shared intimacy was complete. Together, alone, against the world, so close that she could scarcely believe it.

After Ludovic's patisserie-bought dessert, they drank a coffee. Aurore encouraged him to talk. He had been living alone for a long time, knew no one in Paris, and had never met a woman here. It had been three years since she and Richard had made love. Fundamentally, they were very much alike. He was her twin, she was his, and she liked him even more at the thought.

'And you and your husband, you're the perfect couple?'

'Yes. Well, almost.'

She confided that she had not properly kissed another mouth, another body, with such desire, for a very long time. Not for years had she been touched with the eager longing that had seized them both. She and Richard slept side by side like brother and sister, nothing more. There had been tenderness between them, for sure, a bond, but that had retreated further and further recently, like an ebb tide. Talking to Ludovic, she rediscovered all the truths she never uttered, all the things a person never dares admit, even to themselves. She told him that after so many years together, it was impossible to pass from love to a life of routine without a sense of resignation. Ludovic thought that he would have liked to return to his 'life of routine' with Mathilde, all the same.

It was only ten o'clock, but Aurore wanted to go to bed. She would have liked to shower, but it was too cold in this apartment, and she wanted to feel warm. She took Ludovic's hand and led him to the bedroom. They had made love there in recent days, but now, even the simple act of moving towards the bed felt intimidating, far more awkward than the prospect of sex in Kobzham's waiting room, or under a tree in the courtyard. They moved towards the bed like two embarrassed children. At last Aurore removed her coat, her jogging bottoms and T-shirt, and slipped deep between the slightly coarse but clean sheets – like staying in the country. Ludovic found the idea of joining her there, now, impossibly hard to face, like a person diving into a river, who does not know how to swim. He kept his boxer shorts on and slipped between the sheets in turn. They lay for a moment, side by side on their backs, surprised, disturbed by this unaccustomed arrangement. It had been a long time since either of them had got into bed with another person, someone different from the other person they were used to. They were each very far from their respective habits, now – sleeping alone, for Ludovic, and sleeping beside Richard, for Aurore. As if they had to start all over again from the beginning. Make each other's acquaintance. They felt unable to speak, nor to take one another, to touch. At that moment, Aurore's phone buzzed. Her coat lay at the foot of the bed. Ludovic reached to fetch it and pass it back to her. She took out the phone and checked who was calling, before answering. It was Richard. She hesitated, then took the call, as if she were still at home, sick in bed. She asked how their evening had been, talking to each of them in turn. Ludovic listened but gave no reaction, though he was astonished at her apparent ease. She gave nothing away, in fact she lied to them all. She told them she had done nothing but sleep, that she had stayed in bed all day. What else was there to do? Ludovic was surprised at her aplomb. It was a sign that she placed him above them all, that the truth was reserved for him alone. She cut the call, dropped the phone onto the bed and turned to him. There was nothing more to say. She thought how much it hurt to lie. He was already thinking about tomorrow, about Fabian. She would have to grill him quickly and thoroughly, find out exactly what proof he had.

'Look, Aurore, I can take this. It's all on me.'

'What makes you say that?'

'I don't know, just that if things get difficult, you can say you talked to me about it, that one day you told me about their scheme. You were confiding in a neighbour, nothing more. Neighbours chat, don't they?'

'Not really, here, but—'

'Well, if things turn bad, I'll take the hit.'

She closed her eyes. Ludovic was stroking her face. She liked the feeling, the hand that she knew could caress her for hours at a time, the hand she was sure of, a hand that moved so gently, the long fingers framing her face, alighting on the nape of her neck, the hand that calmed her like a drug. And she fell asleep under the touch of his hand on her face, the same hand that had struck a dog and felled a man, the killer's hand that caressed her.

Ludovic could not say why, but to make love that evening would have felt utterly wrong, though for once they had the whole night before them. The ultimate irony. For once they were alone, in peace, with no other commitments, yet to take advantage of the moment would be a kind of sacrilege. He lay still so as not to wake her. He knew he couldn't sleep, there was so little space, he had forgotten how it felt to share a bed, and this bed was not wide. He had slept alone long enough for it to become a habit. He was prepared to spend the night like this, with his back to the wall, mulling things over and trying not to cough – his stubborn cold was no better, and he felt a pain under his rib cage, on his left side. He caressed Aurore's face with the tips of his fingers and felt instantly better. Outside, the big apartment stared down. Through his window, he saw the roofline silhouetted against the night sky, the lights flashing in the sitting room. The apartment was superb, but what had impressed him most was the wall of photographs there in the sitting room, photographs of Aurore, her husband, their children, photographs taken all over the place, in New York, Rio, in country gardens, on boats, in the snow. These people lived lives that were ten times his own. Lives in which he had no place whatsoever. He no longer knew whether he had wanted to help the woman lying next to him, or to challenge her. But he was sure of one thing: he risked tearing her marriage apart when they were a thousand times better equipped to fight than him, incomparably more stable and secure. Compared to that couple, he was a man of straw, a loser, incapable of holding his own. They would crush him. He wanted to draw the curtains, to hide the windows opposite, but it was impossible for him to move. Aurore lay sleeping, nestled against his body. And so he stared at the apartment that looked down on him in the night, with lights twinkling in the windows, and it seemed to him that it loomed closer and closer. He had been wrong to get mixed up with this couple, he had everything to lose. Their world was not his, he should never have got involved, they would grind him to nothing in the end.

It was their first snowball fight. Since that morning, the world had been theirs alone. They had driven at first light through the falling flakes, with no other cars on the road. At about five o'clock that morning, Ludovic had closed his eyes at last, while Aurore lay sleeping deeply at his side. He felt almost proud. Proud of how peaceful she seemed, how she had let everything go, while he had lain awake until the small hours. To have spent a whole night beside her was extraordinary, even more than making love to her. When he woke at seven o'clock, Aurore was already standing at the window, amazed at the spectacle of the tumbling flakes that transformed the courtyard into a cotton-wool fairyland, where people would toss snowballs back and forth. Her apartment receded in the darkness, behind the dense cloud of flakes. It became unreal, lost like an isolated house on a lonely moor. The snow fell harder, covering everything, the rooftops, the courtyard, the trees. Everything was white. Aurore marvelled at the sight of it. She turned to Ludovic. They should take his car and see the sun rise over the snowy countryside, witness the new, clean white morning. Ludovic would have preferred to make coffee, prolong the grace of this shared awakening, stay a little longer in bed, but Aurore said they could have coffee out somewhere, in the snow.

They left the A6 motorway about forty minutes south of Paris, at the forest of Fontainebleau. Since leaving the capital, they had driven through an immaculate landscape, on a motorway barely tainted by the passage of cars. The Île-de-France was waking under a thick, white blanket of snow, spotless, untouched. There was no one about.

The snow fell more gently now. The clouds released a few parting flurries, then thinned to reveal a broad blue sky. Sunlight sparkled on the uniform white world, and in the icy brilliance it seemed everything was born anew. They might have been a very long way from here, lost on the plains of the Far North. Before them, the forest stood like an unexplored land. Ludovic's tyres were unsuited to snow, and the small country roads had not been cleared. It was madness to leave the main routes, but he handled things capably, driving slowly, with no sudden jerks of the wheel.

They found a café open in Barbizon and ate breakfast with guests at the adjacent hotel. Aurore had fixed her hair in a chignon held in place with a pencil. She was still in her jogging bottoms, trainers and mis-matched coat, but she looked elegant, nonetheless. Every movement was a pose, balanced and graceful. Ludovic watched her as he drank his coffee. There were other people around them now and with a fearful lover's caution, he felt unable to draw closer to her. Sitting with her here, early in the morning, on the eve of the Christmas holidays, just the two of them, he felt quite overwhelmed. He did not deserve this moment, still less the freedom he granted himself in reaching to touch her hand. It was a bold move, in a restaurant dining room, in front of all these people, but he needed her touch. He was obsessed by the thought of Aurore's husband, her children, her parents-in-law. They were real, they existed right now, and they would take her back in just a few hours. She belonged to them, in a sense. He was only here by accident. And that was what he wanted to talk to her about now – the accident. He had thought about it all night, but he dared not spoil the magic of this breakfast, the generosity of the sun which shone down on the snow but left it unspoilt.

They emerged from the café into sunlight as bright as a morning in the mountains. Their footsteps creaked in the powdery snow, and they could not resist throwing snowballs at one another. They walked back to the car. Before turning the key in the ignition, Ludovic waited for Aurore to decide if she wanted to return to Paris straight away, take advantage of their morning road trip and call on Fabian. But no, she wanted to make the most of the few hours that lay ahead, enjoy the immaculate scenery before everything turned to mud and darkness fell once more. Away from Paris, she felt extricated from her life, her business, her family, as if she had erased everything, as if her problems had disappeared. Even her flu seemed not to bother her now, though her ears felt as if they had popped. All around her, sounds were muffled. Ludovic noticed that she had received several calls already, but she had simply glanced at her phone, then returned it to her bag. He did not wish to darken the lightness of the moment, but she worried him. It was alarming to see how Aurore seemed to have wiped everything from her mind. She said nothing about Fabian or Kobzham, nor the threats that were closing in around them. Nothing seemed to bother her. Perhaps she no longer needed him, perhaps, on the contrary, he was an encumbrance now. It would be simplest if she ditched him, got rid of him, detached herself from him one way or another. And that made him despair more than anything else – the thought that she might want never to see him again. He did not want to think of this woman as a short-lived fling, far from it, but he knew that it was never wise to get carried away. He knew that he had no one to advise him, to warn him to beware, hold back, and he knew he should have listened to his own counsel, exercised caution, kept his distance.

'Aurore,' he said at length. 'Tell me what we're going to do about Fabian.'

'I don't want to talk about that.'

'I know, but he's twisted, and sly, there's no time to lose. If we don't rein him in, he can quickly become dangerous. He's a piece of filth. If he can get me cornered, he won't hesitate.'

'I'll go to the office later when we get back.'

'I'll come with you.'

Ludovic wanted to protect her, nothing more, but something in his tone worried her.

'Ludovic, please, let's not talk about that now. Come on, let's see if the pond's frozen!'

'What pond?'

She guided him, tracking their location on her phone. They drove out of the trees and straight on for ten minutes, passing no other cars, before entering another part of the forest, or a different forest altogether, he knew nothing at all about this place, had no idea where she was taking him. The signs meant nothing to him and above all, he was concentrating on his driving. The road she told him to take was covered in virgin snow. There were no tyre tracks. There was no serious danger, but driving over the frozen ground with its covering of powdery snow was a delicate business. Everything was white. Aurore tracked their progress on her screen. She was aiming for a narrow track. She wanted to slide over the ice; it had been so cold for weeks that the pond was sure to be frozen solid.

'Have you ever been skating?'

'Never.'

At the Carrefour des Quatre-Chemins, Ludovic glanced at the screen in Aurore's hand to check whether he should turn right. At that moment, her ringtone sounded, and Fabian's name and photograph appeared over the map. Aurore rejected the call immediately.

'You should have taken it.'

'That's the third time he's called. I don't want to talk to him!'

Ludovic felt a sudden urge to snap at her.

'Aurore, if he's trying to get hold of you, something's bothering him, perhaps he has an idea. Don't let him get ahead of you!'

She gave no reaction, but focused on the map, enlarging it with her fingers. She was prolonging the carefree moment. She needed this release, to shake off all the tension, all the others who crowded her life.

The track led to a vast expanse of white amid the trees – the frozen pond, with its covering of snow. Ludovic cut the engine and they got out of the car. In front of them, at the bottom of a slope, a movable barrier lay across their path. A red sign bore a warning in white letters: 'Swimming prohibited'. Aurore took a photograph of it. She was amused by the instruction not to swim in the frozen water. She thought of posting it to Instagram, then realised that everyone would wonder where she was, and what she was doing. She decided to leave her phone in the car, as if even keeping it about her person might compromise her in some way.

They walked around the barrier and drew nearer to the edge of the pond. Timidly, Aurore pressed her foot onto the surface. Ludovic kept hold of her hand, told her this was not a good idea. She ventured a little further onto the ice, not entirely at ease. It seemed solid enough here at the edge. Ludovic held her firmly by the hand, taking care to stay on dry land. She just wanted to try a few sliding steps around the edge. She lifted the snow with the tips of her shoes. The ice was slippy.

'Come on, it's solid around the edge, it's really thick…'

'Aurore, there's no point tempting fate.'

'Don't you want to slide on the ice?'

'Not really, and I'm too heavy. Even you shouldn't be standing on it.'

'Oh, come on!'

'No.'

Aurore let go of his hand and slid a little further out of reach. She worked up some speed and was gliding properly now, back and forth. Ludovic had no desire to follow her, any more than he wanted to tell her to stop. He sat down on the jetty that extended out across the pond. He lit a cigarette and watched Aurore, the grace of her movements, the elegance of every last gesture, even the way she stepped forward now and slid, gathering speed, like a dancer. Even when she lost her balance, she did so gracefully, holding her head up, her neck outstretched like a stem of morning glory, utterly carefree once more. She was the exact opposite of him. He envied her youth, her elegance. This was a stolen moment from a life that was not his, a glimpse of coupledom. Right now, he felt he wanted to live with her, to never leave her, to be bound to her, but that could never be. This evening she would be back in her own apartment, on the other side of the courtyard, impossibly far away.

And yet, bound together they undoubtedly were, and more so than ever. He knew Aurore had feelings for him. She believed he was reliable, unshakeable. It would be a shock for her to discover he was not as strong as all that. He would do everything in his power to spare her that moment of realisation, though he saw clearly that events were overtaking him. Over the last two days, things had taken a sudden turn for the worse, just as they had with Mathilde's illness, and now with his mother, more absent each day. Ludovic dreaded confronting the thing he feared most, all over again: the loss of control, the knowledge that there was nothing he could do.

He knew Fabian had called three times, obviously to talk about the dog. If the dog had reappeared with its maw all covered in blood, Fabian would have no trouble cornering Ludovic, and

Aurore, too – the woman who right now was having fun out on the ice, sliding further and further each time. If Fabian attempted blackmail or went to the cops with something as concrete as a dog wounded by a jab to its jawbone, and all the rest, he would have no trouble saddling Ludovic with homicide. He would see to it that he lost his job with Coubressac, and he would scupper his relationship with Aurore. The fallout was never-ending. Fabian held them both in the palm of his hand. Aurore would be forced to give in, there would be no hope of fighting back, and if she dispatched her lawyers, Fabian would reel off the case for his conviction. Ludovic saw he was the loser, unless Aurore stood back and let Fabian carry out his plans. Ultimately, everything depended on her. His fate was in her hands. He rubbed his forehead until it hurt. It was cold out here on the jetty. He felt he was suffering a kind of punishment, damnation, for a few days of love with this forbidden woman. For a few days of happiness, he was paying a high price. He had brought about a man's death and could wind up in jail. Dear God. He felt cursed, in the grip of an evil spell that followed him everywhere. But how to rid himself of it? All it would take to release him from this nightmare would be to leave her there, to leave right now. The thought occurred to him suddenly. He could save his own skin if he left her here and drove away from this whole business, this vile business that was becoming more toxic by the minute.

'Aurore, I'm not used to asking for help, but it would be good to know why he's trying to get hold of you.'

She concentrated on gliding over the ice, more and more at ease, delighted by her sliding steps, forwards, backwards, just like at the ice rink. She hadn't heard what he said, and she looked supremely unconcerned.

'What was that?'

Faced with such carefree high spirits, he felt a flash of anger

– this had all come from her, it was all her fault, she was the one who had dragged him into this infernal spiral, from the very beginning. Not only had she rubbed his nose in a life he could never aspire to, never enter, but she had got him mixed up in something from which there was no going back. And the consequences were here, now, all around him. He knew that Fabian must have called Coubressac already, to tell him that one of his employees was getting a little over-enthusiastic or working on the side. He would lose his job, the police would be on his tail, and it was all because of her. And so yes, all he had to do, for it all to come to an end, was leave her right here and now.

He watched as she slipped and fell on the frozen pond, decided that he would not move, he would not walk across and help her to her feet. In any case, he was too heavy for this ice. Two steps, and he would sink into the water. He didn't even call to ask her if she had hurt herself, he would let her sink, and it would all be over – for a third time, the thought crossed his mind.

She struggled to her feet, brushed her coat, and glanced at him crossly, astonished that he had not moved. He hadn't even asked her if she was all right, but already she was laughing at her own clumsiness. Ludovic rubbed his face with both hands, closed his eyes and rubbed those, too, and his temples, his neck. His throat hurt, and his chest, he felt a burning sensation with each intake of breath. But above all, he could see no clear way back to the real world, the world of reason. This woman drove him wild. Since he started seeing her, everything had begun to unravel. He had everything to lose. Already a man was dead, and people thought it was his fault – he knew it was his fault – and if he ever got hold of Fabian, he knew he would be unable to keep calm. The fever burned, and he could take the confusion, the doubts, no longer. He just wanted it all to end. To get to his feet and drive away, that would be the simplest solution. But then there came a piercing shriek, short but shocking. The ice had given way, more than ten metres from the edge, and in a fraction of a second, Aurore had sunk in up to her waist. Worst of all, she was frozen, immobile, paralysed with fear and cold, and shuddering now, unable to breathe. Ludovic leapt to his feet, horrified to see her half disappear – she was only up to her waist, but it was still a terrifying sight. He moved across the surface of the pond, clinging to the side of the jetty, putting his weight on the structure, not the ice, as far as possible, but to reach Aurore, who had stopped moving now, he would have to let go. He walked carefully, almost on tip-toe, making no impact on the ice, sliding gently, but five steps further along the ice gave way beneath him and his whole body was sucked down into the cold water. He dropped down heavily – the fault of those blasted shoes, the shoes whose leather was too stiff, whose toes were too narrow, and, now they had filled with the ooze on the bottom of the pond, he was up to his waist in near-freezing water, unable to catch his breath. He smashed the ice in front of him with his hands, and he fought the pain to keep moving towards Aurore. He managed to catch hold of her and pull her towards him, wrapping her arms around his waist. His feet felt like lead weights, the icy water and the pond slime pulled him back with every step he took, he was unable to move, his body seized by the absolute, biting cold. It was hard as hell to hold on to Aurore and move forwards at the same time, and then he saw himself drowning with her, here in this godforsaken spot. The stupidity of it. Aurore was trembling all over, her body racked with convulsions. She was gasping for breath, exhaling violently, then gasping again, then puffing her breath out all at once, and then she began to laugh. She thought it was funny, the sight of them both struggling towards the bank, each as wet and heavy as the other. They were soaked from the waist down, and frozen, but she was laughing.

'You saved my life! You saved my life!'

Ludovic continued towards the pond's edge. He was not laughing. First, because he had been very afraid – afraid of drowning for real – and second, because a stitch was stabbing him like a knife in his side. He felt crushed by the cold. Already, he knew they must take off their wet trousers and shoes and dry everything in the car, with the heating and the fan on full, an almost impossible task. And now, with his practical cast of mind, he was working out how best it could be accomplished.

Back in the car, with the heating on full, their relief was total. Ludovic astonished Aurore by retrieving an old checked shirt, his camouflage trousers and a pair of wellington boots from the assorted bric-a-brac he kept in the back, both in the boot and the dusty space where the seats had been taken out. She peeled off her jogging bottoms and pulled on the coarse woollen shirt. It was too long; she wore it like a dress, though her thighs were left bare. Ludovic handed her his boots. She slipped her feet into them; they were huge around her slender legs, but they were dry and they kept her warm. Never had she worn such an assortment of things. The clothes were rough and uncomfortable, but they had saved her.

'Keep the boots on for now, while your trainers dry out. The jogging bottoms will never dry here.'

She rummaged amongst the pile of junk herself– a big sweater, which she put on; a cloth and a blanket, which she unrolled, revealing a hunting rifle in its holster, hidden under the boards placed across the floor in the back. So that was how he had killed the crows. Ludovic nodded, then wedged her shoes near the fan vents at their feet. His own feet were blocks of ice. After a while, they put their arms around each other. Ludovic was still shaking. The icy water had got into his bones, torn into his lungs. Aurore rubbed his body, but to no effect. His breathing was rapid, and still the pain was piercing his left side. His feet were still frozen, like the rest of him. For a moment, he could neither move nor speak.

'You should take off your sweater, it's soaked through all around the bottom. You can't stay like that, you're shaking all over.'

'It'll be fine, the top part's dry. It's all right. It's just the sight of you sinking all of a sudden... I think I'm in shock.'

Aurore held him close against her, and her fragrance filled his lungs. The warm boots and the thick sweater were reviving her; she was amazed at how intensely she felt their benefit. The transition from the icy water to the all-enveloping warmth of the car had calmed her, like a sauna in reverse. Meanwhile Ludovic was still shaking, with the stubborn air of a man who cannot admit he is cold. She thought of how hard it would be never to see this man again, and yet one day, they would have to part, perhaps even tonight. When he had pulled out the camouflage trousers and gumboots, when she had seen the gun, she realised more than ever how little she knew about him, that they had nothing in common, and yet now, at this precise moment, he was the person to whom she felt closest in all the world. She buried her face in his neck, closed her eyes and told herself, I've known him barely a month, but he has found the hidden door to my innermost self, the door only he could find. They held one another tight, lost for a moment, but beset with questions. She needed stability, direction – too much. She knew that her husband, her children, her work were signposts that marked out her life and kept her from the terror of floating aimlessly, as she had in the past. Whenever she'd lived alone, she had felt lost, incapable of making herself something to eat at night, of getting out of bed in the morning. As if she was drowning in time. She would be utterly lost if she broke away from the structure that had ruled her life for eight years. Even now, just this morning, the mere thought that her family were not at home, that she was separated from them, had alarmed her. Like walking over a void, with nothing under her feet. She clung to this man she did not know. She sat clutching him tight in her arms, but she wanted to call Richard, to know if he was still there, somewhere, loving her, and Iris and Noé too, even Victor her stepson, and her parents-in-law. It was idiotic and understandable all at once, and the feeling inside her was so strong. It was hard to admit, but she needed them so much, needed their presence in her life.

'Ludovic, I'm sorry, but I need to make a call.'

'To Fabian?'

'No, to my husband, my children.'

He made as if to step outside the car in his bare feet, so that she could call them in private. An extraordinarily delicate, thoughtful gesture.

'Stay, you can stay.'

Ludovic fought to control his trembling body. He could not stop shivering. He would have preferred to be outside the car and not hear her conversation, but he was cold, or afraid, or both, he could no longer tell. He listened while Aurore called the people she needed so much. He tried to make himself as small and silent as possible. He was left aside, discarded, forgotten. Aurore must have sensed this. She put her phone on the loudspeaker so as not to exclude him. To involve him in their shared lie. It embarrassed him to hear what was said. Sitting beside him, Aurore's voice changed. She spoke with a gentle, assured lilt. All at once, she was far away, very far away from him. She took his hand. Feeling like an intruder, he listened as she lied. She said she was with her accountant, they were working, and her cold was better. This afternoon she would go to the office and stay there until this evening. They would meet up back at home, or maybe go out to a restaurant. She said nothing about the encroaching apocalypse. Richard told her that he had called the firm of lawyers, he had even spoken to Lathman himself. He said he had briefed him, and they were ready to spring into action. What with the suspicious liabilities, the false accounting, there were plenty of angles of attack; they were certain to bring them down.

'No, Richard, that's not the way... At least – I don't know. It's more complicated than I thought. First, I need to talk to Fabian this afternoon, I—'

'Listen, Aurore, leave Fabian alone, act as if nothing's happened, and next week we'll launch a rescue package, freeze the assets. Then they'll be stuck. Once Lathman's taken a look at the case he'll be sure to put pressure on Kobzham for undeclared income, and VAT carousel fraud. A guy who imports containers to Amsterdam and Antwerp is obviously juggling the VAT.'

'Richard, forget Kobzham, please, just forget him. It's Fabian who's the real problem.'

'But we can get Fabian on embezzlement, bankruptcy fraud, like I said before. Don't worry, we can bring them all down, for good.'

'Please Richard, listen to me, we're not going to do this.'

'Don't worry, Aurore, we're so much stronger than they are. *Winner takes all.*'

Aurore cut the call, laid her phone on her bare legs and breathed a long sigh, as if she had just made a tremendous physical effort.

'I'm sorry about that.'

'About the lawyer?'

'No, I'm sorry for telling lies in front of you. And for lying to them, too. You'll think I'm a natural liar.'

Aurore sensed that Ludovic had withdrawn completely. It had never occurred to her, until now, that he might distance himself, or distrust her.

'Don't tell me your husband is actually going to bring his lawyers into this whole business?'

'I talked about it to him, just once, but I shouldn't have said anything. It was a stupid thing to do, a very stupid thing.'

'Aurore, we need to stop playing games. You know that if you go after Fabian, he'll come down on me. He can wreck my life, turn me over to the police. This is serious.'

'I know. But Richard will never understand if I do nothing. I'm trapped, Ludovic. Trapped. I have no idea what to do... I mean, could a dog injure itself like that?'

'Jesus, Aurore, are you kidding? And the meeting at Kobzham's offices? And the threats I'm alleged to have made: that's a hefty raft of charges, don't you see?'

'But I never wanted you to go and kill him...'

'But I didn't touch him, for Christ's sake!'

Ludovic found it impossible to calm down. He was cold, his throat was sore, and yet all he wanted to do was yell out loud. He contained himself, or his anger would explode. Keep a cool head... Calm the situation...

'Listen, if you throw the lawyers at him tomorrow, I'll be the one that goes down.'

'Ludovic, I can't be seen to hold back and do nothing.'

'This guy could pin a murder on me. This isn't a fucking game!'

'But you didn't do anything!'

'Involuntary manslaughter, failure to assist a person in danger... If he turns me in, I'll go down for five years, because I'll never have lawyers like yours, Aurore. Never. So this really isn't the moment to let me down. Aurore, are you listening to me? We need to think calmly, but you cannot let me down.'

They left the forest behind and found themselves in a small village with a surprisingly large square, flanked to the right by a smart upscale restaurant, La Toque Blanche – evidently a chic, gourmet address – and right opposite, L'Auberge, a traditional, rather shabby-looking place. After a glance at both menus, they chose the second. Pushing open the glass-panelled door with its gingham curtain, they sensed that all eyes had turned to look at them. The old inn was already full. Ludovic, in his camouflage trousers, could easily pass for a forester or a huntsman, but Aurore, in her huge khaki sweater, massively oversized gumboots, and her improvised chignon, was more difficult to categorise. This was an authentic local haunt, frequented by the village's game shooters, the sort of place it was a surprise to find just fifty kilometres outside Paris. Ludovic greeted the men at the bar and took their *bonjour* as a sign of approval. The owner found them a table, the last one available, at the back of the room near the fireplace. Aurore and Ludovic tried hard to look presentable as they crossed the room. Unabashed, the owner held up the menu board and recited the list of starters and main courses in a sing-song voice. They both chose the pot-au-feu. The owner removed the board with a cheery '*Ça marche!*' He directed Ludovic to the wine list.

'I'd go for the Gamay if I were you.'

'Well then, let's say you're me.'

Aurore stared at Ludovic. Since they first met, she had envied his apparent self-assurance, but she saw now that it was all a show. He was pale, and unusually withdrawn. He sat with his head bowed, running his hands continually over his face.

'It's all right, Ludovic. I'm here.'

The owner poured a little wine into the bottom of both their glasses, for them to taste it. Ludovic drank his down all at once and held out his glass for a refill.

'Will that do?'

'Just the one bottle? Not sure…'

Aurore could see Ludovic was doing his best to keep up appearances. He was trying not to let it show but his movements were tense, his face set hard, and she knew he was panicking inside. He drank two glasses one after the other. She searched for something to say, something reassuring. She took his hand.

'Ludovic, what would you do in my place?' she asked, finally.

He knew she wanted to attack Fabian. Her priority was to save her business, and while he would do nothing to stop her, he would show no approval, either. The choice was hers.

'That's up to you, Aurore.'

A waitress brought them a cast-iron pot brim-full of steaming beef and vegetable stew. The owner came over just as she was about to serve them. Already, he was treating them like all the other customers – his regular clientele. He supervised the placing of the meat and vegetables in their dishes, showed the waitress where to sit the marrowbone, went off to fetch the toasted baguette and coarse sea salt himself. A comforting ritual. He noticed that the bottom of Aurore's sweater was damp and suggested she take it off and dry it in front of the chimney. Aurore did as he suggested, embarrassed to be seen in the coarse checked shirt that was none too clean. Ludovic, for his part, took off his shoes and carried them barefoot over to the hearth, where he placed them against the rail. The owner pondered aloud on the reasons why they had got so wet, drawing snide glances from the rest of the room. A stag hunt gone wrong? An exhausting ride? He stared at Aurore and clapped Ludovic on the shoulder as he returned to his seat.

'Ah, but your sweater's wet too, you must get that dried out!'

'No, really, it's only around the bottom, and I've been wearing it for a while, it's damp but warm now!'

'You can never be too careful, don't want to catch a chill, come right up close to the fire, there now.'

The man's jocular, over-familiar tone caught them both off guard in this place where they knew no one at all. Aurore and Ludovic found themselves caught up in the illusion that they were indeed a couple, like any other pair of regular diners. Ludovic filled their glasses as soon as they were empty – Aurore's as well as his own. He wanted her to drink, not to influence her, but to see how far she would go. Halfway through the pot-au-feu, with the bottle finished, the owner fetched a second, automatically, and offered to serve Aurore another glass. She nodded enthusiastically.

'So, you're here for the Daguenau hunt?'

'Don't know anyone by the name of Daguenau,' Ludovic replied.

'You weren't here for the boar?'

'No. We prefer to shoot crows.'

The owner gave a half-hearted laugh at what was clearly intended as a joke, though he hadn't understood. Listening to them both, Aurore thought again about the holster she had seen in the back of the car, the rifle he had used to kill the birds, and it struck her suddenly that Ludovic was armed, like most of the men here, so it seemed.

'Like to know how we prepare crows here?'

'Don't tell me you cook crows?'

302

'Don't tell me you've never heard the recipe for *corbeau-au-feu*? A broth of the usual vegetables, then add your crow, plucked and prepared. They're a bit on the tough side, but it's easy enough to tell when they're done. Just add a good, big stone. When the stone is soft, the crow is cooked!'

Aurore was perplexed by the man's peculiar sense of humour, and sickened by the laughter that rose from the other tables, who were listening in. Ludovic forced a grin, but the stitch was still knifing his left side, as if the icy water itself had pinched a nerve or punctured a lung. He struggled not to show it, but the dip in the frozen pond had affected him far more than Aurore. His fever had spiked, reinforcing the sense of unreality all around him. Everything was strange, and he sensed that for once, he was losing control. He had scarcely finished his glass when he saw Aurore filling it up again and emptying her own, which she refilled, too. He didn't know what she expected of him, nor by what mysterious means she was seeking to rid herself of him.

Alcohol swells the present moment, pushing everything else aside. With wine, there is no future, no past, only the here and now. The only way to avoid reality was to make this lunch last, and never leave. And so they had cheese, and dessert, and two coffees each. Aurore lost all sense of what to do, what to say to Fabian, how to fight him. She was haunted by the vision of the rifle, by the spectre of Kobzham sprawled on the ground in the Bois, and so she concentrated on this meal, this rift in time and space from which she wanted never to emerge, sitting across the table from this man who was so distant, and so close.

While they waited for their clothes to finish drying, the owner invited them to sit in a small room at the back where there were two armchairs and another open fire. Cocooned by the quiet, comforting warmth, Aurore felt suddenly that they would never see one another again. She tried hard not to let it show, but the dark side room felt to her like a kind of antechamber, a departure lounge, as if somehow the moment had come for them to part. To erase the feeling, wipe it speedily from her mind, she wanted this man to talk, to tell her about himself, here in this room, she wanted them to know everything about one another, and she asked him to tell her his most cherished, heartfelt dream, now or in the past, it didn't matter, what was his dream? He told her his dream was to go back home and live in the country again, to start a business, an adventure centre or a gîte in an old carding shed in the Célé valley. That was world enough for him, and never had he wanted to go back so much as now, this minute.

Again, they both realised they had nothing whatever in common, and yet they were twinned in solitude, shared the same sense of isolation. He asked her where Richard was from, and he knew as she spoke that his was a world he would never understand. Richard had been born in the state of Georgia. He had lived in Chicago, Singapore, London and finally Paris. His dream, a few years from now, was to go back to the States, take on a new, even more high-flying role. They would certainly leave Paris one day or divide their time between the two countries. The prospect daunted her; she was worried for the children, how they would shuttle backwards and forwards. She painted the picture of a way of life he could never understand. He had never been to the States; the very thought of it seemed far-fetched. Several times, she said 'I'll show you the photographs later, at the office.' When he saw her drop into the lake, it had occurred to him that she wanted them both to sink down and drown together, for the story to end there. And then there was the way she had looked at the rifle and stroked it with her hand, in fascination. And now he saw no reason at all why this woman should be interested in him, beyond her need for his help in ridding her of all the people who stood in her way. But what he also saw, now, was that the two people who burdened her more than anything in this world, her two worst enemies, were their own two selves. Her very worst enemy was the couple they had made, she and he. He poured more wine, filled her glass, one way to see whether thoughts of this kind had ever crossed her mind, or perhaps whether she wanted to rid herself of someone else, why not Fabian? Perhaps she thought it would all be as simple as it had been with the crows. He no longer understood her at all.

Now that she was tipsy, she seemed bright, almost happy, and the more they talked, the more distant he realised she was. Filled with sudden distrust, he sat waiting for the moment when she would ask him to leave her, to give her some space. She was putting off their return to Paris, making the most of these last moments, a kind of farewell ceremony, and after this, she would cast him off like a piece of shit, ditch him this very evening. And she could do it because she was certain she could get Fabian out of the picture and keep hold of her company. With Kobzham gone, she had nothing to fear; she was the one who would come out on top, while Fabian landed in jail, just like him. The cherry on the cake.

This was all his fault. He had wanted to be part of a world that was not his, a world of rich, wily predators, and he had paid the price. Paris was beyond him, the people, the city; he was in way over his head, he felt small, utterly insignificant in the face of the city dwellers' arrogant cunning. And now, he felt like an idiot, trapped. The pain was growing inside. Every breath was like a knife between his ribs. Worse still was his new understanding that she no longer needed him. On the contrary, he was a burden to her now – a problem vis-à-vis her husband, and Fabian, and the police. A problem. He was just an awkward neighbour she'd be better off without, and that was why she had lured him to the pond.

'Ludovic, you scare me when you look at me like that.'

With a disappointed frown, she reproached him for being absent, serious, gloomy, for not making the most of the moment, and she took his hand again. She smiled and said simply, 'Shall we go?', and he did not feel much reassured.

He followed her like a condemned man follows his executioner. They returned to Paris under dull, grey clouds. The sun had disappeared, and the snow cover was receding in the fields. Along the sides of the road it had become a brown sludge. The virgin snow of that morning was soiled, the pristine white coat turned to mud. The closer they came to Paris the more Aurore felt things were catching up with her. She looked at herself in the mirror. She wanted to face facts. She looked pale, read the fear in her face, felt the dread inside her. It annoyed her, and she clapped the sun visor back against the roof. She knew that she would find it all impossibly hard to face. Everything seemed impossible. Worst of all, as it seemed to her, was the knowledge that once again she held all the cards, right there in her hand. But she was forced to choose between three unbearable losses, three bereavements of a kind: the loss of her company, the loss of her associate, or the loss of this man, the new factor in her life. But to keep him, this man upon whose leg she was resting her hand, she must not only trample her husband underfoot, but also, and above all, set free an associate who had been plotting against her for months. And in so doing, she risked letting her company slip between her fingers. She loved to rest her hand on Ludovic's thigh. She glanced at him. He was absorbed in his driving, his face expressionless, closed. He was somewhere else, almost wholly absent. She loved him, this man sitting beside her. She loved his physical presence, his paradoxically discreet bulk. She had never known anyone so attentive and thoughtful, so delicate, as if he was fragile and vulnerable inside. And perhaps he was. She was ready to protect him, defend him, and at this moment all she wanted was to reassure him, to tell him that she would not let him go, she would not leave him, ever, though they did not live together – far from it. But she could not imagine, one day, making the choice never to see this man again, never to have him there at her side.

'Ludovic, are you OK?'

He did not answer, just gave an unconvincing tilt of the head. He wished he could show more confidence, but he saw no way out of this mess, no way at all, and more than anything, he saw no way to reassure her, to ease this woman's anxiety.

'Ludovic, there's something I've been wanting to say... Lean on me.'

He stared at her in disbelief, as if he hadn't understood, as if he were utterly unable to grasp how she might protect him, when everything was getting worse, when the darkness was gathering all around them. He returned his gaze to the road ahead. But when he thought about what she had said, he saw her words as a kind of promise, a promise he had never looked for, or expected.

Ludovic stood looking at the workshop façade and saw at last just how much was at stake. Above the portico, an iridescent sign bore the name AURORE DESSAGE in neon letters. An impressive sight. Aurore told him to park in the delivery bay, behind the black Smart, 'Fabian's car'. They stayed sitting in the Twingo with the engine off, knowing full well that to get out of the car would mark the official opening of hostilities. She took his hand. He felt exactly as he did on the threshold of an appointment for work, making ready to face every eventuality, never knowing which way things might turn. He was marking a pause, assessing the situation, wondering how to present himself. He knew that pre-meeting mindset by heart, but today he felt his presence was unjustified. More than ever, he felt he was crossing a minefield. The black Smart came as no surprise. A guy like Fabian would drive that kind of car, slightly battered, covered in small nicks and scratches, the sign of an inconsiderate motorist who parked any old how. An unscrupulous, careless type.

'But apart from anything else, is he clean?' he asked suddenly.

'What do you mean, "clean"?'

'Does he… I don't know, does he have any weaknesses? Gambling, alcohol, drugs? He's cornering us for his own entertainment, but perhaps there are things we can corner him with, too.'

'No. We need to stop confronting him, Ludovic, dial down the tension. I've had enough of this game.'

'But the game isn't over, Aurore. We're in it right over our heads. If you can give me anything I can use against him, I swear I'll hit him with it, hit him good and hard.'

'No, Ludovic, we're going to do this differently.'

Aurore opened the passenger door and got out of the car. Ludovic followed close behind. In front of the building, she took a big bunch of keys from her bag and used the biggest one to unlock the door. Inside the entrance, she punched in a code, but it seemed the alarm had already been switched off. Ludovic followed without a word. They crossed the whole of the ground floor to the showroom on the right, a spacious area with tall mirrors and clothes rails. Half a dozen antique fauteuils were covered in spotless white leather. Aurore sprang into action. She seemed quite different now. He watched as she transformed before his eyes, taking off the huge boots, the terrible old sweater and shirt. Then she chose several different dresses, tried on one in black, then another, still black, but shorter. Ludovic was still in his damp jacket and sweater. He didn't dare sit down in this room where everything was pale and immaculate. The walls were painted white, with beige cornices. He stared around as if assessing the value of the property. The room covered at least a hundred square metres. From where he stood, he could see a broad, industrial-style staircase leading to the upper floors, a designer creation in steel and copper. Ludovic walked around the room, not daring to feel the fabrics of the designs arranged in rows along the wall, on gilded hangers. In a space surrounded by mirrors, Aurore was checking the cut and fit of the dress she had chosen. Then she chose a pair of shoes from a dressing room concealed behind one of the wall-mounted mirrors. With these, and the luxurious fauteuils and gleaming copper, everything in the room spoke of perfection and attention to detail. The infinite reflections made it seem even bigger. Wherever you looked, the space was multiplied into infinity. Ludovic imagined the intimate pride Aurore must feel as the mistress of this world-within-a-world – and the unthinkable prospect of being forced to give it all up.

In one way, he found it all quite hard to believe, though he concealed his astonishment. Here, at the heart of her kingdom, she looked even more impressive than usual. This woman had succeeded in building an impressive business, her own small empire, and he felt like a midget by comparison. Even here, standing still in this cold room, he was pouring sweat and running a high fever. He felt the blood beat in his temples, and his vision scattered and span like a kaleidoscope. At last, he dared to sit in one of the armchairs, but even seated the pain was still there, as if a shard of ice from the lake was working its way into his spine. Every movement hurt. Aurore crouched in front of him, leaning back on her heels. She was more fascinating than ever. In her fragile situation, faced with the threat that all this might be taken away from her, that she might find herself locked out of her own company, she cut a poignant, spirited figure.

'I think it's best if I go up there alone.'

'Where is he?'

'His office is on the third floor. You can wait for me here.'

'Whatever you think best.'

'I'm afraid that if he sees you, he'll feel obliged to make things really difficult.'

'He's going to make things really difficult anyway.'

Aurore leaned her head against his knee. Once again, Ludovic was there for her, close beside her, not letting her go. She sighed. She would have preferred him to stay with her, come upstairs with her. She would have felt stronger with him at her side, as she had when they went to see Kobzham.

'This is just so awful. I'm sorry to put you through it.'

'Aurore, I don't know what you're planning to discuss with

311

him, but if he wants to pin Kobzham's death on me, I'd rather he told me to my face.'

She knew Fabian well, the pride he took in never losing his cool. She was afraid of how both men might react.

'Have you got your phone with you?' she asked him.

'Yes.'

'Call me.'

Ludovic frowned.

'You know I don't have your number…'

Aurore took his phone tapped in her own number and answered the call.

'There, you see? It's as if you were with me, in the room.'

She walked out, holding her phone in her hand, and climbed the staircase. Ludovic pressed his phone to his ear, listened to the sound of her steps on the stairs. An image flashed in his mind's eye – a hunt along the banks of the Célé river, when the guns used their mobiles to communicate in walkie-talkie mode. He listened as she climbed the three flights of stairs, heard the sound of her heels echoing along a corridor, on the parquet floor. Finally, he could make out that bastard's voice, though he was hard to picture for the moment. The voice was distant, and interrupted by the rustle of Aurore's dress, until she entered his office, so it seemed, and placed her phone on a table. She would be sitting opposite Fabian, saying nothing, though Ludovic could tell from her breathing that she was nervous. Fabian said simply:

'Did you come alone?'

He could hear the snake clearly now. At last he had something to hold on to, if only his voice.

'You didn't bring your new boyfriend along?'

Ludovic had the vile bastard at last, in the palm of his hand, right there, three floors above, though he was entirely at his mercy.

'Fabian, how long have you been scheming to set this up?'

'What are you talking about?'

'Sinking the company so that you can take it over with them. How long since you hatched the plan?'

'Now Aurore, you're not looking at this the right way, at all.'

'Go on then, explain it to me.'

'Listen, all this, the business side of things, I honestly believe you're out of your depth, and that's perfectly natural. From the very beginning, I've been here so that you can create your designs, your collections, in peace. So that you don't have to worry about a thing, do you understand? What matters is that you should feel able to come up with your designs, and not bother your head about anything else at all.'

'You must think I'm very stupid, Fabian. For six months, you've been doing everything in your power to bring us down, six months spent bringing this business to its knees, so that you can scoop it up, bit by bit.'

'What on earth do you mean?'

'What you're doing, Fabian, is not only vile, it's criminal: overstating liabilities, corrupt practices, breach of trust, bankruptcy fraud, does that mean anything to you?'

'I see Madame has paid a visit to her lawyers...'

'I can put you behind bars for this.'

'No, Aurore. No. I don't think so. Jean-Louis's death changes things quite considerably. Let me see if I can paint a picture of how things stand...'

'Absolutely. Paint a picture, go right ahead!'

'Well, in fact, I can do better than that.'

Ludovic heard Fabian get to his feet and spread out a stack of papers.

'There. Now, what do you say?'

Silence. Ludovic thought the call had been cut, then heard

Fabian hand something to Aurore. His voice was dripping with irony.

'Photographs. The camera never lies. No, wait, I've plenty more!'

'Where is this?'

'Boulevard Suchet, just across from the Bois de Boulogne.'

Aurore had clearly decided to cut the call. Perhaps it cut out all by itself, Ludovic had no way of telling. It infuriated him not to hear the rest of the conversation. Though he had heard all he needed to. He wanted to get up out of the too-comfortable armchair, but the knife-blade in his back was digging deeper and deeper. He found it hard to unbend and stand up straight. Wherever he looked he saw himself, reflected to infinity in the mirrors, hunched over, clutching the small of his back, his swaying stance multiplied every which way. He was unsure what to do. To join her would be an act of stupidity, one more, and he gasped at the thought. He imagined the angry words flying overhead, voices would be raised, they would be shouting, exchanging insults. But no, there was no sound. Even when he held his own breath, there was nothing to be heard. Perhaps she was waiting for him to come upstairs, for him to scare Fabian, like Kobzham. She was expecting him to burst in with his shotgun and rid her of the last man who stood in her way. The car was there, outside the window, and the rifle was inside, she knew it was there...

He called her number, but it went straight to voicemail. He had no idea how Aurore would react now this other piece of shit had played his joker, on top of the eyewitness accounts from Kobzham's assistants, and Kobzham's calls to Fabian to tell him about the threats. There would be other evidence, too, no doubt. Kobzham's entire life had been lived under surveillance cameras. Obviously, that bastard Fabian was going to accuse him of murder. He was master of this game. If Aurore took him to court, he'd tell all, and Ludovic would be investigated. Fabian would go down for bankruptcy fraud, and only Aurore would come out alive. Only Aurore… And that was why she wasn't picking up.

He felt he might beat his head against the wall, but everywhere he turned, he saw nothing but his own image, only himself, bent double, in his coarse, filthy clothes. He was his own worst enemy, the figure pointing at him in the mirror. This was all his fault. He could not stay here. He could not let the rest of them decide his fate. He would not go down because of a piece of filth like Fabian. The room was spinning. He stood with his hands on his knees, trying to catch his breath. He had to get up the stairs and confront them, he had to punch that smug shit-face, the stupidest thing he could possibly do, but the thought of his life in that bastard's hands was more than he could bear. He closed his eyes. He took short, sharp breaths, and his anger welled from deep inside. He made ready to run up the three flights of stairs, burst into that guy's office and lay him out flat, perhaps even the pair of them, he was boiling with rage, heightened by his fever and all that he had drunk in the middle of the day. He took a deep breath and straightened up, then felt the dagger plunge into his back, and the twist of the blade forced him to his knees. The pain was so bad he fell forward onto the cold tiles, shards of ice on a frozen pond that opened beneath him and dragged him down to the bottom.

The scorpion has no consciousness as such, no form of intelligence or reasoning, but while scorpions don't think as we do, they know how to fight. Scorpions kill the instant they are attacked. They have two reflexes, and only two: to respond, and to kill. The same is true of the large mammals that venture out onto the plains. With little cover in the form of trees or shrubs, predators are no longer camouflaged, and their prey is clearly visible, too. There are many splendid animals to be seen, and the buffalo are among the most impressive of all, especially when a herd is on the move, hundreds at a time. Nothing can stand in their way. They are far bigger, and far heavier than any of the fast-running animals. Each weighs about a ton, and though they can run at almost sixty miles an hour, there is one rule they must never forget: do not stand alone. Clearly, the lionesses and cheetahs are powerless against a solid mass of hundreds of buffalo moving as one, batting their attackers away with their horns. But when a single buffalo becomes separated from the group, we know its time is up. The lionesses and cheetahs throw themselves upon the solitary creature and, inevitably, it will die.

Never before had he spent two entire days in bed watching television. Over the holiday season, nature documentaries and old films filled the schedules all day long – animated films, too, but mostly wildlife documentaries, superb images of magnificent beasts hunting in packs. Big cats, their movements detailed in slow motion, single-minded killers intent on spreading death without shame or hesitation, under the watchful eye of the cameras. Ludovic stared at the screen. Knocked out by the opioids he had been taking for two days now, he lacked the inclination or the strength even to switch channels. The buffalo fascinated him, its hide slashed all over by the claws of a pack of lionesses, its legs folding beneath it as it sank to the ground. The narrator's tone hinted that this would not end well.

The day before yesterday, Aurore had gone out to collect his prescription. She had prepared each dose in a plastic pill calendar. It was complicated. The doctor had prescribed antibiotics and ointment, a paracetamol and codeine painkiller, and an opioid analgesic, plus patches to apply if he experienced further pain between doses. The pharmacist had written instructions on the boxes, but her scribbles meant nothing to him, especially since the drugs had knocked him out.

For two days, he had felt crushed, prone and suffering. Whichever way he looked, anxiety lurked – his life, the future of the farm, his mother, his empty existence, the pain that kept him bedridden, the man who had died because of him, and the chaos he had brought into this woman's life. Aurore had come to see him that morning. She told him she would come again that evening, or perhaps sooner, he wasn't sure. For forty-eight hours he had been utterly dependent on her comings and goings. The pain, and the drowsiness induced by the pills, left him barely able to get out of bed. He would never have made it to the pharmacy, couldn't even fill a glass of water from the tap. When he felt the lightning bolt strike his back, two days ago, he had thought straight away of his old injury, the slipped disc, but the doctor had diagnosed pneumonia. He didn't believe that. He knew the pain was the same as before, the pain that had struck him down at the age of twenty-five and forced him to quit playing rugby. Three weeks in bed, hooked up to a succession of drips. Now, the doctor had referred him for an X-ray, convinced there were clear signs of pneumonia. But there was no way he could get out to see to that, and anyhow it was the twenty-third of December, the day before the Christmas holiday, and finding somewhere to get an X-ray would be hell. How could he possibly get out of bed, ride three metro stops, stand in line, organise more appointments, see another doctor. The anxiety gnawed, drove him half-mad. He felt defeated by this sense of helplessness, the absolute lack of control, but above all at the thought of the fucking mess he had left in this woman's life, to the point where he felt unable to look her in the face. At the end of the day he had done nothing at all to help, on the contrary, he had made everything worse, and now he was trapped on all sides, like that ageing buffalo, submitting to its fate on the television screen, while the lionesses tore at its flesh. There was no way out.

All he could do for now was reach out for his pills and capsules. From now on he would take only the two painkillers, the ones that seemed most effective, but he would give the antibiotics a miss. Aurore had told him to take them, but he would do nothing of the sort. As a precaution, he had checked the leaflets that came with all the rubbish he had been swallowing for the past two days. He felt so sick and broken, he needed to know what he was pumping into his bloodstream. And there on the tightly folded slips of paper he read lists of side-effects printed in minuscule letters, and some in very big letters, horrifying warnings of the risks and possible symptoms. Hallucinations. Some of the pills could lead to addiction, even death if taken in high doses. An arsenal of fatal substances there on his bedside table, a battery of poisons. All he had to do was tip out the contents of the gel capsules, dissolve them in a big glass of water and that would be the end of everything.

*

When Aurore came back that afternoon, he asked her to draw the curtains. He did not want to see her apartment opposite, or the outside world, but especially not her apartment, he just wanted to lay low and disappear in front of the bright TV screen. From the kitchen, she offered to make a cup of tea. He accepted. She had been taking incredible care of him for the past two days. When she helped him sit up in bed, he realised he was even drowsier and weaker than he had been that morning. The worst of it was the sight of her coming and going, the unreal sense of a living person around him, another existence. She had prepared two meal trays, one for teatime and another for the evening, so that he would have everything to hand. But it was the lifeline she had thrown him two days ago that he still could not believe. He hardly knew who this woman really was and yet he was certain of one thing, at least, that no one but she could have shown such love. No one else could have done what she did. He had refused at the time, and still he could not accept it. The night before, he had told her not to give up. He had everything to lose in this business, but he wanted her to go after Fabian. It was unthinkable that that bastard alone should get out of this unscathed. She must confront him and bring him down. Knocked back by the codeine, Ludovic told Aurore one more time that she should tell her lawyers everything, she should set the whole pack of them on him; they would bring the jackal down to the ground and eat him alive, like all the animals he'd been watching out on the savannah for the past two days. They would skin his hide. But no, there was nothing he could say to convince her, she would not do it.

'Believe me, Ludovic, I know what I'm doing.'

Above all, she could see he was not lucid. With all the pills he was taking, he seemed distant, floating, half asleep, detached from the real world. She knew what she was doing, and she had dropped the idea of going after Fabian.

Ludovic had no strength to try and persuade her otherwise. He could see she was looking after him, talking to him like a wounded casualty, a casualty she had helped to his feet. She was the one who had driven the Twingo back from her office. They had staggered away from the scene like a couple of wounded soldiers fleeing enemy fire. Because yes, Fabian had called Coubressac and told him that one of his employees was working on the side, issuing threats. Yes, Fabian had a file on him and was preparing to file a complaint, hand him over to the cops. Aurore had told him all this as she supported him back to the car, and the news, and the pain, left him gasping for breath. Then she had helped him up the stairs to his apartment, and called for a doctor, and the medic had given him two injections and prescribed a battery of drugs, and she had gone out to the duty pharmacy and collected all the boxes, and since then he had been scarcely able even to get out of bed, struck down by the pain, and groggy from the opioids.

At least now he felt he was in the clear, as far as Aurore was concerned. He could look himself in the mirror, because again this morning he had offered to sacrifice himself, again he had said to her: 'Aurore, go for it, think about yourself, your own interest. Save the company. Let him report me, I don't care, I can defend myself. Of course, they'll come after me with everything they've got, but ultimately, I've done nothing wrong. I'll lose my job, obviously, and the proceedings will take months, but fuck, I did not kill that man, so go for it Aurore, think of yourself first...' But it seemed she was stronger than him, or more selfless, because her first thought had been to protect him.

Once they had filed for bankruptcy, the company would be relieved of all its debts, which would be rough for the suppliers and their other creditors, but at least the brand would be as good as new for the buyers, and they would have Aurore Dessage all for themselves, to do whatever they liked, dresses, bags, fragrances. In exchange, they guaranteed to inject more cash and keep everyone on the payroll. While the deal was far from clean, at least in the eyes of the commercial courts, the important thing was to save people's jobs. Fabian would take over the company with another partner, not the dead guy, but his brother, and all his staff, because they knew that in business, you should never hunt alone but always with the pack. That in business you should never cut yourself off, never venture out alone without back-up, if you don't want to get eaten alive.

On the third day he was woken by the sound of the curtains being drawn back and felt instantly ashamed to be found still lying in bed. He tried to pull himself up, but the pain stopped him dead. Aurore had just filled the room with light. She stood in front of the window. He could smell coffee. It was broad daylight outside, the sun was shining straight down into the courtyard, and the bright December morning filled the bedroom with the radiance of springtime.

'Did you sleep all right? You know it's Christmas Eve?'

Ludovic was unaccustomed to talking in the morning, especially not the instant he woke up. He forced a smile, blinked in the radiant light from the window, and felt briefly annoyed with Aurore for opening the curtains so wide. But it was ten o'clock already. He found it impossibly hard to focus on his watch. She smiled to see him so groggy. She seemed astonishingly bright and cheerful.

'You know I won't be able to come back again today, so I just wanted to make sure you've got everything you need. For tonight, I've made you a Christmas Eve supper, all ready to go. It's in the fridge – will you be able to make it to the kitchen?'

When someone is ill, they quickly get very tired of being asked every ten minutes, 'Do you need anything? What can I get you?' Better for other people to anticipate, figure out what you might need and bring it. This woman impressed him, though still he did not fully understand her place in his mind, nor what he might expect of her, or she of him.

'Iris and Noé send hugs!'

'Wait, what? You've told them you've been coming over to see me?'

'Yes. We're neighbours, aren't we, even friends? Super-plumber!'

'Sure.'

'And we leave tomorrow. I'll be away for a week. Will you manage?'

He hadn't seen that coming. He felt lost all of a sudden, abandoned for the coming week, and he panicked at the prospect. He hadn't thought that far ahead. A whole week stuck here, in pain, unable to go out, hardly even to get out of bed. An impossible week, and he knew already that he could not face it, especially not here, between Christmas and New Year. A whole week lying here, with thoughts going round and round in his head... It was Christmas Eve and yet neither his sister nor his father had called. They hadn't bothered to find out whether he would be with them for Christmas or not. Perhaps it suited them if he didn't come. His brother-in-law would be delighted not to have him around and his father would prefer it that way too. They could all have a peaceful holiday, no fights. All his father wanted was for the farm to carry on, with his son – or anyone else – in charge, he didn't care about all the rest, and his mother probably didn't even know it was Christmas. He realised that none of them needed him down there. In fact it suited them if he was no longer there to complicate things.

'And what about the ointment, how will you manage that when I'm not here?'

'I'll manage.'

Aurore gave no objection. She pretended to be convinced by his air of determination. To apply the ointment, he had to turn as far as possible onto his side, though the movement hurt him terribly. Gently, she caressed this fallen giant, the muscled valley of pain. Ludovic closed his eyes, said nothing. The drugs, and the massage, left him floating, absent, in a cotton-wool cloud.

There was something she wanted to say before she left. She wanted to tell him that Kobzham's accident had saved her. Without that, she would be facing up to them both, right now, Fabian and Kobzham together. She would be fighting tooth and claw to save her company and free herself from their talons. She would be exhausted, drained. Perhaps she would have brought them down eventually, but to what end, what outcome? For everything to be as it had been before, with her shouldering the burden of the business, more alone than ever, exhausted after the weeks in court, not to mention that she would have had to rebuild everything, earn everyone's trust, remobilise her teams... It would have been too much to bear. And so she told Ludovic clearly how things stood. She told him she no longer wanted to work that way. It was a stroke of luck, an opportunity, to be able to start afresh. Young designers starting out nowadays did so on their own, or with a partner, they were self-employed artisans. She saw that as the ideal way to make clothes on a small scale, and sell them through the right outlets, but never again would she go into mass production. The whole business had sickened her. She hadn't even realised that she was drowning. And now she felt light and unburdened. It was a new beginning.

He listened but did not believe her. She was bluffing, making light of it so he wouldn't feel guilty.

'Honestly, Ludovic, it was the darkest hour before the dawn. I don't want to live under that kind of pressure any more. That's not the life I want to live.'

The balm smelt good, a mixture of camphor and arnica. Aurore concentrated on the gentle caresses she was giving. She felt the muscles relax at her touch. Ludovic lay floating, half

324

asleep. There was something he must hear before she left, but he was fast asleep now. She spoke the words aloud, to herself. As if she wanted him to hear. I can't start my whole life over again, but I can't live without him, his presence in my life is too precious. When I'm with him I feel complete. I feel fully myself. It's a huge decision to leave the person you live with, the person you've made a home and had children with. It's an impossible choice, with so many unknowns. You can break up, and you know your own life will unravel, and the lives of everyone around you. You risk losing it all, losing them, tipping everything over the edge. Or you can leave quietly. Leaving means you can get your life back, and it allows the other person to do the same, it gives a new life to a whole host of people. And that's why men can't do it: they don't know how to give life. All they can do is break things apart. Except this man, here, at the tips of my fingers. I love him far more than he knows, more than he could possibly imagine, but I won't frighten him away by telling him. Not now.

It was hard to be alone on Christmas Eve, knowing everyone was up feasting late into the night. He did not fetch the meal tray from the fridge; he wasn't hungry, and anyway, he still found it hard to move. Facing him, the curtains hung open; Aurore had forgotten to close them. The eight o'clock evening news talked of nothing but foie gras, the *bûches* at a famous Paris patisserie, and Christmas trees. He turned the television off for a moment, so that he could sit in complete darkness and see the apartment opposite. All the lights were on over there. From his bed, he could see heads silhouetted in the windows from time to time. He saw the children moving back and forth, and other people. Clearly there was quite a crowd. It was fascinating to watch, but utterly depressing, too. He watched from his bed, unable to get up, unable to experience the Christmas party he could picture in his mind's eye, right outside his own windows. As if life was passing him by. A life he had failed to grasp. Other people were living their lives, immersed in the real world, but he could do nothing, scarcely even get out of bed. He reached for the packet of Tramadol, popped open two entire strips of gel capsules and emptied their contents into his glass of water. He added the two packs of paracetamol/codeine – big, compressed tablets, hard as stone. He needed them to dissolve, to soak in the water, but they weren't softening. He tried to grind them up with the handle of his teaspoon, but the gesture delivered a slicing sabre-cut to his back. It was hurting badly tonight, the tiniest move felled him back against his pillows, and so he left the glass on his bedside table. The tablets would dissolve in their own time, and then they would dissolve in his body. Sometimes that's all the future there is, just the next few hours. But he did not want to live through the week ahead, a whole week lying motionless, churning his thoughts, his remorse. He would do anything to avoid that. He would not spend this week of all weeks like that.

In the morning, he woke lying on his side. He had no idea how he had managed to turn over in the night, no recollection of it, and yet when he opened his eyes, he was facing the bedside table, with the water glass and its thick, pasty contents right in front of him. The big tablets had melted now; all he needed to do was drink the mixture, mix it with a big splash of whisky, and swallow it down.

He struggled to get out of bed. His movements were slow and cautious. The atrocious thing about this pain was the dread that he would somehow break in two, as if his body might snap clean in half, like a pencil. Reaching for the bottle of Black Label on the shelf, he writhed as if shouldering a sack of plaster, but he did not drop it, and managed to stand it on the bedside table without sitting back down. It took him forever to twist off the cap and fill the big glass brim-full with whisky. He stirred the spoon in the repulsive, gooey mixture. It was eleven o'clock in the morning, but still quite dull. He had slept soundly. The curtains were still open and a few timid snowflakes fell half-heartedly. The sky and the rooftops blended in a uniform slate grey. The lights were on across the courtyard. He hesitated to move nearer to the window for fear of being seen, but at the same time, standing up unsupported was agony. Already, he felt the need to lie back down in bed, and the knowledge robbed him of the last of his morale. He needed a cigarette, so he made his way around the room, holding the wall, as far as his blazer where it lay near the window. He hadn't smoked for three days. The doctor was wrong, there was nothing wrong with his chest, he still felt that avid desire to inhale great lungfuls of smoke. In the inside pocket of his jacket, he found his phone. After three days, it needed recharging. The battery was dead. He hadn't given it a thought. Perhaps they had called after all. With a superhuman effort, he caught hold of the charger cable that dangled over the edge of the chest of drawers and plugged it into the device. It sprang to life immediately with a faint shudder and a short three-note tune. He just wanted to know if anyone had tried to get hold of him. But then he saw the Velux windows opposite go dark. They were about to leave. He couldn't remember what Aurore had told him. He pressed his face close to the glass and saw the twins playing in the courtyard down below. You mustn't call them 'the twins', she said. Never call them that, but refer to them separately, individually, by their first names. Iris and Noé. He remembered that when he saw them. They were dressed in puffer jackets and knitted hats, as if they were up in the mountains, larking about at the bottom of the ski slopes. They had gathered up enough snow to make something resembling a snowman, a fairly good pile. Ludovic leaned forward a little to watch the two small creatures at play, fascinated by their total absorption and dedication to the task. And then, he had no idea why, but suddenly they both jumped up and ran into the middle of the bushes. They had run to hide, but from up here he could see them very well. The windows opposite were all dark now, they were definitely on their way out. Only the Christmas tree lights continued to flash in the sitting room. He told himself that Aurore had left them on for him, a parting gesture. The lights came on in staircase A. The two children were well hidden, no one in the courtyard could see them, but from up above he watched them plot their tiny ambush. The delicate snowflakes twirling in the air lent the courtyard an air of unreality, like a scene in a snow globe. Ludovic could not help but tell himself that the two children down below were Aurore's children, Aurore whom he would never see again, and so he wanted to watch her leave, at least. He looked out for her on the staircase, then looked down at the children again, and he saw that the two little heads were turned up to look at his window. They had spotted him and stupidly, on a reflex, he shrank back into the room, as if they shouldn't see him. But then he thought better of it and moved forward, even forgetting the pain. The two little heads were still looking up at him. Two little heads atop their big, puffy jackets. In a perfectly synchronised movement, like the twins they were, each placed a finger over their lips. They were counting on him not to give them away. Unsure how to respond, he gave an oafish wave of his hand, but already they had returned to their game. Next, Richard's parents – yes, it had to be them – appeared at the bottom of the staircase with their luggage. Richard walked into the courtyard from the direction of the street. He must have been parking the car outside the carriage entrance or looking for a taxi. Ludovic pieced the operation together. Now, they were all leaving the building. The children were still well hidden. Aurore would be the last one down. When she appeared at the bottom of the staircase, he felt guilty and shrank back one more time. He shouldn't watch them any more, he should let them go, let them get on with their lives in peace. Standing back from the window, he lit a cigarette and sucked the smoke eagerly into his lungs. Time enough for them all to leave. The courtyard would be empty once more. He gave it thirty seconds. There was no sound coming from down below. He moved back to the window. Aurore was crouching next to the two children, brushing the dirty snow off their jackets. All three were near the front gate. The two children must have spotted him as soon as he reappeared. They gave him a big, cheery wave, and then Aurore lifted her eyes to where he stood. She looked radiant. Radiant, or relieved to see him up and about. She stood up straight and waved to him, too. From up above, he saw three smiles saying goodbye to him, or perhaps *au revoir*, see you soon, three smiles that were going away for now, but plainly not leaving him for good. They walked out of the courtyard and disappeared under the archway.

Three discreet taps sounded at Ludovic's door. No one could possibly be coming to see him, but another quiet knock came, and his phone, which had gone quiet, began to buzz all over again, as if other lives were reaching out to him from all sides, as if the blood was flowing back to an old, tired muscle. Walking as far as the door was an ordeal, but he wanted to look through the spy-hole and see who was there. A small figure, wearing a fine woollen headscarf, all wrapped up against the cold.

'Mademoiselle Mercier?'

'Ah, there you are, *mon grand*! Our neighbour, the lady from staircase A, has explained it all. You've no need to worry, I'll be taking care of everything. I'll go and fetch some bread in a minute, it'll do me good to get out. So, do you need anything else for tonight?'

'No, really. Just some bread, yes, if you like.'

From the landing she glanced towards his bedroom and saw that his pillow had fallen to the floor, at the foot of the bed. She marched inside and informed him she would make the bed, smooth the sheets, freshen things up a little.

'*Petite Odette*... No, please don't bother yourself, leave it, leave it.'

'I know just how it is. I know you don't like to ask. But consider it a favour returned. One good deed...'

Ludovic had no idea how to behave towards the little woman busying herself in his apartment. He felt utterly ashamed to be seen in such a reduced state and, to make matters worse, she seemed to have abandoned the polite *vous* and was addressing him sporadically with the intimate, affectionate *tu*, apparently unawares. Above all, he felt desperately uncomfortable that she should walk in like this and find him wearing nothing but underpants and a T-shirt, rather than a pair of pyjamas. He supported himself with one arm against the wall, tried to stand up straight, but could not. His phone sounded three times, with the signal for incoming text messages. He picked it up and pressed the screen.

'Oh, but here's your grog. It's gone cold, shall I heat it up, or make you another one?'

Of the three texts, he saw only the most recent, because it was from Aurore. Already, Aurore. He clicked on it straight away: PROMISE THIS SUMMER YOU'LL SHOW ME WHAT A CARDING SHED LOOKS LIKE? PROMISE!! *JE T'EMBRASSE*. He did not know what to think. He had never imagined that Aurore would ever come down with him to his valley. She was so different, so much the opposite of the place he came from, it seemed impossible that she might one day be there with him. And yet she wanted to see it. Plainly, she wanted to see it very much.

He looked at Mademoiselle Mercier. She was sniffing his big drinking glass, with a dubious expression of disgust.

'Well, you didn't answer, so I'm going to throw it away. Shall I? And I'll make you another?'

'Yes, let's do that, Odette. Throw it away.'

'I'll bring you one of mine. Limeflower and pepper. I'll bet you've never tasted that!'

He had never seen his little neighbour like this, sharp and alert, not even limping any more. She tipped his glass into the sink, rinsed it out scrupulously, then left through the still-open front door, turning as she did so, muttering as if to herself.

'So, my infusion, bread, and what else?'

She stood waiting for him to ask her for something else. She was eager and hopeful that he would accept her help. It was not often she got the chance to help another person, and it seemed the idea that she might be of use had given her new strength, new energy, as if the ability to help had brought her back to life. He would not deny her that gift. He would not deny anyone that gift.